Alice Cavanagh

The House That Made Us

SIMON & SCHUSTER

London · New York · Sydney · Toronto · New Delhi

First published in Great Britain by Simon & Schuster UK Ltd, 2023

1 3 5 7 9 10 8 6 4 2

Simon & Schuster UK Ltd
1st Floor
222 Gray's Inn Road
London WC1X 8HB

Simon & Schuster Australia, Sydney
Simon & Schuster India, New Delhi

www.simonandschuster.co.uk
www.simonandschuster.com.au
www.simonandschuster.co.in

A CIP catalogue record for this book
is available from the British Library

Paperback ISBN: 978-1-3985-1056-2
eBook ISBN: 978-1-3985-1057-9
Audio ISBN: 978-1-3985-2237-4

Typeset in Bembo by M Rules

Printed and Bound in the UK using 100% Renewable
Electricity at CPI Group (UK) Ltd

MIX
Paper | Supporting
responsible forestry
FSC® C171272

Alice Cavanagh lives in London and comes from an Irish family. She is a romantic at heart and when not writing, loves spending time with her family and her dogs.

This book is for Matthew, for the last time.
Goodbye, my love.
1970–2021

The House That Made Us

CHAPTER ONE

Tuesday again.

He drives across the flyover and out of the city, onto wider roads. Parking up on the tarmac, scooping the flowers in their cellophane from the back seat, he passes through the wide double doors. Fighting, all the while, the droop of his shoulders.

He finds her in her usual spot, among the high-backed chairs in the pastel rec room. He searches her face for clues to today's mood before she sees him.

'All right?' He bends to kiss her cheek, as usual. He puts the flowers down.

'Look!' She is alight today. Her eyes shine. Years fall away from her gentle, lined face. 'I found this.'

He takes it, turns it over in his hands. 'A photo album.' It is the old-fashioned variety, stiff dark pages, the photographs held down by sticky white corners. It's shoddily bound in dated brown and orange wallpaper. 'Who does it belong to?'

'I've asked around and nobody seems to know. That care assistant I like, Blondie, said I can keep it unless somebody turns up and objects.'

He reads the handwritten label on the front. 'Sunnyside – a love story'.

'But whose love story, eh?' *She blazes with curiosity.*

This is unusual. She has been fading, like a dropped flower, for the past few weeks. 'Shall we find out?'

'I hoped you'd say that.'

'First,' *he says.* 'The all-important cuppa.'

He knows just how she likes it, and he knows better than to bring it with anything other than a modest Stonehenge of Custard Creams. He sets them down within her reach, and begins, awkwardly, 'Actually, there's something I have to tell you.' *He has rehearsed. He didn't expect to be derailed by a photograph album.* 'You may not like it, but just hear me out and—'

'It's like a biography,' *she says, caressing the album.* 'Of ordinary people.'

He gives up. He'll tell her next time. 'No such thing', *he says, 'as ordinary people.'*

'How about we look at one photo each time you visit?' *She frowns, seized by a dark thought.* 'You will come again, won't you?'

'Yes.' *He is accustomed to this question.* 'Every week, regular as clockwork. Promise. Come on, let's see the first snap.'

She holds the album open. Above a small, blurred black-and-white photograph, in the same expressive hand, someone has inscribed, '29 July 1970 – Happiest day of our lives!!!'

'Almost fifty years ago,' he murmurs, aware that she lives in a permanent now.

'A right pair of giddy goats, they are. Is that a wedding dress? It's so short. Not sure she has the legs for it. That must be their house. Just a plain little box, really. The chap looks proud as punch, though. Of her, do you think? Or of the house?'

'Both?' He hasn't seen her so engaged for weeks. 'Looks as if he hasn't a clue what to do with either of them.'

'He's making a right hash of carrying the poor girl over the threshold. Oh, look, there's a nameplate by the door. Can you make out what the funny little house is called?'

'Sunnyside,' he says.

29 July 1970

'Sunnyside!' giggled Marie. 'The perfect name for our new nest.' She bounced up and down, manhandled by her new husband as he tried to balance her in his arms *and* fumble the key into the door.

He dropped her, of course, and she was on her hands and knees on fresh concrete, her veil over her face. 'Jaysus, Mac!' She giggled some more as he hoisted her up into his arms again and dusted her down. 'Don't look so stricken.' Her

3

accent, warm and wicked, was as Irish as her fiery hair and her dot-to-dot freckles. 'I'm grand, I'm grand.' She kissed him, and they were both still.

This is it, thought Mac. *This really is it*. That morning they'd woken up as Ian Mactavish and Marie Neeson; now they were Mr and Mrs Mactavish. *She's mine*, he thought, and the idea was like a balloon in his chest that would never stop inflating. *And I'm hers*.

Hardly anyone called Ian by his first name. He was Mac to all, and now he had a Mrs Mac. He swept her into his arms once more. 'Got to carry you over the threshold, love.'

'We should take a pic!'

'Would you mind . . .' Mac, bandy-legged with the effort of carrying Marie, held out his Kodak Brownie to the man who had emerged from the next house.

'You the new people?' Next Door – he was instantly christened and his name never changed – was small and sour, with the look of a well-squeezed lemon. 'I watched them throw up those new houses. First puff of wind'll take that down.' He looked up at his own place, a holier-than-thou Victorian bristling with detail.

Staggering a little, Mac looked up at the house he had scrimped and saved to afford. It was a white cube, one of three Johnny-come-latelys added to the long terrace of handsome brick semis. The plain door was white. The narrow window frames were white. The garden was a grey slab with a crack here and there but no greenery. It lacked a gate. 'We love it,' he said defiantly.

As Next Door squinted through the camera's viewfinder, he told them: 'Marriage is a mug's game.'

Marie hooted into her bouquet.

Mac fumed, but thought, *How could this funny little fellow know that marriage will save my life?* It was a bridge from the dark chill of Mac's past to the bright stability of family life. The girl in his arms – his beautiful, sparkling wife – was the key to it all. She was a firework that exploded over and over across the night sky of his loneliness.

Next Door saw no firework; he saw what the rest of the world saw. A smallish, plumpish redhead; no beauty. And yet. Her eyes reeled him in. They were kind and they were shining and . . . he gave the camera back. He had more important things to do than stare at this nondescript couple. 'You off on honeymoon I suppose?'

'No,' said Mac, just as Marie said, 'Yes.' They looked at each other and laughed. They did that a lot.

'We've put it off until next year,' said Marie. 'We're going on a cruise to the Isle of Man.'

'That's not a cruise,' said Next Door. 'That's a boat trip.'

'Well, nice to meet you,' lied Mac. He had chosen the Isle of Man because of the puffin colony; he had what amounted to an obsession with the clowny little birds, and his ambition was to see them in the flesh. 'But we should get on.' This peppery little man was raining on Mac's parade. He wanted to get inside his castle, and have his new wife to himself.

Just a few hours ago, his aunt had straightened his tie outside the church, confetti in their hair. 'You're off my hands now, Ian,' she said. She always called him Ian. He'd experienced a sensation of freefall, until Marie slipped her hand into his and Mac landed, soft and secure, in the feather bed of new love.

There had been whoops from her family when they broke the news of the engagement. From his aunt there had been a tiny deepening of the lines between her eyebrows. 'Are you sure?' she'd asked. 'It's very quick.'

But it wasn't quick at all. Mac had waited his whole life, twenty-five years, to find Marie. And now they would fill Sunnyside's square rooms with light and noise. And people. Their own people; Mac was keen to be a father. The role would render him magnificently ordinary once and for all. Wipe away that otherness he felt.

He turned to Marie and said, vehemently, as if telling her off, 'We're going to be happy here!'

'You bet your sweet bippy we are!' she said, and then turned to Next Door, sticking her chubby hand over the hedge. 'I'm Marie, darlin', and this is Mac.' She was unde-terred when he ignored the hand; her good humour was unsinkable. 'He works in the bank on the high street and I'm . . .' She paused for effect. 'I'm an apprentice hair stylist at Vidal Sassoon. You'll have heard of them, of course.' He clearly hadn't, and didn't appreciate what an achievement the job represented for a little terrier fresh off the ferry from Dublin. 'One day I meet this boyo here and he's down on one knee like something out of Shakespeare.' Next Door's carefully bored expression didn't seem to register with Marie.

'I says yes, and next thing you know his auntie lends him half the deposit! There's not a spare penny in me own family, I can tell you, so I never expected to own a little mansion like this.'

When she drew breath – and Mac staggered some more, holding his bride like a sack of potatoes – Next Door asked, in his crab apple voice. 'Are you planning to have children? You Irish are keen on big families.'

'That's just the pope, and he doesn't have to give birth to them, does he?' Marie shook her head. 'I'm ambitious. No babies for me.' Perhaps she felt Mac droop. She added, 'I mean, not yet. Not for years. No babies for a few years, thank you very much.'

CHAPTER TWO

Tea for two, again.

*He negotiates the forest of slippered feet and walking
frames with the tray. She doesn't wave at him; a bad sign.
The staff warned him that she has been 'uncooperative'.
They don't mind, they tell him, it just pains them to see
her with her hair wild when she's so particular with her
appearance. Even Blondie has been unable to coax her into a
fresh cardigan for his visit.*

*The album, however, has magical powers. He opens it in
front of her and there is a sea-change in her eyes.*

'Read the caption to me.'

*Obediently, he recites, '29 July 1971. Our first wedding
anniversary and they said it wouldn't last!!!' He adds,
'They like their exclamation marks, don't they?'*

'The girl's put on weight.'

'Or is she pregnant?' He phrases it as a question; she

becomes upset and querulous when she misunderstands. She
misunderstands so much. Very little makes sense to her on a
bad day. And this could be a bad day.

 He longs to stand on a chair and shout to the room,
'You should've seen her twenty years ago! She was
sharper than me!'

 'Well spotted,' she says. 'The girl's expecting. Dear me,
she doesn't look happy about it. She's just a beach ball on
legs. The dog's a bit of a character, jumping up like that.
He's just a blur.'

 'They've been busy.' He points at the grainy image.
'That's a new porch. Bit wonky.'

 'The window boxes are magnificent. I do love a
geranium. It looks as though they've painted the front door.
Can't make out what the colour is in black and white.' She
considers. 'Could be light blue, maybe.'

29 July 1971

'We should've gone for red woodwork,' said Marie, survey-
ing the house.

Mac kept his head down, busy with the geraniums. He
loved the soft, seasidey blue. Their London suburb might be
miles from the coast, but the blue lent the house a nautical
air that pleased him. No need to say all that: pregnancy
had made his wife volatile. No: *more* volatile. He hoped the
GP was right when he put her behaviour down to 'baby

hormones', but deep down Mac knew he'd simply married a livewire.

And I like it that way.

She had dodged the camera until he insisted that their anniversary photograph was a new tradition, the first one they'd created together. Mac was in favour of tradition, unlike his anarchic other half. 'Just say cheese and it'll go straight in the anniversary album.'

'Exactly! So everyone can see, forever and forever, how fat I am.'

She gave in, though, as he knew she would, and posed ungraciously for the passer-by roped in to help.

'You're not fat, love, you're preggers.' Mac got back to the window boxes, watering, feeding, encouraging. He ignored the orders she gave, to deadhead this or feed that; it was Mac who had the family green thumb.

He longed to tell Marie how beautiful she looked with their baby in her belly, like a walking geranium. Fearful of sounding silly, he kept quiet, even though poetry welled up in him when he watched her doing the simplest things. Right now, his walking geranium was telling the dog he was 'a little eejit'.

Heinz was, appropriately, full of beans. Battersea Dogs Home had warned he was 'lively' – a diplomatic way of warning he would destroy every slipper he found and wage war on the postcode's cats. His complicated heritage inspired his name; Heinz had 57 varieties of dog in his DNA. Clothed in a wire-wool curly coat, he had long stiff legs, a blunt head and a magnificent moustache. If asked, Mac and Marie told people he was 'part Airedale, part poodle, all bastard'.

When Mac had lain in bed as a child, imagining the family home he would one day have, it had always included a dog. Just not this dog.

Heinz was barking and jumping, and jumping and barking. Marie couldn't stoop to pick him up; she was a beachball in her hated maternity dress. She had voted against buying a dog. She'd been wry, nudging Mac as they discussed it in their new double bed, bought on hire purchase, and their very favourite place.

'It'll be me who does all the work, boyo,' she'd said, resembling, in Mac's eyes, Sophia Loren in her nylon ruched nightie, even though Sophia Loren never had roaring red hair and a curler in her fringe.

'I promise I'll train it. I'll walk it. I'll feed it. A pooch'll be company for you, now you've left Vidal Sassoon.'

In the moonlight, Marie had sighed at his clumsy reference to her setback. The salon had been reluctant to let her go, but let her go they must. Marie understood that new mothers must stay at home, devote themselves to the family. But it chafed.

Working for Sassoon was a cherished dream she'd sweated to make real. Arriving in London with no experience – apart from cutting Ma's hair in the kitchen at home – she had begun as a junior. She swept the floor, replaced towels, made hot drinks and trotted out to buy stylists' cigarettes and feed customers' parking meters.

'You're just a drudge,' her housemates would say when she crawled home to her freezing Notting Hill house-share, but Marie loved her job. Mary Quant came in. Twiggy complimented Marie's shoes. One day, Marie would graduate to cutting the razor-sharp, asymmetric bob which was the Sassoon signature, so she put up with the pitiful pay; she lied to her parents about the squalor of the shared loo; she burned with independence.

Now, having fought off eighteen applicants to get her mitts on the apprenticeship, Marie was cast out. On hold, her aspirations grew bolder and stronger. 'I don't want *company*,' she'd told Mac. 'I want *a job*. I'm running back to Vidal Sassoon the moment I can, believe me.'

He believed her, and, eventually, after some kissing that knocked the curler out of her fringe, Marie gave in. 'But you look after this mutt, got it?'

He got it.

Neither foresaw the immediate bond between woman and hound. Heinz hung on Marie's every word; now there were two anarchists in the house and Mac didn't stand a chance.

Turning the corner onto his street was Mac's favourite moment of his walk home. After a dull day in a dull office swamped by dull ledgers, he saw Sunnyside and his heart lifted.

To the Mactavishes, Sunnyside was more than its parts. They saw past the unprepossessing frontage to the hope that held the bricks together better than any mortar could.

Mac's aunt had warned them – how she loved to warn – that homeowning was a costly business, but the reality was even more than Mac had bargained for. Furnishing Sunnyside on his modest salary meant lots of credit, many payday sums on the back of an envelope. And now there was a nursery to furnish. Mac supposed he should be grateful for his firm foothold on the job ladder. *I have a family to keep*, he would remind himself whenever his manager dumped a file the size of a small car on his desk.

Mac's strenuous kindness and need to connect simply weren't nurtured at the bank. Only the cheque each Friday kept him going; he was the breadwinner, and his family deserved the best. He never mentioned the dissatisfaction and wondered if Marie noticed. She was so quick, that cheeky nose of hers in every corner of his life. If she ever brought it up, he would deny it.

Mustn't worry her, not in her condition.

The doctor had a lot to say about Marie's 'condition'.

'Plenty of rest, good diet, not too much . . . um . . .'

'You mean sex?' Marie had squawked.

'Well, *relations*, yes.' The old gent had turned maroon.

Marie was scandalized. 'That's the best part of me day,' she'd harrumphed.

Mac had tried not to look smug. He really had.

Now, as he jogged up the short path, he shook off the bank and reminded himself of the spare ten-bob note in his wallet, ready to put into the jar on the shelf by the cooker.

The handwritten label read 'Cruise!' Coins were dropped

in, joined by the occasional paper note. Marie would shake it every now and then, like maracas, and plague Mac with, 'Guess how much we've saved! Go on, boyo! Guess!'

The jar was raided and replenished, but was redundant for the time being. That same GP had been intransigent: 'No trips, young lady, not with your blood pressure.'

'I don't have any blood pressure!' Marie had argued.

'We'll do the cruise next year, love.' Mac had – with some effort – put away all thoughts of puffins.

'With a baby in tow? Hardly.' Marie had lifted her chin. 'This gives us longer to save, so we can eventually go somewhere glamorous. *Foreign*.' Inspiration struck her. 'The Isle of Wight!'

Mac, who had been to the Isle of Wight, had nodded cagily.

He fished out his key, anticipating the habitual kissy welcome home from his wife.

The door swung open before he touched it.

'Have you forgotten?' barked Marie. 'You've forgotten!'

'I haven't,' said Mac. He endured his wife's Medusa stare for ten seconds. 'All right, I have.'

'Your nostrils flare when you lie.' Marie pointed a mop at him. Suds dripped on Heinz. 'Me sister's coming for dinner.'

'Oh God.' Mac loved Bernie. He really did. She was just a bit *much* after a day's work. 'Do I have to change my clothes?'

'Is that a joke?' Marie looked Mac's smart work suit up and down as if it was a leprous rag. 'Smart. But casual. Don't you dare wear that jumper your auntie bought you.' She paused. The mop lowered. 'Maybe ... the cravat?'

This was an old tussle. 'Nope.' Mac was not a cravat man. Just because Bernie's husband was a cravat man didn't mean Mac could be pushed or pulled into wearing one of those daft little scarves. 'Absolutely and definitely *not*.'

'Love the cravat, Mac,' said Bernie.

'Hmm,' said Mac.

Marie winked at him.

'Very distinguished.' Bernie liked to disguise her Dublin accent; she aimed for upper-crust London but sometimes landed in Wales. Taller than her little sister, she was a Valkyrie. Wide-shouldered, big-bosomed, with hair piled on top of her head. She smelled great, and dressed expensively in satin, fur, leather. All of it was just slightly wrong. She tried; Bernie really did try; but her true self shone through in her walk. It was clumpy, enthusiastic, a carthorse on platform hooves.

Mac adored her, petty snobbery and all.

'Cracking vol-au-vents,' she said. Then, 'Gerroff, Heinz!'

Mac dragged the dog outside, gave him a talking to and a biscuit.

'We're eating in the kitchen?' Bernie drained her glass. 'How cosy!'

Marie bristled. Bernie knew they ate in the kitchen because there was no dining room.

Out in Esher, Bernie and her Londoner husband George had a sunken dining area. Shag pile as far as the eye could see. All mod cons; Mac met his first bidet in Bernie's house.

He heard no malice in Bernie's comment but Marie could be sensitive about the difference in the couples' lifestyles.

'How d'you like being a lady of leisure?' George asked Marie.

'Wouldn't call it leisure,' said Marie.

'Personally, I don't like the whole idea of my wife working.' George put an arm around Bernie. 'It implies I can't afford to keep her.'

'George, she's a wife, not a pet,' laughed Marie.

'You'll see,' said Bernie, in the wiser-older-sibling voice that jumped straight onto Marie's nerves. 'You'll love being a housewife when baby comes. You'll forget you ever wanted to go out to work.'

'Not me.' Marie was adamant. About this, about everything. 'I was built to be out in the world.'

'She always comes back though.' Mac said it aloud as much to reassure himself as anything. Sometimes, he felt he would have liked to marry a home-bird like himself, a little hen content to perch beside him in their Sunnyside coop.

'Remember when you turned up at our door, Marie?' Bernie smiled, nostalgic. 'Fresh off the boat.'

'You make me sound like a waif,' said Marie. 'I only stayed with you for a month or so.'

The sisters painted Marie's decision to leave Ireland very differently. Bernie's version had little Marie following in her pioneering footsteps; Marie described it as an adventure, the polar opposite of Bernie's relocation from their parents' house to George's house.

'I couldn't *believe* the state of that dump she moved into.' Bernie rolled her eyes. 'I sez, are you mad? You'll be cut into bits and left in a bin bag. But no, off she went.'

'It was a pleasure having you at ours,' said George. 'You brightened up the place no end.'

'Thanks, Georgie.' Marie poked Bernie with her foot. 'Aren't you relieved I dodged all those Notting Hill murderers?'

'You wanted to be in the thick of swinging London, and now look at you.' Bernie spread her hands, the nails long and red. 'Pregnant in a suburban two-up-two-down.'

Marie went still. Sometimes Bernie's careless talk cut through. She looked down at her body as if noticing it for the first time in a long time. *Nothing swings in Sunnyside*, she thought. *Except my tent dresses.*

'*This* is an adventure,' said Mac, who sometimes felt as if he were tied to a sled careering down an Alp. 'What could be more adventurous than building a family from scratch?'

'I'll buy the cot, no arguments,' said Bernie. 'Harrods. Only the best. And it can come and see me when it's sad. I'll give it cake and when it's older I'll let it smoke.'

'Bern!' laughed Mac, scandalized.

'You bloody won't,' said Marie. 'Let's have dessert in the garden.'

They stood around in the late, pinky-blue light. Bernie peered at the new fence, its resin seeping out to spoil the blue paintwork. 'You should build a rockery, Mac. Ours is gorgeous at night with all the lights on.'

'It's not Versailles, Bern,' laughed Mac. 'We've hardly room for the bins.'

Marie flashed him a look that parted his hair.

By midnight Mac and Marie were back in their moonlit winceyette nest, picking over their first dinner party.

The dessert hadn't panned out.

Everyone was kind about it as they drifted back indoors. George was especially gallant about the runny lemon posset; Bernie's husband was suave, no other word for it. Black polo-neck. Groomed moustache. Dark hair with a side parting just like those images in barbers' windows. He referred to Marie and Bernie as 'the little ladies', and he liked to keep them happy.

One way to keep Marie happy was never to refer to her as a 'little lady', but Bernie didn't mind; 'He pays the bills, he can call me what he likes!' she'd laugh.

'Saw you having a lovely chat with George,' said Marie, as she shoved Heinz off the bed. 'Asking him how life was in plastics.'

'I never know what to say.' There was strict division in the sitting room after the meal, with the menfolk on one side of the room, the women on the other. All lit by the demonic glow of the new orange lamps, all sipping terrible coffee. 'George only talks about manly stuff.' Mac did a quick impression. It was fond – there was no harm in George – but Mac caught his bluff masculinity perfectly. 'How'd you get here? Take the A308, did you?'

'He's good to my sister,' said Marie, nestling down, finding her spot against Mac's side. 'Did you hear her crack about Sunnyside not having a dining room? She grew up the same as me, stuffed into our little house, no room to swing a kitten let alone a cat.'

Under the bed, Heinz's ears pricked up; he was on constant lookout for those hairy hooligans.

'This little house', said Marie, her voice growing snoozy, 'is a mansion, boyo. When I compare it to that grotty bedsit you rescued me from ...' She yawned. 'I never had a bedroom to meself before this house.'

'Well, not quite to yourself.' Mac kissed the curler in her fringe.

'You know what I mean.' Marie was drifting into sleep, her baby bump a dark hill beneath the bedclothes. 'I grew up in a house where we all lived on top of one another. I couldn't breathe sometimes.'

Mac listened to her breathe now, heard her settle, fall into sleep. He stared at her profile, the up-turned nose, and knew she would be amazed to hear how he envied her.

His history was one of echoing rooms, of whispered conversations amid other people's furniture. Mac was different; his childhood had marked him, whereas Marie had her chaotic, loving family. The Neesons were an open book, perennially short of money, but never lacking noise and laughter and the good-natured teasing common to all happy families.

Mac could not imagine teasing his aunt.

I'm different.

Like a boy grown in a laboratory, Mac keenly felt his otherness. Always, he looked for that moment in the eyes of the people he met – the moment when they realized he was not like them. That he craved their ordinary history. He felt a pang when Marie huffed and puffed about her folks getting on her nerves, wishing he had a family to take for granted.

She stirred a little and did that now, in a drowsy voice. 'D'you hear Bernie banging on about her new car?'

'Typical Bern.'

She had landed with a whump on the Dralon sofa that would take the Mactavishes a year to pay off at ninety pence a month, and eulogized about her personalized numberplate. 'BERN1E. George insisted.'

Marie had said, wry, 'My Mac insisted on *me* having a personalized numberplate until I reminded him we don't have a car.'

They smiled at the memory. Mac said, 'George was adamant that I'll be disappointed if we have a girl. Couldn't convince him otherwise.'

Marie parroted George. 'You need a boy to carry on the family name.'

'Nonsense.' Mac hoped for a girl. A son might expect him to play football, or know about car engines. He had no template for fatherhood, unlike Marie and Bernie, who had grown up in the shade of their giant oak of a father.

Pat Neeson had high expectations of his four children. They must be solid, decent, *reliable*. In return he was all those things, and more. Six foot three of gentleness, with a ham-sized fist that could crush if it chose, but instead held his family gently. Again Mac's thoughts turned to his side of the family tree; there was just him and his aunt sitting on their bare bough. Not too close to one another.

She was all he had.

The story of Mac's parents had hardened into fable. All the details he would ever know he had already been given; his aunt found it difficult to talk about the day she lost both her only sister and her brother-in-law.

Only one photograph of his parents existed – their war-time wedding day. Ed Mactavish spick and span in his army khaki, hair greased, smile wide. A buttonhole carnation frilly on his collar.

And her. Marguerite. *My mother.* Warm dark eyes in a long face. Mac's nose. Mac's smile. His teeth, even. It always pleased him when he stole a look at the framed image to see their shared similarities. As a small child he had tried out names in a whisper as he stroked her flat, sepia cheek. 'Mum,' he'd say. 'Mummy.' He had never called her either. She had gone before he could talk. The man in the photo was also a stranger to his son. *I can tell they loved each other*, Mac would think, communing with the photograph. His father's hand on his mother's shoulder gave him a deep sensation that twinned love and loss.

He assumed they had, in turn, loved him. *Everybody loves their children*, thought Mac. Mac's aunt didn't furnish this level of detail. She was brisk, dealing with his childish questions the way a post office employee might discuss a missing postal order. He could sniff the unhappiness in her reticence.

Tatty can't find the words to tell me the whole truth.

His toddler mispronunciation of 'Auntie', Tatty's real name was lost to history, along with the mysterious truth that squatted between them on their leafless branch of the family tree.

This truth murmured to Mac. It reminded him that he was different. He had heard of babies being deprived of oxygen during birth and suffering afterwards. *I was deprived of love.* With no experience of being parented, would he fall at this vital hurdle?

He dreaded the day Marie would see him holding their child and notice how empty he was, how little he knew about family, how he needed L plates. And she would judge him. And a drop of that love which fuelled Mac through long days at the bank would evaporate.

Mac closed his eyes, but opened them again when he heard a small voice say, into the healing darkness, 'Darlin'? I'm scared.'

'My Marie? Scared? Never.' Mac squeezed his wife, smelled her shampoo smell. 'What's scaring you?'

'The birth.' Marie shrank into him. 'The pain.'

'Why not talk to your mum about it?' Mac leaned on one elbow, looking down at his wife. 'Next time you ring her.'

Once a week Marie traipsed to the phone box on the corner with a pile of change. She would return laden with family gossip – colourful stuff that Mac lapped up: her brother had thrown a beetroot at a policeman; the dry cleaner had ruined a good coat; nobody could locate the cat.

'No point asking Ma.' Nora Neeson was old-school Catholic; her sex education consisted of vague metaphors. 'When we got married she told me to grit my teeth on the wedding night. I hadn't the heart to tell her I tore off your shirt not long after we met.'

Marie turned away, unaware how the gesture hurt Mac. She was standing alone on jagged rocks, unsure where to place her feet. 'All I know is, it'll *hurt*. I can't face it.' She felt him lean against her, hold her tight. 'People say it's worth it when you hold the baby,' said Marie, her voice growing so small it was a mouse-squeak. 'Do you think that's true?'

'I'm sure it is,' said Mac, who wasn't sure.

'Easy for you to say,' grumbled Marie. 'You got the fun part.'

In the dark, Mac blushed. He had never been around a woman who relished sex so openly. Who ambushed him while he was clambering into his Y-fronts. The Mac reflected in Marie's eyes was a sexy piece of work; Mac was still getting used to it. 'If I could give birth for you, love, I would.'

She sat up then, all activity, her usual self. 'You would, wouldn't you? I actually believe you.' Marie laid her hand along the side of his face and just stared at him. 'Promise me things won't change,' she said.

'Of course they'll change. We'll have a baby to look after.'

'I know, yeah, I don't mean that. Obviously. I mean, you, me.' Marie kissed him. 'This.'

23

'Us, you mean? We'll never change, my little love.'

'Promise?'

It was the easiest promise Mac ever made.

They settled down again, closer than close. Just one month to their little girl's arrival, and Mac would like Marie to spend that month swaddled in cotton wool. It was as if a lorry roared towards them.

A lorry, Mac reminded himself, *that'll deliver something wonderful*. But a lorry all the same. He marvelled at her, at all women, for heading towards certain pain with courage and a cavalier swagger. As a man who still had nightmares about his ingrowing toenail, he had nothing but admiration for them all, every last tired, swollen-ankled one of them.

Some things in life are reliably unchanging. The prime minister will always over-promise and under-deliver. The British summer will be Arctic or Balearic. Next Door will never crack a smile.

He was a wet weekend made flesh. Mac had given up early on, but Marie persevered. A few weeks after their wedding anniversary, she invited Next Door and his wife in 'for a cuppa'.

'My *wife*?' He had seemed shocked by the invitation.

'Would be nice to meet her.' Marie had seen a shadowy figure behind the neurotically bleached net curtains.

'My wife is not available for *tea*.' Next Door pronounced the word as if Marie had suggested an orgy. 'And as you well know I never partake of hot drinks before 7pm. When are you due? That baby better not keep me up all night with its crying.'

'This baby will be impeccably behaved,' said Marie. 'I'm not due for another ...' She bent double. She staggered. 'Mac!' she screamed.

He came running.

'It's a boy.' The midwife held up a robotic blob, trying out its arms and legs for the first time.

'It's *our* boy,' gasped Mac.

He was there for the birth; he'd had to argue and cajole, but he took a page from his wife's book and wouldn't take no for an answer. So he heard every grunt and saw all the gore, and his hand was squeezed bloodless by Marie.

Everything the midwife did to help seemed to hurt Marie more. She was the centre of the throbbing room, helpless, and powerful. She was too exhausted to hold the baby, the unexpected boy, so Mac held onto him, gobsmacked, terrified, high as a kite.

The boy grew, as boys will. The health visitor measured him weekly, weighed him, and fell victim to his charms, like everyone else.

At nine months old, Dan Mactavish was bonny and golden and *happy*. As Mac came in from the front garden, he could hear the boy clapping.

'All right, son?' he asked, going to the sink to wash the earth from his hands. 'The wisteria's taking its time,' he said to Marie. 'But that new container of marguerites will be a warm welcome for your family when they get here.'

'Hmm,' said Marie. She lowered Dan into the playpen on the lino. Heinz leapt in after him, and the two of them began one of their companionable, interminable games.

'Lookee here, Marie!' Mac took down the cruise jar and shook it. 'Isle of Wight, here we come.'

She didn't answer. She passed the playpen to open a cupboard, oblivious to Dan reaching up his chubby arms to her.

'Steady, Heinz!' laughed Mac as the dog leapt out of the playpen like a racehorse and dropped a squeaky toy at Marie's feet. He waited, tail wagging, doggy bum in the air, for her to play.

Sighing, not finding what she was after, Marie turned from the cupboard, stepped over the toy and went out to collect the milk bottle on the doorstep.

Mac heard Next Door say a frigid hello; Marie closed the front door halfway through his greeting. The *schlufschluf* of slippers on the stairs told Mac she was headed back to bed.

'How long have we got?' Bernie stood, jacket still on, hands on hips, looking around at the dishes in the sink, and the crumbs collecting in drifts on the lino.

'They get here in two hours,' said Mac. 'I've tried, honest, but Dan needed his lunch and then Heinz had an accident on the carpet and—'

'Right.' Bernie rolled up her sleeves. 'Marie'll never

forgive herself, when she gets back to normal, if the house isn't shipshape for Ma and Da.'

They often talked of this mythical future when the curse would lift, when Marie would be back to normal.

Bewitched, Sunnyside slumbered under a wicked spell cast by some disgruntled fairy. Like Sleeping Beauty's castle, the house was surrounded by thorny briars that blocked the sunlight. Within, the family levitated in a fog the colour of coal, which dulled even the misjudged pink of the nursery.

As yet, no prince had arrived to kiss Marie awake; she didn't allow her husband to come close enough to try.

'I'm bad at this,' muttered Bernie, running the vacuum cleaner over Marie's prized brown and orange carpeting. An army of cleaners dusted Bernie's nooks and crannies out in Esher; only safeguarding her sister's good name could make her pull on a pair of yellow Marigolds. 'Has she been crying?' she asked over the vacuum's greedy roar.

'A bit. Well, a lot. Every day.'

It was a secret, a vice; Marie would turn away, wretched, and shake off Mac's hand.

'This morning,' he said, 'she told me we were wrong to bring an innocent child into an evil world.'

'Are you still keeping her away from the six o'clock news?'

'God, yes. She feels every bit of bad news as if it's happening to her.'

'What about the doctor?'

'The man's *useless*,' said Mac with feeling. 'I went to see him on my own, like you suggested.'

'And?'

'And . . .' Mac told Bernie about the GP's surgery, a chilly room with the air of a headmaster's office.

Looking over his glasses, the smell of whisky wafting from him, the doctor seemed surprised by the question. 'You're here to ask about your wife? Why're you taking such an interest, Mr Mactavish? It's women's business; one can't get too involved.'

'Her business,' said Mac, 'is my business. I'm worried about her.'

'Don't upset yourself. Never heard of the baby blues? The ladies, bless them, can often feel a little down at this time. Giving birth is the crowning glory of their lives, of course, but it's tiring too. And now she's running around after your little chap. Bound to be glum now and then.'

'This isn't glumness. This isn't feeling down. She's depressed, doctor.'

'She'll snap out of it. Give her time. Maybe lend a hand around the house now and then, but do *not* mollycoddle her.'

Hearing this, Bernie's mouth became a hen's bottom of disgust. 'You should have strangled him with his stethoscope.'

They scoured the sink; they scrubbed the table. 'Getting the house Ma-ready,' Bernie called it.

When it was time for Dan to eat, he gurgled and kicked in his highchair, anyone's for a rusk. He was easy-going, one of those dream babies who sleep like a log and eat like a Viking. He was a big hit with the ladies, especially his besotted Auntie Bernie, who kept him supplied with a wardrobe of sailor suits and Harrods bootees. As George joked, Dan dressed like a minor royal from the 1920s.

As she wiped the boy's chin, Bernie said, unhappily, 'What frightens me, is how blank our Marie is. She's always been so interested in everything, in *people,* and now she's not even interested in this little fella.'

'As if,' said Mac, pausing as he dried a plate, 'there's nothing going on inside her at all.'

A floor above them, in the marital bed, a lot was going on inside Marie.

She was terrified.

Of the house, of the baby, of Mac. But most of all of herself.

I'm ruining my milk, she worried. That was today's ugly thought; every day brought a fresh one. Yesterday she had been unable to take Dan to the Co-op because she kept visualizing a car mounting the pavement and hitting his pushchair. Moments ago, in the kitchen, she had imagined her faithful little Heinz sinking his teeth into the baby's arm. No matter how she pushed at these thoughts, they got through.

I'm spoiling my milk with all this crying. Laid out flat as a corpse on the bed, tears pooled in Marie's ears and the creases of her neck. When Mac dared to ask what was wrong, she had no answer. *How can I tell him the truth? That I'm not up to this, that Dan deserves better, that the baby's so-called mother is useless. Pathetic. Not worthy of being alive.*

Marie berated herself in a way she would never do to another person. She had no sympathy for herself, only criticisms. Her sore, wobbly body felt like somebody else's; *I shouldn't be here,* she told herself as she listened to the people she loved most move about the kitchen, taking care of her house. *They'd all be better off without me.*

Bernie was at the bedroom door and Marie dried her tears, brutally, with a fist.

'C'mon, sis, get dressed,' said Bernie, with that fake jauntiness Marie had come to expect. 'They'll be here any minute.'

'Nothing fits,' said Marie. She and her body were estranged; it didn't make sense to her. And it ached.

Downstairs, Mac put away the tea towel and caught Dan's eye.

The child hooted.

'C'mere, you.' Mac bent to pick him up, and walked him, jiggling all the while, around the ground floor. 'Wouldn't Mummy laugh if she saw me in this frilly apron?' Mac was fibbing to his son; the old version of Mummy would laugh, but there were no jokes in the cursed castle. No tellings off, either; Mac was free to put his mug directly on the glass coffee table and he *hated* it.

There was no delight in Marie for the home they had put together so carefully. She had barely registered the new wisteria, half-listening when Mac admitted that, yes, for now, it looked like a dead twig, but it would eventually grow into a chocolate box riot of purple, with blooms dripping from the boxy white front of Sunnyside.

'These ornaments are your mummy's pride and joy.' Mac couldn't see the appeal of the porcelain dancing ladies but Marie – the old Marie, Marie #1 – adored them. 'Ooh, careful!' Dan's chubby fingers reached out and almost toppled a frame.

When Marie had realized Mac owned only one photograph of his parents, she bought an elaborate brass frame and set the wedding portrait front and centre on the mantelpiece over the gas fire.

'That's *my* mummy and daddy, so they're your grandparents, Dan. They'll never meet you but I happen to know they'd love you very much. Nearly as much as me and Mummy love you. Oh look, here's Mummy now.'

Passing through in a shirtdress, its buttons straining and accessorised, as ever, with slippers, Marie barely glanced at them.

Returning to the photograph, Mac schooled his son. 'See the uniform? Your granddad fought in the war, to keep us all safe. He was called Ed and she was Marguerite. Like the flowers outside.' He searched daily in Dan's face to find a resemblance to either of his parents, but Dan was a Neeson through and through. A rakish red-gold quiff bounced over bonny hamster cheeks pink with health, and his blue eyes shone like enamelled buttons.

They wandered to the kitchen, where the radio had been switched on. Loud. Marie stood, arms folded about herself like a straitjacket, gazing out at the garden with a cigarette dying between her fingers, as Michael Jackson, his young voice high and fluting, filled the room.

'It's time for Dan's nap.' Mac held him out to Marie, the child's legs cycling in mid-air. 'Want to . . . ?'

Stubbing out the cigarette to take him, Marie put Dan down in the pink back room. Mac had formally apologized to the baby about the lack of blue when they brought him home from hospital. She tucked him in, smoothed Dan's hair. Efficient. Careful. But mechanical.

Ever amenable, Dan the perfect baby – 'Takes after me,' Bernie liked to say – fell asleep without kerfuffle, mouth open, lashes a-tremble, spatchcocked in his Harrods cot.

The house was silent, Sunday-quiet and stagnant. That wicked fairy really knew her stuff. Mac could practically hear the briars creaking and growing.

But suddenly! Noise, movement, squeals of greeting, and the Neesons were there. A travelling block of Good Times. The doorbell made Marie shrink. The other Marie would belt through the house to greet a visitor, but this one felt the tight elastic band inside her pull even more taut. *Don't cry don't cry don't cry,* she whispered her desperate mantra. For some reason it was vital that nobody know about her agony; *they'll shun me, they'll hate me*, she thought. They could never, however hard they tried, match the hate Marie felt for herself.

She saw the drained woman reflected in the kitchen window and wondered who on earth it was.

I am you, it told her, and she could barely believe it.

Out in the hall, tiny, bird-like matriarch Nora kicked off her good shoes. 'Me feet are killin' me!' she told Mac as she hugged him much harder than those sparrow arms would suggest. 'Are you getting more handsome?' she asked him as she pulled his cheek.

The rooms were suddenly full of humans. It was more of an invasion than a visit. The fridge was opened, cases set down anyhow. Mac was dazed, Heinz was ecstatic, and Marie's torpor went unnoticed alongside the incomers' abundance of energy.

'You've shot up, Adrian!' Mac told his wife's brother. Twelve years old, he was a foal, all arms and legs. 'And Bridget, good to see you.' It wasn't *that* good to see Bridget; she was the human equivalent of a bottle of vinegar.

The television was switched on – *Are You Being Served?* blared out – and the lava lamp was knocked over and tea was requested, nay *begged* for.

When will they notice? wondered Mac, as the Neesons milled in and out and around and about. When would they spot Marie as an impostor, a perfect facsimile with all the spirit sucked out?

Nora Neeson colonized the kitchen. Enormous amounts of food appeared from thin air. Mac sat back from his plate, full as a foie gras goose. Somehow, chairs were found – or approximated; Adrian sat on an upturned bucket – and space was made and they all fitted around the Formica-topped table.

'Another baked apple, Tatty?' Nora held up the dish and winked. 'Sure, they're small.'

'I've had sufficient, thank you.' Press-ganged into

attending – the Neesons didn't take no for an answer when it came to hospitality – Tatty laid her spoon across her plate. She ate sparingly, still trapped in wartime austerity. The teasing to-and-fro of the table baffled her, and Nora's kind insistence that they include her was misguided; Tatty would rather be at home.

Pat was sitting back, dwarfing the spindly kitchen chair, as he gamely tried to engage Tatty in small talk. A big man with a leonine head of greying hair, his tum was testament to Nora's ideas of nutrition. His voice was naturally loud but Mac had never heard it raised in anger. *A real lady*, that was how Pat described Tatty, and now the real lady hid her keenness to be away with a mantle of good manners.

Not so George, who was on his feet, jangling his keys.

Nora was disappointed. 'Ah, no, you're not going, Georgie?'

'I bloody am, Nora,' he said, and she cracked up with cheerful shock. 'You lot drive me bonkers.'

Pat, putting the last baked apple out of its misery, said, 'Yer man makes a good point.'

'Pop up and say goodnight to little Dan,' said Nora. 'He went to sleep like a lamb, he did.'

'But I see him all the time,' said George.

'He's just a baby,' groused Adrian. 'He looks like every other baby.'

'Whisht, you heathen,' said Nora.

'Any idea where that wifey of mine has got to?' George said.

'I'll winkle her out.' Mac was glad to escape the heat of the kitchen.

In the hall, he heard the twitter of sisterly gossip, and followed it upstairs. Through the crack in the door he saw the three Neeson girls – Marie, Bernie and Bridget – sitting close together on the side of the master bed, ruffling the Terylene valance.

Bridget was pious, old-fashioned; behind her back Bernie described her as 'practically a nun'. Her navy twinset was a drab counterpoint to Bernie's Lurex halterneck. They sat either side of Marie, who stared at the floorboards.

'Snap out of it,' Bridget was saying.

Mac flattened himself against the wall and heard Bernie, fiery and protective. 'She would if she could, you massive eejit!'

'Don't you *eejit* me,' said Bridget.

'This isn't a *mood*, Bridget. Marie is sick.'

'Hmm.'

'Take that *hmm* back. I know what your bloody *hmms* mean, Bridget Neeson!'

Nothing from Marie, noted Mac. As usual. He had hoped she might respond to her sisters. *Once upon a time*, he thought, *we discussed every last little thing.* It was only a few months ago, but it felt like a different life. He flinched at the fear that they had lost their rapport, that it wasn't just dormant, but had melted completely away.

Bridget was pontificating. 'Ma had *four* kids, and she never wallowed like this.'

Then Marie did say something. 'But Ma's . . .'

Say it, urged Mac, his back against the still-unpapered

landing wall. *Tell them your ma's stronger than you, that you need help!*

There was silence, broken by Bernie, both triumphant and annoyed. 'Well done, Bridget. You've made her cry.'

Marie spoke. Tears clogged the words she released one at a time, reluctantly. 'I need to sleep but I can't sleep because I watch Dan all night – *all night* – in case he stops breathing.'

'But he—' began Bridget.

Marie carried on, in the same biting monotone. 'I don't know how to look after him. Mac does most of it. I'm so tired and I'm so ... I'm a very bad person and I shouldn't have all this.'

'All what?' asked Bernie.

'This!' Marie was struggling to make herself understood. 'This this this! The house, the love, Mac, Dan! I don't deserve it.'

'You're doing great.' Bernie sounded strained.

'To be honest,' said Bridget, 'she could do better.'

In Mac went, unable to take any more. He was hale and hearty. 'Bernie, your chauffeur's getting impatient, love.'

The trio was broken up. Bernie raced off on her stacked heels and Bridget padded away in her soft-soled slip-ons.

'Marie ...' he said.

She bowed her head. 'Don't,' she said. 'Just don't.' Her language was fierce but she was not. She was listless, hollowed out. 'You'd be better off without me. You know that.'

'Don't talk this way. Please.' Mac felt as if one hand were

tied behind his back. He knew, from recent history, that if he pressed her, she would begin to shake and cry.

'I need ...' She lay back and closed her eyes. 'I need to not be here, Mac.'

He closed the door on her, bewildered, impotent.

The Mercedes purred at the kerb. Mac shut the door on Bernie, who was settling herself on the butter-soft leather seating.

'Mac, don't you let our Bridget bully Marie. She's always had a stick up her arse, that one.'

Wincing, George put the car into gear. 'Good luck, mate. You're a brave man to take on the Neesons *en masse*. Oh, hang about.' The parking brake went on. 'I almost forgot. Did you get that promotion you were so confident about?'

'Nah.' Mac rammed his hands into his pockets. He could feel Next Door's eyes boring into his back through the net curtains.

'Shame,' said George. 'Next time, eh?'

Mac waved them off, but stayed put, reliving the humiliation of being leapfrogged by a junior colleague.

The manager had been frank. 'I'm surprised you even applied, Mactavish. You take all your annual leave in one go after your son is born, despite my protests. Then there's sick leave here, and coming in late there ...'

They both knew Mac was fit as a fiddle and never needed sick leave. There seemed no way for him to explain, in that airless office, about how he had to stay at home to ensure his baby boy was washed, fed, *held*.

'Sometimes I suspect your heart's not in the bank.'

Mac had protested, but secretly he wondered if *anybody's* heart could be in mortgages and standing orders. *My heart's in Sunnyside, with Marie and Dan.*

Oh, and puffins of course.

Marie, Dan, puffins.

When Mac dashed home in his lunch hour, Adrian had just left Sunnyside in Bridget's care to 'do' the sights of London. Mac pitied him; the boy was excited to see Piccadilly Circus, but Mac knew Bridget's itinerary was heavy on cathedrals.

From the kitchen, he heard Pat serenading Nora with 'Danny Boy', his party piece; every self-respecting Irish Da had a party piece. Mac stole a look at Dan in his cot. Just that morning he had seen a property developer look at a pile of cash the way he looked at Dan. As if he were treasure.

Downstairs, he got no greeting from Marie, who hid her silence in Nora's non-stop chatter. He kissed the back of his wife's head. She didn't register it.

Don't touch me, Marie was thinking. *I'll infect you.* The gothic drama within her was at odds with the sunlit kitchen, the romper suits drying on the radiator. Sometimes she felt the paradox would blow her apart.

'Sandwich, Mac?' From Nora this was less of a question, more of an order. 'I was just saying to Marie, good thing she gave up the ould hairdressing. She can't work *and* take care of Dan.'

Marie spoke. 'I didn't give it up, Ma. It gave me up. I had morning sickness, day after day. I had to lie down out the back. I was useless. They had to let me go.'

Pat said, 'Terrible shame, when you worked so hard to get that apprenticeship.'

'She's going back, though,' said Mac. 'Just as soon as we work out some childcare.'

Nora said nothing. But she said it very loudly.

Genial and optimistic as ever, Pat said, 'Vital Sassoon might let you pick up where you left off.'

Marie picked at the corner of a table mat. 'My manager rang last week. Offered me exactly that.'

Startled, Mac said, 'Why didn't you tell me, love? We'll break out the Asti Spumante tonight.'

'I turned it down.' Marie's eyes were dull, as if that wicked fairy had pulled some lever within her, and turned off the juice.

'You didn't!' Mac regretted saying that so passionately; this post-natal Marie was fragile, peculiar. 'Perhaps we can get back to him.'

'I told him to stick it.' Marie's half-laugh was a horrible sound. She cocked her head. 'Is that Dan crying?' She left the room. *Schluf-schluf.*

Nora's face closed up, and she tied a hangman's knot in her headscarf. 'We're out of milk,' she said, and left the house.

Pat laid a heavy paw on Mac's shoulder. 'My poor girl, Mac. She's not herself, is she?'

The sympathy felt like honey to Mac. Honey, sunshine, velvet cat fur; all the good things. He got lonely in the enchanted castle. 'Something's gone awry, deep inside, but don't worry, Pat, I'll look after her.'

'I know that, son.'

Nobody had ever called Mac that before. When he could speak again, he said, 'If this were World War One, I'd carry her off the battlefield on my back. But I don't know what to do, other than wait.'

Lowering his voice, Pat said, 'Her ma was the same after our Bridget.' He put a finger to his lips when Mac drew a sharp breath, and sent a paranoid glance at the door, as if Nora might burst through it with a machine gun. 'Babies didn't happen easily for us. She'll never talk about it, but Nora was just like Marie. Dead inside. Thought I'd lost her. Then, one day, she turned a corner and started to swim back to me.' Pat slapped Mac on the back, winding him. 'So stick it out, Mac. Marie's still in there somewhere.' He rubbed his hands together in a signal Mac understood.

This man-to-man interlude is over.

'I'll walk you back to the bank,' said Pat. 'Might squeeze in a crafty half-pint on the way back, eh?'

They'd reached the corner when they heard the shrieks. They turned to see Marie on her knees, holding a bundle up over her head like a sacrifice.

'Mother of God, is that the baby?' Pat began to run.

'He's choking! He's choking!' Marie screamed like a banshee. 'Help me! Help! He's dying!'

Mac got to her just before she collapsed on the dirty pavement, her limbs puddling.

He snatched the bundle and scrabbled at the blanket over the baby's face.

'Is he breathing?' Pat had caught up.

A passer-by stopped. The lady from the house opposite shouted that she'd dialled 999.

'No, don't, he's fine.' Mac held Dan's face to his and heard him cough. 'False alarm.'

Next Door lingered when the other onlookers went about their business. He and the myriad gnomes in his front garden watched Mac and Pat gently coax Marie up from the ground and support her indoors.

A few minutes later, he could be heard telling his fellow customers in the newsagents that 'her from Sunnyside has gone doolally'.

The house was theirs again. No sudden renditions of 'Danny Boy'. No sightings of Bridget in her curlers.

Mac felt the responsibility of his situation as he trudged home from work. He was once again alone at the helm.

His key in the door no longer brought Marie. It did bring Heinz, who had one of Mac's shoes in his teeth.

'Gee thanks,' he muttered.

She was at the sink, turned away.

'All right, love?' he said cautiously, taking off his jacket, undoing his tie. Something about the set of her shoulders made him pause. *They're not up around her ears.*

She turned. Perhaps it was the eye contact that gave him courage; Marie hadn't looked him squarely in the eye for an age. It was a chink of daylight in the pitch-black of the briars.

'Know what I was thinking about today?' he said.

She shrugged.

But she's still looking at me.

'I was thinking about the night you and I met.'

Is that a smile?

Mac was no good at parties. For one thing, they tended to be full of women, and he was even worse at them.

Pleased with his psychedelic shirt when he left the house, it seemed to fall out of fashion the moment he reached the basement in Notting Hill. Grabbing a beer – he didn't like beer – he began a tour of various walls. First, he stood against the kitchen wall, then graduated to the wall by the coat stand, ending up trapped in a corner of the sitting room. Just him and Che Guevara; the peeling poster hid a damp patch.

He had noticed her earlier and now he saw her again, dancing as if somebody had electrocuted her, in a ruffled minidress and shiny white boots. *She's so small*, he thought. It was like watching a supernova erupt; her energy made its own energy. In the dim light Mac couldn't even make out if the girl was pretty or not.

She doesn't need to be. The little powerhouse made her own rules; he couldn't take his eyes off her. He drank the beer. He was elbowed and trodden on. A man with a beard offered him a spliff. Mac declined; the man looked at him with pity.

Time to leave.

'Oi,' said the girl, who had snuck up on him somehow. 'Do me a favour?'

An accent, he thought, at the same time as he thought, *Oh Christ an actual woman is talking to me*. 'Yeah, sure, if I can.'

'Me ex is here tonight and he's a *monster*,' said the girl. She talked fast, leaning in, looking up at him through spidery false lashes. 'He's desperate to get me back.'

'Um, yeah, and?'

'And if you pretend to be my date then he'll get the message.'

Slightly anxious as to this boyfriend's dimensions, Mac knew manna from Heaven when he saw it. 'Sure.' He smiled. 'I'm Mac,' he said.

'I'm Marie,' she said.

She made him dance with her. He discovered he could do it without hurting himself or anybody else. He discovered he enjoyed it. They both got tipsy. She sent her girl chum home. He wondered how to ask her for her number.

'This boyfriend – did you break his heart?'

'Me? Of course not.' Marie winked and Mac felt his whole body tingle.

'Oh God, he's coming over.' Marie stood on tiptoes; her breath smelled of wine. 'Quick, kiss me and make it look good.'

Her hands were in his hair and suddenly his arms snaked tight around her. The party shrank to where their lips met. He picked her up and she squealed against his teeth. The kiss went on for quite some time.

'Good enough?' he panted.

'I think it did the trick,' she said.

'Remember that kiss?' Mac said to the same girl, only three years older but with all her internal lights switched off. 'It was like coming home. I was excited, off my head, but calm at the same time. I fell in love with you right then, no ifs or buts, like falling off a cliff only to find the sea is made of mattresses. I can't thank that ex-boyfriend enough; he made my life happen.'

Marie looked at him, studying him. Eventually she said – and the voice was Marie's voice – 'Jaysus, boyo, you don't *still* believe he existed, do you?'

And then she laughed.

It wasn't that simple; nothing is. But it was a start. Slowly the curse waned and the briars fell away and Marie slipped into clogs instead of slippers and she took pleasure in Dan and she click-clacked to the door the second she heard Mac's key.

He didn't know where she had been; he was just glad she was back. There would be no more babies, they said. *Just in case.*

Marie didn't look behind her. Who would want to examine such a hard and stony road? She went, as was her habit, full pelt ahead, grateful for being grateful. She didn't share her terror that she might be dumped on that road again. She put her best foot forward. In a clog.

She shook the jar and asked him to guess how much

money was in it. 'This time we'll plan a proper cruise, with a fancy cabin and games on deck and all that sort of thing.'

The future was back, and they linked arms and stepped into it together, Dan in their arms.

CHAPTER THREE

'This photo's in colour!' She is on her feet; he saw her through the glass safety doors as he signed in.

He sets down the tray. 'It's a Polaroid,' he says. 'They're cool again, apparently.'

'Sit! Sit!' She cowers in her chair, stuffing the album down the side of the seat. 'Don't let her see us.'

'Don't let who see us?' He is tickled by the change in mood, and looks around him.

'Don't catch her eye, silly.'

A red-haired woman passes, humming to herself.

'Ah, your nemesis,' he whispers.

'Shush!' She is at daggers drawn with the other resident; a petty battle about portion sizes and chair positions and control of the TV remote. 'It'd be just like her to claim these are her photographs and take them away from me.'

With the danger passed, they find the next page.

'*Oh, they're not at the little house anymore.*' She is
disappointed. '*I do hope they haven't moved. I liked that
funny little place.*'

'*They're on holiday somewhere hot. You don't get
bougainvillea like that in England.*'

'*That's a villa, isn't it? Spain, maybe.*'

'*Just the two of them. Where's the kiddie?*'

'*Do you have children?*' she asks suddenly.

It happens now and again. The acute anguish of
everything they have lost. The memories erased and dumped.
You know me, *he wants to say.* Stop pretending.

*Instead, he says, '*Here, take your tea.*'

29 July 1977

'Grassy arse, *señor*,' said Mac carefully to the obliging taxi
driver who took their photograph.

Wobbling on new rainbow-patterned platforms, Marie
turned to take in the villa that shone a saintly white against
the shimmering blue Malaga sky.

'We're really, truly *abroad!*' she said.

'And we're really truly on our own,' said Mac. 'Your sister's an angel to take Dan off our hands and lend us the villa
for our anniversary. I get you all to myself for a whole week.'

'Can't wait,' said Marie, in the undertone he knew so well,
'to christen the bed. And the veranda. And the pool.'

'Steady on,' said Mac, delighted.

The delight was short-lived. The studded door flew open.

'Welcome to Spain!' yelled Bernie, in a canary-yellow bikini. Dan tore around the side of the house, and behind him came George, in Speedos that would get him arrested back home.

'Oh,' managed Marie.

'I couldn't bear to think of you here on your own, so me and the boys flew out ahead of you to get everything ready.'

'How can we ever thank you?' deadpanned Marie.

'Helloooo!' came a shout from a balcony.

Mac shaded his eyes. 'Adrian?' The boy was a skinny outline against the sun. *Good God, are all the Neesons here?*

There were no more surprises. Adrian had been shipped solo from Dublin 'to get him out of the house' and, as the party convened around the pool, his Auntie Bernie told the newcomers she was committed to finding him a *señorita*. 'Eighteen and never been kissed,' she said, handing round the suncream. 'I'll send him home covered in lovebites.'

'Abroad' was a revelation; so deliciously un-English. Feeling self-conscious in shorts – *Why are my legs so white?* – Mac counted down the hours to his first paella. The scent of bougainvillea battled with the scent of Hawaiian Tropic lotion in the baking heat.

The tiles of the swimming pool reflected the sunshine, and Mac had to reach for his new sunglasses, a £4.99 bargain from Boots in the airport. 'Shame there's no water in the pool,' he said.

'Some kind of fungus problem.' On his sunbed, George gleamed like a slab of oiled teak. 'Bloke's coming to sort it out on Friday.'

'The day we fly home,' murmured Marie, whose ruffled swimsuit felt tight. She checked her watch. 'I should be at work right now.' She stretched, happy not to be in her hated Fresh'n'Fine tabard. The part-time job slotted nicely around Dan's primary school schedule, and Marie brought home tales of staffroom goings-on, along with just-on-their-sell-by-date macaroons. Practically running the place, Marie waved Mac away when he worried she had taken on too much with a job *and* studying for her hairdressing diploma. The local college was no Vidal Sassoon, but the qualification would give her a leg-up when she returned to full-time work.

I want the kids to look up to me, Marie thought, as she ran from Sunnyside to Fresh'n'Fine to school gates to college, and back again. Ambition burned inside her. And now she felt her nose burn as she offered herself to the Spanish sun.

Adrian dribbled a football past, chased by six-year-old Dan, who shadowed his uncle everywhere. 'Ma keeps asking,' he said, stopping to do some keepy-uppies by Marie's lounger, 'when you're having more babies.'

Marie's sunglasses hid her expression.

'Bit personal, mate,' said George.

'Is it?' Adrian covered his mouth. 'Sorry.'

The huge sombrero Bernie wore as she hovered with a tray cast a personal shade around her. She changed the subject; she knew it was a marshy and difficult one for the Mactavishes. 'Booked the famous cruise yet?'

'Norfolk Broads,' beamed Marie. She and Mac had pored over the brochure like medieval monks with a bible.

'Nice,' said Bernie, not very convincingly.

The cruise jar was recovering from recent demands Sunnyside had made on it. The drain problem that had them holding their noses for days on end. The new living room wallpaper Marie so loved; its brown and orange zigzags gave Mac migraines.

'Are we sure about the Norfolk Broads?' Mac's voice was sleepy; Spain had a narcotic effect.

'What you mean is, there are no puffins in Norfolk.' To Marie, puffins were the Other Woman. 'It'll be fun; the boat looks nice.'

They were quiet, neither of them thinking about the Norfolk Broads. They both thought of Marie's diligent, near-neurotic attitude to taking her daily contraceptive pill. Neither could face the so-called baby blues again.

Six years, thought Marie, *but it feels like yesterday.*

Beside her, Mac shivered, as if a ghost had walked over his grave. Baby-making, so straightforward for many folk, was littered with mantraps for him and his Marie. There was no need to rock the Sunnyside boat, no matter how dearly Nora Neeson longed for more grandchildren.

Besides, he thought, watching Dan clamber onto Adrian's back, *where would the extra love come from?* Their little belter of a boy used up every drop of the stuff Mac could find.

Fatherhood had caused an explosion of feeling; Mac simply didn't believe it could happen twice.

'Tell you what I miss out here,' said George. '*Telly*. Spanish TV is all in bleedin' Spanish.'

'You missed a brilliant documentary the other night.' Mac sat up, engaged.

'Was it about birds?' Bernie shared a look with Marie.

'It was about the probation service. Fascinating stuff. They—'

'With all due respect, Mac,' said Bernie, dropping her sombrero onto his head. 'Shut up.'

The bedroom was very different to their room at home – tiled floor, mosquito net, the throb of a warm night beyond the window – but they made a nest of it, just as they always did.

'Happy anniversary.' Marie enjoyed Mac's shocked gasp when she handed him a wrapped rectangle. 'I know, I *know*, we don't usually do pressies, but this is different.'

'Naughty,' said Mac. 'A book?' He assumed it would involve puffins, but no. '*The Language of Flowers*? Love, this book already belongs to me.'

'I know. It's the only thing you took from Tatty's. But I don't think you've ever read the title page.'

Opening the old, yellowed hardback, Mac's face creased with a complicated smile. He followed the handwritten words with a finger. 'To my Marguerite, from Ed'. He couldn't speak for a while.

'You like your pressie?' Marie bounced on the bed.

'I love it,' said Mac.

They made love. They were quiet, freezing each time the iron bed groaned. Afterwards, as Mac drifted off, he felt Marie sit up.

'What date is it?' she hissed in the dark.

'Twenty-ninth, you twit,' said Mac, turning over. 'Our anniversary. Why?'

'Nothing.'

Marie listened to his breathing and lay watching the ceiling until the next splendid day began its march across it.

The busy market smelled of spices and meat and life.

Mac, his nose peeling, tried to stop Dan pinching the fruit piled high on the stalls. The apples were glossy and pneumatic, nothing like Fresh'n'Fine's anaemic offerings. Ahead of him walked the women – his women – hips swinging, gossiping.

Bernie collared Adrian. 'See that pretty little *señorita* on the egg stall? Go and buy half a dozen and ask her to go for a stroll in the square this evening.'

Finding an even deeper red beneath his sunburn, Adrian refused. 'I'm grand, I don't need a girlfriend,' he said.

'Leave him be,' said Marie, her arms a dot-to-dot of mosquito bites. 'He'll find a girl when he's good and ready.'

'Took me until my twenties to find the right one,' said Mac.

'Surely *she* found *you*,' said Bernie, fondling a fig. 'Did I tell youse, Bridget and Ma are jetting over next month.'

'Bridget will suspect the Spanish men of lustful thoughts,' said Marie.

'They're my favourite sort!' Bernie handed a fistful of pesos to the stallholder. 'Poor Bridget. Such a *small* life.'

'Poor Bridget, my eye,' said Marie. 'She looks down on all us sinners. What she needs is a damn good snog. That'd loosen her up.'

Bernie wasn't listening. She was dragging Adrian to the egg stall.

'Cigar?' George tucked one behind Mac's ear when he refused. They browsed a leather goods stall. 'Congrats on the promotion. Assistant Manager! Hope they gave you a decent raise to go with it.'

Mac shook his head. 'Nope.'

George was kind. Which made it worse. 'That's not fair, mate. A title's meaningless without more money. Ask for a raise, so you can move house, stop the girls yakking about Sunnyside being pokey.'

Mac studied an ugly wallet, his thoughts racing. *Has Marie been agreeing with Bernie?*

'Lunch, boys?' Marie bowled up. She had to make two attempts before Mac would give her his hand, and he ignored her questioning look.

George led the way; he knew a little taverna that did a cracking toad-in-the-hole.

Putting Dan to bed was just as much of a performance in the villa. The boy raced through white rooms in the altogether, until his parents formed a pincer movement and got the better of him.

Outside his room, they had a whispered exchange of views.

'I *told you* I did *not* call our house pokey!' Marie stamped her sandal. 'I just . . .'

'Just what?'

Marie stomped through the villa ahead of him, so he had to scuttle to keep up. 'I just said you work all the hours God sends at that bank, you cover everyone's holidays and yet here we are with a crappy car and a porch that's falling off and . . . and . . .' She stammered to a halt, full of pent-up feeling, and threw open the glass doors to the garden. She threw up her arms and looked about her at the bougainvillea, the pool, and Mac heard her loud and clear.

Look at what my sister has!

George, Bernie and Adrian stared, all of them awkwardly negotiating the fruit floating in their sangria.

'Uh-oh,' said George. 'Trouble in paradise.'

'How come you never said this to me?' said Mac.

Bernie butted in. 'Cos she knew you'd be like this, Mac. All stiff, like Heinz when he sees a squirrel.'

'There's nothing wrong with Sunnyside,' said Mac.

Marie ticked a list on her fingers. 'The lino's curling up. The fridge is dying. We still haven't carpeted the landing.'

George went back to his Stephen King, saying, 'You need to walk in to your boss and *demand* more money.'

'That's not how the bank works,' Mac dropped to a sun lounger. He felt small, insufficient, all six foot of him.

Marie bent and took his face in her hands. She was gentle. She kissed him.

And then he said it. Without thinking, without forethought. 'I don't want to work at the bank anymore.'

Marie stared.

'I want', said Mac, 'to be a probation officer.'

'Work with criminals?' Marie gaped at him.

Bernie stood up. 'That'd mean retraining, so you'd get *less* money. You can't, Mac,' she said. 'Not with a baby on the way.'

It was Mac's turn to gape.

Marie closed her eyes and counted to ten.

'Go,' she snarled at Bernie, and Bernie went, hustling George and Adrian with her. 'Sorry, sorry,' she whispered as she closed the glass doors and left them together.

'Bloody Bernie,' said Marie. 'I was going to tell you when the doctor confirmed it but, really, I know.'

'Wow.'

'Wow? Is that it?'

'This is unexpected, love, the pill . . .' Mac decided he should be frank. No shilly-shallying. He picked her up and spun her around. 'This is fantastic!'

Baby number two, still just a speck, unlocked a door inside Mac, and there was the love, luminous as Kryptonite and good to go.

He laughed and she laughed. They were goofy together, and then, as if on a signal, they fell silent.

'What if . . .' she said.

'You get ill again? We'll be better prepared this time, love.' It felt like scant comfort. 'Do you—'

'Don't even ask me if I want this baby. I want it more than I've ever wanted anything.'

'That's good enough for me.' He pulled a face. 'Marie! The cruise! The Norfolk Broads!'

'No way, I'll be sick as a dog by then, you mark my words.'

Bernie was knocking on the glass. 'Can we get pissed now?' she mouthed.

The crickets serenaded the lone figure on the veranda.

The baby had been toasted, over and over. 'You pair of idiots,' George had said, genially. The now-peaceful villa hiccupped quietly in its sleep. Marie hadn't touched a drop. The rocking chair squeaked beneath her and she contemplated the vast black sky, set with diamond stars.

She was happy. She was sad. *Life's like that*, she thought. *Never one thing at a time.*

Marie was a creature of superstition. She trusted her instincts, and her instincts told her not to be frightened, that she wouldn't suffer this time. There was no basis for this; experts would scoff, but Marie tilted her chin and decided not to live in fear.

It was a blessing, this child. *But you're already a tyrant, little one.* The cruise must be cancelled; morning sickness and boats do not mix. She must give up Fresh'n'Fine. She must defer her training. *Again.* The universe was petty; *Why does it keep ruining my dreams, when they're so small they're barely visible to the naked eye?*

Marie stroked her tummy, knowing another universe was forming inside her. There was only one person she'd gladly put those dreams on hold for. 'Welcome to the family,' she said out loud, and the crickets listened.

She sat for a while longer, then she said, without turning her head, 'I know you're there. Come out and join me, silly.'

Adrian slunk out in pyjamas. He sat at her feet, like Heinz. 'Do you ever feel . . .' It took a while but his sister was patient and finally he said, 'Do you ever feel like you don't fit in?'

'I do,' said Marie. She stroked his hair. 'But I'm wrong. I fit in wherever I'm loved, and so do you.'

He leaned back against her legs. He was already a foot taller than her. Vulnerable in that way of boys.

'You fit in here, love,' she said.

They listened some more to the crickets, but Marie felt the first tug of a storm in the air.

London was grey after their week of sunshine.

A casual onlooker might imagine that Mac spent his first day back at work engrossed in bank business. However, the envelope Mac posted in his lunch hour was nothing to do with overdrafts or interest rates.

He wondered, as it left his fingers, if keeping the form a secret from Marie was tantamount to lying to her? Mac's conscience never slept; *I'm a liar*, he decided, as he turned the car towards town.

The lamps were lit in Tatty's small flat. Four floors up, her rent-controlled eyrie in central London was her pride and joy. Pure Tatty through and through, the neat rooms were tidy, somewhat dated. She offered Mac a teacake. Just one.

'You have news,' she said. 'I can tell.' Her response to baby number two was measured, nothing like the Neeson screeching when Marie called Dublin. 'Congratulations are in order,' she said. She asked after Marie's health, and Dan's progress, and they lapsed into silence.

There was so much silence on Mac's side of the family. He had told his parents about the baby, in the dark of the Spanish night, but they had said nothing back. He had strained to hear, but no. Nothing. *I'll be more confident this time,* he had assured Ed Mactavish, frozen forever in his khaki and his carnation. While it was true that Mac didn't have a role model, he *did* have Ed's DNA.

'I planted marguerites in the front garden,' he told Tatty, as a way into the territory he both craved and feared.

'Nice.'

'According to *The Language of Flowers*, they mean "I wait for you",' said Mac. He felt he had waited long enough. 'Did my mother like marguerites, Tatty? 'Cos they're, you know, her namesake.'

He could almost hear a steel hinge snap shut. 'Oh, well . . .' said Tatty.

Why are you like this? thought Mac, suddenly resentful that he must interrogate her to discover the most banal snippets of his history. Surely he owned his own story. Wasn't it his right to know?

Mac often regressed to his schoolboy self in this apartment. Minding his Ps and Qs, he was stuck in the aspic of the other under-furnished rooms they used to share.

Their accommodation had never belonged to them; it came with Tatty's housekeeping positions. He remembered a large attic apartment in Mayfair. An ad-hoc annexe in Pinner. Servants' quarters in a mansion that loomed over Richmond Park.

No front door, no garden of their own. A different bed every couple of years, a different sofa. And none of it new. None of it theirs. To that day Mac couldn't bear rooms in the eaves; Sunnyside's box-like modernity endeared it to him.

'Be good,' Tatty used to say as she left him alone while she went to clean someone else's silverware and serve someone else a three-course dinner. Mac knew what being good meant. It meant being quiet, self-sufficient. Not giving Tatty trouble. No boisterousness. No running around, or kicking a ball.

It meant tidying away any part of himself that needed something. Sensitive little Mac had been contaminated with Tatty's fear of being 'turned out'. The phrase was echoed whenever he and Marie talked about money; she couldn't understand his fear of being homeless.

Marie would say, 'We're young and strong and we'll always keep ourselves afloat!' His wife had a healthy respect for money, but, ultimately, she believed it was *only* money. Mac inherited Tatty's anxious need to save; he knew she had a decent nest-egg, accumulated through thrift and self-denial.

'It's not a difficult question, Tatty. Did my mother like marguerites?'

59

Tatty studied her nails, the way she did when about to say something that mattered. 'Don't look back, Ian. I loathe nostalgia. It's like sitting in the bath after the water's gone cold.'

For all your reserve, thought Mac, *you're a tyrant*. She ruled this silent flat, where the only music was a ticking clock; the place where she could turn her face resolutely from the past.

But what about me? Tatty was keeper of the keys, the only one who could unlock Mac's parents, free them from that one static photograph.

'Did she?' Mac sat forward, far too passionately for a question about flower preferences. 'Did she like marguerites?'

'Yes.' Shocked into answering, there was reproof in Tatty's tone. A little fear, too; as if she felt the freezing bathwater wrinkle her skin.

'The bomb,' said Mac, emboldened. 'The one that killed them, tell me about it. It seemed late in the war for bombs, March 1945.'

A frown from Tatty. Perhaps she sensed he was testing her, somehow. 'It was one of the last V2s of the war. A final grand gesture, I suppose. Spiteful, really.' She exhaled. Realized he was waiting, wanting more. 'It fell early in the morning. The newspapers said it was lucky, as there weren't that many people in the park at that hour. Eighty-one injured. Three killed.'

'Two of them were my parents,' said Mac.

'You didn't have a scratch on you.'

'Lucky,' he said, softly.

'Not a very appropriate word, is it? Not in these circumstances.'

'How come they were in the park so early? Presumably my father was on leave?' Mac never called him *my dad*; that seemed presumptuous, the prerogative of a man who had grown up knowing his parents. Now that he was finally asking questions, it struck him as absurd he didn't know the answers. 'Did Marguerite work? Where did they live?'

Tatty hesitated; she seemed to be resisting the pull of his curiosity. A righteous woman, she didn't resist for long, but she made it clear, with small sighs and her general discomfort, that she would rather leave the past undisturbed. 'She didn't work. She had her hands full with you. You were no Dan, I can tell you. You could be cranky, and as for getting you off to sleep . . .'

Mac felt, illogically, as if he should apologize.

'We all lived together, when your father was home and not with his regiment, in this little one-bedder in Lees Place. Up and down four flights of stairs with that enormous pram. I had the bedroom, and Marguerite slept on a funny old pull-out bed in the sitting room.'

Mac could see it. The dowdy wartime upholstery. The dark March morning beyond the criss-cross of tape on the windows. His young parents, their heads together, as they bent over their baby boy.

Me.

'Why did they go out so early that day?'

'You'd had a bad night; she couldn't settle you. I was just rising, and Marguerite popped her head around the door. She was belting her coat, I remember, a wide-shouldered

61

tweed affair that was far too big for her. She had it on over her pyjamas. *Jimjams*, she called them.'

Jimjams. Mac filed that away. Tatty never called them jimjams. So he didn't either. *I'll bloody call them jimjams from now on!*

'She just laughed when I said she couldn't go out like that. She said a stroll might lull you off. Hyde Park was just across the road, you see. Off she went. I can still hear the pram wheels bumping down the stairwell.'

'And my father went with us. And?'

Tatty blinked. 'And, Ian? What more can I say? There was a tremendous noise, all our windows blew in. The tape helped, but I still got glass in my hair. I ran. Just took off.'

Tatty running? It was unimaginable.

'There was a crater. As if the devil had scooped up a corner of the park. I saw your pram on its side. And then . . .' Tatty swallowed. 'I heard you crying. I heard people saying it was a miracle. I just grabbed you and brought you home, and . . . got on with it.' Tatty slapped her lap. A full stop.

'If I hadn't kept them all up night . . .' said Mac.

If he was waiting for Tatty to say that was nonsense, that he was just a baby at the time, he was disappointed. She was on her feet, brushing herself down, already returned from this unscheduled diversion into ancient history.

'Shouldn't you be getting back, Ian?'

'What?' Her dismissal gave him whiplash.

Perhaps his dazed look touched her. 'I did my best.' She was brisk, staccato. 'I brought you up as well as I knew how.'

'I know that.' Mac leapt in. 'I really do, Tatty.'

As he took the shuddering old lift down to street level, Mac knew the brief window of opportunity had slammed shut. There would be no more disclosures. And yet.

There is more to know.

Mac looked up at the blind, blinking windows of the mansion block. The last piece of the Mactavish jigsaw still sat, hidden, in Tatty's capacious handbag.

Marie was waiting at the door, Heinz beside her.

'Well?'

'Well what, love?' Mac had to squeeze past his wife's folded arms to hang up his suit jacket.

'Did you demand a raise?'

'My manager was off.' Mac withstood the tut. 'Where you going?' he asked as she tugged on her hated, scratchy Fresh'n'Fine tabard.

'Fitting in a late shift before I have to stop earning.' Marie fended off Heinz's berserk affections. 'Feed the dog. Your dinner's in the oven.'

'We're ships that pass in the night,' he said, hauling her back for a peck.

'I mean it.' She dodged the peck. 'Tomorrow, you march in there and *demand* that raise.'

Marie's feet took her to Fresh'n'Fine on autopilot. She loved this area, her adopted homeland, and noticed how it had changed and grown with her little family.

She passed the gates of St Saviour's, where she dropped Dan off each morning, and hurried past the new chain stores on the little high street. Electrical shops, a Dorothy Perkins, none of them challenging the supremacy of mighty Woolworths. It was a palace of delights to Marie, who would let Dan loose in the Pick'n'Mix after a visit to the traditional children's shoe shop down a cobbled alley. She turned down the alley, now, and smiled at how the shoe shop resisted the tide of modernity; matronly staff would measure Dan's little feet solemnly and bring out lace-ups for his approval.

Her reflection in the window, a small, stout woman among the T-bars and lace-ups, stopped her in her tracks. She saw a working woman, a uniformed woman, a woman with purpose. Her tummy already distorted the outline of the tabard.

She hurried on. Wouldn't do to be late.

Mac picked up the phone, and recited the number, still impressed that they had a telephone in the hall and didn't have to jog to the corner to make calls. 'Ah, Pat, hello,' he said. 'Marie's at work, I'll get her to call you.'

'No, Mac, it's you I want to talk to.'

Mac did a double take at the receiver. It was set in stone that neither he nor Pat stayed on the line. They handed the phone to the nearest female relative. That was the rule, in this house and in every other house up and down the land. 'Me?'

A warm chuckle crept through the wire all the way across the water. 'Don't sound so surprised. How're things?'

'Pat, you have no interest in how things are. What's this about?'

'You're right, Mac. I leave the chit chat to Nora and Marie. Well, I call it chit chat; you and I both know it's the important stuff, the stuff that makes the world turn.'

'True.' Mac sat on the too-small wrought-iron stool provided. He could listen to his father-in-law forever. *I wonder if my own father was anything like this?*

'It's about your change of direction, son. The, what is it? Parole officer?'

'Probation officer. You don't need to worry, Pat. I changed my mind.'

'But I do worry. Did you change your mind or was it changed for you? We're lucky to be married to two very forthright women, Mac, but sometimes you have to do what's right for you.'

Mac almost shook the phone. This was not the conservative advice he expected. 'It was my decision, Pat.'

'I heard Bernie stuck her nose in, doing her Queen of England impression. You don't have to please Bernie, Mac. My oldest daughter has many excellent qualities, but when it comes to money she has tunnel vision. There's more to life. Have you and Marie really *talked* about this?'

'Yes and no.' He had told Marie how it felt to discover something he really wanted to do. How sublime it was to realize he had a vocation. *I want to specialize in young offenders.*

He would make a difference, keep them on the straight and narrow. She had been inscrutable as he admitted that the pay would be poor while he was learning. 'I'd be a novice again,' he'd said. 'Not like old George, with his seat on the board.' But the money would improve, and it was steady. It was not just a job for life; it was a fulfilling job.

When Marie spoke she had been calm. 'It's up to you, Mac.'

He could read her mind. She wanted to improve their lot. *She sacrificed so much for me and the children.* All those ambitious little bubbles that were popped over and over. *I owe her.*

'Trust me, Pat,' said Mac. 'Bernie didn't come into it. I thought of me and Marie and Dan and the baby and, well, the decision made itself.'

'Fair enough. But you must be firm, like me. I *never* let my wife bully me.' There was a noise in the background. 'Oh, sweet Jesus, she's coming,' hissed Pat.

The phone was banged down.

They had an early night.

Not one of those sexy early nights so beloved of *Carry On* films. This was a cold-cream on, curlers in, reading the latest Jackie Collins early night.

Mac was just setting aside his Neville Shute when the quiet was disturbed by the shriek of the telephone. Knowing it was his job to answer it, he suppressed a tut and pushed his feet into his slippers.

'Jesus, Mary and Joseph!' Marie grabbed his arm as if she was drowning. 'Somebody's died! Oh God help us all.'

'Love, *love*.' Mac gently pried her fingers off his pyjama sleeve. 'Hey, what's all this?'

'Nobody rings this late! It's always bad news.'

He was happy to prove her wrong; Bernie's wine-infused voice asked if he could settle an argument – 'If a cheetah could enter the Olympics, would it win?'

'She knows better,' grumbled Marie, settling down again, 'than to call at this hour and frighten the life out of me.'

'Just goes to show, love,' said Mac. 'Your Irish pessimism isn't always right.'

Sleepily, Marie found the energy to have the last word. 'You English are no good at death.'

The day began badly.

'Hey, hey, what's all this?' Mac found Marie sobbing over the sink, tears mingling with the suds. *It's starting*, he thought. *Before the baby's even fully cooked!*

'Elvis!' she managed, through a river of snot. 'He's dead!' She put her rubber gloves to her eyes and wailed, 'He died on the toilet.'

'Ah. Your other husband.' Mac understood, and they cuddled until she could speak.

'Today's the day,' she said, wiping her nose.

'I know,' said Mac. He was this side of tetchy. But only just.

The mythical raise that was – apparently – his for the asking was the hot topic in Sunnyside. As if Marie had been contaminated by exposure to Bernie's easy expectation of wealth and ease and *things*. So many things.

Personally, Mac had all the things he needed, and they were nowhere near as important as the people in the allegedly 'pokey' house. 'We do have everything we need, you know.' He felt Marie needed reminding. 'Dan's healthy, we've another on the way, and a safe roof over our heads.'

'And I'm grateful for that. I am,' she said. 'But . . .'

'There's always a but with you.'

She looked at him, stung. 'You go in, you *demand* that raise, got it?' Marie pointed the dish brush. Quite menacingly. 'Or I'll come in and do it for you. I mean it,' she added.

I bloody know you do, thought Mac. He opened the post. 'Just junk,' he murmured, and aimed a balled-up piece of paper at the bin.

Taking his cuppa to the front step, he cursed his timing.

'Hey! You!' This was Next Door's way of saying hello. He held up a red-and-white-striped ball on his side of the hedge. 'I warned you about your lad's football coming into my garden.'

'You did, yes,' agreed Mac, wondering just how heartless a person you'd have to be to take such exception to children playing. 'Sorry. Again.' He held out his hand.

Next Door produced a knitting needle and stuck it into the ball. It deflated slowly as the men watched, emitting a long series of vaguely rude noises.

'There's no need to be like that.' From Mac this was a tongue-lashing.

'He's a bad'un, your boy,' said Next Door.

'He's six,' said Mac.

Marie joined them. She brought Mac a peace offering of buttered toast, and she was sunny with Next Door, asking after his wife, being her usual self.

No need, thought Mac, *to tell her about Dan's ball, in case she strangles Next Door with one of his own cardigans.* He realized Marie was side-eyeing the porch, and knew what was coming.

'That porch is *definitely* leaning to one side. I told you, *I told you*, that builder was a cowboy. Surprised he didn't turn up on a horse. When's he coming to put it right?'

'Not sure. We're discussing a date,' said Mac, who couldn't get hold of the breezy so-and-so.

'You know how I say your nostrils flare when you lie? Well, I could fit Heinz up one of them right now.' Marie kissed him, and tucked an iris into his lapel, from the wilting bunch she'd bought cheaply at Fresh'n'Fine. 'Off you trot, boyo.' She handed him the briefcase that contained only sandwiches and a book about puffins. 'Ring me at lunchtime to say you've done it, and then we can put the porch right once and for all and plan a proper cruise.'

Off Mac trotted. They were both experts in the language of flowers. He pulled in his chin to look at the slightly drooping iris.

I have faith in you, it said.

With one eye on the ledger in front of him, and the other on the gold lettering on the glazed door – MANAGER – Mac couldn't concentrate.

A colleague in a purple suit that had already got him a

warning letter looked up from his work. 'What's that to-do out by the counter?'

There was shouting and there was . . . *barking?* Nonetheless, Mac ignored the to-do, until it seemed to be on the move, and heading for his desk.

'You can't come in here,' someone was saying.

'I can and I am!'

He lifted his head at the sound of that chipper voice. 'Marie?' Mac stood, a pile of documents hitting the floor. Heinz cocked his leg over the umbrella stand. 'Love, it's not lunchtime yet, I haven't—'

'Where's the manager's office?'

Nobody answered the tiny woman who seemed to be emitting sparks. They were struck dumb; the bank was a drama-free space, unless you counted the time the office junior stapled himself to the petty cash book. Marie spotted the gold lettering and knocked. Hard.

'Marie!' Mac was spluttering. 'This isn't the way to go about it.'

She kicked the door open and stuck her head around it. 'Excuse me, but my husband needs the afternoon off. Urgent business. Thanks, handsome.'

To Mac, she said, 'Get your jacket on, you. You have an appointment.' She fumbled in her coat pocket and showed him a creased letter. 'Junk mail, my eye.'

Mac recognized the invitation to attend a formal interview at the probation service headquarters in Westminster.

'Chop chop,' said Marie, and harassed him out of the bank.

Waiting in the Mercedes and blocking the bus lane, Bernie tooted the horn and Heinz leapt into the passenger seat.

'This is crazy,' said Mac.

'No, *I'm* crazy,' said Marie, suddenly close to him. 'I'm so proud of you for wanting to change the world for the better. Just because I have to take a step back, why should you? You support me, I support you, that's how this works, darlin'. Happiness – that's what we're about, not money. No need for Ian Mactavish to stand on his wallet to be a big man. Go, go on, follow your dream, and *make a difference*, my darling.'

'Get in!' roared Bernie. 'Before that bus kills us all.'

CHAPTER FOUR

'You look different today.' She studies him, eyes
narrowed.

He smiles. He nudges her. 'You don't. You look the
same as ever.'

'Oh, you big silly.' She wavers between shock and
delight. She overheard a senior care assistant giggle about
how handsome he was; she feels a prick of pride in her
visitor. 'Tea,' she says imperiously.

He gets it wrong. Too many sugars. 'You've lost your
touch,' she says.

'They're all in black today.' He has cracked the album
open at another Polaroid. 'The woman's all blurred.'

Standing on the doorstep, a mushroom cloud of
wisteria above their heads, the couple she has come to
think of as 'hers' are sombre in dark clothes. 'What on
Earth . . . he has a huge bandage taped across his nose.'

'Walked into a door, maybe?'

'There's the little boy! What a looker. If this is 1979, he's about eight. Their little girl's the only one not in black.'

He isn't studying the photograph. He leans closer. 'Listen, it keeps getting put off, but there's something you need to know. I want you to be prepared; everyone knows how you hate surprises.'

'Do the photographs bore you?' she asks suddenly. 'They do, don't they? It's foolish, poring over these strangers when you come all this way to see me.'

'It's not that far,' he says, before realizing the slyboots has outwitted him.

She will not listen to anything she doesn't want to hear.

29 July 1979

They flapped the flimsy plastic square and were disappointed when they peeled apart the layers.

'You moved, you silly moo,' said Mac. 'Talking, as usual. Let's do another one. For the anniversary album.'

Marie was unwilling. She pulled on black gloves, unsuitable for the weather. 'Can we just, you know, *go*?'

They just went.

A week earlier, she had been in a very different mood. Weekends were the salon's busiest time.

It was only Marie who called it a salon; to Mac it was the

ground floor of Sunnyside. The new hairdressing business meant his life smelled of perm lotion, and his home was dotted with matronly ladies with wet hair.

'Morning, Elsie!' He made his way through an assault course of wider-fit sandals. 'How you doing, Flo.' He flicked the kettle switch, and the kitchen heaved with lust; these women were addicted to tea.

Emma was on a lap.

The baby had arrived on St Valentine's Day, taking them all by surprise. Marie had barely made a start on her heart-shaped box of chocolates before the contractions began. Suddenly, Sunnyside was filled up with the drama of child-birth, its woodchip walls vibrating with Marie's panting.

The midwife had sweated too. 'Baby's facing the wrong way,' she told Mac, who was in charge of clean towels and panicking. 'Might take a while.'

It did, and when Emma eventually emerged Mac held her and cried tears of relief, with some terrified tears bringing up the rear. He keenly felt the responsibility of her little life.

Marie, steamrollered into the carpet, had reached for his hand to whisper, 'I am never ever having sex with you again.'

Like many of Marie's declarations it was soon forgotten, but life with two small children meant it came more or less true.

Now, just shy of one and a half, little Emma was a strawberry-blonde madam, grave-faced and thoughtful. *Clever, my daughter*, thought Mac as he watched her attend to a customer's tale of 'When I was a girl' above the fizz of boiling water.

Whereas my son . . . Dan was gifted with charm. Poncing about in a bow tie, he handed out Jammie Dodgers and accepted the ladies' compliments with downcast, long-lashed eyes.

'Elsie!' Marie put her head around the door. 'I'm ready for you, love.' She shepherded the doddery woman to the sitting room, winking at Mac as she went.

That wink still had power. Perhaps it always would. Mac didn't mind the noise or the fuss or the fact that he couldn't mooch about in his underpants on his day off so long as Marie Neeson-as-was kept winking at him with one periwinkle eye.

He reached for the dog food before he remembered. There was no dog food; there was no Heinz. There had been a rapid decline, some foaming at the mouth, and Mac had taken his little friend/deadliest foe to the vet's for the last time.

They couldn't bear to replace him.

Dan turned up the radio – Abba was playing; Abba was almost always playing – and he danced for the old ladies as they clapped in time.

Mac clapped along, struck anew at how very different a son could be from his father. It triggered the usual speculation about Ed Mactavish: *Am I like him?* And, hot on its heels, *Would he be proud of me?* He shrugged the thoughts away, knowing they wouldn't go far.

'*Voulez-vous!*' sang Marie from the next room. It was the only French she knew.

He yawned over the tea bags. His working week asked much of him. No longer a trainee, Mac was a bona fide probation officer, with a caseload of young offenders. It was his responsibility to discover what had bumped them off the rails, and to come up with ways to keep them from reoffending. It was in the offenders' interests, but it also protected the public; Mac felt as if what he did mattered when he set off each morning in his Bri-Nylon shirt and matching tie.

Each of his lads – there was a lass or two, but they were mainly lads – asked something different of him. Something *real*. Mac took them seriously and they sensed that, even when they turned over tables or called him names he couldn't repeat at home.

The camaraderie in his department was nothing like the worker bee atmosphere of the bank, but Mac knew the others regarded him as a softie because he led with his heart and not his head.

The Mactavishes still suffered the financial consequences of his career change. Marie pointed this out gently, and sometimes not so gently, when Mac griped about the herds of old ladies. They needed her contribution if they were to get to St Malo.

Captivated by the brochure, she memorized sailing times from Portsmouth to France, and eulogized the dance floor (six feet across) and the fine dining option. She didn't listen when Bernie pointed out the fine dining option involved plastic cutlery, and that it wasn't a cruise but a crossing.

Marie's need to earn, to use hard-won skills, mystified Bernie, however much Marie tried to explain. 'Money I earn means more to me; I can squander it if I like!'

'You're mad,' Bernie would say, happy to squander George's income, happy to over-spend on hotpants.

They all wished she wouldn't wear hotpants.

The only one who needed to understand her need to contribute was Mac; Marie knew he was on her team and it gave her confidence.

He hadn't always understood. He had argued against the salon at first, pointing out that she had given birth to their children, and what bigger contribution could there be? He gave in, as he loved to do with his peppery little wife, and had come to enjoy his status as a 'youngster' around her customers.

'My wife's the independent type,' Mac would say proudly to the chaps at work. Sometimes, when he was having a bad day, when some kid didn't turn up and he knew it augured ill, Mac would worry that his independent wife might leave him behind.

This was pooh-poohed by Marie. 'Sure, you're me comfortable slippers!'

This was reassuring. In a way.

Mac stood on the step and toasted the street with the 'Besst Dad in the Wurld' mug that Dan had painted for him, and admired his wisteria.

It repaid the cutting, the pruning, the feeding. People stopped to 'Ooh' at the thick, rough vines that intertwined like lovers. The foamy flowers helped disguise the scars on Sunnyside, where the porch had finally been removed.

Marie's barely mentioned the expensive repair job, he thought. Her silence was strategic. *She'll use it when she's ready.*

Within the house, the Bee Gees took over from Abba. They were 'Stayin' Alive' and they got elderly toes tapping. He heard Marie say, as she backcombed a blue rinse, 'It's all puffins, puffins, puffins with my husband.'

'Hey,' he said, leaning into the sitting room, faux-affronted. 'There are worse vices to have!'

Next Door's elusive wife had been spotted nipping out in a nothing-coloured raincoat. It was one of Marie's ambitions to nab Mrs Next Door, to discover what manner of woman could put up with the endless bad mood.

'We could rescue her!' she would say to Mac.

'Hmm,' he would reply.

One morning, not long after Heinz went to the great dog park in the sky, Mac and Marie took the pushchair to the canal. Since that one genuine conversation with Tatty, Mac couldn't help but see shadows of his parents' last stroll with him just a baby in the pram. Two figures and a treasured little one; one story about to end and the other carrying on. He felt lucky and he felt robbed; it was quite a stew to carry in his head.

Their route was one they'd taken with Heinz, and they were in mid-conversation about the dog when they saw a be-cardiganed man at the edge of the water.

'Isn't that ...?' Seeing him out of context, Marie was unsure.

'Yes, let's double-back.'

'He's seen us,' hissed Marie, pasting on a smile. 'Are you admiring the canal?' she called.

'It's full of shopping trolleys,' said Next Door. His cardigan pocket moved.

'What you got there?' Marie's face lit up when a tortoise-shell kitten poked its head out and mewed at her. She reached out her hand.

'Don't!' snapped Next Door. 'He's condemned.' He took out the little beauty, and it squirmed in his nicotine-stained fingers. 'My cat had kittens. They all went to good homes, but nobody wants this one.' Next Door angled the kitten so they could see its face. 'See? Only got one eye.'

'The poor little darling!' Marie melted. Then hardened, as she caught on. 'You're never going to throw him in the canal?'

'That's exactly what I'm going to do, missus.'

'Give him to me.' Marie bristled. She clapped her hands, the way she did when Dan dawdled in the mornings. 'Quickly.'

'I got a pound for the other kittens.'

'But you were going to drown him!' Marie's lips thinned in anger but she dug out a pound note.

'Seeing as he's special, only having one eye, and you wanting him so much ... let's call it two pounds, eh?'

Certain there was a special circle of hell reserved for Next Door, Mac stuffed another pound into his hand, getting between him and Marie, who might well push the black-mailer into the water.

And so Odin came home with them. Named after the one-eyed Norse God, he was magnificent, noble and, the whole family agreed, the best cat ever.

How it began, neither could say.

Like all the worst marital rows, it seemed to spring to life fully formed, with gripes and irritations locked, loaded and ready to go.

All Mac knew was that when he went to brush his teeth that morning he and his wife were getting on perfectly well, but by the time he pulled on his trousers, World War Three was raging in their bedroom.

'Keep your voice down!' snapped Marie, applying eyeliner at the dressing table mirror with a shaking hand. 'The children don't need to hear this.'

'Perhaps they *should* hear it!' shouted Mac. It was liberating to let rip; he suddenly realized why Marie roared so often. 'Perhaps it's time they learned their father isn't good enough.'

'When did I say that?' Marie wheeled, one eye sultry with black eyeliner, the other still nude and sleepy. 'There you go again, twisting my words.'

Odin hot-footed it out of the room. 'See!' Marie was triumphant. 'You've upset the cat.'

'God forbid I put my feelings above the cat's.' Mac tied his tie as if preparing to hang himself with it.

'This is the porch all over again,' sighed Marie.

'I knew it! I *knew* you'd bring that up.'

'What's the point of it all, Mac, if we can't even go on a bloody cruise? We're cancelling *again*, because of some stupid bloody probation seminar.' She was haughty, huffing at her reflection. 'You keep letting me down.'

That penetrated Mac's carefully assembled armour. He went downstairs, heavy-footed as Frankenstein's Monster. 'Everything's all right, Dan,' he said, pouring out cornflakes for the boy. 'Just a silly grown-up squabble.'

Everything was not all right. Mac battled the unfamiliar sensation of disliking his wife. It felt like black smoke in his lungs. Wrong. Unhealthy. He had to stop himself slamming the fridge door.

He hurried through his breakfast, ate it standing up, hoping to disappear before Marie came down. As ever, she outmanoeuvred him, and plonked Emma in the highchair as he rinsed his bowl.

'Do you ever think,' she said, before he cut her off.

'Clearly, no. You do all the thinking in this house.'

Marie closed her eyes and seemed to count to ten before she tried again. 'Do you ever think I might need a life beyond this house? Beyond the children who arrived perfectly timed to shackle me to Sunnyside?'

'And that's my fault?'

'Did I say that?' They both eyed Dan, who was pretending to read his comic.

Mac said, 'You know I *hate* leaving the kids behind every morning. I miss them all day.'

'That's the solution, then. I'll find a job and you stay at home.' Marie let out a *Ha!* at Mac's expression. 'See? Sheer terror.' She turned her back on him. 'Go on, go. You're dying to get out and leave everything to me, as usual.'

That's so unfair, thought Mac. Before admitting there was some truth to it. 'Have a nice day,' he said as he left, his sarcasm astonishing them both.

Distracted, Mac had to read the file on his new client three times before the information sank in.

Did Marie mean all that? Mac had certainly meant what he said. But only up to a point.

That's what love did, surely? It sanitized the faults of the beloved. Marie's virtues were as towering as her vices. Yes, she was a shouter and a scrapper and she really shouldn't comment on his dress sense in public, but she also loved without limits, was berserkly biased on Mac's behalf, made him laugh, and astonished him with the depth of her generosity and sweetness. On the whole, his towering love for Marie overshadowed her temper, her tendency to exaggerate, her need to blame.

Not today though.

Mac dwelled on her imperfections. *Classic Marie*, he thought, the document in front of him blurry. *Starting a damn row just before our anniversary.*

The desk supervisor looked in through the double doors. 'Your new chap's here. Interview room three.' He watched Mac gather his papers. 'You all right, Mac?'

'I'm fine.' Mac pushed the door of interview room three.

'Be careful,' called the supervisor. 'This one's a tricky dicky.'

She was so flustered she forgot his name, and kept saying to the nurse, 'My husband, he's my husband.' As ever, Emma was on Marie's hip, damp and tossed at being woken from her nap.

Curtains were whisked away to expose Mac full length on a metal bed. His blackened eyes peeped out over a taped bandage.

'Your poor nose!' Marie hung over him, weeping. 'Your *lovely* nose! I love your nose!'

When he spoke it sounded as if he was talking through a flannel. 'Don't upset yourself, love. It's not as bad as it looks.'

'He broke your nose!' yelled Marie, shifting Emma to the other hip.

'It was my fault.'

'You didn't break your own bloody nose, Mac.'

He laughed but that hurt so he stopped. The tricky dicky had turned out to be even more tricky than anyone suspected. Mac had speed-read the bio, forgotten his safety training, and within two minutes found himself pinned up against the wall with a fist meeting his nose.

His old nose. Mac had never really considered his nose before; now he missed it. The new one would be, the doctor said, 'subtly different'.

'I got the poor lad into trouble,' he told Marie.

'Jaysus, the poor lad's an *animal*,' she snapped, as Emma reached out pudgy hands to wipe her mother's tears.

'I didn't handle him properly. I'm meant to be the professional, the adult.'

'I'd like to punch him meself.'

'Don't blame the boy, blame the system.' There was dysfunction in the tricky dicky's family. Drugs. Abandonment. Cruelty that dwarfed anything Mac or Marie had ever been through.

'It's my fault.' Marie slumped into the orange plastic chair at his bedside. 'I was a bitch this morning.'

'Don't be daft.'

'It's true. If I ever make you feel like you're not enough . . . *you*, of all people . . . just remind me how lucky I am to have you, boyo.'

They made love that night for the first time in a while.

It was slightly surreal; Marie couldn't keep a straight face as his bandaged face swayed above her. It was also beautiful, and healing, a renewal of the mutual passion that always amazed him.

His wife was a foreign country, but she was also home.

Afterwards they held each other, settling into their usual position, her head beneath his chin. A church bell tolled midnight.

'Soon be our anniversary, lover,' murmured Marie. 'And I'm sor—'

'We agreed. No more apologizing. Let's forget the steak-house this year, go somewhere more fancy.'

'Are you kidding? I'm already drooling for me prawn cocktail.'

The house ticked. Odin yawned. Outside a fox made a strange cry. Emma stirred in her room, then settled with a dreamy sigh.

The phone rang.

'I wonder who's dead?' smiled Mac, easing out of Marie's grasp. 'It'll be a wrong number probably.'

In three minutes he was back, but he had walked slowly up the stairs, like an old, old man.

Marie sat up. 'Who?'

'Your dad, love.'

The Neeson home on Clonmacnoise Road, Dublin 12, was a typical Irish corporation house. *Why*, wondered Mac, *did the council build houses for Catholic families with only two bedrooms?*

The little place heaved with family and friends. Mac recalled the rattle of earth on Pat's coffin and made for the whisky.

Children ran free-range; there were almost as many kids as grown-ups, and Dan darted in and out of black trouser legs. No need to worry about them here; the kids were everyone's responsibility, and Emma was spoiled rotten.

A cousin – second? Twice removed? Everyone seemed to be a cousin – smoothed Emma's curls, and Mac said, 'We're so glad she got Marie's red hair.'

Intent on Emma's face, he didn't notice the cousin's raised eyebrows and Marie's infinitesimal shake of the head. There was no need, that shake said, to reveal at this late stage in the proceedings that her hair colour came out of a bottle.

Mac slipped a painkiller under his tongue. His nose had throbbed like a Belisha beacon since stepping off the early flight.

Damn, I forgot to cancel the steakhouse.

It was a hell of a way to spend their anniversary.

The rooms were airless beneath a mushroom cloud of cigarette smoke. The piano struck up in the front parlour but somebody said, 'No, not that one, not today,' at the opening notes of 'Danny Boy'.

In the centre of it all was Nora, the remaining one of a pair. Her black dress was neat and her hair carefully waved. She was doing her best for her Pat.

Marie hovered at one shoulder, with Bernie at the other, both of them prescribing 'a nice sandwich'. Their sister Bridget, who had recited the graveside prayers that bit louder than anybody else, stood to attention in a black veil. She refused alcohol, and seemed to judge those who didn't take the same tack.

Saintly spinster Bridget – according to Bernie she had 'never so much as sniffed a trouser leg' – would move in to 'look after Mammy'. The other sisters felt a combination of guilt and relief at Bridget's readiness to take on the responsibility.

Shouldering through the crowd – not easy, everyone wanted to ask Mac, 'What happened to your face?' – he took his mother-in-law's hand and searched her eyes.

They had a moment of understanding. He felt her loss in those cold little fingers, crabbed and bent after a lifetime looking after others.

It was a moment only. Nora went back to being stoic, to looking into the middle distance, to wondering aloud every now and then if there were enough volly-vonts to go round.

Men gathered, ties undone, in the garden. Mac joined them. The conversation was muted. All had a tale to tell of Pat. Even with the whitewash that death brings, his character shone through.

'He was a good man,' Mac managed, emotion stoppering up his throat.

'Yes, aye, yes.' Heads nodded.

'Not many like Pat,' said one bloke.

'What the hell happened to your nose?' said another.

There was a bench at the end of the garden, and Mac found his wife there.

Her eyes were pink with unshed tears. 'I just want to get this over with,' she said. 'And get home to have a good cry.' She patted his shoulder as he sat close to her. 'Right there.'

'What's wrong with my other shoulder? Just as good for crying on. Better, some would say.'

She laughed then, and cried, and laughed again. 'Jaysus,

I've lost the run of meself,' she said, as Bernie lurched across the lawn in heels.

'Guess what,' she said. 'Daddy left us all two grand apiece!'

There was wonderment at Pat amassing such a pile of pennies.

Bernie said, 'I know exactly what he'd want me to do with it. You two take my share and bugger off on a real cruise at last.'

'No, I couldn't let you do that,' said Marie.

'Not up to you. The money's yours, so spend it on a cruise or buy a diamond collar for Odin.'

'Spain! We can cruise to Spain!' Marie closed her eyes, ashamed. 'There's Daddy fresh in the ground and here's me planning a holiday.'

Mac sighed. He wondered what it was like to lose a father. *Or to have one to lose in the first place.* Watching Marie and Bernie hug and sob and giggle and curse, he suspected it was worth the pain.

The volly-vonts ran out. More booze was bought in. Crisps were decanted into bowls. Songs were sung. Mac conceded Marie's point; *the Irish really are better at death.*

The grief was simple and everywhere, and it sat companionably alongside the need to sing.

The contrast with Tatty's flat, with his own family's way of handling emotion, couldn't be ignored. Especially after three whiskies and another Paracetamol.

At Tatty's, no voice was ever raised in anger or song. Mac had seen no tears shed for his parents; Tatty's loss was old by the time he was a boy, and he had never felt able to cry in front of her.

Shame crept over Mac. *It's been too long since I visited Tatty.* The welcome was so pallid, though. No profusion of food or drink or love, like at Nora's house.

And always that fear. That she would tell him what he longed to hear. It was unfair to criticize her for holding back, and then to avoid her in case she gave in and told him. Common sense suggested that there was no big secret, that he was fantasizing.

Since meeting Marie, Mac distrusted common sense; he listened to his gut.

'Say a few words, Mac,' commanded Nora from her armchair throne. 'Pat'd be so honoured.'

'Oh. Um,' began Mac.

'What happened to your nose?' said a small child.

'Whisht,' said an adult.

'Pat Neeson was ...' That past tense reared up at him. His shoulders began to shake. 'Pat Neeson was a ...' Mac let out a sob.

Hands patted his back and slapped his shoulder. His vulnerability was not laughed at nor turned away from. It was admired.

Mac shook himself. He said, 'Pat Neeson was my hero.' He hadn't known it until that moment. He hadn't known he had projected all his thwarted love for Ed onto his father-in-law.

Marie knew. She cried with him.

*

'Always the last to bloody leave,' murmured Marie, watching the priest accept yet another wee drop.

Bernie was murmuring too. It was a day of murmurs. 'Bridget's in her element. *Can I get you anything, Father? Another sandwich, Father? Want me to kiss your behind, Father?*'

'Whisht, youse hussies.' Nora was trying not to smile. 'Have some respect.'

'Oh, Jaysus, he's coming over,' hissed Marie.

They were trapped.

'You remember my sisters, Father,' Bridget said. 'They moved to *London*.' She gave the word an edge, as if they had moved to Vegas to become strippers.

Father Donal took Marie's hands in his. He smelled of mints and incense. 'My deep condolences,' he said.

'Thank you.' Marie looked abashed for mocking the sincere little fellow.

'I sat with Pat after he collapsed. We waited for the ambulance, and I took his hand, just as I'm taking yours.'

All fell silent, drawn in.

'He knew it was his time. All he could talk about was his darling children. He asked me to pray for you. Very little breath, he had, yet he named you all.'

'Oh,' said Marie. It was more of a squeak.

Mac felt hot, as if the white-haired, black-suited Father Donal had taken them time-travelling to Pat's last moments.

'I love them all, Father, he told me. Bridget, Bernadette, Siobhan, Marie and young Adrian.'

A visible jolt ran through the siblings. There was no Siobhan in the family.

The priest nodded solemnly. 'Yes, I know what you're thinking. His mind went a bit, didn't it? He thought he had a daughter named Siobhan. God rest his soul, he was a little muddled. Eh, Nora?'

He turned kindly to the widow in her armchair, but she was sphinx-like.

As Bridget saw the priest to the door, Marie and Bernie stared at each other.

'Did you see Ma's face?' asked Bernie, eventually.

'They lost a baby,' said Marie.

'A baby called Siobhan.'

'Our sister.'

'Siobhan,' said Marie. 'Her name was on his lips right at the end.'

'Your da was a big man,' said Mac, and they understood what he meant. Nothing to do with Pat's height; it was his heart that was huge, with room enough to house a child who never drew breath.

The day outside darkened. Only the immediate family remained. Bridget was clearing up with a martyred air. Bernie had found the brandy.

'Which was your wreath, Marie?' asked Nora, as her glass was brusquely removed by Bridget.

'The zinnias, Ma.'

The Mactavish wreath had seemed modest compared to

the mounds of roses and lilies, but they had been guided by *The Language of Flowers*.

Thinking of you when you are not here.

A glass was tapped. Heads swivelled as Adrian cleared his throat.

'Aw!' Bernie saw her twenty-year-old brother as a toddler. 'Got something to say, pet?'

'Yeah.' Adrian's new suit only accentuated his skinniness. 'Now that it's just us . . .' He coughed, faltered. Picked himself up. 'This isn't about Da. It's about me. I loved Da, but I couldn't say this while he was alive.' He lifted his chin. His slightly spotty chin. 'I'm gay,' he said.

Mouths fell open.

Bernie said, 'No, you're not, you fool.'

Mac stepped closer to Adrian. Laid a hand on his shoulder.

Bridget made the sign of the cross, and they all turned to Nora, who said, 'Sure, I know you're gay, son. We've always known.'

'*I* didn't!' snapped Bridget.

Adrian stepped back, as if pushed. 'Did me da know?'

'It was Da who realized,' said Nora. 'It's bleedin' obvious, love.'

They all laughed then. Except Bridget. She said, 'Thank heavens Father Donal has gone home.'

Bernie kissed Adrian. 'I *love* the gays!' she screeched, and Marie winced.

Mac thought of time wasted, of the conversations Adrian

and Pat could have had. He knew the big man would never have disowned his only son; Adrian's discretion was about protecting his father from discomfort rather than a fear of rejection. Outside the house, homosexuality was illegal, and could mean social ruin. Indoors, though ... *The Neesons do things their own way*, thought Mac. He saw Bridget stare at Adrian as though he was on show in a zoo, and added, *With one exception.*

'Don't you mind, Ma?' Adrian knelt by her chair. He was confused, as if he'd dressed for a typhoon and encountered only a light shower.

'Mind?' His mother rolled her eyes. 'So long as you're happy, I'm happy.'

'I can't give you grandchildren.'

'Sure, I have two and that's plenty.'

'You have to reach out,' said Marie, stroking Adrian's hair. 'Find your clan.'

'It won't be easy,' said Nora, never afraid of plain speaking. 'There's a lot of badness in the world. You keep your chin up, you hear me?'

He heard her.

Outside, in the yellow pool of light beneath a lamp post, Bernie and Marie piled on Adrian in an amoeba of love, kissing him, messing up his hair, making their goodbyes.

'Come and see us soon,' said Marie, backing towards the minicab.

'I'll sort you out a boyfriend!' promised Bernie, clambering into the back seat.

'I've already got one!' shouted Adrian.

Windows were wound hurriedly down. 'What's his name!' shrieked a delighted Marie.

'Adrian,' said Adrian.

CHAPTER FIVE

'Somebody's gone berserk with the bunting!' he says,
putting down the tray.

'It's the year Prince Charles married Lady
Diana,' she says.

Covering his astonishment, he reels at her capacity
to recall historic moments but not his identity, nor the
names of her carers. 'Blondie' was actually Nadia, but
like the others was awarded a nickname that referred
to some physical aspect. 'Our two lovebirds are all
dressed up.'

'Bit old for lovebirds. Her hat with a feather in it
could've come straight from a dressing-up box. Somebody's
left a scooter on its side, look.'

'That laser-eye surgery worked wonders. You could
probably pick out the ants on the crazy paving. Is that the
right name for it?'

'Yes, and crazy's the word for it.' She traces the haphazard shapes of the multi-coloured slabs.

He waits. Sometimes the mist lifts and she looks at him and sees him.

'The kink in his nose,' she says, 'suits him.'

She takes a Custard Cream.

The mist does not lift.

29 July 1981

Marie looked Mac up and down. 'Is that what you're wearing?'

'For our anniversary photograph? Yes. Why?' Mac had dared to think he looked trendy in his jeans and check shirt; his wife's expression chased that little fantasy clean out of his head.

'Wear something smart for once.' Marie shoved him back indoors. 'It's not every day my best friend gets married.'

'One: *I'm* your best friend,' said Mac as he retreated up the stairs. 'And two, you will never meet the bloody woman. Unless she and Prince Charles decide to downsize and move to the suburbs.'

Tying his tie at the dressing-table mirror, Mac leaned in to peer at his new nose; after two years it still felt new. The top of it lurched to the right, but the bottom preferred to go left. Emma called it his wibbly-wobbly nose.

She was there now, leaning against his leg.

'Daddy, Odin says I can stay up late 'cos of Lady Di's wedding.'

The cat only ever spoke to insist on some boon for Emma.

'As usual, Odin's right.'

Emma ran off, a gingham blur, stopping to point at Mac's cassette player and ask, 'Who's that lady singing?'

'That, Emma Mactavish, is the mighty Dolly Parton. Only the most glorious singer ever to draw breath.'

'Mummy likes The Police.'

Mummy fancies Sting, thought Mac. 'Well, Dolly's Daddy's favourite.'

'Big boobies!' yelled Dan from where he hung upside down from his bunk.

'Now, now,' said Mac, pulling at the tie to start all over again. 'We don't say that.'

'*I* do. Big boobies! Massive boobies!'

A shout from downstairs silenced the boy. 'Dan! D'you want me to come up there and teach you some manners?'

'No, Mum. Sorry.'

'Good boy.'

The charm worked on everyone. Even Dan's teachers couldn't help smiling when they warned he needed to knuckle down and 'do some actual work'.

The charm even works on me. Mac ruffled the hooligan's hair as he sped past.

Both children raced everywhere, like small paramedics en route to an emergency. Now they raced out to the trestle tables spread out on the cordoned-off street.

97

Every house was obliterated by bunting. Union jacks fluttered by bins. Schmaltzy portraits of Charles and Diana were pinned up in windows.

Only Next Door opted out of the red, white and blue frenzy. It was business as usual behind the stiff net curtains.

'Potato salad!' breathed Dan, barely able to believe his eyes.

There were mountains of it under clingfilm, alongside all the other food he and Emma considered to be gourmet. Crisps. Sausage rolls. A huge cake Marie had baked, topped with a marzipan Charles and Diana. They looked more like Morecambe and Wise, but nobody said so.

Every sort of chair was pressed into service around the feast. Community spirit had broken out like a rash the moment the royal wedding date was announced. Now the beaming neighbours milled about in their best clothes, and the weather patriotically played ball.

Dan wore sunglasses he had found on a chair, introducing himself as Mister Cool to the other boys on the street.

'Mister Fool!' said one, and some light argy-bargy ensued.

Marie pulled the kids apart, and then straightened her hat.

'Oh blimey,' said Mac, when he saw it, painfully aware that was not the reaction his wife wanted. The hat was a Robin Hood affair, with a feather. 'Very nice, love,' he managed.

'It's an exact copy of one of Di's.' Titchy Marie insisted on emulating leggy Diana. She and Bernie had decided that Marie resembled the princess-to-be. They were wrong. 'I can't wait to see the wedding dress!'

'Won't be as nice as yours,' said Mac, who nursed fond

memories of the eight pounds and fifteen shillings mini dress. He righted Emma's scooter, dumped on the crazy paving. The garish hard surface looked as good as the day it went down.

Unfortunately.

He loathed the multicoloured concrete; Marie cherished it as the height of sophisticated good taste.

'Get a wiggle on, Mac, or you won't get Tatty back here in time for the ceremony.'

And we can't have that, thought Mac, praying for traffic.

The traffic deity ignored his prayer.

Passing sound systems that boomed out reggae and Sinatra, conga lines of children in fancy dress, and the odd dancing constable, Mac delivered Tatty to the sofa in good time to watch live footage of a liveried carriage trundle down The Mall.

'Budge up, Tatty.' Bernie threw herself down beside her. 'Love your hair.'

I don't, thought Mac disloyally. Instead of her habitual tightly wound bun, Tatty had let her hair down, and it fell to her shoulders in a lank, greying curtain. *She's a hair-up kind of lady.* His resistance to change, whether it was Tatty's hair or the lead newscaster on the Beeb, was infamous within the family.

The children sprawled on the rug. Beside them, Odin semaphored his disinterest by turning his back on The Mall and zealously licking his bottom.

'Ooh, look!' squealed Marie, as the cameras gave them a glimpse of the bride, draped and ghostly inside the carriage. Marie perched, vibrating with anticipation, on the arm of Mac's armchair, and he drank in her mingled scents of perfume and BBQ sauce.

'Wish they'd get on with it,' muttered George.

Earlier, over a chipolata on a stick, George had told Mac that Lady Diana was 'a right sort'.

Unable to supply the macho banter required of him, Mac had said, 'I feel sorry for the girl. All this royal wedding hysteria makes me think of public sacrifices.'

There were two Georges; the ladies got the cologne-wearing gent who opened doors for them; Mac got the George of double-entendres and 'Wink wink! Know what I mean?'

On a kitchen chair apiece sat the two Adrians, over on a visit and unwittingly caught up in wedding mania.

Polite, they sat through the coverage without complaint. Adrian Two – aka The Other Adrian – was bookish, quiet, with myopic eyes and a severe hairstyle. He was considered a cut above by the Neesons; he knew about wine and watched documentaries.

'How's your new flat?' asked Mac, eager to move away from rabid discussion of the Queen's matching bag and shoes.

'Grand,' said Adrian. 'Although I miss Ma's breakfasts.'

What he didn't miss, presumably, was the acidic disapproval that Bridget poured out with the tea. It was inevitable that Adrian would move out and escape the prayer books she put under his pillow and the frosty reception she gave his boyfriend.

None of the family enquired if he was sharing the flat with the other Adrian. The discretion was the Neeson way of coping, but Marie fretted privately to Mac that it must make Adrian feel different, left out.

'They'll do just fine,' Mac had told her. 'I know love when I see it.'

And all the while Bernie stole glances at them, as proud of them as if they were treasures she'd found at auction. 'Hold hands if you want,' she said. 'Nobody minds.'

Both Adrians had perfected the inward wince since arriving at Bernie's house.

On the screen, the virgin alighted from her carriage.

'The dress!' shrieked Marie.

'It's all rumpled.' Dan pulled a face.

'She's so beautiful.' Bernie began to sob.

'See those diamonds in her hair? That's the Spencer tiara.' Marie could take a degree in Diana Lore. 'A family heirloom.'

'What's that?' asked Dan. 'Do we have an air loom?'

'Yes, *you*.' Marie bent and kissed him.

'How much longer does this go on for?' Mac refolded his arms, wishing, just this once, that he lived next door, where the wedding was ignored.

The bells of St Paul's rang.

The new couple waved from the palace balcony and shared a suspiciously unerotic kiss.

Music started up in the street, and Dan yanked Tatty out of her chair. 'Come on!'

'Careful!' scolded Marie, drying her damp eyes.

The family treated Tatty like a relic. Old-fashioned all her life, she could be anywhere between sixty and a hundred and one.

'Maybe later, Dan, dear,' said Tatty, and Mac recognized the tone from his childhood.

Aloof. Not unkind. A bruised quality as if little elbows might mark her. The tone that ensured little Mac played quietly, like a child in a picture book. It had no effect on Dan, who went roaring off, tripping over Odin, and bumping into an Adrian.

All the while Emma kept her distance, keeping her eye on Tatty, wary.

'I'll stay indoors with, you know . . .' Mac nodded at Tatty, grateful for an excuse not to join the street party; he had seen the condemned look on the Adrians' faces as Bernie shepherded them out, nipping at their heels like a sheepdog in shoulder pads. He imagined her introducing them to the Ahmeds at number four and the Munroes in the end house as, 'My gay brother and his gay boyfriend'.

The television fell silent. Tatty knitted. Mac thought about work.

I should be there right now. The bank holiday was arbitrary, unwelcome, landing in the middle of a series of cases that needed all his attention. Human needs recognized no schedule; his clients didn't switch off for a royal wedding.

Life as a probation officer was tiring, difficult, and demanded a great deal, but Mac was one of that happy breed, people who loved their job and would do it even if they won the pools.

He shared his small success stories with Marie before bed, enjoying how she punched the air as she applied her moisturiser. Her favourite was the teenaged pickpocket who joined a Youth Opportunity scheme and was now building a flyover with the sort of care more appropriate to the building of the Sistine Chapel.

'Think you'll keep him out of jail?' Marie had asked.

'Hope so.' Experience was teaching Mac that he could nudge and advise, but sometimes the pull of a crooked way of life proved too much.

At such times, Mac didn't like his job so much. *I've failed him*, he'd think, watching a belligerent young offender cuss out the police officer who took him down to the cells. *Like everyone else has failed them.*

Because Mac believed that young people belonged to everyone.

There were fingers clicking in front of his face. 'Earth to Mac!' Marie's feathered hat was askew. 'You're at home, boyo, not the office.' She managed to be both proud of and irritated by her husband's work ethic. 'It's gone seven. Time you drove Tatty home.'

'No need, I have a lift.' Tatty glanced out of the window. 'Ah. Here he is now.'

A shouted 'Hello!' drifted in through the open front door, and Tatty called, 'Come in, Quentin!'

And in Quentin came.

Dan was at his heels, repeating 'Quentin?' with glee; he had a deep scorn for what he called 'posh names'.

The stranger put out his hand to greet the family, who gathered to study him. Even Odin sneaked in to sniff at Quentin's corduroy trousers. His entire outfit was straight out of *Country Living* magazine. Tweed jacket. Checkered cap.

Wrong shoes, thought Mac. The modern slip-ons jarred with the olde-worlde get-up.

'Ready, dear?' asked Quentin, and all jumped at the endearment.

'As I'll ever be!' Tatty was chipper as she took his arm.

The others parted to let them leave, too gobsmacked to say goodbye. At the end of the street, past the cordon, they saw Quentin hand her into a low-slung sports car.

'That Tatty,' said Bernie, 'is a dark horse.'

'I miss the wedding,' said Marie.

'I don't,' blasphemed Mac. He felt at ease, full of roast beef courtesy of Bernie's hospitality, and now seeing out the dregs of Sunday afternoon in a beer garden. He would only discover later that his forehead was sunburned; for now he was a man at peace. All he had to do was keep an eye on Dan and Emma, currently marauding around the adventure playground.

'Di's honeymoon looks a bit crap,' said Bernie, who was pining for the Adrians. 'All Highlands and boats. You'd think Charlie boy'd take her somewhere flashy.'

'Poor Lady Di,' said George.

'Princess Di,' Marie corrected him.

Mac smiled to himself at his wife's devotion to the lady, princess, whatever Diana was. At first, it had puzzled him, even irked him, and he had badgered her with questions about what she could possibly have in common with the privileged, wealthy young woman.

The Neesons were emphatically not royalists; they had a very Irish lack of interest in the doings of the Windsors. Marie was so egalitarian and down to earth, always rooting for the underdog, that her starry-eyed devotion to the blonde aristocrat unsettled Mac. The feeling that he didn't know his wife quite so well as he thought was unwelcome.

But then he remembered how it began. And he understood.

It was months ago, in April. Before that morning, Marie had referred to Diana – if she referred to her at all – as 'Lady Whats'ername, the shy one'. She had shaken Mac awake, the sun slanting into his eyes.

'It's gone, Mac.'

'Eh?' He'd scrabbled to look at the clock. 'What's gone?' Suddenly he understood. 'Oh love, no.'

The baby was still their secret. The least planned of their favourite mistakes. Still just a cluster of cells but most emphatically their child.

He wished she would cry, but she simply flushed the toilet before either of the children saw the blood.

They managed to talk about it. About how their family

hadn't grown in a straightforward manner. There were bumps in the road. Unexpected diversions. There was struggle.

It worried him that Marie didn't cry. Only when he refused to take no for an answer did they talk about it.

'The hardest thing,' said Marie, 'is the suspicion that it doesn't *matter*. There's no card for it in the newsagents. I don't feel I can explain to my customers why I'm sad.'

So she went about her business, perming and setting and tonging, holding the lack inside herself. A future burgled from inside her body. One night she said to Mac, 'I feel like a void.'

He held her until she fell asleep and then did some crying of his own, blowing his new nose like a foghorn in the small hours.

'We'll be open about it,' they decided, only to wish they'd kept it to themselves. Bernie was histrionic; her sincere tears wouldn't stop and made Marie feel worse.

Worse still, Nora was vague, pretending to misunderstand, even though she had gone through something similar. She said, 'Was it even really a baby, love? I mean, it was so small.'

After that Marie didn't call her for a while. She asked Mac, 'How could she say such a thing?' and Mac reminded her that they didn't need anyone's permission to mourn their lost child.

It was then that Marie began to clip pictures of Diana out of magazines.

So, if worshipping the distant, beautiful princess, and believing that 'Diana would understand' helped Marie, that was fine by Mac.

The conversation in the beer garden went this way and that, as conversations do. It turned to Tatty. 'We invited her today,' said Marie, fishing out the slice of lemon in her gin. 'But she's out with *Quentin*.'

None of them could manage to say his ornate name without spin.

'He seems a bit young to me,' said Mac. 'I daren't ask about him. Tatty's very private.'

'Just ask *me!*' Bernie adjusted her strapless dress. 'I rang Tatty and she was gagging to talk. Who wouldn't be? Quentin's a beaut.' She elbowed George, inscrutable behind mirrored aviators. 'Plus, he's loaded. Inherited a pile of property and land.'

'All right for some,' said George.

'He's generous, too. Tatty's bag was stolen and he gave her fifty pounds to tide her over *and* replaced the bag with a fancy new one.'

'See?' Marie, always on the side of lurve no matter now unconventional, poked Mac. 'You've read too many lurid newspaper articles about conmen and little old ladies. The money's going from Quentin to Tatty, not the other direction.'

All Mac could think was, *Why didn't she call me when her handbag was stolen?* The Neesons dashed to the phone if one of them broke wind. 'How old's this Quentin?'

'A lot less old than Tatty,' said George.

'Shush, you.' Bernie rose above their suspicions. 'Their friendship is based on shared interests. They met at that homeless shelter, the one she volunteers at.'

Finds it easier to help people she doesn't know, thought Mac.

'At first, it was just a coffee afterwards. Then they went to a museum. He takes her to stately homes.'

George said, 'Sounds like our Quentin is a little old lady in disguise.'

'He pays for *everything*,' Bernie went on.

'All those small sweet sherries must add up,' said George.

'She wears her hair down because Quentin likes it that way.'

'And do they . . . are they . . .' Mac didn't have the vocabulary to ask.

'Are they snogging?' Bernie did. 'I don't know how far things have gone. Just a close friendship at this stage, probably, but he's certainly woken up Tatty's rusty heart and I say cheers to that!'

Mac didn't raise his glass. 'No, no,' he blustered. 'Tatty doesn't have a romantic bone in her body.'

Marie and Bernie shared a *Men!* look.

'Gin makes Mum sleep,' observed Dan, as his mother snored in the passenger seat.

'I'm bored,' said Emma.

'Ask me questions,' said Mac, his eyes on the road.

'About anything?' said Dan hopefully.

'About puffins,' said Mac.

'Urgh, this is like school.' Dan threw himself back on the seat. 'We *know* about puffins, Dad. You've told us a million times.'

'I want to hear,' said Emma.

'You know why they have curved beaks?' said Mac.

'To pick their noses?' suggested Emma.

'Well, no, sweetie pie. It's so they can burrow into the cliffs and build nice safe nests for their chicks. Puffins are monogamous. That means they only have one husband or wife for their whole lives.'

'Like you and Mummy.'

'Exactly.' Mac wasn't sentimental enough to believe that birds fell in love. It was a matter of practicality. Puffins were good partners. They shared the load.

The first night he spent in Marie's narrow bed, he had woken to find a poster of Elvis sneering at him and Marie standing in her bra, saying, 'S'pose I won't see you for dust now you've had your wicked way with me.'

Privately feeling that the wicked way had been the other way around, Mac said, affronted, 'What do you think I am? A ruby-throated hummingbird?'

Marie had laughed, pulling on his shirt over her underwear, a gesture that made his heart sing. 'I didn't expect *that* answer.'

He had explained how the caddish hummingbird copulated then buggered off, taking no part in nest-building or chick-raising. 'I'm a puffin through and through.'

Dan asked, 'Will you ever see a puffin in real life, Dad?'

'Yes,' said Mac with more certainty than he felt.

With Pat's legacy stashed away, the cruise jar had been plumper than ever. A Teach Yourself Spanish tape was acquired; Marie learned how to say, 'Hello what is the cheapest rosé on the menu thank you'.

Then she bought Dan a bike. Emma came back from nursery to find the pink princess bed of her dreams. Crazy paving appeared. And the boiler decided – with faultless timing – to shuffle off its mortal coil.

The jar was looted. The process began all over again.

'What!' Marie sat bolt upright. 'Wazzntasleep.'

'You snore, Mum,' said Dan.

A raspberry ripple sunset melted over Sunnyside.

Feet tucked beneath her, Emma sat on the sofa in her nightie being very, very quiet; if her parents didn't notice her she might put off bedtime for a few minutes more.

Full length on the rug, Dan put his Action Man through various trials. The loss of an arm and a face covered in felt-tip marks did nothing to dent the soldier's confidence as he stalked a yawning Odin through the sheepskin.

Slippers on, arms folded, Marie was on the doorstep. 'It's late to be gardening, boyo,' she said.

'Just finishing off.' Mac took great care, as he always did. Perhaps he took a little extra care that evening.

'Not at all sure about this,' muttered Marie. 'Making a hole in my lovely crazy paving.'

Patting down the earth with his hands, Mac said, 'Didn't want to put this in a pot.' He sat back to survey the new arrival. 'It's special.'

Marie read the label. '*Magnolia stellata*.'

'Starry Magnolia,' said Mac. 'It'll grow to shoulder height. Lovely white blossoms.' He caught her eye and held it. 'Every April.'

She put her hand to her throat. She couldn't speak. When she turned, he knew she would go straight to the bookshelf and take down *The Language of Flowers*, and read there, *Remember me.*

'Don't worry, baby,' he whispered to the delicate young shrub. 'We always will.'

CHAPTER SIX

'A little birdie tells me you're having a bad day.'

She bridles. She's good at that. 'Well, your little birdie is wrong. I'm having a perfectly fine day, thank you very much.' She softens; perhaps she sees the flicker of hurt on his face. 'Especially now you're here.'

He takes off his jacket. Always takes a while to decompress when he arrives. The atmosphere is so specific. Talcum powder and bleach. Strip lighting and chintzy cushions. 'What are our pair up to today?'

'They're very excited. The lady's in a sombrero. Just back from Spain again, perhaps.'

'That shrub's new. Is it—'

'A magnolia, yes. Last little ragged blooms are about to drop.' She tilted the page for him to see. 'Those two little white rocks are laid side by side. Look as if they're meant to be there.'

'Who knows? This is all a very long time ago.'

She ponders that. 'And, in some ways, just like yesterday.'

'True.' He notices the stain on her collar and his heart falls sideways. He buries his attention in the photograph. 'What's she pointing at?'

29 July 1983

'You ruined the photo. Again.'

Marie was still pointing. 'The taxi's turned the corner!' Gibbering with excitement, she rounded on Mac. 'Sea sickness pills?'

'In the carry-on case.'

'Tickets?'

'My top pocket.' Mac flicked her sombrero. 'Aren't we supposed to buy these in Spain and wear them home?'

'It's to get us in the mood!' Marie clicked imaginary castanets. 'Come on, cabbie!' she squealed as the taxi slowed. 'I can't believe it, boyo! We're really, truly, *finally* going on our cruise!'

The children had been despatched to Bernie and George. Odin would be fed by the lady across the road. Mac's files had been handed over to colleagues, with many annotations and instructions. The jar was empty. The suitcases were crammed with brightly coloured, highly flammable clothing.

'Here we go, love!' Mac pulled at the door of the taxi. 'Eh?' he said, flummoxed.

Out got Tatty.

A different Tatty, in tears, with her head down.

Marie took off her sombrero and set down her suitcase. 'Pay the driver, Mac, and let's get Tatty indoors.'

'So,' said Mac, gently, sitting opposite his aunt at the kitchen table. 'Let's hear it. What on earth's happened?'

Marie put an arm around Tatty's shoulders. 'Take your time. I put our taxi back by half an hour.' She straightened her white lace collar, a copy of Princess Diana's latest style initiative. 'Whatever it is, we'll sort it out right here at this table, you'll see.'

'I fear,' said Tatty, 'this might be beyond the table's powers.' She took a breath and told them all.

The moment she opened the door to him, Tatty knew something was up.

'Quentin, what is it?'

He paced her hallway, dashing his hand through his flopping hair. 'I shouldn't have come. This isn't your problem. It's just that I share everything with you.'

'Sit. *Sit*.' Tatty patted a chair and he did as he was told. The sensation of being in charge of this potent young man gave her a surge of confidence. 'Tell me, and make sure you leave nothing out.'

A land sale had gone wrong. 'I was too trusting,' he said,

and she laughed, because that echoed what she always told him. It was one of their many in-jokes. 'Everything's blown up in my face.' Quentin put his hands over his eyes. His signet ring glittered. 'God, I thought I was so clever! I'm a fool. A *fool*.'

She prised out of him the details of an intricate deal; so intricate Tatty couldn't quite follow. This fellow had said this, another had promised that, blah blah failed acquisition blah blah foreclosing.

'I'm more or less ruined,' he said, miserable. 'Unless I can secure a bridging loan.'

'Will your parents help?'

'I'm on my way there. I'll have to go on bended knee.' Quentin shook his head, dejected. 'God, how they'll love seeing me grovel.'

They had spoken about his parents at length. Tatty was shocked at how little they appreciated their clever, handsome son. 'Are they still in New York?' she asked.

'Yes. So this is a goodbye of sorts, dear.' When Quentin stood he was thrillingly tall. He bent over her wrinkled hand and kissed it. 'I'll be a while. A fortnight at least.'

'But we have tickets for *Oklahoma!*' Tatty knew how Quentin loved their am-dram nights out. 'And you booked Sunday lunch at that charming pub in Brighton.'

'I know, I know.' Quentin flung himself onto a chaise longue. 'Not sure how I'll get through the next few weeks without our little jaunts to look forward to. Think of me, won't you?'

'Every day,' said Tatty, with a little more passion than she meant to. She paused. 'How much do you need?'

'A trifling sum, that's the irony.' He named the sum.

The figure was not, to Tatty's ears, trifling. Coincidentally, it mirrored her own savings. 'Goodness,' she said.

'I can repay my folks in one week, tops, with interest. But they'll make a song and dance of it. You know how they love to knock my confidence.' He waited for her nod. 'Maybe I'll just go bankrupt instead. Move in with them.'

'In New York?' It sounded so far away. It *was* so far away.

'Yeah.' Quentin looked at her searchingly. 'You'll forget me, won't you?'

'As if I could, my dear.'

He stood. He was all action. 'This is goodbye.' He kissed her cheek, let his lips linger for a moment. 'Who knows when we'll meet again?'

He was almost at the door when Tatty said, all in a rush, 'What if I was to lend you the money?'

'No. Absolutely not.' Quentin was resolute.

'But you said you would repay it in a week.'

'That's true, I would. But I daren't complicate this friendship. There are times I think ...' He was dreamy then, taking her in as she stood in her faded skirt, her glasses on the end of her nose. 'This just might be the most significant relationship I've ever had.'

'Oh, Quentin.' Tatty was overcome.

'I know how hard you've saved, how careful you've been with money. I would never accept a loan from you.'

She panicked more with each inch of carpet he covered on the way out of her home. 'Quentin, wait, listen.' He was the first thing she thought of when she woke up. Afternoons with him were shimmering entries in her dull diary. *This is not some fly-by-night thing,* she thought. *I've known this man for two years; I can trust him.* 'Hear me out, my dear.'

She had always tiptoed around naming her relationship with Quentin; she just knew it made her happy. He came and went – there were periods when business interests kept him out of London – but she always knew the exact date when she would see him again. An open-ended parting could not be endured.

Quentin opened the front door and Tatty became imperious; the way she had when young Ian spilled something at the dinner table. 'Listen to me, and listen well. I insist – yes, *insist* – that you accept a loan from me.'

He closed the door, leaned back against it. He kept his gaze on her. His face blazed; he had never looked so lovely.

'There are strict rules, Quentin. I need this money. So it's yours for one week and one week only. I won't accept any interest.'

He ran to her. His arms were around her. He said, 'No, no way. Ten per cent, you deserve it for your generosity.' He held her face in his hands. 'You are an *angel*.'

He took her hand then, whisked her out of the flat and down the communal stairs. She flew along behind him, exhilarated, and turned with him into a travel agency.

'Paris!' he declared to the bored girl at the counter. While Tatty listened he booked a hotel in the shadow of the Eiffel Tower 'seven days from today'. He turned to Tatty. 'To celebrate your kindness and my salvation from doom.'

The girl asked questions. He answered. She filled in a form. 'Double room?' she asked.

'Double room,' said Quentin. He put a finger to Tatty's lips when she tried to protest.

Her lip burned; she could barely remember taking her leave of him on the corner outside her bank.

Mac's face was granite as he listened.

Marie said, 'And that was the last time you saw or heard from him?'

Tatty nodded. She had aged. She was desiccated.

'What do the police say about it?' Mac had one eye on the clock.

'I'm too ashamed to go to the police.'

'The shame is *his*,' spat Mac.

'Shush, boyo.' Marie moved her chair closer to Tatty. She caught Mac's eye and nodded at the bags Tatty had brought with her. 'Have you left your flat?'

'They evicted me,' said Tatty. 'I can't pay the rent. After all those years they just . . .' She slumped a little more, shrank again. 'I had nowhere else to go, I'm so sorry.'

'We don't do sorries here,' said Marie. 'We'll sort this out, don't you worry.'

A whispered conference took place in the hall.

'We're going to miss the Southampton train,' said Mac.

'I've waited for today for years on end,' said Marie.

They were silent. Then Marie said, 'Are you going to say it or will I?'

'We're not going, are we?'

'Cancel the cab, love.'

Dinner was eaten. Lamps were lit. A round of cards was played. Odin slept in the sombrero. Tatty thawed a little.

We should be onboard right now, thought Mac, drying the dishes. To Marie he said, 'Notice she didn't come to us straight away? Only when she was chucked out. When she had literally nowhere else to go.'

Marie took the plates from him and was about to comment that they weren't dried properly, but instead put them in the cupboard. 'She's never relied on anyone,' she said. 'It doesn't come easy.'

The children came back from Esher the next day.

Emma, a homebody, was pleased. Dan, a swashbuckler, was annoyed at having to drop his plan to seduce the older woman – she was thirteen to his twelve – who lived next door to Auntie Bernie.

In legwarmers – 'You rang just as I was getting on me exercise bike!' – Bernie's perm shook as she heard the saga of Tatty and That Bastard Quentin, as he was now known. 'Why didn't she just storm round to his place and beat the shite out of him?'

'Not everybody handles problems the way you do,' said Marie, putting together a hamster cage on the kitchen work-top. 'Besides, it was only when Quentin didn't return that Tatty realized she'd never known his address. He just said he lived "off the Kings Road".'

'And that's a long road,' sighed Bernie. 'Bet you Tatty's not his only victim. Two years is too long to devote to one con. There'll be other Tattys scattered around London. He's probably watching *Oklahoma!* with one of them right now.'

'Keep your voice down.' Marie nodded at the sitting room. It was now Tatty's lair; the television was permanently off and the air sat stale and frigid. 'I reckon he stole her handbag himself.'

'Yes!' Bernie's eyes widened. 'So he could play Sir Lancelot and buy her a new one. What a pig.'

They heard Mac at the gate.

'Did you get it?' shouted Marie as soon as he put his key in the door.

'Yes.' Mac bustled in, pleased with himself. 'One hamster, present and correct.' He decanted a furry ball from a cardboard box and then pulled his hand away, sharply. 'Little bugger bit me!'

'Youse should call it Quentin,' said Bernie.

They didn't call it Quentin. They let Emma name it and she opted for Hammy.

'Jeez, she really dug deep for that,' said Bernie as she left.

'Emma loves her little Hammy,' said Mac, contented, as he and Marie sat in the kitchen late that night, Tatty's snores drifting in from her makeshift bed on the sofa. 'Funny little beast, isn't he?'

'All that energy,' marvelled Marie. On top of the fridge, Hammy was going hell for leather on his wheel. The plan to keep the cage in Emma's bedroom had been derailed by the animal's relentless keep-fit schedule; the noise kept her awake. 'He puts Bernie to shame.'

'All that exercise Bernie does . . .' said Mac.

Marie finished the thought. 'Yet never loses a pound? That's because she rewards herself with chocolate eclairs.' She held up the newspaper. 'Seen this?'

'This' was a picture of Princess Diana opening the wing of a hospital. As Marie waxed lyrical about her bolero, Mac's mind wandered to his office. *Now that we're not going away I might just ring tomorrow, just to check up on things.*

Probation was a curious career; if he did it properly, nothing happened. Nobody went to jail. Nobody set up business as a drug dealer. Nobody hit their partner. *Perhaps I'll call my youngest client, just a quick chat.* To lay a foundation, advise the boy to make decisions that would benefit the future version of himself instead of pressing the self-destruct button.

'Are you even listening to me?' Marie assumed everyone was as fascinated by saintly, chic Diana as she was.

'Of course I am. Um, hospital, and, er, hats.'

'Don't bother trying to lie, your nostrils are inflating.'

Marie wheeled around as Odin jumped onto the worktop and the hamster cage fell, with a clatter, to the lino.

'Alas, poor Hammy, I knew him well,' said Mac, as he lowered the miniscule corpse into the outside bin.

'First thing tomorrow morning,' said Marie, 'you get yourself down that pet shop.'

Mac explained to Emma that sometimes hamsters, when they're particularly happy, change colour overnight.

'Is that true, Tatty?' asked the child.

'Is what true?' Tatty was still in a world of her own. A dreary one, with no dashing young blade to warm it up. 'This frightful cat won't leave me alone.' She pushed Odin off her lap, and the cat glared at her with its one eye.

The hairdressing ladies avoided Tatty, packing themselves into the kitchen. The sitting room became an ad hoc old people's home, with Tatty sitting all day in her dressing gown, cold cream congealing on her face.

Her mantra – 'Just tell me if I'm in your way and I'll go' – was not comforting. Mac told Tatty, repeatedly, that she had a home with them as long as she needed one. He meant it; he really wanted to mean it. He thought of Bridget, who had given up her own life to look after Nora. *My aunt is my responsibility.*

Yet the house was fit to burst, and Tatty affected each corner.

She made a face at sudden noises. With a twelve-year-old

and a five-year-old around, these happened frequently. When Mac said, 'Damn and blast the thing,' about the stuttering TV set, she told him, 'Language, Ian!'

Bed was the only place to escape Tatty's deadening influence. Marie was surprised – and then highly vocal about – Mac's reluctance to make love with Tatty in the house.

'I'm not a *nun*,' she was saying, when the house suddenly creaked, and she sat up like a meercat. Marie was perpetually on high alert for burglars, murderers, all manner of bad men.

'Just Dan going down for a glass of water.' Mac pulled her back down. Her tubby little shape against him helped him think; she was his good-luck mascot. 'Maybe we should extend. Build a granny annexe.'

'Listen, boyo.' Marie's voice was sensible and forthright. 'If we had to take Tatty in, we would. But there's something you're not seeing. Tatty does *not* want to live with us. We're too noisy, too busy. We shout too much and we laugh too much. What's more, Tatty's independent, right through to her marrow. If she doesn't pick up the pieces and get her own four walls again after what That Bastard Quentin did to her then she'll only live a half-life. So, get your skates on and ring that number tomorrow morning.'

'The sheltered housing people?'

'It'll be perfect. She'll have a community she can ignore, and help at the press of a bell if she falls or whatever.' Marie sat up again. 'What *is* that noise? Like a hen's loose in the house.'

'Unlikely,' said Mac, getting up.

The peculiar noise was laughter.

Tatty was out of practice; it sounded as if she was gargling tin tacks. 'You little imp!' she was saying to Dan, who was perched on her blankets. 'He's telling me jokes,' she said to Mac when he appeared. 'Have you heard this one?'

'Dad! Dad! Listen! Knock knock.'

'Who's there?' Mac had one eye on Tatty.

'A little old lady.'

'A little old lady who?'

'I didn't know you could yodel!'

'Isn't he a one?' laughed Tatty.

To celebrate, Dan did his favourite karate move. His foot caught the photograph of Mac's parents and sent it flying from the shelf.

'Careful, son.' Mac, still grinning, still grateful to ebullient little Dan for lifting Tatty's spirits, picked up the frame. He turned to his aunt, opened his mouth to say something about the picture, then saw her face and thought better of it.

Dan's jokes might cheer her up, but the sight of Ed and Marguerite bring the shutters down once more.

He put a hand on his boy's shoulder. 'Bed, you,' he said.

Watering the new planting in the back garden, Mac could hear her yelling from inside the house. Probably all the neighbours could hear her too; Marie was one of life's yellers.

'I'll tell your father and then you'll be sorry!'

Mac waited for the derisive laughter. And smiled.

Neither of his children feared him. They knew his worst punishment was a disappointed look. That was how Mac liked it.

'Big mistake,' said a voice. Next Door squinted through a hole in the fence.

'Oh? How come?'

'Ivy is a pest, nobody *plants* ivy.'

'Except me, it seems.'

'It'll have its suckers all over your brickwork. It'll crawl all over the house. You'll never get rid of it.'

'That's the plan.' *The Language of Flowers* had revealed ivy's meaning as 'Wedded Love'. It was a late anniversary present.

The furious little eye disappeared.

Indoors, he found Tatty knitting, or trying to. She threw glances at the ceiling, her face a picture of distaste.

'You're right, Tatty,' said Mac. 'Dan's playing his records far too loud.'

Already on the boy's case, Marie was yelling again, one foot on the bottom stair. 'Turn down that racket or I'll come up there and pull the plug myself!'

The doorbell rang. Marie jumped, then jumped again at the sight of Next Door jabbing his finger in her face.

'Tell that good-for-nothing boy to switch off that damn punk music.'

It's Madness, not punk, thought Mac. To Next Door, all music other than Cliff Richard was punk.

'Don't you worry,' said Marie. 'I was just about to deal

with it.' She shut the door, turned, and yelled yet again. 'Turn it up, Dan! Loud as it'll go!'

On the day they would have returned from their cruise, Mac took a call informing him that a safe, secure and warm little flat awaited Tatty in Camden.

He was touched by Tatty's happy tears at discovering she could live in comfort – somewhat spartan comfort – for a low rent, with the knowledge that help was on hand if she needed it.

It took little time to move her in. With many a 'Call us if you need us!' on Mac's side and a clear impatience to be alone on Tatty's, she was settled at last.

That evening in Sunnyside was dull and samey. And perfect.

Marie flicked through a magazine with Diana on the cover while Mac tried to follow a drama about an improbable murder. Dan drew something on his own arm. Emma was asleep, or near as dammit, upstairs in her pink bed. Odin stretched and let out a yawn, snapping his jaws shut with a wet sound. A cruise brochure lay, virgin and untouched, on the coffee table.

Dan nodded off, fighting it all the way. His parents smiled at one another over his head. Mac hoisted the boy over his shoulder. Putting him to bed this way was a paternal job he wouldn't do for much longer. *My poor back*, thought Mac as he plodded upstairs.

Bouncing back down, he threw himself on the cushions beside Marie, lips puckered for a kiss.

Instead, she put her hands to her face, horrified.

'Was that . . .' Mac sat stock still. 'Was that a squeak?'

She nodded, hands still covering her eyes.

The next morning Mac was at the pet shop before the owner opened up.

CHAPTER SEVEN

'Go back.' She is peremptory. 'Swap those stupid
Chocolate Fingers for Custard Creams.' She lowers her
voice, conspiratorial. 'You know who's eating them all,
don't you? Just because she knows they're my favourites?'

Her eyes dart to where her titian-haired nemesis sits
with a copy of Woman's Weekly.

The keeper of the biscuit tin admonishes him when
he returns, metaphorical tail between his legs. 'A terrible,
terrible crime to bring her ladyship the wrong biccies.'

'I promise never to do it again.'

'She's a bit full-on today. Don't let it get to you.'

Trouble is, it all gets to him. He is forever battling
with the wrongness of it all. That she – of all people! –
must live among strangers. Attentive, compassionate
strangers, but they didn't know her before. Before all this.

'Careful!' She finds fault with where he puts the plate.

128

Too close to the album, apparently, which is already open.
They have reached 1989. 'The little girl's growing up.'

'Must be about eleven. Is that a hamster she's
holding up?'

'Adorable. The girl, not the hamster. She has braces.'

'The girl not the hamster.'

She ignores his joke. 'The boy's turned out well. Nice-
looking. Hair's rather long, but that was the fashion, I
suppose. I assume that's his girlfriend.'

'Have you noticed the rucksack by his feet? This feels
like a leaving-home photograph.'

'A foot!' She points. 'Who's that standing just out
of shot?'

29 July 1989

As soon as they all said 'Cheese', the girl leaped back into
the family circle and reattached herself to Dan. Red-eyed,
she pressed a disintegrating tissue to her face. 'Promise me
you'll ring every night.'

'Not *every* night.' Dan leaned away, as if she were infec-
tious. 'All right, yeah, sure, SJ.' He gave in as the sobbing
redoubled. 'Every night, honest.'

Watching the tender scene, Marie said, 'Young love's a
beautiful thing.'

Dan's not in love, thought Mac. *He should tell her the truth,*
that he'll have forgotten her by the time his train pulls out of

Kings Cross. 'Thank God he scraped through his O-levels. University might knock a few corners off.'

'Dan doesn't have any corners!' Marie saw all her geese as swans; her Dan was charming and handsome and fun. Mac's Dan was all those things, but he was more besides. And they weren't all savoury.

'This one's the genius in the family.' Mac patted Emma's head as she and Hammy went inside. The child had aced her eleven-plus, and was bound for the local grammar school. 'Although,' he whispered, 'a genius should notice that her hamster is six years old, and their average lifespan is two and a half.'

They were on their eighth Hammy; due to a shortage at the pet shop, it had changed sex.

The desperate SJ had lain hands on Dan. 'Leave me something of yours!' She was a couple of years younger than Dan. Gauche, over-loud, her need to seem sophisticated touched Mac's heart; he guessed there was a story there. 'Give me something that smells of you!' SJ grabbed at his jacket.

'Not the jacket!' Marie was a touch too sharp. The cruise jar had been looted of its last pennies to buy Dan a 'decent' leather jacket for uni. The jar had been putting on weight, heavier by the month, but the car dying on the M3 changed all that. 'Oh Dan, *seriously*?' said Marie, as he dragged a pair of boxer shorts out of his holdall to give to his lady love.

With one last bear hug for his little mum, Dan set off into the next stage of his young life.

Marie scooped up Odin and buried her face in the ageing cat's fur. 'Something in me eye,' she said.

Mac placed a white rock, freshly painted, at the foot of the *Magnolia stellata*. There were almost enough stones to form a circle. 'Eight years old you'd be . . .' He pulled a dry leaf from a branch. He felt for and found Marie's hand. 'Tell you what,' he said to the magnolia, 'your mum looks pretty today, doesn't she?'

And she did, even with red eyes and her mascara leaking into Odin's coat.

The house in Esher had had a facelift.

As had its owner. There was a feline tilt to Bernie's eyes beneath the high ponytail she favoured these days. She was in tartan ruffles, dancing attendance on the Adrians. The couple had come for their annual visit, and Bernie had been quick to say, 'They'll stay at mine, I have more room, after all . . .'

They brought Nora along for the ride, and she seemed glad to escape Bridget. Even Nora, a daily mass-goer, was exhausted by her daughter's appetite for Catholicism. Now she sat on Bernie's velour sectional seating sipping a cocktail, very happily pagan.

'Show them your photos.' Nora nudged her Adrian, the original Adrian, and beamed at the family as he produced a paper wallet of snaps. 'There was this march, all about gayness, in Dublin. Sure, the fellas had a grand day out.'

It looked like a *very* grand day out in the small, colour

pictures. A sea of denim, many a moustache, and hand-made banners.

'It was . . . emotional,' said Adrian. 'First time we ever held hands in the street.'

Marie swallowed hard. She was proud. She was scared. She wondered how it would feel to be with your other half for ten years and still be reticent to touch them in public. 'We're getting there,' she said. 'You boys hold on, you'll be married someday.'

'Now now, sis,' said Adrian. 'Don't be silly.'

'What the divil's going on in Germany?' Nora peered at the television.

'The Berlin Wall, Ma,' said Adrian. 'It's coming down at last.' He cheered, and so did the other Adrian. They never strayed more than three feet away from one another.

'Go on, lads! Push that wall down!' Marie stamped her feet, and her bouffant George Michael 'do' wobbled. She looked around for Mac, but he was out on the terrace, near the new outdoor dining set (they all knew to the penny how much the built-in barbecue had cost), staring into the middle distance.

Bernie sent George after him, like a mountain rescue team. George grumbled, but went, bringing an anecdote about the one-way system around Walton-on-Thames.

'How's work?' George asked the mandatory question as the others drifted out to join them, leaving Berlin's falling masonry behind.

For once, Mac told George exactly how work was. 'I've

got this client,' he said, and he sighed. Mac sighed every time he thought of Josie Craig. 'I can't reach her. Can't help her.'

'Our Mac's a workalcoholic,' said Nora, approvingly.

'Josie's still at school. Seventeen. A kid, really. Family are new to the area. Good student, quiet type, till suddenly, overnight, she changes.'

'Nobody changes overnight,' said Adrian Two.

'Her family — nice, unremarkable people, apparently — can't cope with her. She bewilders them. Out of the blue, Josie began shoplifting. A watch. A handbag. The police were called one night when she smashed all the ground-floor windows in her house. Goes to a private school, and she attacked her mother at the gates one morning. Blacked her eye.'

'Jaysus!' said Nora.

'Sounds like a charming young lady,' said Bernie, draining her glass.

'Do you ask her why?' said Adrian. 'Why she suddenly became her parents' worst nightmare?'

'I try.' Mac sighed again. 'She barely talks. She's full of . . .'

'Rage?' suggested Adrian Two.

'Exactly,' said Mac. 'There are other children in the family, and she lashes out around them. Her father's worried sick. I can't get Josie off my mind.'

Bernie, fixing her ruffles in the glass of the new patio doors, asked, 'Is she pretty?'

Silenced, Mac thought hotly, *What manner of question is that?*

'Hey, now, whoa.' George waggled his cigar at his wife.

'I'm just saying,' said Bernie, unrepentant, 'forty-four's a funny age for a man.'

'*Any* age is a funny age for a man,' said Nora.

Scandalized, Mac looked to Marie for support, but she was staring out at the garden.

'Only kidding, Mac.' Bernie draped herself around him; the rush of Calvin Klein Obsession almost knocked Mac out. 'Everyone knows you're one of the good guys.'

That night, pulling wet washing from the machine, Marie said, 'I know the house.'

'Sorry, love, what?' Mac was changing a plug.

'The Craig house.'

'Oh. Do you?' Mac felt he had missed a scene. They hadn't mentioned Josie's case since they left Esher.

'It's *big*. Changed hands about a year ago. I wondered who could afford a mansion like that. They totally refurbished it.' She struggled with a duvet cover and Mac helped her. 'High walls all around.'

'I'm going there tomorrow, to discuss home schooling with the parents.'

The phone interjected. It was Dan.

'Darlin'!' sang Marie, and angled the phone so Mac could hear Dan's excited summing-up of the past week. 'All these parties sound grand, love, but you're keeping up with the work?' she said.

'Yeah, yeah, 'course. You know me.'

That's the problem, thought Mac. *I do know you*. He waited for it and it came.

'Actually, Dad, you couldn't see your way clear to bunging me a few quid, could you?'

The Craigs' sitting room was stylish. A fire sprang to life in the grate at the touch of a button. Only the colourful plastic toys underfoot subverted the magazine-cover feel.

'What age are your other kids?' asked Mac. He took in the family photographs crowding every surface. He thought of his one and only photograph of Ed and Marguerite, and suppressed an ignoble twinge of envy.

'Lucy's three and Jacob's one. We always say we have two families,' said John Craig, his eyes cagey for this polite intruder. 'There's Josie, then the other two. Perhaps that's it. Perhaps she's jealous.'

'Rarely that simple, in my experience.' Mac felt over-large and awkward; he would never be invited into this palatial house if it wasn't for the catastrophe slowly unfolding within its walls.

'She's angry with us,' said Angela Craig, dragging on the cigarette between her fingers. 'About *him*.'

This italicized individual turned out to be Josie's boyfriend.

'A bad lot.' Angela bit her lip as if she could say much more. 'Infamous in our corner of Devon. To think, we gave Josie everything, the best education, all our attention, and she seeks out this lowlife . . .' She turned away. Her narrow back was eloquent.

'My wife's right. *He's* where the rot set in,' said John. 'We banned her from seeing him and she sneaked out. Came back stinking of drink and weed. We moved two hundred miles to put space between him and Josie, but she's worse, if anything. The school have washed their hands of her.'

Mac scribbled in his trusty, ever-present notepad. 'That's why I'm here, to set up home tuition. We must make sure she gets her A-levels and—'

'I want her out of the house,' said Angela, resolutely facing away from Mac.

Mac's pen paused.

'We know how that sounds,' said John. 'Believe me, we don't want this. But Josie's started . . .'

Angela turned to face Mac and jabbed the cigarette in his direction. 'She started hurting the little ones. She grabs Jacob when my back's turned. I hear little Lucy shouting "Stop". Jacob's barely one; I have to keep him safe.' She was stiff, exhausted. 'I want my daughter out of here, Mr Mactavish.'

'I helped her pack,' Mac told Marie.

'It's not right. A child belongs with her family.'

'Yeah, but it's complicated.' Mac's job had led him into homes so broken he was surprised the roofs stayed put. 'Don't judge the Craigs, love.'

'Sometimes,' said Marie darkly, 'people *should* be judged.'

'Behind those high walls, the house is like something out of a movie. Josie's room is twice the size of ours. And then I had to deliver the poor girl to an A.P.'

'You and your abbreviations.'

'Sorry, love: approved premises. At such short notice, I could only get her into the place by the new shopping centre. It's not one of the better ones. Institutional, you know. Her bedroom's a cupboard.'

'It's not right,' repeated Marie.

'It's not,' agreed Mac, wishing for the umpteenth time that he was a bigger cog in the huge infernal machine and could truly change things. He bent to stroke Odin.

Old Odin miaowed, content, knowing nothing of such matters.

'Venice!' said Marie, suddenly, as she washed a regular's scant hair at the kitchen sink. 'That's where we'll go! A cruise to Venice!' There was just about enough for a deposit in the jar. 'The baroque splendour! The Italian fellas' bums!'

'Lovely,' murmured the regular, shampoo in her eye.

As soon as the last customer left Sunnyside, Marie hot-footed it to the travel agency. Emma went too, Hammy in her pocket; she needed new school shoes.

'Oh.' They halted, confused, outside the traditional shoe shop down the cobbled mews where small Mactavish feet had been measured for almost two decades. It was dark, dusty, deserted. 'Couldn't stand the competition,' said Marie. Their suburb was known as a 'nappy valley'. Families moving in. Gentrifying. Knocking through reception rooms and crowding the pavements with pushchairs. The big-name stores had followed, in the pale temple of the shopping centre.

'Come on, Mum.' Emma pulled at her mother's arm. 'Oh no. *What?*' She knew that look on Marie's face.

Transfixed, Marie pressed her nose to the dirty window. 'I wonder . . .'

'But you *have* to come to Bernie's with me,' said Marie, hands on hips. 'This is our last chance to see the Adrians and Ma before they fly home.'

'Sorry, love. It's an emergency.' In a new, Marie-approved jumper, Mac was overdressed for visiting an A.P. 'Josie Craig's started staying out all night and the manager wants to chuck her out.' He paused, and eyed her. 'You do understand? I can't say no.'

'You *can*.' Marie was tart. 'You won't though, so go on, skedaddle.' She kissed him. It was perfunctory, so she hauled him back and did it again, properly. 'This girl is getting to you.'

They all get to me, thought Mac, hurrying out into the November night.

'Isn't Bernie's house a *palace*!' Nora Neeson was proud of the detached five-bedder. 'She's lucky to have an earner like George.'

'Mmm,' said Marie as she helped stack her mother's Crimplene pleated skirts and sensible shoes in the old-fashioned hard suitcase.

'Where's Mac, love?'

'A work thing.' Marie gathered up her mother's talc and cotton-wool balls from the en-suite. Marie would kill for an en-suite. 'Bridget'll be missing you.'

'Bridget'll be at Mass round the clock,' said Nora. She lowered her voice, looked to the door as if ears might be pressed against it. 'She's gone a bit funny,' she said. 'About the boys.'

'Adrian and Adrian?' Marie frowned. 'Funny in what way?'

'That AIDS,' said Nora. 'Bridget washes all the doorknobs after they visit. And they visit *all* the time. Such good lads.'

'You can't catch AIDS off a handle, Ma. Tell Bridget that from me.'

'She says it's God punishing the gays.' Nora looked hurt as she folded an ancient cardigan with great care.

'God doesn't seem like that sort of bloke to me. AIDS is just a disease. Terrifying but not supernatural.'

'It was when Rock Hudson got it that she sat up and took notice,' said Nora.

'I've been trying not to think about it,' said Marie. She turned to her mother, her frail, indomitable mother. Some things Nora just wouldn't discuss. This might be one of them. 'But I'm scared for Adrian, Ma.'

'Me too, pet, me too.'

Jaysus, she's shrinking, thought Marie as Nora embraced her.

'She doesn't keep her room clean. She's downright rude to me.' The manager of the approved premises ticked off Josie's sins on her fingers. 'Curfew means nothing to the girl.'

Mac turned to Josie, studying her bitten nails in a corner of the manager's office. 'Where do you go at night?' he said. 'You can't afford to get into trouble with your shoplifting case pending.'

'I'm already in trouble.' Josie shrugged. She was tall, spare, dressed in shabby black bits and pieces, with a new nose ring through a scabbed hole in her dainty nose.

Leave-takings on the drive.

Bernie cried as if waving the Adrians off to war. George disattended.

Adrian punched Marie gently on the shoulder. 'Stop it! I know what you're doing.'

'I'm not doing anything!' Marie punched him back.

'You're studying me. *Examining* me.' Adrian grinned at her mock-innocence. 'I'm *fine*, sis. Me and Adrian are monogamous. We're safe.' He rubbed one eye with the heel of his hand. 'More than can be said for some of our friends.' He listed two or three names.

With a start, Marie recognized one. 'Not your little bald pal from Terenure? He's *dead*?'

'Yes. And it wasn't pretty. We looked after him as best we could. His folks just turned their backs.' Adrian hugged her suddenly, and hard.

Mac walked Josie back to her room, six square metres of stained woodchip. 'Help me keep you out of prison, yeah? Only you can determine how your life goes from here, Josie.

I want it to be a happy life, a fulfilled life, and I can show you the tools to—'

'God, stop, puh-lease!' Josie threw a Doc Marten into a corner. 'My life's already messed up. It's too late.'

'At least tell me where you get to after curfew.'

'So you can come and drag me back to this dump? Nope.' Josie was wry. 'Trust me, I don't go anywhere exciting.'

Needing to be active, desperate to shake off the spectre of the big disease with the little name, Marie stripped the bed Nora had slept in.

'The cleaner'll do that!' called Bernie from downstairs.

'I've practically finished.' Marie, nosiness running through her veins along with the tea and blood, hoicked open the wardrobe door. *Bernie's overflow wardrobe*, she thought, with a mixture of mild envy and grudging admiration.

A coat with a suede trim. A kaftan embellished with sequins. A collarless jacket. Skirts. Trousers. A slagheap of designer handbags beneath them.

Hang on, thought Marie. There was a price label on the coat. Another on the kaftan. Marie checked every item, and none of them had been worn. She tore open drawers stuffed with pristine, sumptuous garments. The shoes in the bottom of the wardrobe had unsullied soles.

'Incredible, isn't it?' George was there, all of a sudden. He picked up a heap of bangles that jingled merrily in his hand. 'Don't say anything, please. She goes up like a firework if I mention it.'

'But why?' Marie held a fake fur cape to her cheek. 'There must be thousands of pounds worth of clothes here.'

'She says it's to fill a hole.' George looked different when he was sad. Older. A bad caricature of himself. 'She says it's *me*.' He left the room.

'Josie told me where she goes at night,' said Mac, getting in Marie's way as she trotted around the kitchen, doing the thousand-and-one things necessary to keep a house afloat. 'She climbs the tree outside her family home, and sits in it, looking at the lit windows.'

'Aw no, that's sad.' Marie shoved him away from the fridge. 'She misses them.'

'But when they let her in she causes havoc. The little ones, Lucy and Jacob, are scared of her. What a decision for the parents to make. To protect two children at the expense of the third.'

Marie shoved him away from the sink. 'Don't forget your own child in all this.'

'Emma?'

'You said you'd help with her biology project.'

'And I will! The life cycle of the puffin. We're doing a poster and—'

'She handed in the project today.'

Mac sat at the table. He had been the last to leave the office each day that week. 'I'll do better next week,' he said. 'I promise.'

Marie relented, sat on his lap.

Like a little puffin of my own, thought Mac, glad of her change in humour.

She said, 'Just remember, this is a *job*, Mac. You know what happens when you lose focus.' She stroked his roller-coaster nose.

'Luckily,' said Mac, 'I don't have another nose to break.'

Hammy was on Tatty's lap.

Little sod's looking peaky, thought Mac, bringing Tatty a pre-roast snifter.

Apron on, Marie joined them from the coalface of the kitchen. Sunday was no day of rest; the success of her home salon meant she must cram in all the weekday chores around cooking a rib of beef that could feed the whole street. 'How's your new neighbour?' she asked Tatty, alighting, ready to dash back to tend the joint.

'Seems like a respectable lady.' Tatty's hair sat coiled in a bun, as it used to do pre-That Bastard Quentin. 'I can't tell you much about her. I keep myself to myself.'

My wife would know the new neighbour's inside leg measurement by now, thought Mac. 'I'll get that.' He rose to answer the phone.

As ever, Marie hovered, hating not knowing who was on the other end, what they were saying. 'Is it work?' she hissed.

Mac waved her away, turned his back. 'Yes, yes, I'll be there,' he said.

Tatty was politely put out. 'But, Ian, this is our one Sunday a month.'

Marie's face was demonic as she flung his coat at him. 'You *know* how much I have on me plate today and now I have to look after Tatty too.'

Even Emma's goodbye was long-suffering. *All the women I'm related to are mad at me*, thought Mac. He caught sight of the framed photograph. *Except her.*

Marguerite grinned at him, and it encouraged him to go to Marie and say, 'Look, love, I *have* to go. Josie's father caught her breaking into the house and the police were called.' He took a deep breath. 'I suspect he wasn't exactly gentle with her. This'll impact all the work I'm doing trying to keep her out of youth court.'

Marie, stirring with one hand, basting with the other, had her back to him. 'Just go,' she said. Then: '*Is* she pretty, Mac?'

He didn't answer.

It was late. The Mactavishes were having one of their moon-lit bed-chats. There was no spooning tonight, no warm and lazy kisses.

Mac tuned out, then heard the dreaded words: 'Are you even listening to me?'

'Yes. No. I mean ...'

'I'm telling you something important about Bernie, and as usual you're away with the fairies.' Marie turned and punched her pillow.

'Bernie? She's not ill?'

'No, she's ... it's weird, Mac, but I don't want to share it with you while your head is elsewhere. This Josie needs you, but so do we.'

'You don't think I know that?' It was odd, disfiguring, to be sore at Marie. His little puffin, his queen. 'Josie's case is unusual and takes up a lot of my time. It has nothing to do with whether she's pretty or not, *that* I can tell you.'

There was silence from the other side of the bed. A deep, heavy silence.

'I mean, Marie, where's the trust? And where's the compassion for a girl in trouble?'

'And where's my husband?'

'It's ... I'm ...' Mac had wondered the same: *Why am I so drawn to Josie's case?* He had come to the conclusion that it reminded him of his own childhood. The sense of a central mystery, one unspoken truth.

The air bristled between them.

The doorbell rang.

Both sat up. Mac raced downstairs and Marie listened, quivering.

'You!' she heard Mac say. 'What are you doing here?'

The fluorescent light lit the kitchen with unsparing honesty, and revealed the mauve shadows under Marie's eyes and the deepening lines on Mac's forehead as they struggled to understand.

'I don't get this. When, exactly, did you drop out of your course?' he asked.

Dan, looking far too relaxed for the situation, shrugged.

'A couple of months ago. I didn't tell you 'cos I didn't want to upset you.'

'Ha!' snorted Marie. She was ambivalent, checking her son for signs of malnutrition, longing to kiss his stubbly cheek, and also longing to kick him up his lazy, entitled bum. 'You lied to us, you mean. He doesn't get this slyness from my side of the family.'

It had long ago been agreed that all the children's virtues came from the Neesons, everything else from the Mactavishes.

'So you're not in student digs anymore?' said Mac.

'I've been sofa surfing.' Dan's charisma was the oil that greased his life. 'My mates have been great.'

'What are you doing for money?' Mac felt uneasy. His son's life, which used to be so known to him, was now cryptic. He felt a chasm between them; this confident, reckless boy was doing his own thing, and Dan's own thing scared Mac.

'I've been promoting bands. Leeds has an amazing music scene.'

'How do you make money doing that?' asked Marie. 'Sounds like you're bumming around to me, young fella.'

'I get by.'

'Then why are you here?' Mac had never been so sharp with Dan. A creeping sensation was claiming him, inch by inch, as he struggled to respect his son.

Dan smiled. A *What am I like?* smile that riled both his parents. 'I ran out of sofas to surf. It's just temporary.

I have plans, big plans. Uni's not for me. I'm not like you, Dad; I'm not a tortoise; I'm built to go at a hundred miles an hour.'

While Dan showered, Marie told Mac, 'He's going off the rails.' She dug Mac in the ribs. 'You two need a man-to-man chat. Tell him what's what, order him to get his act together.'

'*Am* I a tortoise?' asked Mac.

'Here he comes.' Marie hurried out. 'Read him the riot act.'

The riot act took ten minutes, and then Mac lent Dan ten quid from the cruise jar to get a taxi into the West End.

'Mu-um,' said Emma, from the corner of the office. 'I'm bored.'

'Whisht,' said her mother, who was listening intently to the man in a suit.

Unsure what 'solicitor' meant, eleven-year-old Emma only knew that this tedious man had her mother's rapt attention.

'Thank you,' said Marie at last, and pulled on the Diana-style military coat she had just bought from a catalogue. 'I'll be in touch.'

Walking home, Marie said, 'Don't tell Daddy about all this.'

'Please stop being annoyed with Dad. I hate it.'

'Who says I'm annoyed with Dad?' Marie smiled at Emma's perfect, Neeson-esque roll of her eyes.

*

Mac faced Josie across the tomato ketchup bottles and ashtrays of his favourite café. The girl was full-on Goth; kohl-edged eyes and a ratty, black-dyed nest of hair. He hoped the pallor was make-up.

They talked of her accommodation – 'It's shit' – and her new college – 'It's shit' – and the fried-egg sandwiches – 'You're right, they're the best.'

'Tell me,' said Mac, wiping grease from his chin.

'Tell you what?'

'Tell me *why*.' Mac felt it was time. They had road behind them. They had trust. She was bursting with the why of it. 'Tell me why you stole from shops.'

It all came out. Matter-of-fact over the mugs and plates. 'They stopped giving me money. That was no big deal, not really. But then they stopped feeding me.'

'They what?'

'They starved me. I had to eat on my own, and it was scraps. I had to stay in my room. The *fuss* if I looked in on Lucy and Jacob. They told Lucy I was bad, and mad. That's why she tells those tales about me. When I argue with my folks she thinks I'm being evil. They were punishing me, you see, about *him*.'

'But you stopped seeing your boyfriend when you moved from Devon.'

Josie's black-painted lips curved into a sardonic smile. 'Not *him*. They're punishing me about Jacob.'

'Your little brother?'

'My son.'

*

The phone call was fraught, the line crackling with Marie's disappointment. 'I know, I *know*,' said Mac. 'I promised I'd be home on time all this week, new leaf and all that, but there's an emergency.' He paused, listened. 'Yes, love, it's Josie.'

Afterwards Mac couldn't recall if he'd said goodbye or just slammed down the phone.

Even for a man accustomed to difficult conversations, the meeting with Josie's parents was taxing.

John Craig wouldn't accept the legal realities. 'To all intents and purposes,' he told Mac, his face grey beneath the interview room's strip lighting, '*I* am that child's guardian, his adoptive father.'

'That's simply not true.' Mac was repeating himself; he did his best not to sound weary. 'Jacob's birth was registered under the names of Josie and her boyfriend. She is his mother and she has rights. This isn't up to you, Mr Craig. Josie has the last word in where her son lives, and what she wants is this.' *Listen to me, man*, begged Mac. He was throwing the family a lifeline. 'Josie wants to remain in the family home, so Jacob can have you and Mrs Craig and little Lucy around him. She insists, though, that she is recognized as Jacob's mother from now on, and *I* insist that you treat her with respect and see to her needs. Meanwhile, I can work with Josie on getting her out of the system. Myself and my superiors feel confident that your daughter won't reoffend if she can establish a secure home life with her baby. You look reluctant, Mr Craig. Why?' Mac sat back. Threw up his hands. 'You have plenty of space, after all.'

'It's not about having the space. It's about Josie getting her own way. After what she did!'

'Having a baby isn't a crime.'

'It was worse than a crime. Hanging around with that scumbag, then declaring she was pregnant. I *mattered* in our old town. People looked up to me.'

'So you covered up the pregnancy,' said Mac, working hard to keep his tone level. 'Moved miles away, to London, where you could disappear. Then you passed Jacob off as your wife's child.'

'Sounds crazy when you say it out loud, but it was for the best.'

'And starving your own daughter? Punishing her for every infraction of your preposterous rules?' Mac gave up with his tone. Heard his voice raise. 'Denying Josie even the touch of her son's hand? Your daughter has sat in this room and cried about how it felt hearing Jacob call *her* mother "Mama", when she knows that your wife is ashamed of him! It was about control, Mr Craig, and you have to accept that Josie's life is her own to manage as she sees fit.'

He could've gone further, and described the rage Josie felt, the sense of injustice that powered the window-breaking and the defiant clothes, the love within her that had nowhere to go.

But that might expose how deeply Mac empathized with

a fellow seeker for family truth, and it would definitely bring his boss barrelling in to put a stop to the meeting. Instead, Mac simply asked John Craig one last time if he would consider letting Josie return to the family home as Jacob's mother.

With Dan lurking in his old bedroom, Sunnyside bulged at the seams.

'What time did his lordship roll out of bed today?' asked Mac as he arrived home on the dot of six.

'Not too late,' said Marie. She had forgiven her son; Dan was the golden boy once again. 'Don't nag him, Mac. He's trying.'

'Trying my patience,' said Mac, always ready with a dad-joke. He wasn't angry with Dan; he was disappointed. Dan took the easy way, the crooked way, the way that stayed *just* this side of decency. *I need to look up to my son.*

'He thinks I don't know he's smoking out the window,' said Marie.

'Silly boy. You know everything,' said Mac. The banter was welcome. Like the old days, if the old days could be said to be a fortnight ago. 'Josie got the keys to her council place today. Miniscule one-bedder, couldn't swing Odin in it, but she's so happy. Still on probation, of course, but it'll all work out, I can tell.'

A key had turned. Josie's life had clicked into place. It would be challenging, but it would be real.

'So your involvement's more or less over?' asked Marie.

She asked it nonchalantly, which meant the answer was very, very important. 'She's a matter for social services from now on?'

'Still some loose ends to tie up,' said Mac.

'You're only my second visitor,' said Josie. She wasn't the typical sunny young mum of TV advertising, with her fingerless black gloves and her jet-black beehive, but she held Jacob tight as she showed Mac around the three bare rooms on the twenty-first floor.

'Quite a view.' Many other residents in the tower were known to Mac, who had already checked the double-lock on the front door. 'Are you in touch with this little 'un's dad?'

'He knows Jacob exists. He can find us if he wants.' Josie fiddled with her nose ring. 'But he won't want.' She looked at Mac, her black-rimmed eyes urgent. 'Do you think he loved me a little bit?'

'That I can't say, Josie. But I do know this; there'll be plenty of love in your life, and in the meantime, Jacob there is overflowing with the stuff.'

Josie kissed the one-year-old's impossibly round and pink cheek. 'I'll be off your hands soon,' she said to Mac, as she pulled the boy's dimpled arms through the sleeves of a hand-knitted jumper. 'So I just want to tell you that you've been an example of how real men behave. You're nothing like my ex or my dad. You're a gent, Mr Mactavish.'

*

'You're home early!' shouted Marie, as she combed a client's hair, deft and kind as always. Other ladies were ranged on the sofa like battery hens.

'C'mere, you!' Mac bent her over backwards and kissed her. The comb fell to the floor.

'Aww!' clucked the hens as one.

'I love you, Marie Mactavish,' said Mac.

The hens applauded.

'Eurgh, pack it in,' said Emma.

They whispered together, man and wife, in front of their enraptured/disgusted audience.

'Only one person knits baby clothes in brown and bloody orange,' said Mac.

'I'm so sorry for asking if Josie was pretty. That was grotty of me.'

'Forgiven, all forgiven. How'd you get her address?' He held his wife at arm's length. 'Never mind, forget I asked, you know everything.'

Later, he discovered Marie had also given Josie a Tupperware vat of Irish stew, and their home phone number.

'That's strictly against the rules,' Mac said during their moonlight chat. A slightly breathless one. There had been activity beneath the duvet.

'You know me and rules,' giggled Marie.

A voice rang out from Dan's room. 'Keep it down in there, you two!'

'Mrs Mac, we need some "us" time.' Mac had seen this

phrase in one of Marie's *Woman's Weekly*s. 'How about bringing that cruise forward, love? Next stop, Venice!'

Marie said, 'About that, darlin'. Can you meet me after work tomorrow?'

They met at the corner of the cobbled passage. Mac let her take his hand and dragged him to the door of the much-loved shoe shop.

He took in the empty windows. The post piled up inside on the mat.

'It went bust? What a shame. Hey, love, don't do that!'

Marie was trying the door.

Mac looked up and down the alleyway. 'That's private property.'

She produced a key. She walked in. She did a twirl in the middle of the floorboards. 'Come in, boyo. This is no shoe shop. This is me new salon.'

He wanted to return her smile, match her enthusiasm. But he knew they couldn't afford the shop. 'Does this mean we're not going to Venice?'

'I only took out a tiny loan. Teeny.'

'You should've consulted me.'

'But you'd have talked me out of it.' The logic seemed clear to Marie. 'It'll take off, Mac, I promise. It's my *dream*.'

He smiled then. He knew about dreams. 'It's fabulous, love,' he said.

CHAPTER EIGHT

'The funny little woman's in a tunic. One of those tabard things. Brown and orange.' She thinks hard, rummaging for the reference. 'She's working at Sainsbury's!'

'She has a nice face, doesn't she? Approachable.' He pauses. 'How are you feeling? After . . .'

'After what?'

'We can talk about it. People have disagreements all the time. Ups and downs.' He hesitates. 'They said you were crying after I left.'

'They said, they said, why not listen to what I say!'

He realizes then that she can't remember. On his previous visit he had cornered her – gently, gallantly – and insisted – gently, gallantly – that there were changes in store and she needed to listen to him.

The red-haired arch enemy had thoroughly enjoyed the

*spectacle that followed. Shouting. A cup turned over. It
was the talk of the rec room for days.*

*And now she is all smiles. The one slim silver lining to
her condition is that she forgets the disagreements.*

*'What on earth,' she says, 'is that green thing at the
edge of the photograph?'*

'Looks like ... yes, it's a bath.'

'A bath?' Her eyes widen. 'In the front garden?'

29 July 1992

'Good riddance!' yelled Marie, as soon as the camera clicked.

The avocado bath was dragged to the dump truck, along
with its good friends, the avocado sink and the avocado loo.

'There was *years* of use left in that suite,' said Mac. He was
experimenting with a moustache; nobody was sure about it.
'If you recall, the "gorgeous" avocado bathroom was one of
the reasons you wanted to buy the house.'

'Yes, boyo, but that was twenty-two years ago.' Marie was
cock-a-hoop. '*Everyone* has a white suite these days.'

Mac had stood his ground about installing a bidet. *Not on
my watch*, he thought, with a shudder. It was a pyrrhic vic-
tory; Marie would use it as a trump card to get something
else she wanted. 'The new bathroom's turning out to be
pricey, love. I hope your bubble baths are worth putting off
the cruise yet again.'

'The salon's going great guns. As soon as the loan's paid

off we can start saving again, and we'll soon be as rich as Bernie and George.' Marie picked up her handbag. 'Right. Chop chop.'

'Don't chop chop me, woman. It's you who has to beetle back to work. This is my day off.'

'That's what you think. Me junior's rung in sick.' The spotty, monosyllabic junior was the bane of Marie's life. 'Which means, you've just got yourself a Saturday job.'

'Hair by Marie' buzzed.

The phone on the reception desk never stopped ringing; satisfied ladies trotted in and out, past the cascade of plastic vines and pearly sinks set into the wall. It was only after Marie chose her uniform that she realized the brown and orange palette echoed Sainsbury's; she laughed that off, too busy revelling in her tiki-tiki fake bamboo panelling to worry about it.

Marie was a blur. She was a wife, a mum, a proprietor, and a cutter of (mostly grey) hair. Holding herself to impossible standards she would never ask of other people, the fuel that propelled her was the urge to make them proud. Mac. Her sister. The children. *Especially Emma*, she would think. Her girl would grow up with a strong, independent female role model. *Even if it kills me.*

'This way, Mrs Levinson, my junior will shampoo you now.' Marie handed a startled-looking woman over to Mac. 'Try not to scalp this one,' she said under her breath.

'This way,' said the oldest junior in town. They passed

157

Odin reclining on his special cushion. The cat's magnificent fur was a little ratty these days; Mac knew how he felt. At forty-seven, Mac felt fifty breathing down his neck.

'Comfy?' he asked, as he settled Mrs Levinson in at the sink, tucking the towel too tightly and treading on her feet. He tentatively washed her hair, feeling this was too intimate an activity to be doing with a lady he had only just met.

Christmas lights twinkled on the roadworks. They would be late. Tatty wouldn't comment. But she would notice.

These visits were a duty, like going to church. Although, as Marie said, at least they gave you wine at church.

On the backseat, in dungarees and her hair tied up in a floppy bow, fourteen going on forty, Emma stroked Hammy #12. The blonde was gone from her hair, along with the red tones. A brunette, the girl had Marie's blue eyes and her father's original nose. A strong face for a strong character. 'Wish we were going to my other auntie,' she said.

'That's next week,' said Marie. 'I wonder why Bernie's throwing a party? She's having us over at Christmas a few days later, and it's not a birthday.'

'Does our Bernie need a reason?' asked Mac. 'She opens the champagne if there's a vowel in the month.'

'This is a big deal, though, caterers and everything.' Marie sat up, happy, realizing, 'We can tell everyone about your big promotion.'

'My big-*ish* promotion, love.'

'Dad never blows his own trumpet,' said Emma, allowing Hammy to nibble her bow.

'Nobody knows your dad even owns a bloody trumpet.' Marie fiddled with the radio. 'I hate them Smiths. That's the one good thing about Dan moving out; we don't have to listen to Morrissey whingeing all day and night.'

Mac put his foot down and left the roadworks behind. Privately, he felt there were other benefits to Dan moving on. No lingering smell of weed outside his room. No late-night, heavy-footed stumbling up the stairs. No encountering young women on the landing in their underwear. 'Dan's twenty-one now. About time he paid his own way.' *That came out wrong,* thought Mac. It wasn't about money. It was about accountability.

Emma let out a sudden scream; she and her friends were prone to these. She leaned forward between her parents' seats. 'What the hell? Hammy is, like, *nine*! How is that possible?'

They told her the truth on the Hammersmith flyover.

Emma didn't speak to them at Tatty's, and only relented the next morning when she asked Mac for a lift to school. 'I will never, *ever* forgive you and Mum,' she told him.

'Rightiho, love,' said Mac.

The wisteria was pre-menstrual.

Just like Marie, thought Mac, with affection. He knew how to deal with the plant from long experience dealing with his wife; ignore the huffiness, the turning away, the bristling and the fading. He trimmed and fed it, stopping short of bringing it a hot chocolate, which worked wonders on Marie at her time of the month.

The magnolia was December-bare, but no less beautiful to Mac than when it shook out its robes in April. 'Terribly sad,' he said to it, as he fussed with its branches. 'Next Door's wife dying suddenly like that. The ambulance came in the middle of the night, but it was too late. Your mum sent flowers – you know your mum – and brought him some stew. He sent it right back. Doesn't know how to accept kindness, you see.'

The blue lights striping the bedroom wall had made Mac face the thought of losing Marie. The pain – even imagined – floored him. *To the whole world,* he thought, *she's only one person, but to one person she's the whole world.* The fragility of the framework that held up his heart was too frightening to contemplate.

The one person who was Mac's whole world sprinted out to him, yelling, 'Look! Emma taught me how to vogue!'

The song blared out and Marie began to – badly, hysterically – ape Madonna, while Emma looked on, bent double, hooting.

They made Mac join in.

Next Door pulled his curtains together with a vicious swipe.

Crouch End was up and coming, according to Dan, who knew about such things. He frequented wine bars Marie read about in gossip columns, and wore clothes from designers just before they burst onto the scene. He had a 'nose' for snuffling out talent, apparently, and this nose won him a job in the A&R department of Wasp, a major record label. 'Artists and repertoire, before you ask, Dad,' he'd said.

In his sharp suit and sharper haircut, Dan sought out new talent, nurtured it, styling it into something saleable.

Despite his flashy way of life, Dan's bachelor pad was a damp slice of an ugly house near a roundabout. 'He's more junior than he's letting on,' said Mac, as Marie tried desperately not to jump up from Dan's lumpy sofa, and tidy the magazines and bottles on the coffee table.

'The Christmas tree's a nice touch,' she said.

When they looked closer they saw the decorations were beermats with telephone numbers written on them.

'You still out every night, love?' said Marie, as Dan appeared from the kitchenette with mugs of what might be coffee. 'You need a good night's sleep to do your job properly.'

'Going out *is* my job, Mother.' He was in indie clubs every evening, chasing the next big thing in a whirl of sticky floors, plastic beakers, and girls. Lots of girls.

'Going steady with anyone? How's that nice SJ?' Marie was hopeful. 'Is she still on the scene?'

'Nobody says "going steady" anymore, Mum. And SJ ... well, she's SJ,' he said, and he was quiet for a moment.

'D'you like this girl, son?' Mac was hopeful too; hopeful that Dan would show a gallant, sensitive side at some point.

''Course I do. SJ's gorgeous, and we've been on and off forever, but I don't have time to get serious. I'm finding my feet in the industry.'

'Don't forget to fall in love,' said Mac, as he and Marie left.

'Christ, Dad, you're *so* soppy.'

Mac eyed the tins of eggshell lined up and ready to go. He had done his best but Marie had prevailed. Played that trump card. The kitchen cabinets would be orange, and Sunnyside would slide a little further down the style slope. 'Things are changing, aren't they?'

'How'd you mean?' said Marie.

'Well, Dan moving out, and Emma spending all her time in her room.' He missed their David Attenborough binges on the sofa.

'Things are supposed to change, love. Imagine if we were still the same two idiots who got married back in 1970.'

Mac did imagine it. It felt nice.

'Is it Viennetta tonight?' Emma swung in. At Marie's queenly nod, she said, 'Fabulous! We had it all the time when Dan was back. Obviously. As he's the *favourite*.'

'We don't do favourites here,' said Mac, taking her seriously while Marie cackled.

'He gets away with murder. Just 'cos he's got dimples and he can pick Mum up and swing her around. I'd never get away with stuff like he does.'

'But you never put a foot wrong,' said Mac.

*

Fashion baffled Mac.

This party could be a funeral, he thought. Somebody had flicked a switch at the beginning of the nineties and suddenly everyone wore black. The ground floor of Bernie's house heaved with black velvet and black chiffon and black leggings and – *Dear God,* he thought – the hostess was in black over-the-knee boots.

Marie was dancing; her black tulle skirt made no sense to Mac, who was self-conscious in a new suit. Double-breasted, black of course, it turned him into a Mafia don.

He browsed at the buffet, mourning his moustache. He had shaved it off earlier, convinced he'd heard Emma giggling at it. Mac missed it now; the moustache had been comforting to stroke at moments of high pressure, such as staring down a violent offender, or trying to find a compliment for Bernie's outfit. *Where's old George?* He couldn't see his brother-in-law in the crowd. Taking a sausage on a stick, he prowled the perimeter, dodging the elbows and feet of the dance floor.

George was probably hiding, as Mac longed to do. He felt a rush of empathy for the man; although dull and status-aware, George put up with a lot.

Newly installed lighting made the night-time garden a multi-coloured daytime. Dan shivered over a cigarette. Mac knew what his son's dilated pupils meant; being a proba-tion officer often entailed checking people for signs of drug use. Marie, oblivious, had cooed over how handsome Dan looked; Mac saw past the satin jacket.

'Anything you want to talk about?' Mac sidled up to Dan. That approach worked with his clients. Sometimes.

'Big deal coming up, Dad.' Dan spoke fast. 'Make or break. I found this band. You'd love them. Really seventies. Silverskin, they're called. I've polished them, turned them into louche rock gods. I'm expecting a call from LA tonight. I've asked for a £30k spend. I can turn that into millions.'

'Goodness,' said Mac, aware it was an inadequate response.

Dancing over, glass in hand, Bernie chucked Dan's cheek. 'Here he is, me little movie star. The ladies love him, Mac. He's danced with all my mates.'

'Happy to help,' said Dan.

'Where's George?' Mac felt the need of a sardonic take on the event.

'C'mere!' Bernie waved Marie out to join them on the terrace. Emma, in black satin, was wearing lipstick for the first time in her life, and seemed both embarrassed and elated. 'You got yourself a boyfriend yet?' asked Bernie.

'I don't want a boyfriend,' said Emma, pointed little chin up.

'She means,' said Dan, 'nobody's stupid enough to ask her out.'

'Shush, you,' said Marie, pushing him.

'I'm too busy to bother with a boyfriend,' said Emma, looking daggers at her brother. 'I want to do really well at school.'

'Attagirl,' said Mac.

'She's ambitious,' said Marie. 'Like her ma.'

'God, no, Mum,' said Emma. 'I don't want to be a *hairdresser.*'

'I'm not just . . .' Marie lost faith in that sentence. Downed her drink in one.

'Emma'll change her mind about fellas,' said Bernie. 'When some hunky sixth former comes along.' She seemed sure of this.

Equally sure, Emma said, 'Not all women get married. I'm going to be independent.' She eyed Dan. 'And if I wanted a boyfriend, *I'd* ask *him* out.'

'Woooh,' said Dan, holding up an imaginary handbag with both hands.

Emma fumed; her big brother pressed her buttons in a way nobody else could.

'Shit!' exclaimed Dan. 'The time! Auntie B, can I use your phone?'

'Sure.'

'He's ringing LA,' said Mac, ever-conscious of phone rates.

'Ooh!' Bernie was thrilled.

'Where's George?' asked Marie, then, suddenly, ecstatically, 'They're playing "Vogue"!'

She was off, along with the rest of Mac's womenfolk. He lurked – no other word for it – in the circular hallway, where it was cool and the music was just a thumping rumour.

Dan raced down the stairs, shrugging on a coat.

'Where you off to? It's only ten,' said Mac.

'They went for it!' Dan clapped his father on the shoulders.

'The deal, Dad! It's on. It's bloody *on*.' He opened the double doors, and freezing December rushed in at them. 'Gotta find the guys in town and celebrate.'

'But your aunt's party,' began Mac.

The doors slammed and Dan was gone.

The music stopped. Chatter replaced it, then Mac heard Bernie shouting, 'Whisht! The lot of youse!'

He stood at the edge of the party-goers in the opulent room and watched his sister-in-law clamber onto a table.

'I've something to say.'

She's nervous, thought Mac. He had never seen Bernie unsure of herself before, and his heart went out to the tall, clumsy, well-meaning, infuriating woman.

'You've all been asking what this party is *for*. Well, I'll tell you. It's to celebrate a new phase in my life. It's a divorce party.'

She held up her glass triumphantly, but there was silence.

Mac felt a hand steal into his. Marie, her eyes full of questions, had found him.

Bernie steamed on, determined to rally the crowd. 'It's time to find myself! George clipped my wings and now it's my time to shine.'

There was a murmur then, a trill of excitement; she was winning them over.

Not the back row, though. Mac, Marie and Emma stood together, thunderstruck.

'Why didn't she tell me?' whispered Marie.

'This is the last party in this house. I'm selling up and I'll buy an apartment, and I hope to see you all there, because, believe me, I ain't gonna stop partying!'

The music struck up, and people roared, and Bernie was mobbed.

Marie sat upstairs in a spare room, the wardrobe doors open to reveal the cache of unworn clothes. Her tulle skirt had wilted. 'This isn't the way to go about divorce. Announcing it like she's running for president.'

Mac, on the bed, his shirt collar chafing, agreed.

'Everyone gets divorced now,' said Emma. 'Auntie B might be happier on her own.'

'*We* don't get divorced.' Mac felt insulted. 'You don't have to worry about that, love.'

'I don't,' said Emma, matter of fact. 'Can we go home?'

'Not until I've had a word with madam,' said Marie.

Marie had a word. Madam was not contrite. Madam was high as a kite on the success of her party.

'Leave me be, Marie. You're just mad I didn't tell you first.'

'That's true, I *am* mad about that, but most of all I'm worried this is another one of your crazes. Like the time you wanted a horse, or thought you could speak Italian because you watched *The Godfather*.'

'It's time for me to—'

'Shine, yes, I heard all that bollocks already,' snapped Marie. 'What's really going on? Is it, is there, are you . . .'

'Mum means do you have a lover,' said Emma.

'I wish!' said Bernie, with feeling. 'Neither does George, before you ask. We both agreed. It's over. The forms are signed, Marie. This is no passing fancy.' She had drooped slightly.

Those over-the-knee boots must be killing her, thought Mac. 'We're only saying all this 'cos we care,' he said.

'I know,' smiled Bernie. 'But you don't need to worry.' She let out a weary little *woohoo!* 'I'm so happy.'

'Where the hell has George *gone*?' Marie's hands were on her hips; never a good sign. 'Did you just leave him out for the binmen?'

'George is fine. He's starting afresh, just like me.'

'You're blaming him for everything, I suppose,' said Marie. 'That's what you did with me, when we used to share a room.'

Bernie's lips thinned. 'And there was me thinking you might actually support me.'

Emma went to her aunt, put her arms around her. 'I understand,' she said. 'You have to live your own life.'

'Exactly, pet,' said Bernie, staring smugly over Emma's head at Marie.

'Marriage is a marathon, not a sprint,' said Marie. 'This is so *you*, Bernie. Trading something in because the glitter's worn off, when it still has years of service left in it.'

They found the car where they'd left it, all three of them silent, chastened. Marie had embraced Bernie, of course, told her she was 'there' for her, but Bernie's flippancy hadn't faltered. She behaved as if divorce was a huge lark.

His own marriage was Mac's foundation stone. It felt attacked by Bernie's determined whimsicality. He struggled with the car key; like Mac, it didn't react well to cold. He heard Marie say, 'Isn't that . . . it is! George!'

'Looks like the party's over,' said George sheepishly, coat collar up, hands in pockets.

'How're you doing?' Marie was shivering.

'You know . . .' George was a dry, bloodless version of himself. 'Up and down. Bit of a shock, all this.'

Mac longed for the old George. The boring one who asked if there was traffic on the A3. This man was defeated. Sad. 'Listen, maybe this isn't the end.'

'It's Bernie's decision and I respect that.' George backed away. 'I shouldn't be here, really, but something draws me back.' He looked up at the house, where lights were going off, one by one. 'She'll be still dancing, in her stockinged feet,' he murmured.

'Oh, love, come home with us,' said Marie.

'No, no, I'll go. Please don't tell her you saw me. Let me have some dignity.'

Marie said nothing; when she went to the phone the moment they got home she defended herself by saying, 'No, Mac, I didn't promise George I wouldn't tell her. Bernie should know what she's doing to him, how unhappy this stupid divorce has made him.'

There was a brief conversation. It didn't go well.

'He what? Jaysus, the git,' said Bernie.

'He's heartbroken,' said Marie.

They agreed to disagree.

Later, in their moonlit lair, Mac snuggled up to his wife. 'So,' he said, 'my glitter's worn off but I still have years of service left?'

'Exactly,' said Marie.

CHAPTER NINE

*Blondie is in his chair. She is gesticulating, her face
bright as she tells a story. She laughs, sees him approach,
and leaps up.*

'Sorry! There you go! Madam's ready for you.'

*'Smashing girl, that Blondie,' she is saying as he wiggles
out of his jacket.*

*'Sure is,' he says. 'Shame she's leaving.' It's out of his
mouth before he can rethink. He sees her blink, shudder.*

*'Leaving? She can't.' There's a hysterical note just below
the surface of her voice. 'Who'll put me to bed?'*

'Well, they're all pretty nice, so . . .'

*'They are not. That one with the glasses smells of
chewing gum, as if we're all idiots and don't know she pops
outside for a smoke every few minutes. And as for Big Legs,
I won't have her in my room.'*

'Shush!' He looks around neurotically in case Liz — for

that is Big Legs' real name – can hear. 'Just because you
can't remember her actual name, you can't call the poor
woman Big Legs!'

'But she has got big legs.'

There is a second when they are in a stand-off, but then
the giggling begins. It builds. He is helpless. She slaps the
photograph album. They guffaw.

'What's so funny?' smiles Big Legs as she passes them.

'Nothing,' they say together, and that's it.

They're off again.

29 July 1995

'It's our silver anniversary,' said Marie. 'And here we are,
gardening.'

'*I'm* gardening, love. What you're doing is called watching. We've taken our photograph, the restaurant's booked.
Everything's tickety-boo.' He snipped off a particularly fine
geranium and handed it over, with a courtly bow.

She smiled. Smelled it. 'According to *The Language of*
Flowers, the geranium stands for foolishness. So let's do something wild and foolish for our anniversary.'

'We talked about this. What with the kitchen extension
and everything, we can't afford to throw a party. It's the
steakhouse as usual.'

'Sod the steakhouse,' barked Marie. 'Let's have a barbecue!
Today! Now!'

'If we must.' Mac was bad at barbecues.

Calls were made. Bernie was summoned from her modern apartment in Chelsea. Dan was ordered home from Notting Hill. A taxi was despatched for Tatty.

'Pity Emma's too far away,' said Marie. 'She loves a sausage.'

After her reign as Head Girl, Emma had delighted them all by getting into Oxford to read English Language.

'Typical,' Dan had said when he heard.

The youngest Mactavish was 'no trouble', as her doting grandmother, Nora, liked to say.

'We'll see Em soon enough,' said Mac, who missed his daughter more than he liked to admit, even to Emma. He'd been disappointed when she announced she was staying in Oxford for what she called the 'vac', but the offer of a plum role assisting one of her tutors with research into early medieval lyric poetry was too good to turn down. 'Might surprise her one Sunday with a visit.'

'Burgers.' Marie was writing a list in the hellhole that used to be their kitchen. 'Buns, posh ones, not cheap ones.' The orange cupboards were already in a skip, the room just a dust-filled cube separated from the elements by a flapping tarpaulin. 'Potato salad. Coldslaw.'

'Coleslaw,' said Mac, automatically. He'd been correcting that word since they met.

'And don't forget salady bits.' She handed him the torn-off piece of paper.

'Oh, *I'm* going for this, am I?'

'You are,' said Marie with a smile. 'And then you're going to cook it. I'll drag the barbie-thingy out from the shed.' She wrapped her arms round herself. 'I can't *wait* until me new kitchen's in!'

She had exploded one day over the stew, screaming that she couldn't cook in 'this old-fashioned pigpen one minute longer'. When – if – the workmen finally finished, she would have a glossy white tundra with sliding doors out to the garden and – cue celestial angelic voices – an integrated washing machine.

'The food'll taste the same,' Mac had kvetched, as costs piled up and the original estimate became a laughable ancient document.

The charcoal was lit.

The July sun beat down upon the garden chairs and the rubble from the hole in the back of the house.

Tatty moved her chair into the shade.

Bernie sprayed herself with suncream. Her lips were new and it was still impossible not to stare at them. They were part of a three-year post-divorce overhaul that had seen her breasts inflate and her teeth glow in the dark.

Dan paced the lawn, Motorola to his ear.

His female relatives watched him. Tatty with misgivings; Bernie in awe of his effortless cool. Bernie had begun to say 'cool' a lot; it made Emma want to scream.

'Ow,' said Mac, from the mouth of hell, or, as others called it, the barbecue. *Why*, he wondered, *are men assumed to be natural barbecuers?* He sucked his burnt finger and eyed the rows of burgers and chipolatas as if they were armed and ready for a knife fight. 'Who wants a burger?' he called, a shout echoed in many gardens up and down the street that peerless afternoon.

'Two please,' said Dan, looking up from his call.

'Dazzy Mac's a growing boy!' laughed Bernie.

Mac hated the nickname bestowed on Dan by his colleagues at Wasp Records. At fifty – *half a century!* – Mac was at pains to resist becoming a grumpy old git, but there was something un-serious about Dan that rankled. Something uncommitted. Dan worked hard, that was clear, but his ambitions were for a corner office, a bigger expense account. Mac fretted about such hollow aspirations, whereas Marie was merely proud of their boy; Mac tried to relax and do the same. It didn't come easy.

'This looks delicious,' said Marie, as they sat down to the smorgasbord. She over-praised his grilling efforts every time. 'I declare my husband king of the tongs!'

'Twenty-five years ago today you were just saying your vows.' Bernie, rarely nostalgic, was soft-eyed.

'I meant every word,' said Mac.

'Aw, Dad, such a softie,' said Dan, attacking his burger.

In Dan's mouth it sounded like a criticism.

'Jaysus, who's that, the minute I sit down?' Marie sprang up at the sound of the doorbell.

There were joyous shrieks from inside the house, and soon she was dragging Emma out into the sunshine. 'Look who's here.'

'Oh.' Emma stopped dead, a beribboned box to her chest, when she saw the table, and the barbecue. And Dan. 'I didn't realize . . . when did you plan all this?'

They all felt it. The queasy frisson of competition. Between the Favourite and the Other One. *All nonsense*, thought Mac, rising awkwardly from the lawn chair. *But it hurts her all the same.*

'Spur of the moment, love.' He could see she only half-believed him. 'Honest, we thought you were in Oxford so we didn't—'

'Happy silver anniversary.' Emma, with bad grace and a heavy heart, held out her gift. 'I thought I'd be a nice surprise.'

'And you are!' Bernie leapt up, manhandled her into a chair, kissed her, petted her like a kitten.

'Yo, Em.' Dan took in her ragged jeans. 'See you dressed up, as usual.'

Emma half-smiled. 'See you came in costume as a dick-head, as usual.'

It was papered over. Happy families can do that.

'Where's Odin?' Emma, who did indeed love a sausage, was on her fourth.

'In heaven,' choked Marie. Odin had fallen asleep on his cushion for the last time earlier that week. Their grief was tidy; the cat was sixteen. 'He's irreplaceable.'

'Especially his smell,' agreed Dan.

'Let me cut your hair,' said Marie, impetuously, to her daughter.

'Nope.' Emma was adamant. Hair by Marie churned out identikit perms and sets; she had outgrown her mother's skills.

Marie nursed deep misgivings about Emma's straightened shoulder-length hair, clipped tightly in place either side of her fringe. 'You look like a serial killer.'

'Gee thanks, and it's still no.' Emma caught Dan's eye; Marie's mission to drag Emma out of the nineties and back to the seventies was a favourite topic between them. 'Hey, music mogul, how's SJ?'

'She's annoying, clingy and shouty, but thanks for asking.'

SJ was the only constant in the whirligig of women. The couple were on-again, off-again; the family had the impression that SJ would make their relationship permanent if Dan would only play romantic ball.

'Why does she bother with you?' mused Emma, feet up on the table. 'Why does any girl bother with you? You're like a bee going from flower to flower.'

'I suppose they like the way I buzz.' It was infuriatingly hard to irritate Dan, whereas Emma would go up like a rocket. She did it now, when Dan said, 'How about you? Still dazzling the Oxford men with your witty feminist repartee?'

'Jesus, Dan, you say feminist like it's an insult.'

Dan put his hands up in surrender. 'Relax, relax.'

'*Relax?*' shrieked Emma.

'Don't start, you two,' warned Marie.

A heroine emerged to save the barbecue from descending

into the sibling quarrel they all knew so well. 'Did I tell you about me latest fella?' asked Bernie, and, without waiting for a reply, told them about her most recent Lonely Hearts Column date. 'He *counted* his chips when the meal arrived. Then wrote down how many in a special notebook.'

'Talking of serial killers . . .' murmured Dan.

'Don't see him again.' Marie had sleepless nights when Bernie was 'off gallivanting' with the men she found in the back of the *Guardian* newspaper. 'One of these weirdos'll chop you up into little pieces, Bern. Remember that one who said he was forty years old and six foot?'

'He was sixty years old and four foot,' laughed Bernie. She waved away Mac's offer of supermarket trifle for dessert. 'I've gone low-fat,' she declared, then changed her mind and grabbed the little plastic pot. 'I never fancy the ones who fancy me.' She ate in a peculiar way these days, to accommodate those enhanced lips. 'The ones I like don't call.'

'More fool them,' said Mac. Secretly, he felt that if he saw Bernie waiting for him at a candlelit bistro table he'd jump through the nearest window, but he longed, all the same, for his sister-in-law to find the love she craved. *And deserves,* he thought, aware of Bernie's big heart that needed no silicone implant.

'Me last one, the baldy bloke, you know, with his own pest-control business?' began Bernie.

'Sexy,' murmured Dan, taking the last trifle.

Bernie swatted him. 'Third time we met, he brought me a present. Lovely pendant. *Diamond.*'

'A diamond on the third date?' Marie was amazed. 'I'm twenty-five years wed and still waiting for a diamond.'

'I believe I gave you two.' Mac pointed at Dan and Emma with his spoon.

'Aw,' said Emma.

'Urgh,' said Dan.

'I was *delighted*, as you can imagine.' Bernie re-enacted her own extreme delight. 'And then I see it in the jeweller's window. Knocked down to a third of the price.' She lifted one eyebrow before the killer blow. 'And not a diamond at all. Believe me, all the good men are taken.'

Marie winked at Mac.

Dan had a solution. 'Next Door's available.'

'Don't say his name,' warned Emma. 'It makes him materialize, like a demon in a horror movie.'

Loss had not softened Next Door; it simply meant his curtains grew more and more dirty. Mac had invited him to the barbecue, certain of a refusal but wishing to extend an olive branch. Next Door just laughed, and said, 'I told you so,' about the ivy that had turned the back of the house green with its leathery leaves.

'So, this cruise:' Bernie lifted her chin. 'Any chance of you two actually setting foot on board before one of you drops dead of old age?' She fixed her sister with a beady eye. 'When are you going to let me give you the money and just *go*?'

'Twelfth of never,' said Marie. 'We're getting there, aren't we, boyo?'

He couldn't lie in front of his offspring, so Mac busied himself with wiping a spatula. The kitchen renovations and the revamp of the salon – now red and black and chrome, like a Duran Duran record cover – had dealt the cruise jar yet another body blow.

'Are we still talking Venice?' asked Dan. 'I went there for a music biz shindig.'

Emma tutted.

'This time next year we'll be there,' said Marie, Venetian stars in her brilliantly blue eyes. 'The bridges, the gondolas, the seafood, the mist rolling in from the sea.'

'It stinks, you know,' said Dan.

Emma didn't want to go and see Dan's new flat, but she was jollied into it by Bernie, who bundled her into the passenger seat of her Alfa Romeo. With a toot of the horn, they set off, tailing Dan in his equally show-off motor.

Mac's car wouldn't start. He knew how to cajole it, but as he was horse-whispering the engine, Marie got out and approached another car, parked down the street.

'Well I never …' said Mac, as George unfolded himself from the driver's side.

There was back-slapping and hand-pumping. 'What brings you here?' asked Mac.

'I have a pal in the area.' Perhaps George saw Marie's expression. 'Who am I trying to kid? Bernie. It's Bernie who brings me here.'

'She'd flip her lid,' said Marie. She seemed torn. 'It's not the way to go about things, George. I know you're hurting but no woman wants to be followed.'

'That makes it sound creepy,' said George. He was greying. Some of his swagger had melted in the three years since Bernie. 'I worry about her. All these guys, Marie. They can't care the way I do. You know how I feel about her.'

'I do, I do.' There were occasional phone calls, long ones, when Marie listened patiently to his anguish. 'She hasn't found anyone. There's still hope for you, George.'

Mac wasn't so sure. Accustomed to giving hard advice to his troubled clients, he said, 'Best thing to do is to try and build something of your own, George. Make a life and then, who knows, you and Bernie might get together again, but if you don't, you still have something solid of your own.'

Like much of the advice Mac gave, it went down badly.

'You're saying give up on the love of my life?'

Mac stayed schtum. The words of his bosses rang in his ears: *You're a probation officer, not a therapist.*

'You won't tell her I was here?' George was pained. 'I hate to make liars of you, but . . .'

'We won't.' As ever, Marie answered for Mac. 'You look after yourself, George.' She was thoughtful all the way to west London. 'That man's falling apart,' she said, as they braked by a row of stately white houses. 'Bernie broke his heart. And for what? Dinner dates with losers.'

'Have you clocked the name of this street?'

Marie gasped. 'Jaysus, boyo. You used to wait for me on this very corner.'

The coincidence went farther. Not only was it the street Marie lived on back in 1970, but Dan now lived on the top floor of her old rooming house.

'Changed a bit,' whistled Mac, taking in the wedding-cake facade of white stucco and gleaming black front door. Their son's address was one of the chicest in a chic post code.

'That window used to have a sign.' Marie was solemn. 'No Blacks. No Irish.'

'You used to cover up your accent.' Mac remembered, and it stung.

Out on the sliver of roof the estate agent had referred to as a terrace, Mac found himself tete-a-tete with Bernie.

'Isn't it swish?' She was impressed with her little movie star's progress. 'Dan the man's done it again.'

It was all a bit monochrome for Mac's taste. He appreciated, though, the signal it sent. Dan was a success in his chosen field; no doubt his salary outstripped Mac's. 'The boy gets what he wants.'

Bernie looked out over the W11 chimney pots. Her eyeliner was smudged.

'How are you, Bern?' Mac added, 'Really,' before she could gush. 'Because you look tired, love.'

There was a moment when she seemed to decide whether or not to blow a gasket at such honesty. She decided against it. 'I'm *knackered*, Mac. I'm on a diet and I'm getting fatter. I'm looking for love and I kiss a frog a week. I'm almost fifty and I feel a hundred.'

'You've always got us, you know. No need to turn over every stone looking for a boyfriend.'

'Easy for you to say. You've been married since they invented the wheel. You have someone in your life who puts you first. I don't and I need that, Mac.' Bernie was not generally so frank. 'I *need* it.'

'Yes, sorry, I can see that.' Mac had been fearful when she announced her divorce. *What if it's contagious?* It was exhausting just watching the treadmill Bernie found herself on. 'You must be sick of us all telling you to slow down the search for a bloke.'

'You don't know what it's like. It's a jungle out there, Mac. Men have such high expectations of women, yet they turn up looking like they've slept in a hedge. I just want someone to cherish me.' Bernie looked up at him from under false eyelashes that reminded Mac of tarantulas. 'The way you cherish my sister.'

'She cherishes me back.' That felt important to say. He asked, ready to duck, 'Is there no way back for George and you? I'm sure he'd be open to a reconciliation.'

She looked hard, as if considering something. 'He used to beat me,' she said.

'He what?' Mac was sure he'd misheard.

With a furtive glance indoors at the others taking a guided tour of the three-roomed flat, Bernie said, 'Never where it showed. Sometimes he raised his hand – or his foot – because I didn't cook shepherd's pie and he was in a shepherd's pie mood. Sometimes it was because I didn't pay him enough attention. He never liked me visiting Sunnyside on my own – did you not notice? That man knocked me to the floor once a week, whatever the weather. Sometimes you and Marie'd be in the next room. And every time it happened I skipped off to a shopping centre and dragged home some consolation prize. But I could never bear to wear any of the clothes or the jewellery. They were all soaked in blood.'

'Bern ...' Mac's body revolted against the revelation, so clearly true, so clearly painful. 'You should've come to me.'

'I was trapped, Mac. I had to get myself out. I had to rescue *myself*. And I did. So *please* don't ever suggest I get back with George as if I just wantonly ruined some kind of perfect marriage. Okay?'

'Of course.' He felt impotent. He felt angry. A pacifist, Mac had sudden visions of drop-kicking George over the balcony.

Bernie's face twisted. 'Don't tell Marie. She'll just get upset and George ... he's not all bad.'

Mac gawped. 'He's a monster.'

'No, no, I have my moments, too.'

'No.' Mac shook his head. 'Absolutely not. The blame is his. The shame is his. A man who's "not all bad" doesn't hit his wife.'

'At least he's stopped stalking me,' said Bernie. 'That restraining order did the trick.'

She told him, then. Told him everything, and he shielded her from the others as she wept.

184

CHAPTER TEN

For a change, they are in the garden.

It's a pretty space. They circle the sundial with ponderous steps. He has her arm in his, and feels her lean on him. He likes that. Beneath his other arm is the album.

There are snippets of news. He talks of a day trip to York – 'Very historic,' he tells her – and of his newfound love of green peppers, after a lifetime of strict avoidance. It's far from engrossing, and she asks no questions.

She never does. Perhaps questions would expose her ignorance of his life, her vast attics full of forgotten facts. It is gothically horrible that he has never told her of the recent death in their family. A person who meant a lot to them both is no more, wiped away like a cat swatting a chess piece. She will never know; she will never care.

'Let's sit.'

They find a bench next to a rosemary bush.

'Our lovely folk are galloping through the 1990s,' she says. 'The girlie's the image of the father. Well, hardly a girl, a young woman by now.'

Sometimes having a foot in two timestreams confuses him, but she slips easily between them.

'The fellow must be her boyfriend,' he says. 'Good, solid-looking individual.'

'Who's this other glamorous creature? The son's girlfriend, no doubt. She seems upset.'

'Something about the son,' he says, 'tells me there's always an upset lady within a few hundred metres of him.'

29 July 1997

They had congratulated Dan on his sudden promotion, heard all about his new LA office, wondered at the vastness of his salary, but still Mac and Marie couldn't grasp what it was their son actually *did* at his record label desk.

'R&A,' they would muse. Then, one of them would say, 'Hang on, it's *A&R*.'

Whatever it was, Dan was strutting like a peacock about his move to the States, champing at the bit to get away from London.

From us? wondered Mac, who felt he should have a speech prepared, some sort of paternal advisory mono-logue, for the boy who confounded him. So much spirit and magnetism. And kindness too, but well hidden beneath the arrogance. Mac longed to beckon out that soft side of Dan, but it was heavily armoured with silk-lined suits and a cock-of-the-walk bravado. *Besides, the 'boy' is twenty-six years old*; the person he was least likely to listen to was his tortoise of a dad.

There were times – so many times – when Mac would have welcomed a fatherly pat on the back, or even a fatherly reprimand. He had yearned, since he first studied the faces in his parents' wedding photograph, to know what they thought of him. He knew, instinctively, that Ed would have been a shining example, a mentor in how to father. But that was not to be, for Ed or Mac.

He shook off such sepia gloominess, to smile into the lens of Dan's high-tech new camera.

Beside him, Marie, her red hair choppy with a straggly fringe that Mac tried and failed to like, revelled in having all her ducklings around her, and the sorrow of waving one of them off across the Atlantic. 'Look at my babies, all grown up!'

'*Mum.*' Emma, who had finally introduced her boyfriend to the Mactavishes, said, 'Ollie will think we're crazy.'

'Nah, you sound just like my mum, Mrs Mac.' Ollie Jones had won Marie's heart the moment he arrived, handing over chocolates and a bottle of something, and taking a heavy minimart bag out of her hands. He was gallant, but within the strict parameters acceptable to independent-minded Emma. He was handsome too, always a plus for Marie, who longed to get her hairdresser's hands on his short dreadlocks.

'Sorry, only my barber's allowed near. Afro hair's different to your hair.'

'I'll learn!' Marie had given up on Emma; she would never be permitted to chop her daughter's long hair into a Rachel, and had to stand helplessly by as it grew and grew and *grew*.

The cab was late. Dan checked his enormous watch – it was, thought Mac, like a town hall clock – and cursed, as SJ tailed him, pawing at him, begging for affection like a cat.

A voluptuous Renaissance creature reimagined in black Lycra, SJ had a high-voltage, carefully curated sex appeal. 'You promised!' She addressed, as ever, Dan's retreating back. 'You said we'd go for dinner before you left.'

'I forg—' Dan thought better of that excuse, grabbed her, kissed her. 'I'll make it up to you.'

She turned to his parents then, who jumped. 'See? This is what I get from him, from all sodding men! I love them, I do everything for them, and they don't love me back.'

'Dan ...' tutted Marie. She and Mac often shook their heads over SJ's great neediness, knowing it would never be met by their son.

Emma was curt. 'Why do everything for them, SJ? They don't appreciate it. They just walk all over you.'

'Hey,' said Mac, defending his gender. 'Some of us appreciate it.'

'Do you appreciate it enough to fill the dishwasher once in a while?' asked Emma.

'We don't have a dishwasher,' said Mac, hoping Emma wouldn't interrogate him about the last time he washed a cup. He made a vow to himself not to leave his mug in the sink next time, but to rinse it under the tap and dry it. A vow he would break within the hour.

'Where's that damn cab?' Dan had ants in his pants, itching to get away from England, from SJ, who stuck to him like a shadow.

SJ appealed to Mac and Marie, who jumped again when she said, 'He should stay here, shouldn't he? He should put down roots, start a family. He'd make a great dad, wouldn't he?'

'Well . . .' said Mac, who couldn't agree.

No matter. SJ moved on, gabbling to Dan, 'I have a friend in LA. She'll tell me what you get up to. I know what you're like.'

'If you know what he's like,' said Emma, 'why don't you dump him?'

'I love him,' said SJ. 'And he loves me. He just doesn't know it yet.'

Marie nodded approvingly. 'Sometimes, they need to be told,' she said, as if men were some dim form of life found in the backs of cupboards.

'Rubbish,' said Emma stoutly.

'There's no need to tell me I love you,' said Ollie.

They all felt it. The change in the air. They all guessed that Emma and Ollie had not yet used that word to each other.

Emma stared at Ollie. He stared back.

Mac felt he should look away but he couldn't. *Her face . . .* He loved Emma too, of course, and more than ever when she softened like that.

'Get a room, you two,' said Dan.

They'd all heard the origin story of Emma and Ollie. How, celebrating her internship in an architectural conservancy agency, Emma met Ollie in a W1 pub.

They talked in a corner of the bar. Emma drank too much; odd for such a self-possessed woman; she would never admit how nervous the handsome stranger made her feel. He saw her back to her friend's place, held her hair while she vomited into her handbag, deposited her on the sofa and left. When she emerged from her coma, she didn't remember the tall, wide young guy. She didn't remember his name, nor that he was a painter and decorator, a son of Jamaican immigrants, three years older than her. She vaguely recalled someone being calm, funny, with a low centre of gravity who spoke slowly and concentrated on her when she talked.

A ring on the doorbell had forced Emma from the sofa. Miffed to find nobody at the door, she looked down and saw a new handbag, very similar to the one she'd desecrated the night before. It contained a note asking her out to dinner.

Now, as Emma and Ollie gazed at each other, as something important was born, Dan broke the spell by yelling, 'Cab's here!'

He left.

SJ accepted Marie's hug as well as the offer of 'a nice roast lunch' sometime soon. It had been noticed that, on the rare occasions Dan brought her over to Sunnyside, SJ was always reluctant to leave. She clearly craved something she found in the little house, something warm, something reliable.

When Emma left, Mac and Marie were quiet. Los Angeles was a long way away. Their susceptible son, so impressed by sparkle, must navigate its highways and byways without them.

'Tell you something,' said Mac, leaving his mug in the sink. 'If I had a lovely-looking girl like that SJ mad about me, I wouldn't stand her up.'

Marie threw a *People's Friend* at him. Overarm.

'That hurt!'

'It was meant to, Casanova.'

Leaving Sunnyside to its own devices, they made for the sea.

August was bowing out with skies so blue they seemed fake. Southwold welcomed the three of them – Mac, Marie and Tatty – with open, old-fashioned arms. The weekend was her treat, a sign that she was financially on her feet again post-That Bastard Quentin.

'This town's a very Tatty-ish place,' said Marie, unpacking in their hotel room. 'A pier, beach huts. All very proper.'

Finding it impossible not to be charmed by Southwold's wholesome *joie de vivre*, the trio took sedate strolls along the promenade and sampled the local ice cream, cold on their parched tongues.

The town was indeed Tatty-ish, but it embodied all her best characteristics – the classic British Tatty, not the tight-lipped, food-rationing Tatty.

After a fish-and-chip dinner – 'My cod was more of a whale!' Marie reminisced – Mac and Marie were alone in their room. That nice half-hour before bed, when Marie rubbed cream into her face and pushed at her hair in the mirror, and Mac folded clothes and enjoyed the feel of his toes in his slippers, as the radio burbled in the background.

'S'pose', said Mac, investigating the in-room safe and wondering if it was ever used, 'this is the only getaway we'll have this year.'

It was unspoken but nonetheless true that Hair by Marie was faltering. She regularly sat up late at the kitchen table with a calculator, jotting down and crossing out, covering her sums if Mac came near.

She gives her all, he would think, setting down a mug of tea at her elbow. Just the way she liked it. Strong, three sugars. Some days his wife was a blur, racing from house to salon. *All those discounts* ... Any business manager would advise Marie to harden her heart but she saw her cosy premises as a neighbourhood hub, a place where good things happened, where her creaky customers felt accepted, and she permed away their troubles.

The cruise jar was raided. Rebuilt. Attacked again.

'We could go to LA,' said Mac.

Dan had offered to send tickets. Marie's reply of, 'Don't go wasting your money on us' was exactly what Nora said if they offered to help her out. Mac didn't point out Marie's growing similarity to her mother; he didn't want his nose broken a second time.

'Hmm,' said Marie, which meant 'No'.

Photographs of Dan were stuck to the wall in Hair by Marie. He beamed out of the images, leaning on gleaming cars, framed by palm trees and kaleidoscopic sunsets.

Nobody, thought Mac, *could be as happy as Dan looks*. Manic, open-mouthed. 'Look at me!' the photographs said.

Marie turned, stricken, from the dressing-table mirror. She was white beneath her freckles. 'I just had the most awful feeling.' She looked terrified. 'Something's coming, Mac. Something bad.'

He was immune by now to her Irish superstition. 'Don't be daft, love. The Adrians are fine. Your mum's hale and hearty. Both the kids are okay.' He turned back the covers on the big hotel bed. 'Hop in, love.'

She didn't. 'Something's coming, I can feel it inside. Something bad is coming for someone I care about.'

Saturday brought cold beer and cream tea and the purchase of postcards. Southwold baked merrily in the last of the summer, seagulls celebrating noisily along the front.

All the while, a dark imp sat on Marie's shoulder. *She can't shake off last night*, thought Mac, unwilling to admit she had spooked him. When Tatty suggested a walk – 'Just the two of us' – after dinner, he was loath to leave his wife in the guests' lounge.

'Go, go,' she laughed, shooing him away.

A lighthouse striped the dark sea. It was chilly, now that the day was done. Mac walked on the sea side of the road.

Tatty said, 'I haven't been well, Ian.'

Marie was right. The thought sprang, fully formed.

Tatty went on. 'I found a lump.'

They all lived in fear of lumps. Mac went hot, and kept his eyes on her lined face, familiar and remote. 'And?'

'I had it checked out. It's benign.'

'Thank God.' *Marie was wrong!*

'It made me think. If anything were to happen to me, Ian, you'd never know the truth. That wouldn't be fair.'

Now that the moment had finally come, Mac wanted to run. Just take off, sprint into the water with his fingers in his ears. He did none of that. He simply listened as Tatty unwrapped the missing jigsaw piece, her voice just audible above the susurration of the waves.

'The bomb, that hateful bomb, the one that killed your mother . . .' Tatty swallowed. 'It didn't kill your father.'

'What?' It was all he could muster. '*What?*' he repeated.

'Ed wasn't with her that morning.'

'You said . . .'

'I know. I killed him off to avoid telling people the sordid truth. Ed Vole came into Marguerite's life after he was wounded in France. Shrapnel, to the leg. Privately, I felt he exaggerated the limp, but I never said so.'

A penny dropped. A large penny, one Mac should have noticed long ago. 'His surname was Vole? Not Mactavish?'

'Ian, *my* name's Mactavish. Marguerite was my sister. How could it be your father's name too?'

'I didn't think . . .' *I'm a fool*, thought Mac. There had been so little paperwork, all of it allegedly lost in the chaos of war-time moves. In a flash Mac realized he had always known of the discrepancy, but had suppressed it. His stomach moved. The truth was coming for him at a hundred miles an hour. *I need Marie's hand to hold.* 'Go on,' he said.

'The wedding photo *is* a wedding photo, but it's not Marguerite and Ed's wedding. That was taken the day they met. She was bridesmaid, and he was best man. One of those hurried, wartime ceremonies. I never actually told you it was their wedding photo, Ian. You just joined the dots as a child, and, well, I never corrected you. Ed was Canadian, invalided out of the army, and at a loose end in London. Marguerite felt sorry for him. She was just like you, a heart as soft as butter. Soon, she was singing her way through the day, madly in love. And he was too. They laughed a lot. They danced, him with his bad leg, her leading.'

The night thickened around them, as if leaning in to hear.

'Then, well, Marguerite found herself in the family way.' Tatty blinked, uncomfortable. 'She told Ed. He seemed very pleased. Shocked, of course, but pleased all the same.'

'They weren't married yet?'

'No. I remember how relieved Marguerite was when Ed said he'd stand by her. She'd heard of girls being abandoned by their beaux. Wartime … things get sloppy, Ian. People come and go. The morning after she told him she went off to meet him at their usual spot. Speakers' Corner, by Hyde Park.'

'Don't tell me he didn't turn up.'

'I'm afraid he didn't. Not that day. Nor the next. She kept going to Hyde Park, though, day in, day out. She said it helped.'

The fabled early morning walks, so central to Mac's personal mythology, was no rosy-cheeked family time; they were his melancholy mother's attempt to walk off rejection. *He left her because of me*, thought Mac. *Ed Vole didn't want me.*

'It was a difficult pregnancy. Not helped by the rumours that Ed had gone back to Canada. You came along, and that changed things. There's no time to moon about with a baby in the house.'

Moon about? thought Mac. *I hope that's not how you described it to my mother, Tatty.* With a rush of empathy, he imagined how Marguerite felt, sharing two rooms with her buttoned-up sister, a woman who knew nothing of love. 'Did Ed break her heart?'

The question seemed to puzzle Tatty. 'She was certainly very upset.'

This, Mac realized, had been Tatty's strategy all along. *Only answer direct questions.* He had filled in the background details of his life story, and now he felt them melt, slip away like the black tide out in the bay. 'She loved me,' he stammered. 'Didn't she?'

Emphatic in her quiet way, Tatty said, 'Ian, you were the crowning glory of Marguerite's young life.'

Even though I was illegitimate. That mattered back in the

forties. Mac imagined the stigma. He saw his conservative Tatty through new eyes. *You bore it, too.*

She was exhausted. They turned back.

In the hotel's guest lounge, a sleepy, low-lit place where the clientele retired to digest their four courses plus cheese, Marie had lined up three Irish coffees.

As Marie and Tatty planned the next morning's schedule, cream moustaches on their top lips, an idle thought stopped Mac in his tracks.

My father might still be alive.

He wanted to jump out of his wing chair and bolt to the hotel's 'business centre'. Actually just a cubby hole with a phone and a PC, it was perfect for his needs. An internet search for Edward Vole might answer his question.

If I want it answered.

'Anything from Bernie?' asked Marie, gesturing at his phone squatting among the potpourri.

'Not yet, love.' Mac had been reluctant to have a cell phone, until it became necessary for his work. Now he wondered how he'd ever got by without one. Tonight, like every other Saturday, they spent the evening on stand-by for a text from Bernie.

An early adopter of mobile phones – Marie prophesied they would never catch on – Bernie would appraise her blind dates, then text either 'Good!' or 'Stinker!' to Mac's mobile. Occasionally she'd tap out 'RESCUE ME' and Mac would call her with some trumped-up emergency that required her immediate presence.

Come on, Bern, he thought. The sooner Bernie texted the sooner Mac could usher the ladies to bed, freeing him up to set sail on the world wide web.

'She has high hopes for this bloke.' Marie was dwarfed by her leather chair. 'A pilot, apparently.'

'So he says. You can claim to be anything online. Bernie claims she's in her late forties.'

'So she is. *Very* late forties. So late they're her fifties.' Marie's laugh died in her throat; she remembered her premonition. 'What if he's a maniac? What if he throttles her outside Pizza Express?'

'Bernie knows the rules, love. She told us where she's going. Relax. Maybe this pilot is The One.' Mac was picking up Bernie's lingo, talking like a magazine article. 'Although there've been a few The Ones.'

'Bernie's so full-on. Dresses differently for each chap. Remember all the power suits and the fake glasses when she met the architect?'

'Took him a couple of weeks to suss out she didn't actually like going to art galleries, and preferred Coronation Street to French cinema.'

'And then we went through the flimsy dresses phase when she fell for that younger guy. He let her pay for *everything*.'

'So?' Mac was wry. 'What happened to girl power?'

'Even the Spice Girls let a man pay for the first few dates,' said Marie. She worshipped the mouthy quintet, and quoted them often, as if they were philosophers. 'Ooh!' she said, as a text landed.

'Looks like the pilot's a wash-out.' Mac held up the phone. RESCUE ME, it begged. He stood and went into the lobby to liberate Bernie with a sorry tale of a flooded kitchen.

It was after midnight when Mac and Marie escorted Tatty to her room. She had been unusually talkative.

Relieved probably, thought Mac, hoping tipsy Marie would fall like an oak when they got to their turret.

But no. 'Shame to waste this big bed,' she said, embarking on an impromptu strip tease. She toppled over while tugging seductively at her control tights and he caught her and one thing led to another and it was 1am before she began to snore those gentle little mouse snorts Mac loved so much.

Down in the business centre, as the building shifted around him in its sleep, Mac found the answers he needed with just a few keystrokes of the computer.

A picture flashed up.

My father.

Alive and well, and staring back at Mac with Mac's own eyes.

A desultory search revealed that Ed was already married when war broke out. *Did my mother know?* Mac suspected she had no idea. He grappled with this bitter titbit.

Feet on the stair. Marie in her nightie by the business centre, a white flash like a ghost. 'Her car crashed! I told you! Oh God, Mac, what if she dies?'

The receptionist came out from behind her desk, her face wet with tears.

'Bernie?' Mac was astonished by the receptionist's high emotion. 'But, but I spoke to her and—'

'*Diana!*' Marie and the receptionist hugged each other. 'A crash, in Paris, with him, that Dodi fella. It's serious, Mac, she might die.'

They drove home in silence.

'Those poor boys of hers,' said Marie. 'What'll they do without Diana?'

Tatty kept her counsel. She couldn't condone such out-pourings for a stranger.

Carrying her bags to her door, Mac told her he'd found Ed Vole.

'Will you get in touch?' Tatty seemed nervous. She searched his eyes; eyes that must have reminded her of Ed Vole over the years.

'You're all the parent I need,' said Mac.

She was awkward, then, and looked away, but as he turned to go back to the car, she said, 'You're a good boy, Ian.'

Sunnyside welcomed them back with quiet acceptance. If their mood didn't match the weather, the house didn't notice.

Mac could not sit still. Up and down the stairs, in and out of the shed, he bent his thoughts towards his father. Ed Vole.

I'm a Vole, not a Mactavish.

He couldn't see Marie okaying a name change, not to Vole. It didn't feel as if it was his name to take; Ed had never even seen baby Ian. The insult to Marguerite that was implicit in Ed's choices was too painful to grasp all at once. Mac picked at edges of the picture, all of it ugly.

He might have looked as if he were simply watering the garden, but Mac was spinning in space. The central story of his life was rewritten. *I used to think my childhood was dreary,* he thought. *It feels positively cosy compared to the truth.* Mac hadn't been denied a childhood with doting parents; he'd been disowned by a brutally indifferent man.

One email could reunite them. *Although you can't reunite two people who have never met.* Mac went to and fro, backwards and forwards. He wanted to confront Ed; he wanted to hug him; he wanted, above all else, to ask why. *You fool, you just want Ed to love you,* he told himself, and over-watered the japonica.

Mac had his father's eyes: *What if I have other attributes of his?* Never confident of his parenting skills, Mac now knew he was the son of a callous man. There had been fifty-two years for Ed to get in touch, but no, nothing. *He's no puffin! My father's a ruby-throated hummingbird.*

From the house came the sharp crash of a dropped cup. He heard Marie curse.

The two sounds together made up his mind. He was needed here, in Sunnyside. He would comfort his wife in her shock about her lost princess and call his son in America and invite his daughter and her solid young man over for dinner.

A door slammed on Edward Vole. Mac's place was with

his family. The love was all in that one circle. He knew who he really was.

I am not my father.

Bernie arrived. 'God rest her soul,' she said solemnly, and waited a respectful twenty minutes before telling them all about her date with the pilot. 'He smelled of mothballs and divorce.'

Half-listening, Marie made a tour of the sitting room, righting a cushion here and a terrible ornament there. She paused at the shelves. 'Where's the . . .' She stopped short; it was up to Mac if he wanted to take down his parents' photograph.

A shout came from outside, one of those high, yelping, male shouts that brings everyone to their window in the hopes of witnessing a brawl.

'Jaysus, that's my Mac,' said Marie, her nose against the glass. She strained but couldn't hear what he was shouting.

'Take that back!' Mac ran at George like a bull at a toreador, stopping just short of him, his fists balled. 'You do *not* refer to Bernie like that in my hearing!'

'Calm down, mate. This isn't like you.' George backed away, bemused.

'I asked you politely to leave,' said Mac, following George around his car. 'You know you shouldn't be here. Get in your stupid, overpriced sports model and leave her alone.'

George raised his voice, glanced over at Sunnyside. 'The old slapper's at the window. Ask her when she'll see sense and realize nobody wants her except me.'

Mac charged.

They fought.

Neither knew how to do it. Soft punches missed. There was a great deal of grunting and eventually, just as Marie came running out to separate them, Mac pulled George's safari jacket over his head.

CHAPTER ELEVEN

He tries not to show how tired he is, how out of sorts. Some days the journey takes an age; today is one of those days.

She's not fooled. 'What's the matter?' she asks, more than once. She puts a hand on his forehead. 'Are you unwell?'

'Me? I'm never ill,' he says.

'I'm serious.' She dislikes being fobbed off; after all these years he should know that.

The biscuits help. And the anomaly with the photo album. 'This is the first photograph that wasn't taken on their anniversary,' he points out. 'It's New Year's Eve 1999.'

'Millennium Eve!'

'We thought the planes would drop out of the sky, and all the computers would crash.'

'They've put fairy lights everywhere, and a big bow on the magnolia tree.'

'I reckon,' he says, 'they're throwing a party.'

'And they're still kissing,' she says. She seems entranced.

'After all these years.'

31 December 1999

A stolen moment in the chaos.

'Come on.' Mac pulled Marie through the crowd so she tottered behind him in her heels. He needed a blast of cold air. The only one not boozing at his own party, his ears rang with the insistent thump of dance music.

'Oops sorry!' They bumped into a dark shape in the front garden.

Emma disengaged herself from Ollie's arms. 'Look!' She waved her left hand in Mac's face. 'We're getting married! He proposed! Mum!' She disintegrated into wordless squealing and Marie did the same.

'Congratulations, son.' Mac pumped Ollie's hand, both of them trying not to show the other man the tears in their eyes. 'Look after her, won't you?'

'Oh, Dad, you dinosaur, we'll look after each other.' Emma looked small next to her Ollie. 'I wish Auntie B was here.' Bernie could be relied upon to over-react to all family news. 'How's her date going? Have you had the text yet?'

'Nope.' Marie expected a RESCUE ME any moment. 'This man's her worst nightmare. Older than her. White hair. Bit fat, so she says.'

'Why'd she agree?'

'Well, she felt as if she had to. He arranged his millennium around her after a handful of emails.'

'At least he didn't lie about himself,' said Ollie. 'That's a big tick.'

Snuggled into Mac's side, Marie said, 'Bernie should be here with us on Millennium Eve. Not out with some stranger.'

'Everyone's a stranger at first,' said Mac. 'I was a stranger when we met.'

'Nah, boyo. You were always mine.' She leaned up to kiss him and they both jumped at the flash as Ollie took their photograph.

Later, with midnight drawing near, and the party revving up to the big countdown, Mac said, ever so casually, 'Surprised a chap like Ollie didn't ask me for Emma's hand. Formally, like.'

'You're disappointed!' Marie was tickled. 'Don't deny it, your nostrils are flaring and we know what that means. Youngsters don't do that anymore, Mac.' She was coquettish. 'You haven't mentioned my millennium dress. Do you like it?'

'It's gorgeous, love.' It looked like tin foil scrunched up by a toddler, but Mac had long ago given up on fashion.

'Those nostrils are flaring *again*.' Marie was piqued. 'Your problem, Ian Mactavish, is you have no style.' She stalked away, hips swinging, and Mac was almost tempted not to tell her that her dress was tucked into her knickers.

*

'Great party!' said the man from number twenty-three.

'Thanks, Happy New Year,' said Mac, knowing his guest had been seen snogging the woman from the end house; the new millennium would start with a bang when number twenty-three's wife found out.

He struggled through the scrum of revellers, nodding and smiling and wondering if *he* looked that daft after a few beers. *Very probably*, he decided. He looked for Marie; he liked to know where she was, like sailors with the North Star.

The revelation about his parents' relationship had hit Mac hard, but as the clouds cleared, there had been an epiphany. The truth was icy, like the first slap of winter weather, but it was bracing too.

The truth meant little, in the end. He would always – *always* – resent the affront to his mother. He would always wish she had lived long enough for him to make things up to Marguerite, to make her proud, to *love* her.

As for Ed, though, Mac felt liberated. He no longer mourned a perfect man; instead he made the choice to ignore a deeply flawed one. *I could call him, now, this minute, but I don't need to.* He saw Marie's back, busy at the sink in her finery, and he threw his arms around her.

She tutted, batted him away, and Mac felt the euphoria of knowing exactly how she would react. The joy of truly knowing another human being.

'Ow! What the hell was that!' came a cry from the hallway.

Toulouse had claimed another victim. The Siamese cat

sat beneath the half-moon hall table, slashing at legs as they went past. Acquired at great expense a year before, Toulouse looked right through people with his blue, blue eyes. Haughty in his coffee and cream furs, he carried himself like a young prince, and spat and hissed at anyone who was not one of his courtiers.

He adored Tatty, and he found her now, weaving his way through the throng, to where she sat nursing a sherry.

'Hello, your majesty,' she said, and patted her lap.

Mac found Tatty's eye, checked in with her. He had promised to drive her home after midnight – hence the No Booze rule – and he would wait on her step while she checked the windows and dark corners of her small flat. It was a spartan, clean space; the smell of cleaning products brought him back to his childhood. She was happy there; as happy as Tatty could ever admit to being.

Another thumping began, below the disco bass of Marie's playlist.

Next Door, thought Mac, *communicating via the shared wall, as usual.* They had invited him – 'Bugger off!' he'd said – and brought him a glass of champagne – 'Muck!' he'd said. *He drank it though,* thought Mac.

'Ten!' shouted someone. 'Nine!' everyone else joined in.

'Eight!' Marie grabbed Mac as she shot past, and dragged him into the street, tripping on the crazy paving. 'Seven!'

Bonhomie reigned. The road was rammed with people, sparkling-eyed, arms about one another, jumping and jiving to some inner music. 'Six!'

Marie frowned at her phone. 'Nothing from Bern,' she said. 'That's not right, Mac.'

'Five!' yelled Mac. 'Text her, love.'

'Four!'

'URgeNT ru ok@?' typed Marie.

'Three!'

Emma was on Ollie's shoulders.

'Two!'

Toulouse yawned on Tatty's lap.

'One!'

Fireworks shattered the sky. Car horns blared. 'Auld Lang Syne' broke out up by the minimart. London exulted and Mac got into his car.

All the way to Mayfair, Marie speculated.

'She'll be trussed up in the boot of a car by now. Or dissolving in a bath of acid. These psychopaths prefer spectacular crimes. Bernie could be known as the Millennium Murder.'

'Or she might be on her fourth negroni,' said Mac. 'And too pissed to text.'

'There! That's the restaurant!' Marie jumped out while the car was still slowing down.

'So he's your psycho.' Helpfully, the homicidal maniac had booked a table by the window. He was, as advertised, white-haired and overweight. 'Look, love.' Mac pointed.

Bernie's hand lay over her date's on the tablecloth.

'Let's rescue her,' said Marie.

'Look at her face.' Mac yanked his wife back to his side by

a handy frill on her Bacofoil dress. 'Bernie's *glowing*. Either that old bloke has drugged her, or your sister is *happy*.'

They crept away.

Marie rattled the salon door the way she always did after locking up for the day. She leaned against it, her forehead against the glass, and its gold lettering: *Hair by Marie*.

'I did me best,' she whispered.

'You did, love. You did.' Privately, Mac wished Marie had given in a couple of years ago. She was worn to a thread, and the spiralling salon had leeched them dry. The offer from a giant sports chain to buy the lease could not be ignored, but it rankled with them both that the beloved little shop would be used for storage.

'Trouble is,' said Emma, as they trailed away over the cobbles, 'all your customers are dying off, Mum.'

Mac sent a message with his eyes. *Not the right moment for this rant, Em.* His daughter's belief that her parents were embracing middle age – late middle age? – a little too enthusiastically was one that depressed Mac and Marie. *So what if we favour an early dinner and an* Antiques Roadshow? 'It was rising rent and business rates that killed off your mum's salon.'

Marie paused at the corner for one last look, then lifted her sharp little chin and led her daughter to the wedding dress boutique at the other end of the high street.

That's my girl, thought Mac.

*

Bernie awaited them in The Frockery. She had picked out a few designs, all of them instantly dismissed by Emma with a comment of, 'I'm the *bride*, Auntie B, not the cake.'

Seated on brocade chairs with a glass of dreadful prosecco, the sisters *ooh*ed and *aah*ed at Emma as she stood on a dais in a procession of white/off-white/oyster creations. They disagreed on each one. They were having the time of their lives.

'Ma would've loved how Emma's doing everything the old-fashioned way. Marrying young, planning babies.' Bernie crossed herself. 'God rest her soul.'

Nora Neeson had died quietly, with minimum fuss. It was expected, even wished for; she deteriorated badly in her last months. None of that detracted from the heavy, metallic tang of loss for her children.

Each of them handled it differently. Mac, always curious about siblings, assumed Bernie and Marie would dilute their grief by sharing it, but it didn't work out that way. Their anguish was bespoke, personal. He respected it, and let it work its way through his wife.

Emma stomped up to the dais, Doc Martens peeking out beneath a frothy hem. 'Dan's making noises about not coming to the wedding,' she said, as she bent her head for the shopkeeper to pin a veil to her hair. 'Says he can't get time off.'

'He'll be there,' said Bernie. She still saw the best in her nephew. 'Nothing would stop my Dazzer Mac attending your big day.'

'Except his problem with Ollie,' said Emma, shoulders

drooping as she took in her reflection in a baroque mirror. 'Christ, I look like a bag of expensive washing.'

'What problem with Ollie?' Bernie looked to Marie as Emma lifted the dress knee high and stalked back to the changing room.

'Emma reckons Dan's a bit, well, *jealous*. Because Ollie's so sensible and sorted and grown up.' Marie squirmed at accusing her son of such immaturity, but Dan's devil-may-care pursuit of a good time made him seem that way.

'Nonsense.' In Bernie's universe a Los Angeles-based record executive could *not* be envious of a Balham-based house painter. 'My Dan'll be at the church.'

'Is Angus your plus one?' Marie was arch, looking the other way as if the very important question barely mattered.

'Maybe.' Bernie had amazed herself, on that millennium date, by saying to the old fart across the table that they should do this again sometime.

He had said, 'How about tomorrow?'

Bernie and Angus saw each other a couple of times a week. He would motor up from Henley in his gleaming old Bentley, or she would catch the train down to visit him in the flat above his bookshop that smelled of cigars and good meals.

'Well?' Emma put her hands on her hips. She was corseted in lace.

'That's the one,' said Marie and Bernie together, bursting into tears.

*

Toulouse kept swatting the keyboard and directing them to random websites.

A new cruise was in the planning stages; as usual, they had scaled up their plans.

'Just humour me,' said Mac, holding Toulouse to his chest with one hand as the other clicked on the mouse. 'Look. Lundy Island. It's National Trust, very prestigious.'

'And full of puffins.'

'Well, yes, there are puffins, but the accommodation is old and beautiful. I guarantee Bernie will never have been there; you'll have bragging rights, for once.'

She looked closer at the screen. 'The electricity goes off at night! And there's *one pub*. Are you mad, boyo? It's Venice or bust.'

The new double glazing had set them back, but now Sunnyside was draught-free and they were snug as two bugs in a rug as they roamed the internet, daydreaming in the golden hour before *Antiques Roadshow*.

'Is this carbs?' Bernie looked down at her plate. She had discovered the Atkins diet, but could never quite work out what a carbohydrate actually *was*.

'No,' lied Marie. 'Shut up and eat it, it's costing us twenty pound a head.'

The wedding meal was as strictly conventional as the white lace dress and the groom's buttonhole. Emma had gone Old Skool for her big day.

Apart from the Jamaican touches. Marie had been thrilled

to discover that both parents were expected to accompany the bride down the aisle. She opted for the curried goat instead of the roast beef, and had developed a taste for rum.

Mac wished he'd gone for the goat; the beef was tough. He sat back, feeling faintly preposterous in the embroidered waistcoat Emma had prescribed for him, but also feeling perfectly *right*. He loved his new in-laws; he felt at home with them. And every other person in the banqueting hall seemed to be a Neeson, bringing with them their patented brand of good cheer that threatened to raise the roof once the band got going.

If only Dan was here. Nobody quite believed the pressures of work he blamed for the no-show. The extravagant present couldn't mitigate Emma's disappointment. 'Typical,' she'd snapped; Mac saw through the mask of irritation and glimpsed the hurt.

He's opting out of the family, he thought, watching Ollie's two brothers, jackets off, ties undone, sit either side of the groom and tease him.

'Is *this* Atkinsy?' Bernie held up her champagne, still reeling from her discovery that white bread was the big baddie of the carb world; Mac knew she would trade every last one of them for a slice of jammy toast.

'Why do you diet, darling?' Angus, her Plus One after all, was on his second helping of goat.

Marie sat up abruptly, signalling to him with swivelling eyes not to go any further. But Angus was a newcomer to Marie's signals and didn't understand. He went on.

'I like a curvy woman,' he said.

They awaited the throwing down of cutlery. The tearful march to the loo. Bernie could not abide being called 'curvy' or 'shapely' or even 'normal'. She longed to be thin. If anybody advised her not to diet, they should damn well follow it up by saying she had no need to.

'Oh dear,' muttered Mac.

But Bernie's cutlery remained in her grasp. She was smiling. 'Oh *you*,' she said, flirtatiously, bumping shoulders with Angus.

Marie kicked Mac under the table. He kicked her back. *This relationship*, those little kicks suggested, *is different*.

The DJ stopped taking requests from Bernie after *Oops I Did It Again,* never imagining that she knew the entire dance routine.

Out of breath, in the ladies' loo, Bernie leaned on the basin until she could speak. 'I love that Britney,' she said, eventually.

Reglossing her lips, Marie said to the mirror, 'You love that Angus, you mean.'

Bernie blushed.

'Jaysus, you *do*!' squawked Marie. She had been fishing; she didn't expect to be right. 'Hang onto him, Bern. He's a dote.' To a Dublin woman of Marie's age there could be no finer compliment.

'He proposed.' Bernie hoisted her cleavage.

'Congratu— oh.' Marie grimaced. 'You said no. Is it the age difference?'

'I *love* the age difference. It does what plastic surgery does, but it does it for free: I'll always be his younger woman. No, it's because he'd get bored of me in ten minutes.'

Marie looked closely at this woman, who was surely an impostor. Lack of confidence was not one of Bernie's issues. 'He's cracked about you, you eejit.'

'For now. But Angus leads such a full life. He goes to concerts on the South Bank. He's in a choir. He *cycles*.'

'Angus isn't giving into age.' Marie approved. 'I'd rather live like him than ...' She hesitated. 'Well, like Ma, in her last years.' Nora had greeted old age with open arms, with slippers, medicines piled up by the bed, TV in the afternoon. 'Angus is interested in everything, but especially you.'

'It's not like it was with George.'

'Men like George don't come along every day.' Marie was unaware of her double meaning. 'I hope he finds somebody; he deserves it.'

'George never *talked* to me like Angus does.' Bernie stumbled, choosing her words carefully. Perhaps she was aware of how Marie stopped, lip-gloss in mid-air, to properly listen. 'George talked *at* me. I'm not used to being listened to.'

Marie seemed confused. 'But George was lovely, I mean, until things went wrong between you.' She stopped. Shook her head. 'Never mind the past, Bern. If this man makes you happy, keep it simple and marry the poor sod.'

They laughed. Ollie's mother came in and all three of them screamed that scream of delight women do in the loos at weddings.

'Shall we tell her, sweetheart?' Ollie's mother asked Marie.

Marie nodded, and together they whispered – very loudly – 'Emma's expecting!'

He felt ridiculous.

'Ask a man of Angus's age about his intentions?' Mac had put his foot down. 'I will *not*.' Marie had trodden on the foot he put down, and here he was, pulling up outside the quaintest shop he'd ever seen outside of a Richard Curtis movie.

Mullioned windows in a two-hundred-year-old facade offered a patchwork glimpse of piles and piles of books.

'This is a surprise!' Angus walked Mac through his crumbling realm. 'Looks a mess, I know, but I can put my hand on any title you ask for.'

A kettle balanced on an atlas. Two cats fought beneath a stool that supported Trollope and Dickens and Zadie Smith.

'D'you have a birds section?'

Angus waved a hand. Picked out a cloth-bound book and handed it to Mac. *'Life Histories of North American Wood Warblers* by Arthur Cleveland Bent. Some nice illustrations. Rare. It's yours.'

'I couldn't,' said Mac, trying not to drool.

'Please. It's my gift to you, for welcoming me into your family.'

'About that . . .' Mac was uncomfortable. 'I've been sent to discover your intentions.'

'My what? Do men have those these days?'

They sat outside in the sun, on two wobbling wooden

chairs, and Mac asked about Angus's divorce. 'What happened, if you don't mind me asking?'

'I don't mind at all, dear chap. It was a very long time ago. There was no philandering or bestiality involved, if that's what worrying Marie. We just sort of stopped noticing each other, I suppose.'

Good answer, thought Mac. 'And those intentions? I need an answer, or Marie'll turn me round and send me back.'

'That's simple. I intend to love Bernie forever, with all of my heart.'

This was more than good enough for Mac, but later, over dinner, Marie bemoaned the lack of detail.

'Typical man,' she said.

CHAPTER TWELVE

Something called Swimmersize is going on in the new pool.
The smell of chlorine leaks into the rec room, along with
snatches of chart music.

'You didn't fancy Swimmersize, then?' He's wry.
Swimmersize was her nemesis's idea; she would rather eat
her own feet.

'Not really.' She is correct, her language careful. 'Did you
come far?'

'Same as usual.' He pauses, mid-sugaring and milking.
'Hey, it's me. Me.' He repeats it yet again, and it sounds
nonsensical. 'It's me!'

'Ah, yes, of course. You.'

It is a mistake to expose her like that. She shrinks inside
her handknit. They are pretending now, both of them – she
has no idea who is taking tea with her.

The album lies, ignored, by her chair.

Minutes tick by. She won't respond to him; it's as if he's badgering a stranger at a bus stop. He takes the album onto his lap and opens it at the latest photograph.

She taps her fingers on the arm of the chair, looking around, hopeful for rescue.

'Another anniversary,' he says to himself. 'Thirty-three years.' He lets out a low whistle. 'Quite an achievement.' He side-eyes her when he says, 'What a delightful baby.'

There is a twitch of interest, but she still refuses to look his way. 'Wonder how old it is?' he says. 'Looks about one.'

'Rubbish.' She can't resist correcting him. 'That child's at least two.' She is captivated. That change of mood again, the rapid about-face. 'Such chubby arms! Must be their grandchild.'

Just like that, she is back.

29 July 2003

Abbo sat placidly on his Gramps's knee. He reached for the laptop screen; at two, he didn't know what a wellness blog was, but he enjoyed the colours and shapes.

Mac caught the little hand and kissed the dimpled fingers. Between the cat and his grandson, it was tricky to concentrate. Both creatures seemed envious of the attention he gave to the computer; one tried to leave sticky fingerprints on it, and the other mewed at it.

'Gerroff, Toulouse.' The blog had a self-assured tone,

complacently dispensing instructions on life. The modern habit of making heavy weather of, well, just *living* perplexed Mac. Sunnyside had survived the decades without being cleansed with burning sage; he'd never witnessed Marie in a downward dog; the life-affirming quotes in a curly font just affirmed that Mac hated life-affirming quotes.

The young – and at fifty-eight Mac had burned his passport to that generation – seemed certain that other people were desperate to hear all about how they went about their days.

'Even my daughter,' he said aloud to the cat and the tot. 'Judging by the comments on Emma's latest post, she's right.' They all agreed with Emma's assertion that 'fast food is as much a threat to society as Class A drugs'. She no longer loved a sausage.

Abbo griped, but smiled when Mac said, 'No no, what's all this?' The child never wanted to cry; he wanted to be happy. Mac's adoration of Abbo was pure and clean and overwhelming, like standing beneath a waterfall.

Having sole charge of the little fellow had sounded daunting. 'You sure?' he asked Emma, when she swanned off to a health farm with her mother and her aunts. As he waved them off, Marie had realized too late that it was their wedding anniversary. 'I forgot! You forgot as well, boyo.'

'Silly us,' said Mac, who had remembered, and would ambush her with a card and roses the moment she returned. A hasty photograph – *We can't break with tradition!* – had been taken.

'Lunchtime, Abisai.' Toulouse jumped, yowling, to the carpet as Mac rose, the boy on his hip. He relished his grandson's full name, a Jamaican favourite according to Ollie. 'But first, there's someone I want you to meet.'

Out in the front garden, little Abbo Jones grabbed a magnolia bloom, and it fell apart in his grasp.

'It's like a hotel,' Marie told Mac, when she called to let him know she'd arrived safely; all car journeys longer than ten metres were potentially disastrous to Marie. 'A hotel where they take you into small rooms and do bizarre things to you.'

She wasn't sure how she felt about her mud wrap. She'd been wrapped in mud; that was it. The benefits, rattled off in a bored voice by the therapist, weren't yet apparent. She was neither more youthful nor thinner, but she did have mud in her eyebrow.

She joined the others on rattan loungers overlooking manicured grounds. 'Ooh,' she said, when Emma handed her a glass of champagne. It felt indecent to drink fizz while wearing nothing but a bulky towelling dressing gown, but Marie was keen to get with the programme, and if that's what they did in these places, so be it.

Emma and Bernie, aficionados of spa culture, looked perfectly at home; the same could not be said of Bridget.

The three-day Wellbeing Odyssey was conceived as a treat for 'poor Bridget', the sibling who martyred herself to look after Nora and now lived alone in the family home.

Poor Bridget didn't bother to conceal her horror as

Bernie and Emma discussed the electro-facials in the brochure. Bossy Emma underlined something called 'Full Body Ritual' and told – told! – Bridget she would book one on her behalf. Bridget held the champagne away from her as if it might burst into flames; she had never tasted the stuff before. She would later confess to Marie she preferred Tizer.

Covered up her whole life, the God-fearing spinster had never worn a swimsuit, never mind offered up her naked body to a stranger's touch. She was a handful of twigs in her robe, her grey curls cut short and her cold, Celtic face pale, except for those blazing blue Neeson eyes. They widened now, as a man padded past en route to the pool, in nothing but swimshorts and flip-flops.

Marie and Bernie exchanged a look, both of them positive that was the nearest Bridget had ever been to bare male legs in her life. Bernie, in particular, was rudely fascinated by her churchy sister's virginity, hypothesizing that Bridget's 'down there' smelled of incense.

They listened to a long tale of hers, about the 'new father' at St Thomas's, the church around the corner that loomed large in Neeson childhoods. The smells. The shadows. The droning sermons. And, for Marie at least, the brilliant colours of the stained glass when the sun hit. The feeling of belonging. The warmth of her father's hand holding hers.

'The new priest's very *groovy*, as they say. He wears an anorak and plays the guitar.'

'He's practically Mick Jagger,' said Bernie.

Bridget didn't laugh. 'Marie, Mac tells me you've booked a cruise.'

'That's right. To Venice!' Lundy Island had never been a serious contender. 'We're shelling out for a snazzy cabin, and I'm going on every single shore excursion they can throw at me.'

Bernie was wry. 'She could be on board right now if she'd take Dan up on his offer. You know how generous he is, Bridget.' They ignored the scornful noise Emma made in her throat. 'He goes, *What's wrong with a little instant gratification, Mum?* but she won't let him pay for it.'

'He looked a bit strained under his tan.' Dan's visit had been too brief for Marie's liking, cut short in typical Dan-style by a work emergency. 'I hope he's eating properly.'

Another noise from Emma; difficult to spell, probably something like *fttth!*

Bernie said, 'Only you could worry about a young gun living the dream in a Los Angeles penthouse.' She stretched out her legs, newly fake-tanned and smooth as Abbo's bottom. 'I could get used to this, eh, Bridget?'

Bridget sniffed.

'Let's come back here,' said Emma, 'before the wedding.'

'Ooh, who's getting married?' Bernie sat up.

'You are, Auntie B, if you'd only make an honest man of Angus.'

Bridget sank a little. She knew Bernie was 'living in sin' with Angus, but the family didn't discuss it in front of her. A shame, really, as she never heard about the jolly life Bernie and Angus had built in the cosy flat, with long meals and lazy Sundays in bed and the match of a good cook with an appreciative eater. Angus especially enjoyed Bernie's soda bread, made to Nora's recipe, right down to the slashed 'x' across the top of the loaf 'to let the fairies out'.

A big hit with the family, Angus was already one of them. There was no need for a marriage licence, except for the fact that he yearned to marry his 'girl', as he called her.

Bernie sat back and seemed to turn something over in her mind. 'I know you all want me to tie the knot, but . . . since George . . .' She looked to Marie, her eyes huge, as if asking to borrow some courage.

'Go on, Bern. Since George what, love?'

'You can talk to us, Auntie B,' said Emma, even though Bridget was pretending to be engrossed in the yoga class timetable.

George's death had shocked them all. Nobody knew how ill he was; there were no goodbyes.

Death sanctified him in Marie's eyes; ignorant of George's abusive alter ego, she could not forgive Mac for that pathetic fist fight. 'Hitting *George* of all people!' she'd yelped. 'Him with his poor broken heart, just trying to get a glimpse of Bernie.'

Bernie inched along, word by word, finding her way. 'George and I, we didn't, we weren't, it wasn't as . . .'

Wincing at the pain on Bernie's face, Marie reached out and put her hand over Bernie's. 'We get it, love. Deep down you still love him, and it's too soon to remarry. We understand.'

It wasn't often that Bernie fell completely silent.

Bridget said, 'Angus might stop proposing, and then you'll be sorry.'

Bernie found her voice. It was waspish. 'Says you, with your huge knowledge of romance.'

Emma raised her eyebrows at the cruelty, and Marie let out a small tut, but Bridget was not insulted. At least, not in the way they imagined; the sarcasm whizzed over her head; she took Bernie literally. 'Pardon *me*,' she said, all acid. 'What are you insinuating? I have stayed well away from men and their lusts. The minute I turned down Tony Cassidy, that was the end of all that love nonsense for me.'

Bernie dropped her glass. 'Tony Cassidy? *The* Tony Cassidy?'

'Tony Cassidy who everybody fancied?' Marie remembered him well. Tall, mischievous, the focus of every local girl's fantasies. She doodled his name on her maths book. Bernie believed the sight of him in his football gear was her one truly religious experience.

'I told him: no, Tony, no,' said Bridget. 'I can't marry you. I knew what he expected from me.' She pursed her lips. '*Bed*, and all that.'

During her massage in a curtained cubicle that smelled of lavender oil, Marie, who would have crawled over hot coals for 'bed and all that' with Tony Cassidy, pondered how the darkest of dark horses can be stabled in your own family.

*

Abbo was most attentive to his Gramps's guided tour of important local landmarks, twisting in his pushchair to gaze upon the minimart.

'That's where your Uncle Dan shoplifted a penny chew, and I warned him he'd become one of my clients at the probation service one day. And that's the park where Uncle Dan tied your mummy to a tree with her own skipping rope. Look over there, that used to be our local swimming baths, where I taught them both to swim.'

'Where cat?' asked Abbo. He had grown fond of Toulouse, who ignored him.

'At home. We'll see him soon.' Mac turned the pushchair, with one last look back at the hoarding that had sprung up around the baths. The advertising for the new luxury apartments was seductive, but Mac could think only of the sticking plasters that used to float past in the shallow end.

'See there, by that car, Abbo?' They turned into Sunnyside's street. 'That's where your Grammy told me I was a ruffian and a disgrace because I biffed a man called George on the nose.'

'Biff!' yelled Abbo.

'Biff!' yelled Mac.

He had pleaded, more than once, with Bernie, 'Just tell Marie! Tell her about the A&E visits after the family get-togethers, about the despair you smothered by buying clothes that didn't even fit.'

Bernie refused. She didn't want to upset her sister; Mac intuited that Marie's sympathy would break Bernie.

*

'All girls together!' said Bernie, as the women assembled in Emma's room to prepare for their last supper.

On stylist duty, Marie was straightening Bernie's hair. 'You next, Bridget.'

With clear misgivings, Bridget acquiesced, and her mannish cut was softened with just a touch of the heated appliance.

'Takes years off you,' said Bernie.

'What's the point of that?' Bridget was immune to flattery. 'Sure, isn't me birth certificate available for all to see?'

Emma held her aunt's chin, tenderly, and looked at her. 'Your skin is like a teenager's after those facials.'

Pink, Bridget seemed confused by the compliments.

'Your turn, love.' Marie snapped the straighteners at her daughter.

'I'll do my own.'

'Which translates as I'm too naff for you.'

'Are you still in a huff 'cos I laughed when you bought matching kagoules for you and Dad? Christ, Mum, if Goldenballs Dan had laughed you'd have laughed with him.'

Marie couldn't win this one; Emma's conviction that Dan was the favourite was immovable; there was no way to tell the girl how much it hurt her feelings.

Emma went on; she could rant about Dan the way Marie ranted about Prince Charles (everybody avoided the name 'Camilla' in Sunnyside). 'Bet he didn't tell you SJ finally gave up on him. She just stopped getting in touch. If Dan has such a thing as a heart, I'd say it's broken.'

Bridget stood up. 'Jesus, Mary and Joseph!' she exclaimed. 'I'm late for me Intense Body Ritual.' She raced out of the room.

'We've created a monster,' whispered Bernie.

Their last morning in the spa, and Bridget was squeezing in one more treatment. It involved high-pressure water jets, and to Marie it sounded like the sort of thing Amnesty International protested against.

She found Emma in a corner of the orangery, where the smell of blossom fought with the tang of chlorine. 'You doing your blog, love? Or can I . . . ?' Marie pointed at the empty chair.

'Sit, sit.' Emma closed her laptop. 'I'm just bashing out two hundred words on the eight-glasses-of-water-a-day challenge.'

'Also known as the in-the-loo-every-five-minutes challenge. Fancy a smoothie?' Marie was glad when Emma demurred. She secretly hated smoothies, and how they tasted of the kitchen bin. 'Wonder how our little Abbo's doing.'

'Having a whale of a time, being spoiled rotten by his dad and his Gramps.'

'How'd you find the time to work and raise a child and write that blog, Em?'

'Because I ask for help. Those two afternoons you come over and play with Abbo make all the difference, Mum.'

There was a moment when Marie could have said that she didn't just *play* with Abbo, that she fed him and bathed him and did the laundry and gave the kitchen a good going-over, but the moment passed. Marie was not a petty woman. She said instead, 'It's my pleasure, darlin'. I have plenty of time on me hands since the salon went bust.'

'Don't say it went bust. You worked your heart out, but it wasn't enough. So many businesses failed. Not your fault.'

'Feels like it.'

'Why don't you find a part-time job in a hairdresser's?'

'Couldn't do it after being me own boss. Unless Vidal Sassoon want me back!' joked Marie. She took in Emma's shock. 'You knew I trained at Vidal Sassoon.'

Emma shook her head. That piece of Mactavish lore had passed her by. 'You? Vidal Sassoon?'

The naked disbelief made Marie bridle. 'Yes, me, your antiquated old mother. If I'd had my own mum nearby to help with the childcare I might still be there. Looking after children is just as – sometimes *more* – demanding than going to work, but it's unpaid and unnoticed. That's why I can't let you go the same way, Em, why I help out.' Marie waved a hand at the laptop. 'Although you're so organized and energetic, you'd find some way to juggle it if I wasn't here. I wish I could say I see myself in you, love, but no, it's all *you*. I'm so proud of you.'

'Mum, are you nuts? I'm *all* you. I watched you work all through my childhood, and still churn out three meals a day and kiss my knee when I fell over and tease Dad out of his anxiety and chase after Dan and walk the dog and and *and*.' Emma leaned closer. 'Mum, you do know you had PND after Dan was born, don't you?'

'Pee enn what?'

'Post-natal depression.'

'How'd you know about that?' Like most parents, Marie underestimated what her children knew about her. 'It was just the baby blues.'

'I don't know the full story but to call it the baby blues is an insult.' Emma saw Marie's head droop. 'I understand if you don't want to talk about it, but it sounds like a classic case. Guilty feelings, low mood, tearful all the time, unable to cope. I mean, come on: Marie Mactavish, unable to cope? You were ill, Mum, and if it happened now you'd receive therapy and medication and support, not some condescending claptrap from your doctor. You had to manage on your own.'

'Not entirely. Your dad was with me every step of the way.' Marie felt a sudden fierce homesickness for Sunnyside. 'So, other mummies get this post-natal thingummybob?'

'Many, *many* women suffer with post-natal depression.' Emma was vehement. 'And it's me who's proud of *you*, Mum, for surviving, and thriving.'

'Girl power, eh?' Marie knew the Spice Girls reference would irk her daughter.

'Yeah, whatever, Mumsy. Girl power.'

She's been back less than an hour and already found me a job to do.

Mac was tasked with clearing out Emma's old cubbyhole of a room. It was his den these days; his wife called it a man-cave.

'Those drawers are full of crap,' called Marie from where she was turning the mattress in their room across the landing.

'I have a system.' Mac was haughty. 'I know where everything is.' This was a lie; he had sleepless nights about where his passport might be. It was, he knew, in a safe place. *Safe even from me.* 'Bridget enjoyed herself, then?' he called.

'She's a new woman. Bought a box of essential oils to take home.' Marie stood in the doorway, her fringe standing on end with the effort of the sudden spring clean. 'Typical Bridget, she was all set to get on the plane without so much as a hug. I thought to meself, *If those masseurs can touch her then so can I.* I grabbed her and so did Bernie and Emma, and she *let us.*'

Mac opened a drawer. Another priceless Mactavish archive: greetings cards from the kids.

'She said she might come for Christmas.'

'Oh. Lovely.'

'I hear the fear in your voice, boyo. Don't worry; she won't be able to tear herself away from St. Thomas's.'

One stack of cards was tied up with ribbon. Father's Day cards. The bottom ones were handmade, falling apart now, and shedding sequins. They grew more professional and more tasteful towards the top of the stack. Mac traced the embossed lettering on the most recent one.

Happy Father's Day to the Best Dad in the World.

Apparently, that's me! he thought, happily.

Each Father's Day, Emma made a huge fuss of Mac. Marie would shed a tear for dear Pat. Dan would pretend he hadn't forgotten and cobble something together.

But I've never written a Father's Day card.

As a child he'd found the day difficult. No father to eulogize, he would, even as a man, find himself envying those lucky people with both their parents intact. He would imagine how they'd still be together, him and Ed, if that bomb had fallen a hundred yards or so farther down Park Lane.

Six years ago another bomb had fallen, when Tatty detonated the truth, and these days Mac felt nothing on Father's Day. Nothing at all.

Mac shut the drawer, knowing that wasn't quite true. One of the challenges he set his young clients was a remorseless inventory of their souls; he did one now, and admitted he felt resentment where he used to feel a poignant sense of loss. Even the dark happiness of imagining the what–ifs was denied to him since Tatty revealed all.

It was a second betrayal. First, Ed Vole had abandoned Marguerite, and then he trashed their son's idealized image of him by emerging from Tatty's story as his real, cruel self.

I'm not like him. So prone to self-doubt, Mac held Ed at bay. *But is he coming out in Dan?*

Marie plugged in the vacuum cleaner and shouted over the din. 'Did you pay the deposit on the cruise?'

'What? Oh, you bet, love.'

Mac knew wartime made its own rules. His parents had turned each other's heads, fallen for each other while the world burned. *But only one of them was free to fall.*

In an effort to absolve his father, Mac imagined how it

must feel to encounter an amazing woman when you are already spoken for. He imagined meeting Marie – that five-foot-nothing force of nature currently hoovering the curtains – while married to someone else.

He knew what he'd do in Ed's place. *I'd stick to my vows.*

His wife shouted again. 'Nothing'll get between us and this cruise, Mac. Nothing. Is that a vow?'

'It's a vow,' said Mac. 'We sail on our anniversary.'

CHAPTER THIRTEEN

'Another kiddie!' she exclaims. 'A little girl. Very serious. About five or six, I'd say. How come we haven't seen her before?'

'Our couple look shell-shocked.'

'Can't be theirs, can she? Wonder what's going on? Wish we could ask them questions.'

'I've a question for you.' He sees her bristle, brace herself. She has always hated being interrogated, and she loathes it even more now that her brain is disobedient. 'Don't panic. It's an easy question. Are you happy here?'

'What makes you ask that?'

'Nothing.' It keeps him awake at night; he needs an answer. 'Well? Are you? You'd tell me, wouldn't you?'

'Why wouldn't I be happy? You and your questions.'

She makes it clear that's all he's getting.

He gives in.

29 July 2004

Houses are sticky.

Even though the Mactavishes were Venice-bound, gagging for sun on their faces and the ship's gourmet buffet, they found a dozen last-minute tasks.

'Come on, *come on*,' nagged Marie. 'Get Toulouse into his carrier. Is the back door locked?'

A shouted 'Hello?' from the open front door brought them to the hall.

They recognized the woman. They didn't recognize the large-eyed little girl leaning against her legs.

'SJ!' Courtesy and impatience battled in Marie's tone. 'Lovely to see you, but this is a bad time. Who's this pretty little lady?'

'She's your granddaughter. Say hello, Lottie.'

Lottie said a tiny 'Hello', and with that one word, Sunnyside turned upside down, to land with a jolt back on its feet, everything in the same place but all of it subtly changed.

The luggage glared balefully from the bottom of the stairs, and the kitchen table, scene of so many powwows, braced itself for a biggie.

Flint-faced, Marie folded her arms and sat opposite SJ, who was spidery in black leggings and oversized brilliant white trainers.

Opposite Lottie, Mac smiled at the child, whose expression didn't change. She studied him, as if memorizing him for a police photofit.

Checking her watch at ten-second intervals, SJ told them her story. 'I was pregnant when Dan left for the States in '97. Neither of us knew.'

'Hmm,' said Marie. It was a catch-all word, one her children feared.

'He more or less dumped me when he got there, like I knew he would. I called and called, but I gave up, because, well . . .' She shrugged. 'So, when I found out Lottie was on the way, I decided not to tell him.'

'Hmm,' said Marie, again.

'I know that was wrong, but the rejection of me *and* Lottie would've hurt too much. I couldn't trust Dan to do the right thing.'

That makes two of us, thought Mac. 'Should I take Lottie out to the garden?' This was adult stuff for such small ears.

'She knows everything. No fairy stories for my little girl,' said SJ. 'Eventually I *had* to tell Dan, when Lottie was about two. I couldn't make ends meet. A music career and a baby don't exactly mix.'

Marie's third 'Hmm' was softer. 'Must be hard, bringing up a child alone.'

'My folks help out but they don't approve so that's, yeah . . .' SJ didn't elaborate.

'Has Lottie met her dad?' asked Mac.

SJ shook her head.

There had been opportunity; Dan made regular if erratic trips to London. *A chip off the old Vole block,* thought Mac.

The clock on the wall, reliably ten minutes slow, told them they should get a move on if they wanted to make their plane. All the same, Mac said, 'Tell us about Lottie,' and smiled at the quiet, biddable girl holding a beaker of squash with both hands. She wore dungarees, and what Mac would call bovver boots. She leaned against SJ, whose arm lay across her like the wing of a mother hen.

'Tell your grandparents how old you are, cupcake,' said SJ.

'Six.' Her voice was small.

'Lottie's not like me or Dan. She's a reader, a thinker. A proper little lady. It's always been just me and her, but now it's time Dan did more than send a cheque now and then.'

So he sends money; that's something. Mac checked the clock. It had nothing good to tell him. 'What can we do, SJ? Why are you here?'

Pushing Lottie's dark hair from her forehead, SJ said, 'Like I say, it's just me and her.' She swallowed hard. 'But now I have to do this. For myself, sure, but really it's for both of us. Opportunities like this don't come round often.'

'Have to do what?' Mac hoped against hope that the South Circular wouldn't delay them on their way to Gatwick.

'Take this job. You know I'm a singer?'

They politely pretended.

'And you know Yazz Toon? Huge R'n'B artist.'

Again, the pretending.

'I'm on backing vocals for his European tour. It's epic. Three months. Twenty-two countries. Chance of a lifetime. At last, after all these years of scraping by, it feels like things are moving.'

'Congratulations,' said Mac. To Lottie, he said, 'Don't you have a clever mummy?'

Lottie nodded. Burped. Blushed.

'Being a mum holds you back. Don't get me wrong, Lottie's the best thing that ever happened to me, but I've had to turn down so many offers, and I don't want to get older and say *what if*.'

Marie nodded. 'Nothing worse than regrets,' she said.

Mac gave her a wondering look. Then he looked at the clock, and wanted to swear. He didn't: little ears, and all that.

'So I signed the contract, and Lottie was all set to stay with my mate, but now she's got a new boyfriend and he's anti-kids, and my folks moved to Spain, and so I decided: time for Lottie to stay with Daddy for a while.'

Lottie's eyes grew larger and her mouth disappeared altogether.

'It's not ideal,' said SJ. 'All very last minute, but hey, that's our life, isn't it, cupcake? I know Dan came back to live here, but – typical Dan – I don't have an address. I thought maybe Lottie could wait here for him to collect her?'

As if sharing the one thought with her husband, Marie stood and held her hand out to the child. 'Want to come into the sitting room and meet our naughty cat?' Lottie must not be subjected to the bad news they were about to dish out. 'Is Lottie allowed a biscuit?' Marie had been trained by Emma not to offer sugary treats willy-nilly.

'Yeah, whatever,' said SJ.

Mac spoke low. 'Dan's not here, SJ. They offered him a better position in Los Angeles and he stayed put.'

'No, he can't be, my flight . . .'

And our flight!

SJ fought high, hot emotion. 'I have to do this. Not just for me but for Lottie. For our security. Because men aren't the answer. I really thought my last boyfriend would be her daddy, but that fell apart. Like everything falls apart.'

'I wish Dan had stepped up.' Mac wasn't doing his thoughts justice; he came up against the poverty of language every day in his job.

'It's only three months. Couldn't you . . .' SJ put her hands together in supplication.

He explained. About the cruise. About the cruise's history. About how they only had minutes to spare.

'Understood.' SJ sat back. Exhaled. 'I'll let you get away. Bad timing.'

'And you?'

'I'll have to let them down.' SJ wiped her face roughly with the back of her hand. 'I'll keep going, though. Keep hoping. I've got good at that.'

Lottie had made friends with Toulouse, a minor miracle given the cat's infamous irascibility. Marie brought cat and girl back to the table and held up one hand.

'I don't want any arguments from youse. I've cancelled the taxi. Three months isn't long.' She reached for Mac's hand. 'She's our flesh and blood, SJ. You've done this alone for long enough. You run off and sing your heart out, love. You chase your dream.'

Once again my little sorceress has read my mind, thought Mac, fit to burst with every shade of feeling.

The leave-taking was necessarily rushed. SJ was a bottle of champagne about to pop, kissing and hugging and picking up and putting down Lottie as she bustled down the crazy paving path.

'Slow down!' Marie caught her by the elbow. 'Tell me about Lottie – what she likes to eat, what time she goes to bed, everything!'

'She eats anything; she's the most easy-going kid ever. Lottie's used to making do, fitting in. We've been on a mattress in a squat before now. No particular bedtime; she falls asleep wherever she is, even under the coat pile at parties.'

Only at the gate did SJ pause. She squatted and took Lottie's face in her hands. 'Three months'll fly by, cupcake. I'll call all the time. You be good, you hear?' She looked up at Marie, suddenly desperate. 'I don't want to go.' She began to cry. 'Shit, I don't think I can go.'

'Mummy,' said Lottie. 'Go.'

The spare room had morphed into a junk room, the bed hemmed in by cardboard boxes full of *What, exactly*?

wondered Mac. An exercise bike, its saddle a virgin, idled in a corner.

Bernie, turning up to collect Toulouse and discovering the strange turn of events, took matters in hand. By 7pm the room had been pinkified, with fairy lights swooping across the ceiling and a dolls house at the foot of the bed.

'Consider me', said Bernie to Lottie, 'your fairy god-auntie.'

Lottie said one of her tiny 'Thank you's, but seemed trepidatious of climbing into bed.

'Go on, pet,' said Marie. 'This is your room now.'

'All mine?' Lottie was incredulous.

'All yours,' said Marie. She added, quietly, 'For three months, anyway,' as she stole downstairs with her sister to break out the booze.

Tucking in his brand-new, surprise granddaughter, Mac asked if she'd like a story.

'Mummy sings to me,' she said.

Flippin' heck, thought Mac. *I don't know any songs.*

From the depth of his memory, something surfaced. A lullaby Marie had sung over the kids' cots, that used to drift through the house as their little eyelids closed.

'I can't sing as beautifully as your Mummy,' he warned.

Lottie didn't seem to mind. Her small eyes were shutting before he got to the chorus. *It's been a big day for such a little girl*, thought Mac.

'*Be still,*
And hush.

Be warm,
And slumber.
Who's my baby?'

Lottie touched every moment of every day.

Mac called twice as often from the office to ask, 'How's tricks?' and find out what Lottie was up to. He saw how tired Marie was when they sat down to rampage through a box set in the evenings. Just because she didn't own up to being fifty-six didn't change the truth; she was past the age when anyone expects to be responsible for a small child.

'Stop fussing,' she'd say, when Mac brought it up. 'It's only for three months, and she's a dote, she really is. I'm happy to help out.'

When she was more forthcoming, she admitted how she looked forward to getting her life back when SJ came back from tour. 'But,' she would always, *always* add, 'we'll keep in touch with them both. They need our support, Mac. They're family.'

SJ called every day, and Lottie sprinted to the phone, Toulouse drooping in her arms like an apostrophe. Girl and cat went everywhere together; he slept curled around her in the pink cavern.

'Brought you a chum,' said Mac one night, pre-lullaby, holding up a stuffed puffin. He had noticed the absence of soft toys in Lottie's hold-all. 'What'll you call him?'

'Jeff,' said Lottie, and once again Mac regretted allowing a child to name something.

He sang – if you could call it singing – the lullaby, before tiptoeing out of the room, closing the door on his grand-daughter's gentle, even breathing.

Be calm,
And dream.
Drift,
And wander.
Who's my baby?'

Sunnyside was bathed in a talcum cloud of peace.

A peace broken by the telephone.

'Dan, love!' Marie got there ahead of him. 'You got our message?'

Mac stood over her, and she twisted and turned to ignore his face, a face that plainly told her not to let Dan off with a rap on the knuckles this time.

'Lottie's *adorable*,' Marie was saying. 'Of course we can cope.' She ignored Mac's truculent exhalation. 'But when can you come to see her? Oh. Right. Yes, well . . . Hey!'

Mac had snatched the phone. 'Why didn't you tell us about her?' he asked without preamble.

'Dad, look, it's complicated.' Dan spoke as if he had only one foot in the conversation. Mac imagined him leafing through a magazine or, more likely, texting somebody. 'I didn't want to worry you.'

'Didn't want the roasting, more like.' Mac saw his wife scowl. 'You need to come good, Dan. This is a little life you're playing with. Not to mention the extra stress you've simply dumped on your mother and me. We should be on a cruise liner right now, not clearing up your mess.'

'Hey,' said Marie. 'Go easy.'

He couldn't go easy. Ed Vole and Dan were fusing in Mac's mind; *Blood will out*, he thought, returning the receiver to Marie, unable to listen to Dan's mealy-mouthed excuses as to why he couldn't come and see his own daughter.

Two months passed.

Sunnyside smelled of bubble bath. Marie imposed her own brand of mothering. Togetherness. Structure. Discipline. Good food. Cuddles. And Princess Diana.

Abbo was overwhelmed with love for his new cousin and toddled after her; Lottie returned the compliment and couldn't hide her pride when she was allowed to 'help' with the boy.

'She's so good,' beamed Marie, as she and Emma watched Lottie drag Abbo around the garden in an old cardboard box.

'She's *too* good.' Emma took another non-gluten, organic, multigrain cookie. Her wellness blog had gained traction; her fans demanded recipes and Marie was often the taste tester. 'Too quiet.'

'Some kids are naturally quiet!' Marie was on the defensive; it was on the tip of her tongue to say the biscuits tasted like insoles. Later, when Emma left Abbo with her, she would introduce him to Viennetta, a foodstuff both Marie and Mac believed to hold the meaning of life.

'Lottie never goes against us, Mum. Never says no. Like she's scared to upset us.'

'You speak like Lottie doesn't know she's loved.'

'No, *no.*' Emma seemed troubled by another of those chasms that could open up suddenly between her mother and herself. 'Lottie's always felt duty-bound to be quiet, to be no trouble for SJ. Sounds as if they slept on other people's floors and might be asked to leave at any moment, or that's how it seemed to Lot-Lot.' The family sometimes borrowed Abbo's mangling of Lottie's name. 'I love to see a girl stomp her feet and make demands now and then.' She nudged her mother. 'Like you and me.'

'Yeah, we're stompers, all right.' Marie was easy to win round.

October was bright, sharp.

Marie put away her summer clothes. Deferring the cruise for another year gave her time to lose that stone, the one she'd been losing since Emma was born.

Presents arrived from all parts of the globe, at random intervals, addressed to Ms Lottie Mactavish. A book, a Yazz Toon tee, a face-paint set.

'Not long now,' said Mac, as he tucked in Lottie, switched on the nightlight, kissed Jeff; each step of their nightly ceremony must be respected. 'Mummy'll be back to collect you soon.'

'Mummy didn't ring today,' said Lottie. 'Or yesterday.'

She hasn't rung for a week. Mac was trying not to worry about that.

'Be still,

And hush.
Be warm,
And slumber.
Who's my baby?

Be calm,
And dream.
Drift,
And wander.
Who's my baby?'

October bled into November.

Like mercury, SJ was impossible to pin down during the brief, increasingly infrequent calls. The Mactavishes were tense, and hiding this tension from the pretty little cuckoo in their nest only made them more so.

That's why that row blew up between Marie and Emma, thought Mac.

Emma had been incandescent; 'Who gave you permission, Mum? Who? *Who?*'

Abbo, wobbling with the drunken body language of all three-year-olds, stood between them, lip quivering.

'It's just a trim!' Marie yelled too. For such a shortie she had tremendous lung power. 'I'm a hairdresser, remember! And do I ask permission to come to your house early and stay late so you can work? I'm not slave labour, Emma, I'm your mother!'

'I know you're my mother!' Emma was screaming

now. 'And I really appreciate everything you do for me!' she shrieked.

They had to laugh.

They hugged. Emma said she loved Abbo's hair but to ask next time. Marie said, 'Why not let me have a go at your fringe?' and Emma told her not to push her luck.

'Girls,' said Mac, forgetting that Emma hated it when he called them that. 'Look.' He held up his phone.

Marie snatched it. 'A text!' she snapped. 'She lets us know by bloody *text!*'

'That's the way these days.' Mac didn't feel like defending SJ, yet he did just that. 'A world tour, how could she say no?'

'Like this.' Marie shouted 'No!' at the top of her lungs. 'See? Easy! Especially when you have a little girl counting down the days until you come and get her.' Marie covered her face. 'How're we going to tell Lottie, Mac? How do we say she won't see her mummy until March?'

'We don't. Not all at once.' Mac felt the weight on his shoulders, of Lottie's expectations, of his wife's exhaustion, of his own exasperation at the cavalier behaviour of SJ and Dan. 'Tell you what though,' he said, determined. 'If Lottie can't see her mummy, she's damn well seeing her daddy.'

For once, the appeal to Dan's conscience worked.

Within a week he was ensconced in a London hotel, and a roast was roasting in Sunnyside's oven, and his favourite Viennetta – mint, since you ask – was in the freezer.

His sister insisted on being present when he met Lottie.

'To support her,' said Emma, fearlessly voicing the lack of confidence they all secretly felt about Dan's ability to live up to such a critical moment. 'That's if he turns up.'

He turned up.

He was taller, somehow; he took up more space. Tanned, be-suited, Dan smelled like a lemon grove.

'A lemon grove full of money,' was how Emma put it when she hugged him, and held on for a second or two more than was necessary.

'And this must be Lottie.' Dan squatted, face to face with his daughter. 'Hello, funnyface.'

Lottie laughed.

'Thought you might like *this*.' Dan produced something glittery from his breast pocket, and Lottie gasped.

'Is that real gold?' Marie was perturbed.

'What else?' Dan fastened the charm bracelet around Lottie's wrist.

'Dan, she's *six*,' said Emma.

'And she's all mine!' Dan hoisted her into the air and kissed her cheek.

'Another female won over by the great Dazzer Mac,' murmured Emma.

'I love you, Daddy,' said Lottie, so quietly nobody heard. Except Mac. He heard.

Later, after the lullaby and a special double tucking-in from both Mac and Dan, the adults talked in an adult tone, about adult matters.

'You're doing brilliantly,' Dan told his parents in their sitting room, which seemed to both shrink and date with him on the sofa. 'Lottie's so *happy*. Bloody SJ, she should've—'

'No,' said Marie, shaking her head. 'Not in this house. We don't criticize Lottie's mummy.'

'Yeah, sorry.' Dan looked even more handsome when contrite. 'But you have to admit she's crazy. I always said so.'

Emma pounced. 'Crazy! That's the word men use when women don't behave the way they want them to. According to you, all your girlfriends are crazy, but the common denominator is *you*. You drive them crazy, Dan.'

'Remember the one who took his central heating control with her when she left?' said Marie, almost fondly. 'She turned it up every night of the heatwave.'

'She was great,' said Dan, nostalgically. 'Listen, you can't hold me responsible for this mess. SJ didn't tell me about Lottie until she was two. She never wanted us to meet. She's been more of a direct debit than a person to me. Sometimes I wonder if—'

Emma interrupted, her voice like ice. 'If you're going to say you're not sure that she's yours, please stop right there.'

'She's the image of you,' said Marie.

'She is, isn't she?' Dan sat back, pleased with himself.

'Typical,' said Emma. 'SJ does all the work, and Lottie ends up looking like *him*.'

'Go on, Dad.' Dan turned to Mac. 'Get it off your chest. I can practically feel your disapproval cutting a hole in the side of my head.'

'We must make plans, son.' Mac wondered if Dan knew how badly he needed to admire him. 'Lottie's here until March. That means she needs to go to school, she needs to be settled.'

Marie grasped the nettle; she was better at it than Mac. 'What your father's trying to say, darlin', is you need to come back to London and take care of your daughter. We'll help.' She and her husband had privately agreed they'd watch him like hawks. 'But Lottie needs you, Dan.'

Mac's fingers were entwined so hard they were white. *Come on, step up*, he begged his son as the silence lengthened.

'There's nothing I'd like better,' began Dan.

'Great!' said Marie.

'But I can't.' Dan was grave, explaining it would mean demolishing the career he'd built. There was no position in London for him. He was in the midst of myriad deals. 'And,' he said, reluctantly, 'I'm overstretched financially. I can't afford to take a sabbatical. You know how it is, Dad.'

Mac, who didn't know, felt sick at his son's transparency. Dan would allow his parents to look after his child; he would live in a different time zone; he would not disrupt his hedonistic schedule.

Emma said, 'Mum and Dad have done their child rearing, this isn't fair. What about their cruise?'

'SJ'll be back in March and by July I'll be sipping margaritas on board!' Marie, as ever, recovered with miraculous speed.

Mac, who took longer, who wondered why Dan put such

energy into doing the wrong thing, said, 'Lottie has to go to school. It's the law.'

'Vine Road Primary beckons!' said Dan.

'No.' Marie was emphatic. 'We'll send the child to St Mungo's.'

'That private school?' It was the first Mac had heard of this. 'Why?'

'Yeah, Mum, why?' asked Dan. 'Vine Road was good enough for me and Em.'

Emma backed her mother. 'You and I had a different start in life, Dan. Vine Road's enormous, and Lottie ... there's a fragility to her.'

'Rubbish!' said Dan.

'Your sister's right,' said Marie. 'Lottie needs attention, and careful handling. She's still in her shell, even after four months. I don't want her being jostled.' She turned to Mac, chin up, fire in her blue eyes. 'We'll send her to St Mungo's.'

'Shall I just step outside and shake the money tree?' asked Mac.

'Yes,' said Marie.

'Dan should pay,' said Emma, gleefully.

'Yeah.' Dan nodded emphatically. 'Don't be proud, Dad. Let me help.'

'Proud?' Mac hated the way Dan used words to manipulate; he would prefer a straight argument. 'Who said I was proud? This is your duty, and you're not going to "help", son. You're paying for all of it.'

*

252

The front door was chipped, in need of a fresh coat of paint. Despite Marie's pleas for purple, Mac rebelled and brought home the same seaside blue from the DIY shop.

'Am I a good helper, Gramps?' Lottie handed him a rag to wipe his brush.

'The best, poppet.' Mac saw her swell with the praise. Her eagerness to please, her fear of being a bother, reminded him of another small child.

Me.

All through his childhood, Mac had watched Tatty closely, fearing she would stop loving him if he caused her any trouble. Like him, Lottie had spent much of her short life in other people's houses, there on sufferance, trying to be invisible.

Mac's knee twinged when he rose. *Sixty next year*, he thought, *and raising a six-year-old*. 'Run and fetch me the bigger brush.'

Off she shot. He watched, envying her vim. *She's like the ivy*, he thought. *She's taken root in my heart.*

'Am I, though?' asked Marie, standing at the end of her bed in the new dress. 'Just be honest. Am I fat?'

'You're gorgeous,' said Mac, who wasn't ready to navigate his wife's body issues before his first cup of tea. The shoe she threw just missed his head. 'Mercy, woman! You're not fat! You're just right!'

Marie tore off the dress as if it were full of poison ants. She kicked it into a corner. 'I've lost touch, Mac. I don't know what's in and what's out any more. I'm over the hill.'

'There is no hill, silly. The hill was made up by women's magazines.' Mac patted the bedcovers and she came and sat against him in her sturdy underwear.

'The youngsters wear such revealing clothes,' she said. 'I'd happily reveal myself if there was less of me.' She sighed. 'D'you know what I really, really want? A nice new kagoule.'

The forms were filled in. The uniform was bought. Lottie worshipped her new piped blazer and tried to wear it to bed.

Mac took a call at his desk one morning, just before he went in to interview a sixteen-year-old whose list of convictions would make Al Capone blush, and said to the aggrieved person on the other end, 'I'm sorry, that should've been dealt with by now.' He put down the receiver, took it straight up again and dialled a long number.

'Dad? It's 3am. What's happened?'

'You haven't paid the deposit to St Mungo's, Dan, that's what's happened.'

'Christ, tell them to calm down. They'll have it next week.'

'They needed it last week. They won't hold Lottie's place.'

'Tell them to—'

'I won't tell them anything. I'll pay the deposit and you can pay me back.'

'Dad, you're a star.'

'I'll need you to repay me, son.' Mac cupped his hand

around the phone. 'Or is there anything you need to tell me? Can you afford this school?'

'Of course I can. Now let me get back to sleep, Dad, and you get back to turning young lives around.'

The way he says it, thought Dan, *makes it sound like a joke.*

Lottie loved St Mungo's. She loved the routine, the lessons, the teachers. She had a best friend and an almost-best friend. She tried to smuggle Toulouse in her book bag.

Christmas surprises came wrapped in ribbon from Los Angeles and Singapore. There were long chats on the phone on Christmas Eve with both Dan and SJ, and Mac reprised his role as Father Christmas in the small hours.

Just like Dan and Emma before her, Lottie twigged it was Gramps behind the cotton wool beard, but played along.

In January, Mac paid St Mungo's for the upcoming term. Dan promised to 'see him right' for that, and for the first term's fee. Marie snatched the phone and asked, in a special tone she brought out very rarely and which was more feared in Sunnyside than nuclear war, what the hell was really going on.

She summarized Dan's answer to Mac over the strongest pot of tea she'd ever made.

'He's broke. The eejit sank every penny he had into some "amazeballs" tech deal, some revolutionary piece of film equipment, only to discover somebody had already patented it.' Marie rolled her eyes. 'Why wasn't he straight with us in the first place?'

'I see it every day with my clients. They keep going with the fibs until they're backed into a corner and then – bam! – it all comes out.'

'Can we afford St Mungo's, Mac?'

You know the answer. Mac lied, as was required of him. 'Of course.'

They would manage. And meanwhile Dan's life of limos and Rolexes would carry on. 'All smoke and mirrors,' he told his mother.

'Let's not ask Dan to contribute again,' said Mac.

Marie agreed. 'I couldn't deal with another lie,' she said. She took Mac's hand. 'Don't think too badly of him, love. He tries his best.'

No, thought Mac, hating the truth. *He doesn't.*

Resplendent in her new kagoule – a Christmas present from Mac – Marie was chivvying Lottie into her blazer. 'Come on, this isn't like you,' she said, as Lottie wriggled and writhed. 'We'll be late for school.'

Mac poked his head round the door. 'Chop chop, Lottie.'

'Go away!' Lottie tore off the blazer and threw it at Toulouse. 'I'm not going! It's counting today and I hate counting!' She jumped into her wardrobe and it shook as she banged the doors shut.

Mac and Marie gaped at each other. They wanted to applaud. The little girl trusted their love enough to misbehave.

Marie crept on all fours and knocked on the painted wood. 'Is there someone called Lottie Mactavish in there?'

'I'm sorry, Grammy.' The voice was full of tears.

They scooped her out, smothering her between them, until she couldn't help but giggle.

'Tell us what the matter is,' said Mac.

'I miss my mummy.'

'I'll tell you a secret,' said Marie, her mouth close to Lottie's ear. 'I'm an old lady and I still miss my mummy. We'll miss them together until yours comes back. Deal?'

'Deal,' said Lottie.

They were only five minutes late for school.

CHAPTER FOURTEEN

'Where have you been? Why didn't you come last week?'
He is still yards from her corner of the rec room when she lets
him have it. 'Don't make promises you can't keep.'

'I was here last week. Remember?' He keeps his face stoic.

'I . . . well.' She finds it hard to climb down from her
high horse. 'Sit, sit,' she grumbles. 'Everyone's looking.'

'They're your friends! Especially that lady who knits.'

'Not anymore. That's all she talks about. Knitting!'

He remembers how she used to knit. He picks up the
album; hopefully it can save their afternoon. 'Look, they're
not in front of the house this year!'

'They're off somewhere tropical.' She is intrigued; she
resembles her old self when a fire is lit within her. 'The
lady doesn't look convinced by her sarong, does she? Not
comfortable at all.'

'Nearly as awkward as our man in his white suit.'

29 July 2006

'Welcome to paradise!'

That was how Bernie welcomed them at the airport, tucking oleander in their hair and neglecting to help them with the luggage. St Lucia *was* paradisical, its powder-fine sand a white stripe beneath untroubled blue skies.

'It's a garden of Eden,' marvelled Mac, as the minibus turned off the potholed road onto the luxe tarmac of the resort. 'The greenery, it's so profuse.'

'Perfuse,' said Abbo, from the seat behind. At five, he had taken to repeating Gramps's longer words.

'*Profuse*,' Lottie corrected him, the wiser older woman of eight.

'Nothing but the best,' said Marie, already sweating like a wrestler and inclined to be sardonic, 'for my sister's wedding.'

After years of prevarication, Bernie had turned to Angus in Lidl and said, 'You haven't asked me to marry you this week.' So, he asked and she said yes, and they went to the checkout with a crate of Lithuanian champagne.

The minibus disgorged them at a white bungalow. 'Blimey, this must be costing Angus a small fortune,' said Mac, standing on the veranda to take in a view of the sea that must surely be CGI.

Angus never baulked at Bernie's demands, even though he had the sort of genteel taste that favoured country cottages and old Barbours. When it came to his wife-to-be he wore rose-tinted glasses; Bernie got on everyone's wick sooner or later, but not Angus. He just loved her.

'Look!' Marie got to the towels shaped like swans before Lottie did. 'Everything's so *posh*.'

'Knock knock!' Bernie barged in. 'We're like footballers' wives, Marie! They even put rose petals in the bath.'

Mac said, 'Don't rose petals in the water get up your . . .' but went no further. He didn't understand luxury. It was usually uncomfortable.

The next two days were one long rolling buffet of ripe fruits and colourful drinks.

Mac kept an eye out for the St Lucia parrot. When he finally snapped one, he punched the air. Marie tutted and adjusted her sundress straps, her back and shoulders already criss-crossed with a fluorescent design on red skin.

The resort was dotted with deckchairs complete with their own petite awnings, and Mac sought out his favourite one, on a terrace that offered him a V-shaped chunk of the Caribbean Sea framed with rowdy vegetation. At his feet, Lottie sat stringing beads; she was making bracelets for the whole party. Jeff the puffin was at her side in lieu of Toulouse, who was currently plotting his revenge in a costly cattery.

The first bracelet had been wrapped up and sent to her mother. SJ alighted in London now and then, always at short notice, never for long. She breezed in and out of Lottie's life; Mac and Marie dealt with the tearful aftermath.

Now Lottie held up the latest bracelet, showing Mac its harmony of reds and golds and greens.

'Lovely, Lot-Lot,' he said.

The lush beauty of St Lucia intoxicated Mac, but he was uneasy about the five-star bells and whistles. The heat got to him; like his wife he was designed for a temperate climate. As for the shorts Marie foisted on him . . . Mac preferred to keep his knees to himself.

He thought about the wisteria at home. Even at its best it was nothing like the abundance here. The magnolia had done him proud this year, but it was a whimper compared to the Bird of Paradise plants all around him. *Infinitely more meaning, however!*

There was an itch in Mac's soul at being away from Sunnyside. As if it might falter without him, a chimney drop off, the whole house list to one side. It was silly, he knew that, but humans tend towards the silly.

The cruise would take them away from home for much longer than this wedding. *If it ever happens.* This year's plan had been scuppered by the costly Caribbean fandango; Angus's largesse had stopped short of flights. The jar had stood more or less empty since Lottie's arrival three years earlier; Dan contributed very little. He was 'stretched,' he said; *Aren't we all?* thought Mac, who had stopped broaching the topic of money with his son, which meant it was never mentioned at all.

Marie dropped into the adjacent deckchair.

'Grammy, for you.' Lottie handed over a poorly made bracelet.

'Wow, that is *beautiful*,' said Marie. She dug out her trusty Jackie Collins novel. Jackie was Marie's Dostoevsky; she read all the titles back-to-back, starting again at the beginning when she got to the end. She waved at Emma and Ollie, gliding past on a tandem. Sporty, active, they rose early each morning to take the little ones paddleboarding; they were planning a hiking holiday – two words that Marie felt did not go together *at all*. 'Emma updates her website every day, even here,' she said.

'You don't get into the *Sunday Times* round-up of best wellness sites by sitting on your hands.' Mac had framed the article. He was proud. And yet ... a little wellness went a long way. He had felt his daughter's eyes boring into his back as he dolloped a spoonful of double cream onto his breakfast porridge. She'd told him he might as well mainline heroin. 'Is Emma still making Abbo keep that journal?'

Marie tutted. She could produce many shades of tut – scornful, disappointed, shocked – but this one was fond. ''Fraid so. I says to her, that child's *five*, much too young to keep a one-line-a-day journal about his mood. She asks him how he feels, and then she writes it down for him, and one day hopefully he'll write it himself. She said she has to live up to the mantra of her website.'

They quoted her together: 'You're never too young to start living well.'

Marie found her page in Jackie C. 'If living well means no Viennetta, then I'll live badly, ta very much.'

*

Leaving the huddle of lodges behind, Emma lifted her face to feel the sun. She was recharged, every inch of her fit, firm frame pulsing with wellbeing.

The tandem veered slowly to the right. Ollie was in charge. He was strong, healthy; her desire for him had never waned, although life got in the way of their once-daily lovemaking. Since arriving on the island they had resumed their old ways, connecting and merging in the pink hours of dawn.

Not today though. Today Ollie was out of sorts. It wasn't easy to converse on a tandem, but Emma persevered with asking what was up; it might be the only pocket of privacy they would manage.

She got a little bit more than she bargained for.

'My family?' Emma felt attacked. 'What about them? Mum and Dad bloody worship you.'

Ollie braked. Turned. They both straddled the cumbersome bike. 'Don't get all defensive. Mac and Marie are great, but do they have to play such a huge part in our lives?'

'You know I couldn't work without Mum helping with Abbo.'

'Girl, he starts primary school in September.' Ollie laid the tandem on its side, like a sick horse, and they sat on the grass beside it. 'You and your mum seem to bicker half the time anyway.'

'So?' That was their love language; Emma and Marie took care to argue within very defined boundaries. It did them both good to holler at one another. 'It's all right for you,

Ollie, you swan off to work without ever worrying about who looks after Abbo.'

'Don't make this a man/woman thing. This is a family thing. It's time we put the plan into action.'

The plan was their secret. It involved moving out of London to somewhere their budget would buy them a larger house with lots of garden. A paddock was part of the plan, although neither of them was sure what they'd do with one.

'Or is the plan just a fantasy?' Ollie pulled apart a blade of grass as he spoke.

'No, I love the plan. It's just ...' A city girl, Emma distrusted the countryside. Where were the takeaways? The streetlamps? What if she needed an emergency mascara at 5pm?

'Don't get me wrong. Your parents are diamonds. They're family to me, but family don't need to live on top of one another. Jesus, if I let my mum have her way, she'd run our entire lives. We've saved and worked so hard, Em, isn't it time we made the change?'

She couldn't answer. They cycled back to the resort. Independent, outspoken, Emma couldn't countenance moving away from Mac and Marie. The apron strings she ridiculed were still tied tight, all the stronger for being invisible.

The wedding-eve supper was laid out on a long table, the diners lit by flaming torches.

They all had a touch of the sun. The Adrians looked like

an advert for menswear, and even Tatty was improved by the oleander in her hair.

St Lucia has loosened her up, thought Mac, gratified. His aunt, so averse to luxury, was won over by Bernie's generosity, and now she sipped at a cocktail the size of her head, served in a coconut. *Please, nobody tell her it's called a Slippery Nipple.*

Keen to get full value for her new boobs, Bernie sported a new sarong every day. Hair swept up, shoulders bare, she was happy. Showing off, naturally, but so keen to share her good fortune that it was difficult to carp; she was the heaviest, and the happiest, she had ever been. 'Hey, you!' She dragooned a waiter into taking a snap to send to Bridget, who had declined the invitation as, 'it's not a proper wedding'.

With the children in bed – Mac had sung the lullaby three times – Emma brought up the elephant in the room: Lottie's future.

'Do we have to do this now, over dinner?' said Marie. 'Like we always say, Lottie has a home with us for as long as she needs one. End of.'

'Dan should take this opportunity to start over with his little girl and get it right this time. Don't you agree, Adrians?'

The Adrians did agree, but with less heat than Emma. The second Adrian suggested encouraging Dan, instead of insisting.

'You *have* to insist with Dan. He ignores bloody suggestions,' said Emma.

'My Dan?' Bernie was his family PR spokesperson, as ever. 'He's a sweetheart.'

'If he's such a sweetheart, why isn't he here to see you and Angus get married, Auntie B?'

Although proud of his daughter's honesty, Mac wished she could show a little more tact; Bernie fell abruptly silent.

Clearly trying to sound as if he believed it, Angus said, 'Emma, poor Dan is *devastated*. Apparently the wedding clashes with his moving date. He's found a fabulous apartment for himself and his paramour, and he just can't get away.'

Emma said, 'I see, he can shell out for a swanky flat but he can't afford to educate his daughter?'

Rallying, Bernie thought she was defending Dan when she said, 'His girlfriend's a stunner, she's off some reality programme.'

The original Adrian said, 'She's twenty-one to his thirty-five, Bern. Funny how Dan gets older but the paramours remain the same age.'

Tatty sat forward; perhaps the Slippery Nipple emboldened her. 'Dan is Dan. We must accept the boy as he is.'

The older Adrian said, 'Ah, nature versus nurture. Are people born the way they are, or can they redeem themselves? Can anyone truly change?'

The other Adrian put his head on Adrian's shoulder. 'Don't *you* change. I like you the way you are.'

There was toasting after that, and Angus was prodded to his feet to make a speech. He spoke of his satisfaction in finding a family so late in life. He thanked them for accepting him, for folding him up in their hearts.

Just the sort of speech Mac liked, it would have forced a happy tear out of him if he'd been listening.

Instead, he was thinking of Dan, and how they'd all known he would stay away. *A family wedding can't compete with flashy parties in Tinseltown.* Nature versus nurture? Mac had reared his children the same way, in the same house, but Dan persisted in emulating Ed Vole, the grandfather he'd never met.

Neither man looked over their shoulder to glance at the little child in their wake.

It was as if the ocean belonged to him.

The waves whispered in Mac's ear as he stood watching the black water stretch away to an invisible horizon. He felt small and far from home, but peaceful. As he turned to go back to the lodge and his sleeping grandchildren, he sensed somebody approach along the dark sand.

'What's all this?' he asked Bernie. 'The bride needs her beauty sleep.'

She took his arm, in the companionable way she always did, but this time she held it tight, and leaned in. 'I'm thinking, Mac.'

He understood. 'About George?'

'It was good once. Perfect, even. It could've been good forever. Why did he do it? Why did he make me so unhappy I had to leave?'

Working with destructive people had given Mac a theory.

'George was in pain, love. He wanted to spread it around. That doesn't excuse him, but it might explain him.'

'I loved him, you know.'

'I do know that, Bern. Maybe he didn't know what to do with the love, and ended up smashing it on the floor. Look at you now, though. On your feet. In love with a man who loves you back.' Mac hesitated. 'At least I hope you are. This is love, isn't it, Bern?'

'It's love, Mac. Angus is the only man who looked at me and thought *you'll do*. No demands. No complaints. I love him madly, completely.'

'Phew. Thought you had cold feet.'

'Sweaty feet, certainly, but not cold. The only thing holding me back was Angus's age, until I realized that one good year with him would be worth a lifetime with someone else.'

'He's lucky to have you, Bern.'

'We all know that's not true,' laughed Bernie. 'But Angus believes it, so let's not enlighten him.'

They turned, as if on a prearranged cue, and began to plod up the sand to the bungalows.

'If we have half the marriage that you and my sister have,' said Bernie, 'we'll do all right.'

They took their seats in the front row of white slatted chairs.

'I phoned Toulouse,' said Marie.

'You whatted Toulouse?' Mac assumed he had misheard.

'I rang him. At the cattery. He sounds fine.' Marie pulled tetchily at her sarong. She was not one of nature's sarong wearers. 'Trust Bernie to choose our wedding date to get hitched. She'll hijack every anniversary from now on.'

'It's a sweet gesture.' Mac was uneasy in the white linen suit his womenfolk had stipulated for him and Ollie. A few seats along Ollie looked dashing, as opposed to crumpled; Mac noted with satisfaction that Ollie held Emma's hand.

He saw how Ollie allowed Emma her enthusiasms; the little family were vegan now, much to Marie's consternation and cries of 'But my daughter loves a sausage!' Ollie was strong, but never hard. Mac admired him, and he knew that Dan's teasing – when he called Ollie a 'new man' it was with heavy irony – stemmed from envy. Ollie had found what he wanted – Emma and Abbo – and hung onto them. There would be no more babies; 'one and done' was how Emma put it. Her blog bristled with such zeitgeisty phrases.

An Adrian fanned Tatty, while the other Adrian made jokes with Angus, who was by far the most relaxed and affable groom Mac had ever seen.

The music struck up.

They all stood.

Down the sandy aisle came Abbo and Lottie, both in white satin with scarlet sashes, strewing petals – none too tidily – ahead of the bride.

Bernie ran the last few paces, and let out a hiccupped sob as she reached for Angus.

'I do,' they agreed. They kissed and Mac got something in his eye.

*

269

Out on their veranda, they were both tipsy.

Mac wanted to go to bed and sleep off the rum punch. Marie wanted to go over every detail of the day. Marie won.

'What did you think of the bridal sarong?' The moonlight lit her face strangely. 'The bejewelled flipflops were plain silly. Gave her cankles. The vows were so makey-up. *I will help you be the best possible version of yourself.* Honestly!'

'Hey now.' For Mac this was a harsh reprimand. He didn't want to hear sarcastic criticism, not tonight. 'This is Bernie's wedding, not yours, and she loved every second of it.'

Marie said, chastened, 'And so did I, if I'm honest. I'm being Bridget, aren't I?'

'A bit.' Mac patted his lap and she leapt onto it. He hoped he covered up his shocked *Oof!* as she landed. 'Give us a kiss, Mrs Mactavish the first.'

Her lips tasted of mango. 'We haven't done so badly, have we, boyo?' Her face was close to his.

'*I* haven't. Not so sure about you. Thirty-six years ago today I won the lottery.'

'We were so young.'

'You haven't changed a jot, love.'

Marie thought of her sagging jawline, her wardrobe of elasticated waists, the laughter lines that weren't bloody funny. '*You've* changed, Mac,' she whispered. 'You've got lovelier.' She put her head on his shoulder, and they were both glad that they had been together forever and neither expected this tender moment to translate into sex; they needed to sleep off the long wedding day and the dancing and the singing and the emotional rendition of 'Danny Boy' by Adrian.

Mac felt her grow heavy against him. This was the moment to say it; if she didn't hear he could convince himself he had tried and need never mention it again.

Softly, into her hair, he said, 'Remember Lottie's birthday party? All her little mates came over the last Saturday in May, and we had a clown and Toulouse walked over the cake.'

'Hmm,' said Marie, drowsily.

'I did some adding up, love.'

She was wide awake, as if jump-started. She stared into his eyes. 'Me too.'

The cat was decidedly out of the bag.

Mac said, 'If Lottie was born on 31st May in 1998, ten months after Dan left for America, then she can't be his.'

'Nor ours.' Marie was grave. She looked her age. She felt it, too. 'I've known since just after Lottie arrived. I ignored it.' She widened her eyes at her own foolishness. 'As if that could make it less true! She doesn't look like Dan, not really. It's just coincidence and wishful thinking.'

'As usual,' said Mac, 'it took me a while to catch up with my good lady wife.'

They heard Lottie's gentle snuffles on the baby monitor.

Sore feet forgotten, Marie left Mac's lap and paced the veranda. 'SJ lied, of course. No woman makes that mistake about their own baby.'

'Why do it?' Mac had assumed SJ to be transparent, artless. 'Is it because Dan's theoretically loaded?'

'Maybe a little of that.' Marie had had time to come up with theories. 'But mainly it tells you a great deal about Lottie's birth father. Imagine what kind of character he must be for SJ to prefer Dan, the guy who broke her heart and left her flat on the floor.'

'I see what you mean. SJ certainly never has anything good to say about her exes.'

'And then there's us,' said Marie. 'In handing Lottie to Dan, she can't genuinely have expected him to drop everything and look after her. Remember how SJ used to love Sunday lunch at our place? Didn't want to leave? She was giving Lottie the family she never had by making us grandparents.'

'You're right, love.' Mac saw it clearly now. 'SJ was doing her best for Lottie, even if it meant lying to us.'

'And to the child,' said Marie. 'Whenever the phone rings at home, half of me hopes it's SJ so Lottie can chat to her mum. Half of me hopes it *isn't* SJ, in case she says she's coming to take her home.'

How quickly the unexpected burden had become their chief joy.

'What do we do now?' said Mac.

Marie was ready with the answer. 'I've worked it all out. We tell SJ we know. We ask her what she means to do in the long run. It'll break my heart, but we encourage her to tell Lottie the truth.' With a sigh, she closed her eyes, and let her head hang back until she could speak again. 'If I've learned anything from watching you spin in the fallout from Tatty's fibs, it's that we all deserve to know where we come from. Poor little angel, she has to know who her daddy is. She has to know that Dan's not her daddy.'

'I'm not her Gramps.'

'Oh yes you are, boyo, and I'm her Grammy. Blood might be thicker than water, but my stew is thicker than both, and we love that little girl. For now, we say nothing and carry on as normal. Agreed?'

There was part of Mac that wanted to keep the lie going, a part he was ashamed of. *Tatty did me untold damage by trying to protect me.* He opened the door to the room where Lottie and Abbo slept, and felt the rich texture of the children's dreams in the dark.

He offered up a futile prayer, that nothing should ever hurt Lottie.

'Night night,' he whispered. 'Who's my baby?'

CHAPTER FIFTEEN

'The little girl's growing up fast,' he says. 'I wonder what they're all looking at? It's as if they've all turned at once and are staring into the road.'

'When can I come home?' She slams the album shut with a sure hand. When she accepts a cuppa the hand shakes; when she wants to vent it does not.

'Oh, well . . .' He opens the album, finds the page again. He regards it doggedly. 'The lady hasn't really changed, has she? Even though nearly forty years have passed. Funny how some people remain the same all through their lives.'

She harrumphs. 'Do you really think it's that easy to distract me? Answer my question. I don't like it here. When can I go home?'

'You do like it here.' It's idiotic to inform a person they like something when they tell you the opposite. But she chops and changes so much, he has no option. The staff reassure

*him she is doing fine; she reassures him of the same thing.
Until, every so often, she declares her hatred for the residential
care home. 'How about a nice drive? You love a drive.'*

*'Don't tell me what I love.' She pushes at the album and
it skids along the coffee table. 'Take this when you go. Bin
it. Why do we waste our time looking at photographs of
strangers?'*

*'They don't feel like strangers anymore. I've got to know
them. I like them!'*

*'Get it away from me.' Her face tells him she still has
autonomy, even in this place.*

29 July 2009

Jangling his car keys, Mac loitered in the hallway of the
shabby house. It smelled of cabbage, with undernotes
of biscuit.

The resident was too frail to make it to the front door. A
customer of Marie's new mobile hairdressing business, she
was a Saturday-morning regular.

Hardly a business, thought Mac to himself. Prices were kept
so low it just about broke even. The profit was all in the satisfaction Marie took in reaching forgotten people, cheering
up elderly ladies whose bodies no longer reflected how they
felt inside. Sticks to get around, slippers cut to accommodate
widening feet, but a smashing shampoo and set to look forward to, courtesy of Marie Mactavish.

Mac was never prouder of his wife than when he stood waiting for her while she made her customer one last cup of tea, and had one last belly laugh with them. *Something ageless about my Marie*, he thought. She would never wither; she would always be the ball of fire he met at a party.

'Come *on*, boyo.' Marie whisked past as if he had kept her waiting.

They took the long way home. Mac had things to do in the shed, but he knew his wife loved to tootle along with the radio turned right up. Today Lady Gaga entertained them, with her 'Pokerface'.

They were given one day's notice.

The text landed the day before their wedding anniversary: 'Hi guys!!! Coming back from tour tomorrow to see my cupcake!!! Tons of love SJ xxxxxx'

They knew SJ had a new husband; they didn't know he drove a Jeep worthy of a *Mad Max* movie. It rolled down the street like a tank, braking loudly just as the family posed for the traditional photograph.

The vehicle throbbed with the booming bass of dance music and brought Next Door to his window. The new husband stayed within when SJ hopped out.

At first, Lottie was shy of her mother. Mac saw how that wounded SJ. 'She'll soon warm up, love, don't worry.' He took the massive puffer jacket SJ wore despite the sunshine.

'Hey, Lottie, I love your hair,' said SJ. To Marie, she said, 'She's so *tall*.'

Eleven now, Lottie bit her lip and pushed the toe of her right sandal into the floor, a sure sign of inner tumult.

Mac put a hand on her shoulder, and Lottie leaned into him.

They were wary, the Mactavishes. Neither knew what this visit meant; they made SJ welcome, and Marie fussed with cups and plates.

Before long, Lottie's excitement cancelled out her shyness. She babbled to SJ about her classmates, and Toulouse's habits. Showed her a dance move she and Abbo did at family get-togethers.

Making polite conversation, Mac wanted to stand up and yell, *Please don't take her away from us!*

'Won't your husband come indoors?' asked Marie.

'Damien's not sociable,' said SJ, smiling as if this was a lovable quirk. 'Doesn't like new people.'

'Hmm,' said Marie.

'He'll like this one, though!' SJ put her forehead against Lottie's. 'He already *loves* her.'

Judging by the jewellery that weighed SJ down like gold shackles, the man-child out in the jeep was wealthy.

'That thing we discussed,' said SJ, with clear sub-text. 'I'm doing it here, today.'

'Right now?' *She's going to tell Lottie Dan's not her father, just like that?* Mac managed to cover his panic; Marie could not.

Quivering, Marie said to Lottie, 'Run and fetch my blue cardi, love, it's on my bed.' The child, always eager to help, dashed out. 'Let us listen in, SJ, to support the child.' Marie was urgent; it came out like the prayers her mother used to gabble in church. 'We know her better than you do by this stage. I know you don't want to hear that, but it's true. Let us *be* there.'

'Nope. Sorry. I'm Lottie's mum and I'll do this my way.'

Marie started forward, but Mac caught her arm. 'SJ's right. She's Lottie's mother and what she says goes.'

'And us?' Marie could barely keep a lid on her distress. 'What are we? SJ, you led us to believe we're her grandparents, let us take complete responsibility for her these past five years. It's been a privilege, she's the light of my life, and I don't begrudge a moment of it.' Tears spilled; Marie struggled on. 'I've bathed her, dressed her, sat by her bed when she was poorly. I'd do it again in a heartbeat. But who will I be to Lottie after this conversation, SJ? Who am I?'

'You're my Grammy,' laughed Lottie, turning up with the blue cardigan in her hand.

'C'mon, cupcake.' SJ pulled the girl to her. 'We need a chat.'

It only took ten minutes, but Lottie returned to them a different person.

She had a blank look, as if waiting to reboot. She flew to Marie, and buried her face in her chest, eyes squeezed shut.

Also dazed, SJ jumped at the honk of the jeep's horn.

Next Door banged on the wall.

'I should get going.' SJ was hoisting herself up by her bootstraps, calling on those resilient reserves she'd had to use so often.

'You've only just got here,' said Mac. He was hanging onto his manners; SJ pushed them all to the limit with her careless self-interest.

'Damien's on a schedule.' SJ was flustered, torn. 'Hang on.' She dashed outside and returned with a man who was much older than her, and might have been older than Mac. It was impossible to divine the age of a face so expertly rearranged.

Polite, but betraying his desire to get away, Damien shook hands with Lottie. 'I've heard all about you,' he said. 'Aren't you gorgeous!'

Mac said, 'She *is* gorgeous, but she's also very good at maths, kind to animals, mad about history but especially the Tudors, and she always, *always* knows when you need a hug.'

'Like now,' said Lottie, and reached up to cuddle Mac. He heard Damien say, 'Time's getting on, babe.'

'Show her the jeep, babe,' said SJ. 'Please?'

Neither Damien nor Lottie were keen, but they trailed out together all the same, Damien tapping his watch when he thought Mac wasn't looking.

SJ spoke fast. 'It went okay. She's shocked, but she'll be fine.'

'Fine? Just like that? How did you put it?' asked Mac.

Speeding, SJ ignored him. 'Quick, let's pack while she's out there. I've told her we're just going for a drive. I can explain what's really happening later.'

Marie stiffened. 'What *is* really happening?'

'I told you. I'm sure I said. Didn't I?' That vagueness again.

'Oh God, I'm so crap. Sorry. I've packed in the singing. Damien's looking after me and Lottie now. We'll have a real home with a real daddy.' She took in their faces and backed away. She appealed to Mac. 'I thought you'd be happy for us.'

'We are, love, but—'

'She's not a book we borrowed!' shouted Marie, and Toulouse shot out through the cat flap. 'You can't just drop by and take her back. Lottie has a life here. School. Little mates. *Us!*'

Mac felt a fault line open in his heart. A crack that might engulf him. 'Listen, why don't we sit Damien down and we can discuss it calmly, make plans. Lottie will need time to acclimatise.'

'Better to make the break.' SJ was restless, testy.

It was the behaviour Mac saw in his clients en route to a bad decision.

'Just let me pack her stuff and we'll go, yeah?' SJ looked anywhere but at Mac and Marie.

As she ransacked drawers upstairs, there was a hissed con-flab in the kitchen.

'We have to put a stop to this.' Marie stabbed at her phone. 'Let's get Dan involved.' She put the phone to her ear. 'It's gone to answerphone.'

Of course, thought Mac. 'What can Dan do? We don't have a leg to stand on, love. Nothing written down, no contracts, no adoption. SJ has rights.' He stilled his wife, put his hands on her shoulders. 'And that's the way it should be. She's Lottie's mother.'

'What about *our* rights?' Marie shook him off. 'Aren't you going to fight for our girl? *Rights?* Don't give me rights, Mac. Rights come from *here*.' She struck her chest so hard it hurt. 'SJ's not thinking straight. She's here, there and everywhere, as usual. That bloke looks dodgy, all fur coat no knickers. We can't let them take Lottie. We can't give her up.'

'I'm imagining,' said Mac, 'how I'd have felt if my mum suddenly turned up at Tatty's.'

Marie was wretched. 'I'm not stupid. I know we have to let her go. I know this is SJ's decision to make. I know she's not perfect, which mother is? God knows I'm not. But . . .'

'No tears, love.' Mac was gentle. He heard SJ's feet on the stair. 'For Lottie's sake. Not until she's gone.'

Gone.

Such a black hole of sadness in four letters.

Eyes on the floor, SJ held a pink suitcase. 'Thank you,' she said. 'That sounds ridiculous. How can I ever thank you?'

'We don't need to be thanked, love,' said Mac. 'We've done it happily. Lottie's a great person. A credit to you.'

'And to you.' SJ bit her lip the way Lottie did when words wouldn't come, when her feelings outran her eloquence.

'What we do need,' said Mac, 'is respect. Which means a relationship with the child who's become the centre of our world.'

'If that's what you want,' said SJ. 'Sure.'

'We want to be her grandparents,' said Marie.

'Look, I get it, I do, and you are her grandparents. That

won't change.' SJ was suddenly fidgety, as if the attention she'd allotted to this trying episode was running out.

They followed her to the door. 'When can we see her?' asked Marie, shredding a tissue in her hands.

'Anytime.' SJ waved at Lottie, who jumped down from the driver's seat. 'Just fly over.'

'Fly?' Marie repeated the word as her stomach plummeted.

'To Sydney. That's where Damien's based. I did tell you.'

'You did *not*,' said Marie, hotly.

Lottie crossed the crazy paving, avoiding the lines as she always did. She didn't see Damien discreetly take her case and stow it. 'Fish fingers tonight, isn't it, Grammy?'

Marie nodded.

'Great.' She turned and dashed to the car, with no idea of the momentous farewell taking place. She bounced on the high back seat. She didn't wave.

'I can't do this, Mac,' stammered Marie.

They watched the huge vehicle lumber down the street, and pause at the junction.

'Turn around, Lottie, please,' begged Mac under his breath.

She did. Just as the jeep took a right, Lottie waved Jeff's wing at them.

Marie did jumping jacks.

Mac whispered, 'Be calm, and dream. Drift, and wander, my darling Lottie.'

Emma's first question was, 'What did Dan have to say about all this?'

'He was shocked.' Marie was low, two days after what she referred to as Lottie's kidnapping. It had happened so fast; she and Mac re-enacted all the ways they could have changed the outcome. Blocking the door. Telling SJ some home truths. 'Dan said if only we'd given him some notice he'd have come over, tried to reason with SJ.'

'Woulda shoulda coulda,' said Emma, unimpressed.

'He's processing.' Mac was uncomfortable with how Emma demonized Dan, even though he tended to do the same. 'We don't all react in the same way.'

'New girlfriend, I'm guessing?'

Marie slapped her with a tea towel. 'You have a bad mind, missy! But yes. Only ten years younger this time.'

'Oooh, he's improving. Let me guess; she's a top cardiac surgeon?'

'She's a model,' said Marie reluctantly.

'Quelle surprise.'

Trailing down the stairs from Lottie's room, Abbo asked, disconsolate, 'She's really not coming back?' At eight, he was lanky as a new pony, with unfeasibly long arms and legs. He wore a pair of angel wings left behind by SJ, in her haste. He was the sort of boy to bend double when he laughed, a sensitive but bold character. He didn't laugh now.

'Not for a while.' Marie stripped him of his wings. 'These are for girls, Abbo.'

Emma wore them instead. 'We don't differentiate, Mum. You know, pink for girls and blue for boys kinda thing. We let Abbo express himself.'

'I used to love playing with guns, meself,' said Marie.

'Explains a lot,' said Mac. 'Em, why not come over for Sunday lunch and keep us oldies company?'

'Can't, Dad. I'm playing catch-up with work and the website.' Her site was turning a good profit, but August was a hungry mouth that demanded a daily feed of fresh content.

'You work too hard, madam.' Marie accused her daughter of her own crime. Overwork was a Mactavish trait; except for Dan, who sweated the least and earned the most.

'Feels like a treadmill,' said Emma. 'I can't get off. We're saving so hard.'

'For what?' asked Marie.

'This and that,' said Emma, as Abbo said, 'A house.'

Marie was alarmed. 'You're moving? Where?'

Mac saw how Emma withdrew. 'Ooh, it's just talk for now.'

To save her from further interrogation, Mac said, 'We'll invite Tatty for a roast instead. She'll have to find out about Lottie sometime.'

Emma said, 'Will it hit her hard?'

Mac shrugged. 'Hard to tell, with Tatty.'

'She's such a heroine,' said Emma. 'A real Boadicea.'

'Tatty?' Mac wondered if they were discussing the same person.

'The way she sacrificed any notion of marriage to bring you up, Dad. She never farmed you out, she kept you close.' Emma hugged herself to illustrate her point. 'Worked hard, no man to support her at a time when women were expected to simper about at home. Made sure you were educated. Tatty's a Valkyrie!'

Mac knew Emma was merely riffing, stringing together throwaway thoughts, but they sparked a change inside him, a deep churning turn.

'No wonder,' said Emma, 'she's a bit emotionally unavailable. I would be, too, if I'd been through all that.'

Talk turned to other matters. To Abbo's eczema, what Princess Diana would think of Prince William's girlfriend, whether the sitting room needed a makeover.

'Hmm,' said Mac, and occasionally 'Good point', but he listened to none of it. Inside his head, he watched Tatty take a small step to the side, and be bathed in an entirely new light. She firmed up, became a three-dimensional person, with personal Tatty hopes and personal Tatty fears.

I remember all too well the cold bedrooms and the lonely rainy afternoons and the lack of goodnight kisses. He had forgotten, however, the hot meal on the table come what may, Tatty's tired face after another long shift, the books she put into his hands on those rainy afternoons.

He looked at Emma, as she campaigned for a new mantelpiece in the (now unavoidable) sitting room refresh, and saw her differently, too. He saw how she empathized, and how that empathy was sometimes so cluttered with smart remarks and her disfiguring jealousy of Dan, that it was overlooked.

I see you, my darling, he thought.

Out in the front garden, goodbyes took forever, as usual. Marie kept remembering something she simply *had* to tell

Emma, Abbo was admonished for disarranging the white rocks – twenty-eight of them now – beneath the magnolia, and they all turned to watch the harried-looking woman pelt out of the house next door with her head down.

'Meals on Wheels,' said Marie. 'Next Door can't get about anymore. Needs one of them walkers. So he gets free meals. The delivery ladies always come out looking like they've been to war.'

A thwack. A groan. Next Door, desperately eavesdropping, had fallen by his front door.

'We've got you!' Emma bounded over the fence.

Hauled up, dusted down, Next Door pointed out that Emma had trodden on his gnome and went indoors.

The years do not ask permission, they make their way onwards without our say-so.

It hurt the Mactavishes to put months between themselves and the last time they saw Lottie. The house in Sydney was soon sold in favour of a house in Perth. Damien was restless, and his new family moved in his wake. Phone calls were rare; the time difference cited as a reason, when everyone knew SJ had consigned them to the past, a difficult past she didn't care to revisit.

Mac and Marie found a consolation prize in at last planning their cruise with some confidence. With no school fees to pay, they dared to look at a premium sailing.

'Peru to Panama,' said Mac, drawing up a list of birds he would spot. *No puffins, though*, he thought, as he used the pen with the puffin eraser Abbo had brought back from a school trip.

He and Marie worked hard to convince each other that the cruise would soften the sting of losing Lottie, and perhaps it would.

Then again, perhaps it wouldn't.

Marie tapped Mac's nose. 'Your nostrils are dilating,' she said.

2010 was a bully. It bullied Mac right out of his job.

'I might be sixty-five according to the calendar,' he sighed, sloughing off his coat as he returned home after his last day at the probation service. 'Inside I'm still starting out.' He managed a smile for his wife. 'Thank God you listened to me when I said I didn't want a big retirement party.'

'Well . . .' Marie threw open the sitting room door.

'Surprise!' yelled the thirty people crammed therein.

'Admit it, you enjoyed it,' said Marie, during their moon-lit bed-chat.

'I enjoyed it,' said Mac, and felt a burp building. He had drunk too much; he'd pay for it tomorrow. *I'd have enjoyed a quiet evening with my Marie even more.* 'While we're admitting things, you admit the party was an excuse to show off the new sitting room.'

'How dare you,' smiled Marie. She was a recent convert to the church of minimalism. The brown and orange swirls were finally banished and the ground floor was a sea of beige.

Tasteful pale rugs were layered over tasteful oatmeal carpet. The new suite was cream leather, and the curtains had been somewhat calmed. The new stone mantelpiece was bare of ornaments.

'Here's another confession,' burped Mac. 'I bloody hate beige.'

No longer a PSO – Mac abhorred abbreviations and had always written Probation Service Officer on forms – Mac was now, well, *Mac*. No casebook. No agenda. The job had changed mightily in the three decades since he'd joined up. Far more paperwork, far more blame when events went awry, and far more qualifications necessary. A young Mac just starting out would need a degree. He had, he felt, winged his career, using common sense and compassion.

Every morning he felt relief at being able to turn over and go back to sleep at 7am. That lasted thirty seconds before the feeling of something misplaced or lost, a small bereavement, as he mourned the sense of purpose that fuelled him for so long.

When they called Australia – and, hallelujah, someone actually picked up – it was often to find that Lottie was on a sleepover or at netball practice or indefinably 'busy' in a way no other twelve-year-old ever was.

Even though SJ was upbeat, they smelled blood in the water for her marriage. Mac tried not to tremble about what that might mean for mother and daughter on the other side of the globe. He imitated Marie, who remained jaunty throughout; she didn't seem to let the worry worm its way through her defences. He envied her.

Love demanded so much of Mac. Constant anxiety. Constant recovery. How much easier not to love! How relaxing that would be, to whistle his way through life, hands in pockets.

Ah yes, but think of what I'd miss! Mac passed an open door and glimpsed Marie folding clothes and putting them away. Newish wrinkles creased her familiar face. Her T-shirt said Don't Worry Be Happy. Her slippers were fake fur, and would be shucked off if anybody came to the door.

Mac gave the specific little secret smile Marie always evoked as he turned away.

Marie folded a small dress. It was satin, with a red sash. A bridesmaid dress, with a mango stain on the front. She held it away from her, then sank her face in it and soaked the fabric with her tears. She wondered if the ache would ever settle, if the memories would ever stop ambushing her. Careful to protect Mac from her sadness, she was glad he didn't seem to miss Lottie with the same acute anguish.

'Love!' he called, and she knew that tone of voice.

'What?' Marie flew downstairs as speedily as her slippers would allow. 'Tell me! What?'

'Read that.' White-lipped, Mac turned his laptop so she could see the screen. He put a hand to his chest. It was tightening, hot.

She squinted at the computer, then reared back. 'Jaysus,'

she said, then read it aloud. 'You are invited to Edward Vole's ninetieth birthday celebration.' She turned to Mac, ready to be sardonic, but was instead alarmed. 'Mac? Boyo? What is it?'

He felt something land on his chest. An anvil. A wardrobe. Mac staggered, and saw tiny white stars before he saw nothing at all.

CHAPTER SIXTEEN

They both stare at the photograph marked '29 July 2011'.

'Oh no. Please no,' she says eventually.

'The lady's never on her own,' he says. They glance at each other, rattled. 'This is just her and the cat.'

'Why?' She puts her hand to her mouth. 'Where is he?'

He goes to turn the page, check out the next photograph. She taps his hand, dainty but determined. 'No. Don't.'

'Just this once,' he says. 'Just to reassure ourselves.'

'We'll stick to the routine,' she says. 'One snap at a time.'

'Okay.' He always gives in.

They discuss the lady's smile. They don't like it. It's forced, they agree.

29 July 2011

Traditions must be upheld.

The anniversary photograph must be taken. *I'm not alone*, thought Marie. She was brave; it was second nature. Which is not to say that it was easy. *I have Toulouse.* Marie wielded the new selfie-stick, tried to contain the yowling cat, and smiled. After a fashion.

Next Door was at the hedge. 'Left you, has he?'

She was saved from answering by the squeal of bicycle brakes.

'Em! Ollie!' Marie let Toulouse go and threw out her arms.

'We were passing,' said her daughter.

'Pull the other one, girlie.' *They won't let me spend this day on my own.* She looked up at the clouds, and wondered if Mac was looking down on her. She decided he was.

Mac was not looking down on Marie.

The flight path from Heathrow to Calgary did not take in Sunnyside. As Marie sent him the anniversary snap, he was high over Wales, accepting a dolls' house bottle of wine from an attendant.

Mac had not travelled solo since his marriage. He was clumsy with his safety belt and had gone the wrong way in the airport, despite the clear signage. *Marie always knows what to do*, he thought, before immediately contradicting himself.

The day he collapsed to the kitchen floor, she had come

undone. Screaming over him, the screeches landing on his ears as if he were trapped down a deep well. One moment Mac had been standing, reading the birthday invitation; the next he was flat on the tiles.

Marie had fallen apart; she had fallen apart even more when he shook his head and sat up. She wound around him like a koala, repeating 'Thank God, thank God', until he could stand.

'No doctors,' he insisted, when she gathered her senses. 'No fuss. It was shock, that's all.'

She had stroked his face then. 'Trouble with you, my lovely boyo, is you feel too deeply.'

He touched his cheek where her fingers had caressed him, and opened his laptop, to seek out, once again, the email sent with the invitation.

'Hi, I hope you don't mind my getting in touch, but I believe we are related. My name is Glen Vole, and I am Ed Vole's youngest son.'

On its umpteenth reading, the declaration still had the power to move Mac. *In other words, he's my half-brother.*

Glen's sensitivity shone through the short, careful message. He wanted to 'bring Dad's life full-circle while there's still time. The family only learned of you and your late mother when our mom passed, three years ago this spring. Dad has always felt terrible about what happened, and his 90th celebrations feel like the perfect moment to reunite you both.'

Another thought always intruded at that point: *You can't reunite people who have never met.* Mac carried on reading, aware that the man in the adjoining seat was half-turned towards him, like a dog begging a treat.

'Dad's marbles are intact – to say the least! – and he's fit and healthy, despite suffering with heart problems, as do I.'

Mac felt his fellow passenger's eyes on him. He panicked. *Do I speak to him? Do I ignore him?*

He made a fatal mistake. He offered the man a handshake and his name and that was that, for the next nine hours. By the time Mac made his connecting flight he could have aced *Mastermind* on the subject of his fellow passenger's life.

Emma turned up her nose at the contents of Marie's fridge. 'Seriously, Mum, would it kill you to have a spirulina smoothie now and then?'

'Would it kill you not to wear Lycra now and then?' Marie would not be bullied; she clung to her chocolate milk and her stash of Choco Leibniz. 'You can't be en route to the gym *all* the time.'

'It's called active wear. It's not just for exercise,' said Abbo, in hoodie and leggings like his parents. He shared a secret look with his grandmother, one that poked gentle fun at Emma's tyrannical wholesomeness. 'Any news from Lottie, Grammy?'

'She's doing great, pet.' Marie had no idea how Lottie was doing. The lack of communication was like a thorn in her underwear; it never stopped smarting. She hurried on before Abbo could ask his standard, eager question – 'When's she coming to see us?' – and said, 'I bet your poor grandfather's chatting to some eejit right now. I usually protect him from the mile-high bores.'

Ollie said, 'You know what they have in Canada, Marie? Puffins!'

'Dad'll see one at last!' said Emma.

''Fraid not,' said Marie. 'Ed Vole lives somewhere called Edmonton, and the puffins live in Labrador. Mac had visions of hiring a car and driving there, but it's three and a half thousand miles away.'

'Bloody hell. Canada's *big*,' said Ollie. 'I can't believe old Mac actually caught that plane. I half-expected him to cancel at the last minute.'

They all knew that Marie had 'the divil of a job' convincing Mac to accept Glen's olive branch. She said, 'I knew his father's desertion affected him, but the depth of it only really came out when we discussed going to Canada.'

'He's angry with Ed,' said Emma.

'And he doesn't *want* to be angry with Ed,' said Ollie. 'He just wants to love his dad without complication.'

'You've hit the nail on the head.' Marie patted her son-in-law's meaty shoulder. 'We sat and talked and *talked*. We brought old Ed to life between us, right here, at this table.' She tapped the chipped wood. 'It brought Ed out of the shadows, you know? We built him into a real person, not some panto villain. There's more to Ed than just being the rotter who ran away.'

'Maybe Ed had PTS.' Abbo was proud to add something to the conversation. At ten, he was precocious; he had the only-child habit of voracious reading. 'Soldiers get it, and they keep imagining they're being shot at, and stuff.'

'Maybe,' said Emma. 'I'm not making excuses for the guy, but Ed was displaced by war, and trapped far from home in an exploding world. He was weak, yeah, definitely, but perhaps he didn't mean to be cruel.'

'I told Mac he holds his father to very high standards, and that's not fair. Parents are people too. He went off willing to hear Ed's side of the story. That's all the old fella can expect.'

She was glossing over the hours they wrangled.

Marie had argued there were many reasons to say yes: 'Not least because retirement's boring you.'

'I don't have time to be bored,' he'd laughed. 'You keep me busy.' There was always a picture that needed hanging, a box that needed fetching from the loft.

She'd brought out the big guns then. 'The real reason, the *only* reason to go to Canada, is the fact that not having a father has dogged you all your life. It got even worse when you realized he's alive. If Ed wants to make up for bolting, why not let him try? Yes, it means the cruise is scuppered again, and yes the trip will clash with our anniversary, but the man's ninety – there's an eleventh-hour feel to this. What if you regret saying no?'

That had clinched it.

Ollie wanted to know, 'Will Mac call him Dad?'

'He's never called anyone that,' said Marie. She reached out and tugged at the hairband in Abbo's hair. A wayward afro, his hair was a supernova around his lean, clever little face.

'Don't say it, Mum.' Emma was wry. 'Boys can wear hairbands if they want to.' She took out her phone, aimed it. 'Abbo, this light is fabulous, look at me.'

'Stop, Mum.' Abbo put his hands to his face. 'I don't want to be on your stupid website.'

'That stupid website pays for your trips to Disneyworld, matey,' said Ollie.

'Yeah,' said Abbo, offering a surly glimpse of the teen he would one day become, 'and when we get there, we have to take *more* stupid photographs for the stupid website.'

'Hey, manners, please.' Emma seemed taken aback by his outright rebellion.

'He's tired,' said Marie, also surprised. It wasn't like Abbo to cheek his mum.

As the Joneses filed out, back onto their inevitable mountain bikes, Emma asked what Tatty made of Dad's decision to meet his father.

'Who can say? You know how she is; your dad craved a thumbs up but she was non-committal.'

'Can I visit my new great-granddad in Canada?' asked Abbo, swinging one leg over his steed.

'Give your old grandmother a kiss first!' Marie grabbed him before he could complain.

Canada was fresh, clean, welcoming. Different but not different. Like the United Kingdom in a good mood.

Mac showered, shaved, snoozed in his hotel room, and was woken by a call from the front desk.

Glen Vole sat waiting in reception, jumping up when Mac stepped out of the lift.

Big, bluff, in pristine pastels, Glen's face was pink and earnest. They shook hands, both of them energetic and awkward. As they walked to the parking lot, Mac searched Glen's features for a similarity to his own, but found none.

The wide car bowled along wide avenues, as Glen filled in the family tree.

I have a half-sister, too. This new cast would take some getting used to.

'You'll love her!' Glen extolled his sister's sense of humour. He was as nervous as Mac, clearly desperate for this trip to be a success. 'You're the best birthday present Dad could wish for.'

'Maybe,' said Mac, 'I should jump out of the cake,' and Glen endeared himself even more to him by laughing extravagantly at the feeble joke.

'Home sweet home.' The car braked by a large, modern house. An architectural tour de force, its plate-glass front juxtaposed a wall of flintstone boulders.

'Blimey,' said Mac. Sunnyside would fit into the porch. He had assumed the Voles were workaday people, like himself and Marie.

'Before we go into the party ...' Glen turned to Mac, the leather upholstery squeaking beneath his bulk. 'I should warn you ...' His pink face was clouded. 'Kinda, well, not everyone's stoked about you being here.'

'Look, I don't want to cause any trouble.' Keenly aware of his outsider status, Mac had decided to speak when spoken to, keep his head down. Naturally modest, he had the added feeling of attending a concert without the proper ticket; *I'm an interloper, the outsider.* Marie had scoffed, insisting, 'These people are your blood,' but now Mac could see that 'these people' lived in stupendous houses and were not entirely welcoming.

'It'll be fine, honestly.' Glen seemed contrite, sorry he'd brought it up. 'I'm a fusspot, Ian. It'll be okay, it's just . . .'

Spit it out!

'My sister, Meredith . . . she's somewhat . . .' Glen didn't seem able to describe her. 'She's a bit wary. But me? I'm just pleased I found you, Ian, and that you were brave enough to come over. We're family, you know? This is the right thing to do. Your situation has weighed on Pop all these years and now he can redeem himself.' He slapped the steering wheel. 'C'mon! It's gonna be great!'

It was a catered affair.

Mac felt underdressed, and worried there was shaving cream on his neck – *I need Marie to make sure I'm presentable!* – as a bow-tied waiter handed him a glass of champagne.

Knots of guests parted for them, as Glen led Mac through the partygoers. They were older folk, on the whole, dressed with quiet taste, and as he passed he heard them say, 'That's *him*!' or 'It's the son from London!'

Rooms opened out, one after the other, each a luxurious

space hung with modern art. Mac was disoriented, as if heading deeper into a labyrinth, and had the crazy desire to leave a trail of breadcrumbs.

So I can get out again.

At the centre of the maze, he would finally find his father. The profundity of Mac's quest was out of kilter with the tinkling jazz.

Glen pushed a heavy door into a study. A tall woman stood with a glass in her hand, but the epicentre of the room was the elderly gentleman in a plush armchair.

'Pop!' Glen was proud, nervous. 'This is Ian.'

'Please, don't get up,' said Mac, as the elderly gentleman pushed down on the arms of his chair. *He's so small*, he thought. *And fragile as a dry leaf.*

Dapper at ninety, Ed Vole insisted on standing. He was a trifle bent over in his smart trousers and braces. 'Welcome, son,' he said.

The unexpected title – *Son!* – meant Mac took a moment before grasping the gnarled hand offered to him. The handshake lasted. And lasted.

Mac's initial impression of fragility was confounded. *He's strong*, he thought, feeling something wild and strange happen between him and Ed. The rushing in his ears only faded when Ed relinquished him, and the hovering woman fussily settled the old man back in his seat.

She came into focus for Mac.

Meredith was a long-nosed woman whose face made no secret of her disapproval, and although Mac said, 'Pleased to meet you, what a beautiful name,' he would soon come to feel differently.

'It was my mother's name,' she said, as if Mac had committed some crime with the compliment.

'Lovely house you have here . . .' Mac tailed off, realizing he had not rehearsed how to address Ed. Dad? Too intimate. Father? Weirdly formal. But calling him by his first name disrespected their blood tie.

'Thank you, son,' said Ed, with no such qualms. He appraised Mac, enjoying him, as his hands rested, bent, in his lap.

'It *is* a lovely house,' said Meredith. 'I'll save you the trouble of looking up its value. This place, our family home, is worth just over a million dollars.' She waggled her head. Her make-up was pearly and her hair was lacquered; she was a female Glen, but with none of his agreeability. 'Want to jot that down?'

Mac kept smiling. He had brought no dagger to this fight.

'Show my boy round, Glen,' said Ed. 'Then bring him right back to me.'

'Pop likes you,' said Glen, sotto voce, as they dived back into the guests, all of them trying not to stare at the prodigal son.

His mind fluttering like a torn flag, Mac barely took in the garden room, the cavernous kitchen, the endless nooks.

He scanned for clues; what did Ed read? What food was in Ed's fridge? Did Ed have a green thumb, too? The garden was pleasant without being memorable. No magnolia. No white-painted rocks. A pang of longing for home shot through Mac, and he had to remind himself that this, too, was home now.

I am in my father's house, he thought, and had to hold on to the banister for a second.

The last of the guests gone, the family were left behind.

This included Mac.

'My wife was a great one for parties,' said Ed, from his armchair. His grown children stood one either side of him, arranged as if for a portrait. Mac stood opposite. Still outside the charmed inner circle. 'I don't really care for big events.'

'Nor me!' Mac reminded himself to tone down the delight each time he found the smallest affinity between himself and Ed. 'My wife throws a party at the drop of a hat.'

'Marion, isn't it?' Ed took the correction. 'Sorry. Marie, of course.' He had a good head of hair; it was dyed, Mac noticed. Father and son were unalike in vanity.

'Here.' Mac rummaged in his wallet. 'Pics of your grand-children, um, Ed.'

'None of that. Call me Pop. That's what this crew call me.'

Glen beamed, gave Mac an encouraging nod. Meredith – who had overindulged on the eggnogs – shuffled nearer to Ed.

'This is Dan. That's Emma.' Mac handed over the photo-graphs. 'And then there's the next generation.' The treasured snaps of Abbo and Lottie were put in Ed's lap.

'Lovely, lovely, great kids.'

Perhaps, thought Mac, *his eyesight's weak and that's why he barely looked at the photographs.*

'These jokers,' said Ed, gesturing at his middle-aged posse, 'haven't stumped up one grandchild between them. Can't hold down a marriage.' He poked Glen, who flushed an even deeper pink. 'When're you gonna grow a pair, eh?' Ed laughed the whole while, his veneered teeth large in his shrunken face. Perhaps he saw Mac's discomfort. 'Oh now, Ian, you mustn't mind my teasing. We're all family here. What's family if we can't tickle each other now and again?'

'My Marie,' said Mac, 'is big on teasing.'

'Yeah, whatever,' said Meredith, with teen rudeness shocking from a forty-something. 'When do you go back?'

'He's only just arrived!' squeaked Glen.

'I'm here for a week,' said Mac. He had worked out how to handle Meredith. He reacted to each sour comment as if it were a pleasantry. Her enmity was understandable; as living proof of their father's infidelity, he made her uncomfortable. Mac hoped to win Meredith over by being as non-threatening as possible.

'A whole week?' she snorted.

'Check out of that damn hotel,' said Ed. 'We have plenty of room, and I want my boy near.'

Don't cry again! Mac was worse than a toddler on his first playdate. Each confirmation of his position in this family – of his right to be a Vole – went straight to his tear ducts.

*

In a hushed voice, Mac described the spare room to Marie. 'More of a suite. Did I say there's a housekeeper? She asked me for my *breakfast preferences*!'

Marie's afternoon was Mac's early morning; she found that perplexing. 'What's Ed like?'

It wasn't easy to describe the big character in the small frame. 'He's nobody's fool. A proper, no-nonsense, old-style head of the household. The main thing, the *amazing* thing, is Pop really wants to usher me into the family, to atone for leaving me and my mother.'

It's 'Pop', is it? Marie felt a stirring. A vague disquiet. *He's always wanted a strong male role model.* Now he had one, and it occurred to Marie that Mac might not have his wits about him, that he might not use the intuition he'd fine-tuned through his years in the probation service. 'The bed's awful empty without you, boyo.'

'Drag Toulouse in there with you.'

'Oh, love, I wasn't going to say, but Toulouse has gone to heaven.'

Mac slumped. The price of loving pets was high; they didn't last as long as humans. 'How?'

'He died the way he lived. Being a complete sod. He was stalking a little sparrow with a broken wing when he keeled over.' Marie sniffled. 'Don't know what I'll do without him, getting in me way.'

'I miss you,' said Mac.

'I know,' said Marie. 'And I miss you. Ooh! Guess what!' she squeaked, cheery again. 'I saw our Lottie!'

'She's *there?*'

'Well, no, I saw her in *Hello!* magazine. A guest at some famous singer's wedding, just in the background, with SJ and that Damien. She was wearing lipstick.'

'She's too young for lipstick.'

'She's thirteen, love. Growing up.'

'They all do that, the cheeky monsters,' laughed Mac. 'What's that noise? Sounds like hammering.'

'Just the decorator.'

'Eh?'

'God, I knew you'd be like this.'

'Like what? I literally said "eh"!'

'I'm having the sitting room de-minimalized. I can't stand good taste, Mac. That oatmeal carpet's already up.'

'The new carpet's orange, isn't it?'

'A bit,' said Marie. 'I've ordered a lovely rug.'

Mac knew the rug would not be lovely.

When the call ended, the hush of the Vole house roared in his ears. The friendly chaos of Sunnyside seemed – indeed *was* – very far away. The smell of baking. The loud castigation of the cat. *Rest in peace, Toulouse*, thought Mac.

He tried to use the trouser press. He ruined his trousers.

There were outings, dinners, drives to see the sights.

Ed always sat at the head of the table. He always sat in the front seat of the car. Schedules ran to suit him; his children were careful not to tire him out.

The great solicitude impressed Mac; he shared some DNA

with these people, and it was good to discover that they were kind to Ed.

Not to me, however. It quickly became clear that Glen – decent, keen-to-help Glen – had projected his attitude onto Meredith. He could only imagine the arguments sparked by Glen's campaign to usher Mac into the fold.

If left alone with Mac, Ed would say, 'She'll come around, she'll come around.' He drawled, and liked to lift his chin to drink Mac in. 'She's jealous. You know that, son.'

'That's silly,' Mac would say.

'Is it?' Ed liked to withdraw after a rhetorical question. He came and went, literally and metaphorically. Mac tried to grasp him, but he was vaporous; *I wonder if Mum felt the same.*

He understood why she fell for him. He was charismatic, yet throwaway. Despite the doddering walk, the use of a stick, he was perpetually one step ahead. Each pat on Mac's back, each uttered 'son' made Mac feel more and more accepted. *This is who I should've been all along,* he thought. *This man's son.*

Glen lapped it all up, urging on their growing rapport.

And Meredith? She nursed an abnormal interest in Mac's financial affairs. In the interim between one four-course dinner and a ride on the High-Level Bridge Streetcar, she researched what a PSO earned. She was a mutterer; she muttered how Mac 'fell on his feet' when he discovered Ed was his father. She muttered that 'a million divided by three is a lot less than a million divided by two'. There was more, about how 'some people just turn up for a piece of the pie', and Mac pretended not to hear any of it.

'Sit here, beside me,' Ed said, every time.

Gingerly, Mac would take the honoured place. He moved with caution, mimicking his half-siblings, and the staff. It was a house where people moved on soft soles. The politeness Mac saw as a national characteristic was exaggerated around Ed; his children were Sunday-school reserved with him.

'I see a lot of myself in you, Ian,' Ed said one evening as the clan gathered on the back stoop.

'Really?' Mac choked on his iced tea at this eulogy. He had longed to be *like* someone all his life. Instead he had been singular, a sore thumb sticking out. *Not any longer.*

'Oh come *on*, Pop,' said Meredith. 'That's laying it on a bit thick.'

'Whereas Meredith,' said Ed, still regarding Mac, 'is nothing like her old pa. I never stuck my nose in the trough the way she does. I worked for what I have.'

Mac blinked at the disrespect – for his daughter! – but Ed carried on.

'My Meredith just loves to count my money. Doesn't she, Glen?'

'Oh, Pop, now, I wouldn't . . .'

'If we could find a goose,' said Ed, ''ole Glen here wouldn't say boo to it.' He darted forward and shouted, 'Boo!' in Glen's face.

Meredith tittered. Glen tried to do so. Mac didn't find it funny.

'But you, Ian,' Ed went on. 'You're cut from the same cloth as me.'

'I see something of you in Dan,' said Mac.

'Dan?' Ed shrugged. 'Oh, yes, your son. He's the decorator, yes?'

'No, that's my son-in-law.'

When he was alone with Glen, Mac would agree that, yes, Ed's hearing was deteriorating, although they both knew he was sharp as a tack, and simply didn't listen.

'Dan Mactavish,' said Ed wonderingly. 'Now, why isn't he Dan Vole? Why aren't *you* a Vole?'

'It was my mother's decision,' said Mac.

'Huh,' said Meredith, making Mac curl his fingers. He had assumed that even Meredith would leave his mother out of it.

'That was Marguerite's prerogative,' said Ed, and like so much of what he said it sounded like a decree. 'If this youngster, Don – sorry, Dan – expects to be remembered in my will, then maybe he can do me the honour of taking my name.'

Meredith looked as if she wanted to pull out a gun.

A laugh was forced out of Mac. 'Dan has no expectations at all!'

'Then maybe I'll surprise him,' said Ed, head on one side, staring indulgently at Mac. 'There are others who have high expectations of a legacy, believe me. I just hope none of you inherited my heart troubles.'

'Not me,' said Mac.

His phone dinged. It was a photograph. Marie, sprawled alluringly on a brown and orange carpet.

'Who's that?' said Ed. 'Marion?'

A farewell feast was planned in Mac's honour. He smelled the cook's wizardry as he packed. Keen to get home, he was also sad to leave.

It would be impossible to explain to someone who had always fitted in. Mac was glad that his own children couldn't fully grasp the significance of his rollercoaster trip. *They don't know what I've been through – the loneliness, the search for a stable identity.* Mac had done his job; he had been a heedful parent. *Now it's time to let Ed father me.*

A knock on the door, and before Mac could call, 'Just a minute,' Meredith strode in and found him in his boxer shorts.

'Oops!' said Mac, trying to alleviate her embarrassment.

Meredith was not embarrassed. She leaned back against the door as he scrambled into his trousers. 'I want a word before you leave,' she said. 'I've been, well, hey, let's be honest, I've been a bitch, Ian.'

'No, no,' said Mac, turning away to button his fly. 'It's not easy.'

'Glen was so full of you when he found you online.'

Meredith toured the bedroom, picking things up, putting them down. She was tall, overbearing and, despite his gratitude at this last-minute rapprochement, Mac felt invaded.

'He told us you were a great guy,' she said. 'But Glen . . .

he thinks *everyone's* great, so I had to see for myself. Because Pop's a wealthy man. It doesn't bring out the best in folk.'

She could be talking about herself. Mac began to say she didn't need to worry, that he wanted a family not a cheque, but Meredith was broadcasting, not receiving.

'Like the women,' she said, and her eyes, so like Ed's, glittered. 'Gold-diggers, every one of them. Oh, I'm not saying your mother was in it for the dollars. I'm just saying she wasn't the only gal on the side. There were many over the years. Mom pretended not to know.'

'Christ,' said Mac.

'And who knows how many other little Ians are out there? How many other Vole bastards?' Meredith's tour took her back to the door. She opened it, paused. 'So when Glen seemed to feel that you, for some reason, mattered, I couldn't agree. See you downstairs for a martini.' She smiled. '*Bro.*'

It was as the gravy was handed around that Mac realized something.

I've stopped searching for similarities. He could see nothing of Ed in himself, and didn't want to. He could, unfortunately, see a resemblance between himself and Meredith, but that was purely physical; Mac had none of that woman's bitterness.

Odd that she should grow up in her father's house and feel bitter, but I was abandoned and I feel none! Then the second realization landed, and with such a bang that Mac almost dropped the gravy boat.

My little family is the sort of family I grew up envying.

'Shame you don't live in Canada,' said Ed. As ever, he ate little, dabbing his mouth with his napkin, watching his children with a canny eye. 'After all, you're my eldest.'

Meredith dropped her fork.

'Something special about the firstborn,' mused Ed.

'I don't differentiate between my two,' said Mac. 'Something special about all babies.' He said it lightly, and felt the frisson of shock at the table as Ed was contradicted.

'I do wish you'd take my name, Ian.'

This was a subject Ed returned to regularly. It always made Mac uncomfortable, but tonight he felt a twinge of irritation.

Ever fearful of conflict, Glen slapped Mac on the back. 'Old Ian's one of us no matter what his surname, eh, Pop?'

'Eh, Pop.' Meredith impersonated her brother, with no fondness.

He sets them against one another, thought Mac. An observation Marie would have made in the first five minutes.

'Now that you're in my will, perhaps you'll reconsider?'

Meredith pushed her chair back from the table. 'Congrats, Ian,' she said, standing up. 'You sure got what you came for.'

'She'll be back,' said Ed, as they watched Meredith bang out through the doors to the garden. 'Ian Vole. I like how it sounds.'

'Let's not talk about wills on my last night,' said Mac, still light, still cheery.

'What we talk about at my table', said Ed, 'is up to me.'

Mac wondered for a moment how that would go down

at Sunnyside if he tried it. *Not well*, he decided, with relief. 'You've made me so welcome,' he began, in an effort to turn the tide. 'I don't—'

'That's because I want to make amends.' Ed's eyes flickered, lizard-like, to where Meredith lurked, eavesdropping. 'I've changed my will, Ian. One third of my entire estate will go to you.'

'Why, Dad?' shrieked Meredith, barging back in. 'He's nothing to you!'

Glen stood. 'Jesus, Meredith, have some respect!'

Ed ignored her, carried on talking to Mac. 'You're a Vole, Ian. That's all I ask of you in return for, well, Meredith can tell you to a cent how much you'll get.' Mac's frozen face seemed to puzzle him. 'Let me do this, son. I feel bad about what happened to you.'

Mac folded his napkin. It was embroidered with a scarlet 'V'. 'It didn't *happen* to me,' he said. 'You did it to me.'

Glen said, 'Please, Ian, that's our father you're talking to.'

'He's not *my* father.' Mac spoke as if someone else pulled his levers and made the words come out. He was fluent, honest. 'I'm grateful to know you, Glen, and I appreciate your kindness in getting in touch. This visit could've been about love and respect and second chances. We could get to know one another. But that's not why Ed brought me here.' He turned to the top of the table. 'I'm a pawn in a family game of chess. You pit me against your son and daughter. Glen's too good-natured to play along, but poor Meredith falls for it every time.'

'Damn cheek,' said Meredith.

'Be quiet, girl.' Ed banged the table with that strong, crooked fist. 'If I'm not your father, how come I'm leaving you a fortune?'

'What I really want from you is something you can't give me.'

'Fine words!' Ed sat back. 'So you won't mind if I cut you off?'

'You're right; I won't mind a bit.' Mac stood up. 'Now, if you'll excuse me, I have to get home. To my family.'

CHAPTER SEVENTEEN

The album has to wait; she has news; a terrible scandal has erupted in the care home.

His heart sinks. After all the vetting and the heart-searching . . . 'Tell me.' He is grim.

'Well, lady muck, you-know-who . . .'

'Is this a story about your red-haired nemesis?' He almost melts with relief.

She nods. Lowers her voice. 'She rigged the bingo!'

'Never!' He gives her the reaction she craves. 'Disgraceful! Appalling!'

'Isn't it just? She rigged the whole thing and waltzed off with the top prize.' She pauses for effect. 'A brand-new hot-water bottle.'

'She should be jailed for life.'

She laughs, delighted with the hyperbole, and flicks through the album. 'I think we're up to 2017.'

'Before we look at the photo . . .'

'Yes. What?'

'Let's take a moment, just to talk. We do need to talk. There's something I haven't told you and soon we'll have to—'

As if he hasn't spoken, she finds the right page. 'Ooh, a big gang. I love it when they're all together. And a skinny grey doggie, too.' She turns the album on its side, checking their progress through the pages. 'We're almost at the end.'

A question occurs to them both.

What will they talk about when they finish the album?

29 July 2017

Battersea Dogs Home had changed.

More like a hotel these days, thought Mac, as he walked out of the gates with his new little friend. Shelley, the elegant, tippy-toed, silver-grey lurcher was on her way to a new life of soft beds and incessant compliments at Sunnyside.

'Brace yourself, girl, we've a full house today,' he told Shelley as she hopped daintily into the passenger seat. 'You're Marie's anniversary surprise.'

He chatted to the dog as they crawled home in heavy traffic, apologizing that he had been instructed never to let her off the lead. 'Feels like clipping your wings, but apparently you'd just run and run.'

Meeting Ed six years ago had emancipated Mac.

The weight of wondering was taken from his shoulders; *I know exactly what manner of man my father is*. Ninety-six now, Ed had not been in touch, and Mac was glad. Perhaps Ed would live forever; Marie half-seriously floated the notion he was a vampire. Whatever life was left to the old man was nothing to do with Mac.

It was liberating. But it was also deeply sad. Like so much of life.

'Be honest, Dad.' Emma cornered her father as the rest of the family welcomed the dog. 'How's it *really* going, having Dan home again?' She pointed at his nose. 'Your nostrils are flaring! You're about to lie!'

'I love having Dan to stay.' Mac's nostrils threatened to engulf his face. 'Look, put it this way, I *want* to love having Dan to stay. What's that saying? Home is the place where, when you have to go there, they have to take you in? Well, Dan ran out of options in America and I'm only too glad to help him out, set him on his feet again.'

In hot pursuit of Shelley, Abbo zipped past, a free-wheeling mix of maturity and childishness. The youngest Mactavish turning sixteen was a family milestone. Abbo could marry, give blood, drive a small tractor; the boy had googled it. Wonderful and disconcerting; Mac saw the slight retreat from the elders of the tribe, the tendency towards secrecy. *My grandson is becoming himself, creating another Abbo, who belongs to the world, apart from us*. It was natural. Desirable. But it stung.

The Joneses' move from cramped terrace to echoing barn conversion had coincided with these changes in Abbo. New mates were made, but none of them were introduced to Emma and Ollie. He was gnomic about where he went – 'Here and there,' apparently – and who exactly he'd been 'here and there' with. Mac was relaxed about such typical behaviour, as was Ollie, but Emma quivered with the need to know.

'You're meddling,' Ollie would castigate.

'I'm taking care,' she would respond.

The other junior Mactavish was often on Mac's mind. Extraordinary that their little Lottie was now nineteen. He had only two hopes for her – that she was happy, and that she might get in touch.

And so the family wagon rolled on.

The table was properly laid for the anniversary meal: 'napkins and everything,' as Marie put it.

'All right, Gwyneth?' Dan greeted his sister as he took his seat, in crumpled sweats, with stubble dotting his jaw.

'Ha bloody ha.' Emma would welcome the comparison to Ms Paltrow from anyone else. 'You're just jealous 'cos I live thoughtfully and eat clean, Dan. You should try it.'

'I meditated all morning.' Dan threw out his hands. 'And look. I'm still in the shit.'

'Hey!' said Mac, nodding at Abbo.

'I hear worse at school, Gramps,' said Abbo. 'Anyway, meditation *is* shit.'

'Ab-*bo*,' said Marie from the stove with a hint of menace.

'Don't be cursing and don't be mocking your mum's way of life. She's the perfect advertisement for healthy living.'

It was true. Emma was lithe and well and her face shone. How she managed this without the consolation of profiteroles was a mystery to her mother. Emma threw a bread roll at her brother. 'Can't say the same for you, Dan. Are you allergic to showers?'

'Shut up,' said Dan. They reprised their childhood dynamic at Sunnyside. It could be cute. It could give Mac a headache.

'Jesus, Dan, you're such a cliché,' said Emma. 'A mid-life crisis? Couldn't you be a bit more original?'

Mac said, 'I never had time for a mid-life crisis.'

Marie, trotting upstairs to redo her lippy, said on her way out, 'Too late now, boyo. Unless you live to be a hundred and forty-four.'

'It's your Uncle Dan's favourite for dinner tonight,' Mac told Abbo, who looked up from his phone for two, possibly three, seconds. 'Irish stew.'

'My favourite,' said Dan, 'is the albacore tataki salad at Kiriko in LA. Bit beyond Mum's skills.'

'Mum thinks your favourite is stew, so let's not burst her bubble, okay?' Mac couldn't help sounding peeved. He knew his son needed gentleness to recover. The tearful long-distance phone call – 'Dad, I've screwed up big-time' – had come out of the blue, and yet wasn't unexpected.

The boy was burnt out. *Can a man in his forties be called a boy?* Dan was disillusioned. Apathetic. He was in touch with nobody from his old life. The girl of the moment had vapourised. 'A month, tops' in the spare room was now six months and counting. Marie told anyone who asked that Dan kept himself to himself; she didn't share how demanding and disruptive he could be.

They shushed Emma when she periodically huffed, 'Just chuck him out! He can cope!' She didn't know about Dan's debts, only just covered by the use of the cruise nest egg. 'Peru to Panama' shimmered, once again, just out of reach.

Mac slapped his lap. Stood to let Shelley out into the garden, enjoying having a dog around once more. 'Good girl,' he said, his knees cracking: his seventy-second year was one of novel noises from his joints.

Dan joined him on the grass. He spoke low, his voice dead and flat, a contrast to Emma and Ollie joking indoors at the table. 'Listen, sorry about that crack about Mum's stew. I know I disappoint you.'

'Don't talk daft.' *I thought I hid it better than that.* 'You're the golden boy, Dan. You'll soon be back on your feet.'

'Whatever that means.' Dan lit a cigarette. Blew a smoke ring. 'I don't know what I want, that's the trouble. Always has been.'

'Hey, look at me.' Mac had to repeat it before Dan turned to face him. 'You're fine the way you are, son. There's nothing to prove. Not to me, not to Mum, not to anyone.'

'Jesus, Dad, you're so positive, so full of advice, and you really think it helps, don't you? If anything, you make matters worse.'

If Dan was a client, Mac would have simply absorbed the rudeness. But Dan was his son and Mac had gone to the wire for him more than once, so he said, in a most un-Mac tone, 'Cheers for that,' and went inside.

'Sit! Sit!' Marie was back and flapping her hands. She put the stew – two pots, one tofu and one beef – in the centre of the table with reverence. 'Save something for Viennetta!' She winked at Emma. 'And a slice of mango!'

The stew was good – one of Marie's best – and the family banter chugged along the usual paths. Dan called Emma 'the patron saint of detoxing'. Marie tried to brush Emma's hair. Emma took the hairbrush and spanked Ollie with it. Abbo stole the last spoonful of stew. They all slipped Shelley titbits under the table, sparking a lifetime of bad doggy habits.

A bowl of Viennetta was despatched to Next Door. Abbo was grumpy about being the messenger. 'But he smells.'

Marie tutted and propelled her grandson out of the door. 'How's Abbo doing at the new school?' she stage-whispered when he left. 'Still hanging out with a bad crowd?'

'There you go again,' said Mac. 'Leaping to conclusions.'

'It's the only exercise I get,' said Marie.

'They wear *hoodies*,' said Emma.

Ollie shook his head. 'You say that like they carry machine guns.'

Dan asked if Emma still 'made' Abbo keep his 'one-line-a-day diary thing,' and rolled his eyes when she said, yes, she did. 'You need to ease off, Em. He's a teenaged boy. He doesn't want to be *in touch with his feelings*.' Dan found the phrase disagreeable. 'I certainly didn't.'

'And look how that turned out.' Emma was always sharp when attacked.

'Hey now,' said Mac.

'If only I could get my hands on that diary,' muttered Emma. 'It might shed some light.'

Ollie looked at her as if he'd never met her before. 'Promise me you won't read his diary. I'm serious.'

Emma squirmed. She and Ollie only ever presented a united front at the Mactavish table. 'I only—' she began.

'No, it's not right.' Ollie looked away, as if dismissing her, and the conversation was done.

'And give the poor kid a day off from being *perfect*,' said Dan. 'I looked at your website and he's all over it.'

'It's cool, though,' protested Emma.

'Jesus, when do parents and kids ever agree about what's cool?' said Dan.

Marie screwed up her face. 'Is it even cool to say cool?'

They all laughed, glad of her attempt to draw a line beneath the quarrelling. Abbo returned, with a tale of Next Door's staggering rudeness; the day was back on track.

But all the while Dan said nothing to Mac, and Mac said nothing to Dan.

Have I let him down? The question whirred in Mac's mind like a pebble in a tumble dryer. What if his fathering contributed to Dan's waywardness?

Life's big questions could strike at any time. This was an anniversary like all their others, but family life had reached a hinge, a moment when things could change. *Is Abbo going off the rails?* thought Mac. Then, with real trepidation, *Does Dan love me?*

The wild ride of Dan's life had been a mindless trolley dash; *If he'd enjoyed the hedonism, that, at least, would be something.* But no. Riddled with insecurities, Dan had forgotten to grow up.

There was much to do if Dan was to make something of himself, to 'find himself', as Emma's blog would no doubt put it. *But apparently I can't help with that*, thought Mac miserably. *I make matters worse.*

Summer flared and faded. Autumn was bright, crystalline.

Dan was 'up to something': that's how Marie put it. 'Mark my words, my boy's *back.*'

Mac kept his thoughts to himself.

'I'm moving out,' said Dan, one morning.

'Oh. Rightiho.' Mac kept reaction to a minimum; he had learned to edit himself around his son.

'Got yourself a little flat somewhere local, love?' asked Marie, already wistful that she wouldn't be washing his smalls.

'Nah. A farmhouse in Cornwall.'

Sounds expensive, was Mac's first thought.

'You're a townie through and through!' Marie flicked him with a tea towel. 'You take taxis. You go to clubs.'

'I used to, Mum.'

Only 'cos you can't afford it anymore, thought Mac. *Cocaine doesn't come cheap.* He had discovered a lot about Dan's former lifestyle when paying his debts.

'I'm leasing a cottage for next to nothing.' Dan produced estate agent particulars of a hovel in the middle of nowhere. 'A few coats of whitewash and it'll look like a stylist's dream. I've got backing for my venture, the packaging's designed, I have outlets interested.' He was the old Dan, hurtling at a hundred miles an hour.

'What venture is this?' Marie was concerned.

'I'm going to make cheese,' said Dan.

'Cheese?' Emma laughed herself inside out.

'I love cheese.' Bernie was still Dan's greatest defender. 'And so does my current husband.' She could speak about him that way because she patently adored Angus. Confident of his love, Bernie had made peace with her body. Striking, queenly, she linked arms with her sister and her niece as they strolled by the river. She had taken to Henley-on-Thames like a duck to water; Angus's friends were enthralled by her spirit and her outspokenness. 'You wait and see, Dan'll have a cheese empire in no time. Heard anything from Lottie?'

'Not much.' Marie skimmed a stone across the river. It sliced and slid; she was skilled. 'SJ texts me pictures now and then. I ask for details, about college and what-have-you, but she just fudges. The marriage is kaput, surprise surprise.'

'When she's older,' said Bernie, 'Lottie will find her way back to us.'

'Hmm,' said Marie.

The farmhouse turned up in one of the Sunday supplements. Mac and Marie turned the glossy pages in wonderment, Shelley whining unheard for her walk.

'Look at the style of him!' Dan, last seen in an egg-stained tracksuit, stood in front of his ancient new home in corduroy and tweed. The rough-plastered rooms were simply furnished. Dandelions massed in the field outside; 'They stand for happiness,' said Mac.

There was a shot of gleaming copper piping and a photogenic cow. Dan was quoted as saying his new cheese would be in Harrods come Christmas, and it would be called Sexy Farmer.

'He's smiling again.' Marie stroked the colour portrait.

'Nah. He's smiling for the first time, love,' said Mac.

In the run-up to Christmas, Sexy Farmer seemed to be everywhere. A pop star mentioned it in a vlog. A supermodel broke her diet to eat it. A minor royal served it at her wedding.

Yet none of the family had tasted it. 'It's doing so well, it must be delicious,' said Tatty from the back seat as Mac drove her and Marie and, *d'accord*, Shelley, to Emma's for the festivities.

'It's PR genius, not the quality of the cheese,' said Emma, when they arrived. 'A new product usually takes *years* to develop, but Dan knows where the bodies are buried. He knows all the celebs' secrets and he's blackmailing them – subtly – to promote his stupid cheese.'

'Have a little faith,' said Mac.

'Come and see our *fabulous* new en-suite!' Emma dragged them to the master bedroom, up in the beamed roof. The barn had been comprehensively refurbished, its comfort and style testament to Emma's eye for detail. She had blogged the whole process, of course, pictures appearing in the self-same magazines now fawning over Sexy Farmer. '*Voila!*'

The reclaimed bath and sink and loo were green. Avocado green.

'Lovely,' managed Marie.

Wonder if it's the one we slung out nearly thirty years ago, thought Mac.

Christmas Eve brought Bernie and Angus, arms full of presents, both of them gagging for a stout gin and tonic.

'Nothing like a real fire.' Angus settled himself by the hearth, their very own red-cheeked, platinum-haired Santa. 'The newlyweds send their love.'

The Adrians had finally tied the knot; Marie and Mac had stood by and wept, and Bernie and Angus were fresh from visiting them on their first anniversary.

'Amazing, how times change.' Bernie adjusted her sequinned neckline. 'Never thought I'd see the day when gay marriage was legal in Ireland. *Sláinte,*' she grinned, raising her gin.

Abbo, winkled out of his room, was sent in with a tray of vegan *amuses-bouche*, which Bernie said didn't amuse her boosh *at all*.

He sidled back to his boy-lair, as Christmas Eve, that glowing precursor to the main event, rolled out in a firelit haze of nibbles, games and slightly too much booze.

'Dan better turn up tomorrow,' said Marie, discreetly, to Mac, as they watched Bernie cheat her way around the Monopoly board. 'Em's gone to so much trouble.'

'I'm off to bed.' Mac stretched. 'That drive wore me out.'

'It's early,' protested Marie, who was always Last Woman Standing at family get-togethers.

She and Bernie agreed after he went up the new oak stairs; Mac was looking peaky.

Tatty disagreed; Mac was fine.

Emma arbitrated. They were all correct, she said. 'But Dad's just tired after the long drive. He'll be himself again tomorrow.'

Christmas Day outlined the bedroom curtains in cold white.

Mac confronted himself in the full-length mirror. Thanks to the flattering lighting in his daughter's house, he looked his best. Which wasn't saying much. 'O Love of My Life,' he said to Marie as she did battle with her Spanx, 'are we *old* yet?'

'Not me,' panted Marie, jumping, tugging. 'I'm in denial. As far as I'm concerned, people assume I'm your second wife – you know, the younger woman you met online.'

There was a family-wide ban on mentioning that Marie would be seventy on her next birthday. *Seventy is already in my rear-view mirror,* thought Mac. He slapped his jowls, watched them wobble. True, he bothered the doctor more often than he ever had, and it took a couple of jump starts to get him going these wintry mornings, but deep inside he was unchanged. His exhaustion of the day before was vanquished by sleep. 'I quite like being an old guy,' he said, turning to the side and pulling in his tummy. 'I embrace it.'

'Not me!' squeaked Marie; she had beaten the Spanx but had to lie down to recover.

'Amazing, isn't it, how your hair has stayed the same beautiful red, love? Not even a touch of grey.'

Marie said nothing.

Nothing at all.

'He's here!' yelled Abbo, skittering down to the five-barred gate. 'Uncle Dan's here!'

Marie dashed out, Shelley barked, and Bernie hobbled over the gravel in her fluffy mules to help him carry in the gaily wrapped gifts.

Each of which turned out to be cheese.

'Ah!' said Bernie, cupping a hand to her ear. 'The traditional Christmas Day row has broken out.'

'Shush,' said Marie, who didn't find the screaming match between Abbo and his mother at all funny.

'They'll make it up before lunch.' Bernie leaned against the Aga, already on the Buck's Fizz.

Ollie let out a long sigh as he checked the nut roast. 'She won't let him be,' he said, just as Abbo burst into the kitchen.

'She followed me!' he yelled.

'First,' said Ollie, pointing a wooden spoon, 'take down that hood. And secondly ...' He was lost. There was no secondly. 'Em ... ?' He was confused as Emma joined them, red in the face.

'All right, yes, I followed him,' she said, over-loud, still in fighting mode. 'I saw him with this *gang*, and they all met up in a car park and they handed their money to this older guy and off he went and, well, we all know what that means.'

'Do we?' asked Tatty, from where she and Shelley were sitting out the drama in a window seat.

'Drugs!' said Emma.

'Drugs?' Dan was wry. 'Jesus, Em.'

'You weren't there.' Emma rounded on him. 'They were shifty. Looking around. *Smoking.*'

'In other words,' said Dan, cosying up to Bernie by the stove, 'typical sixteen-year-olds. You've got no proof of *drugs.*' He rolled the 'r' theatrically.

'Don't I?' Emma was suddenly calm. Eerily so. She took a slim book out of her jeans pocket and held it up like an exorcist wielding a bible.

'I hate you,' spat Abbo. 'I hate you, Mum. I really hate you.'

'Son, don't,' said Ollie, but the boy was gone.

Shelley whined; she hated it when her humans raised their voices. She had been through stuff before she came to the Mactavishes, and sometimes it showed. Marie laid a hand on her delicate head. 'Is that Abbo's diary?' she asked, fearful of the answer.

'Look, look.' Emma flipped through the pages. She seemed unaware of the change in the room. Of the disapproval mingling with the aromas of lunch. 'Every time he sees these guys he writes the same letter. D.' Emma seemed to expect a gasp. 'D for drugs!'

'D stands for many things,' said Angus from the fireside.

'You promised,' was all Ollie said before following Abbo upstairs, where slammed doors drowned the sound of carols on the radio.

Lunch was a subdued affair.

Emma's rebellious expression – part guilt for ruining Christmas, part righteous certainty – obviously masked a desire to cry.

'No turkey?' asked Tatty, with some of the incomprehension Mac felt.

'Nut roast is much better for you,' said Marie. Later she would treat Tatty to a contraband turkey and cranberry sandwich that lay cling-filmed in her overnight bag.

Every so often, to break the un-festive silence, somebody would come up with another suggestion for what Abbo's D might stand for; the boy himself had taken a plate to his room.

'Dancing!' was Marie's contribution. Angus proffered, 'Discotheque,' and during dessert Bernie shouted, 'Dominos!'

Emma barely touched the Christmas pudding she had stirred so optimistically back in October.

Just a light snooze, Mac promised himself in the den, as he stretched out among more cushions than he had ever seen in one place before. It was odd to be tired again after a lay-in. *I can't even blame a heavy lunch*. He anticipated the late-night sarnies with something akin to lust.

Just as he closed his eyes, the door to the snug opened and closed.

Emma knelt by him. 'Dad, look.' She held out Abbo's diary.

'Em, love, *give it back*.' Mac was past the age when he expected to explain the difference between right and wrong to his children. 'I don't want to look at it, it's private.'

'The D is for drugs, Dad, and here's how I know.' Emma held open a page.

Mac gave in, read the sentence scrawled in capitals. *AM I ADDICTED?*

Mac sat up. However Emma came by the evidence, it must be acted upon. He had seen too many promising lives disappear down the Class A plughole.

'Will you talk to him, Dad?'

Talk about a poisoned chalice. 'Of course.' He had his training to fall back on.

And love, he thought.

*

There was a rustling in Abbo's room when Mac knocked.

'Go away.'

'Sorry, can't.' Mac waited. As he knew it would, the door opened a sliver. This was their Abbo, after all. He said, 'You and I need a little chat, young man.'

'God, no, can't you just ... Mum gets everything blown out of proportion.' Abbo was one big wince, bending this way and that in his desire to be anywhere but there.

Mac held up the diary. 'This is yours. It was wrong to take it, but ...' Mac held it open. 'Am I addicted?' He handed back the trouble-making little book. 'That's a big question, Abbo. Are you?'

Abbo's face seemed to boil with feeling. His large brown eyes met Mac's tired blue ones. 'I think I am, Gramps,' he said, and held the door wide.

He sought out his daughter.

Just back from walking Shelley, Emma was hanging up the dog's tartan coat when she glimpsed Mac's face. 'Oh shit,' she said. She began to shake.

They found a sofa, not hard in that house of many corners. Emma put her feet in Mac's lap, just like she used to. He rubbed her socked toes and warned her not to open her mouth – 'Not a peep!' – until he had told her all.

She closed her eyes and heard about her son's new friends.

They were more streetwise than Abbo; 'But, then, Gramps,' Abbo had said, 'everyone is! Mum mollycoddles me.'

331

He liked their swagger. He emulated it, and their clothes. He was becoming one Abbo at home and another at school.

'Moving here from London,' Mac told Emma, 'meant that Abbo was the new boy, with a chance to start over. Nobody knew him here. Nobody laughed at him the way they did at his last school.'

'They didn't laugh at him,' said Emma. 'Did they?'

'They did. Because ...' Mac hesitated. 'Because they followed your website and listened to your podcasts. They all – friends and bullies alike – saw him making vegetable smoothies and doing yoga and running in slow motion.'

'But he loved doing all that!'

'Em, just *listen*. Abbo did not love all that. It was fine when he was small but he was getting older, finding his feet, and that sanitized, organic, soft-focus version of Abbo got him ridiculed at school.'

'I didn't know.' Emma's face crumbled.

Mac carried on. Better to rip off the plaster. 'So when you moved, he told nobody about his mum's funky website, didn't boast about you like he used to. He was just Abbo Jones, the guy with the big hair who was great at skateboarding. He made friends, but you never met them, not because they were skanky but because you might tell them about that other Abbo, the goodie-two-shoes Quorn-eater.'

Abbo had gone to pains to defend his mates. 'They're not, like, *criminals*. They just hang out and we talk crap.'

'Sounds great,' Mac had said. 'But the addiction, Abbo?'

'He confessed all,' Mac told Marie, and felt her brace. 'He's addicted to Kentucky Fried Chicken.'

'You what, Dad?'

'You were right, that D stood for drugs. But the fried, greasy kind. The fast food you've always referred to as "worse than drugs". Abbo *adores* it. When you saw him hand his money to the bigger guy, it was for a family bucket of hot wings. Sometimes it's McDonald's. He dabbles in Nando's, too, when he has enough cash.'

Mac had seen this before; *deny a child something and they want it all the more.*

Emma was stunned. 'Fast food,' she said, wonderingly. Then they came, the tears, spilling down her cheeks. 'I've been too hard on him, Dad. I've leaned on him. I didn't hear him, did I?'

'No, love, you didn't.' Mac had too much respect to sugarcoat the pill. 'He's on the verge of manhood. He can eat saturated fats if he wants to. He can wear a hooded sweatshirt. And you can't read his private diary. But I don't need to tell you that. You know it already.'

'I'm a terrible mother!' Emma began to wail. 'I've ruined his life.'

Mac was stern. His instinct to protect Emma from these strong feelings wouldn't help her in the long run. 'You're not a terrible mother, love, but this isn't about you. It's about a conflicted boy who adores you and who's sitting in his room suffering because he thinks he's let you down 'cos he likes a Happy Meal now and then.'

'I have to apologize.' Emma sprang up. 'About reading the diary. About lots of things.' She went, then dashed back, kissed her father on the forehead. 'Christ, Dad, what would we do without you?'

Mac stood up. No longer tired, he knew he was duty-bound to get Christmas back on track. 'Right!' he roared, rubbing his hands together. 'Where's that karaoke machine?'

Peace restored, Christmas got rowdy.

Abbo was front and centre in the strange orange and brown yuletide jumper his Grammy had knitted. He handed round a platter of Sexy Farmer with one last drinkie-poo as the fire died in the grate.

Emma was on Ollie's lap; they were back in harness, and Mac recognized the elastic properties of long-standing love. He trusted his daughter not to backtrack on the promises she had made to observe a clear divide between her online life and her family.

Relaxed, gregarious, Dan went to bed early, worn out with winning every round of charades.

'He's *happy*,' slurred Marie.

'He's healthy,' said Emma. Her party hat had slipped over one eye. 'Running every day. Eating properly.'

'He hardly touched the champagne.' Tatty was impressed.

'No too-young girlfriend on the scene.' Emma paused, then said, in a small voice, 'I prefer the old Dan.'

'He's boring!' hooted Marie, putting her hand over her mouth at such blasphemy.

They laughed together, but then somebody mentioned the cheeseboard and the laughter stopped.

'His cheese,' said Tatty carefully, 'is interesting.'

Ollie said, 'Sorry, Tatty, I have to correct you. Sexy Farmer is disgusting.'

'It tastes of socks,' said Abbo, even though he had praised it to the skies, along with the rest of the family. Shelley had found a sliver on the rug and promptly thrown up on Mac's new slippers.

'How does it sell so well?' Even Bernie, who had really, *really* tried to like the cheese, was incredulous.

'Marketing,' said Ollie. 'Dan's a genius. Did you see that article about the influencer who married herself? He catered the reception.'

'Will we have to pretend to like it every Christmas?' asked Angus.

They would. There was no way out of it.

Again, Mac tried to be proud. But again, that worry that Dan's success was smoke and mirrors, the result of sleight of hand rather than hard graft.

New Year's Day always meant a call to Glen. Or 'Poor Glen', as Mac and Marie called him.

A puppy among vipers, Glen had wanted a sibling he could love without complications, and Mac did his best to fulfil that role. They didn't speak of Ed, beyond the barest update: Mac had come to terms with his father's true nature. It didn't pay to dwell on it, or to pretend that theirs was anything more than a biological bond.

That New Year's Day, however, Glen called before Mac had a chance to dial his number. 'Glen!' he said, full of cheer. 'I was just about to ... oh.'

Marie hovered.

'I see,' said Mac. His grief surprised him. It rolled over him, spun him round and knocked the breath out of him.

And with that, it left him.

'God rest his soul,' said Marie, which was the nicest thing she'd said about Ed Vole in years.

'So, it's over,' said Mac. He felt Shelley nuzzle his leg. Sweet animal, she always knew when he needed a tender touch. 'He's gone, and what really hurts is the fact that he gave my mother *nothing*.'

Marie disagreed. 'He gave her *you*,' she whispered.

The phone rang again. Mac snatched it up. 'Dan, hi,' he said, then, 'What? Really?'

'Tell me!' barked Marie, grabbing at the phone, done with hovering.

Covering the receiver, Mac mouthed, 'He's paid us back, love!'

'The cruise is *on*!' Marie did a lap of honour, Shelley at her heels.

They were on the high street, chattering like children, talking about the round-the-world trip that was, as of an hour ago, booked for a month's time.

'Mister Mactavish?'

A woman hailed him, and he turned.

'It is you, isn't it?' she laughed.

'Good God, Josie Craig!'

His erstwhile client, possibly his most memorable one, was no longer a goth, but a polished woman carrying one of those monster handbags that baffled Mac.

'Jacob's thirty now, but he still has that story book about puffins you gave us as a moving-in present. God, that little flat . . .' Josie shook her head. 'Do you know you changed my life?'

'Oh, now,' said Mac.

'Actually, you *saved* my life!'

The long years of unpaid overtime and battling regulations and having his nose rearranged were worth it.

Josie – and all the other Josies – made it worthwhile.

'I don't like the look of you,' said Marie.

'Charming,' said Mac.

'Get to bed,' she told him, and he did as he was told. Because, in truth, Mac didn't like the look of himself either.

He didn't hear her call Glen and ask some questions about how Ed Vole had died.

'Congenital heart failure,' said Glen, and then, in answer to her next question, 'Yes, sad to say, it does run in families.'

CHAPTER EIGHTEEN

He sits heavily. He keeps his coat on. 'Okay, so, today's the day.' He rattles on, knowing how expert she is at deflection. 'It can't wait any longer. I have something important to tell you.'

'It can wait until after today's photograph!' She is bright. She means to jolly him past whatever is making him so grave.

'I've been trying to tell you for a while now.'

'Have you?' She knows he has. There is no mist today. She is neat as a pin, and every bit as sharp. She opens the album. '2018. This one's all out of focus. Our man looks different here,' she says. 'Sitting down? That's not like him.'

'He's put on weight,' he says, drawn in, despite himself. 'He's gone all puffy in the face.'

'Something's the matter.' She draws back, as if the image has malevolent power. 'Something's wrong.'

338

29 July 2018

Marie took a selfie of them both to mark their anniversary. It would turn out badly; Mac was the photographer in the family.

At the fence, Next Door shuffled closer. He was unkempt; his clothes spoke of neglect.

'Morning, love,' said Marie, whose fingers itched to knit the old bugger a jumper.

'I see someone's been overdoing the cakes.' Next Door pointed a yellow fingernail, and presumably the noise he made was a laugh.

'Yes, that's right,' said Mac affably from his chair.

Marie was not affable. Marie was furious. 'My husband's sick, and if you had one ounce of decency ...' She gave up and went indoors.

'How was I to know?' Next Door banged the rubber handle of his walker. 'I've not been well meself, but what does she care?'

I could challenge that, thought Mac. *I could remind you that Marie waited with you for the ambulance when you had that turn. I could remind you of the bowls of stew she hands through your window, and the groceries she picks up for you.*

Mac was breathless these days, and saved his puff for more important conversations.

There were quite a few such conversations coming up, he suspected.

*

'Not how we wanted to spend our anniversary,' smiled Mac, sitting across from the specialist.

The joke was lost on the humourless doctor, who was keen to begin.

Mac kept tight hold of Marie's hand as the doctor found a number of ways to tell him what he already knew; he was very ill indeed.

'Looking through your notes, I see your father died of congenital heart failure.'

Ed had bequeathed something to Mac after all.

'If your problems were the result of damage, there would be some chance of a cure, but as the condition is innate, I regret that's not possible. Congenital heart failure can continue undetected for a lifetime, and make no real difference to your health. With you, unfortunately, it has pounced in your seventies, and, well, the symptoms are all too familiar to you by now. The lack of breath, the inability to exercise. I see you've gained weight; that will continue.'

'His ankles,' said Marie, 'are awful swollen.'

'We can mitigate that – a little – with medication, but we can't erase it completely. How's your appetite?'

Marie answered for him. 'He's off his food.' This hurt her terribly; it was a mortal sin to throw away a decent dinner.

'That's to be expected. We can get you started on supplements. Coughing? Restlessness?' The doctor scribbled as Mac nodded. 'Any confusion?'

Mac shook his head passionately. He dreaded the loss of

his reason. He and Marie watched Bernie navigate Angus's increasing dementia, and saw what it took out of her.

He made himself ask, as they were standing to leave, 'Life expectancy, doctor?'

Marie froze.

The medic was shifty. Repeated he was a 'severe case', and left it at that.

'You're a sight for sore eyes!' Mac was pleased to see Bernie waiting outside Sunnyside.

'We cancelled the anniversary, Bern.' Marie tried and failed to be annoyed. Her sister fizzed like the champagne she held in her paw.

'If there's one thing life has taught me,' said Bernie, 'it's to celebrate *everything*, so happy forty-eighth anniversary to the both of you!'

They asked after Angus, and received only the most positive spin on the situation. After a lifetime of attention-seeking, Bernie had tapped into her reserves of stoicism. 'He sits by the shop counter and chatters away. He still knows where all the books are, but doesn't always remember customers' names. We don't let him work the till. He keeps asking me to marry him.' She looked inward for a moment, staring into her drink. 'I always say yes.'

They talked of Lottie, twenty now and a stranger. The family no longer emailed pictures from magazines to show one another; no need; Lottie was so successful there were images of her everywhere. She was edgy, feminine, modern.

With that vulnerability around the eyes that models must have to do well.

'Can't help wishing,' said Mac, knowing the women were keeping careful watch on him as they sat together in the brown and orange sitting room, 'that Lottie had a more secure job. Something not so glamorous that'd help her set down roots.'

'She's tough, that one,' said Marie. 'She'll be fine.' Her tone betrayed nothing of the melancholy she admitted only to Mac, of her wish that they saw Lottie now and again, if only to prove that the years Lottie lived with them meant as much to the girl as they did to Marie. She changed the subject. 'Tell him, Bern,' she said, 'tell him we have to cancel the cruise. It's only a month away.'

Before Bernie could meddle – and oh how Bernie loved to meddle – Mac said, holding up his hand as if in court, 'We're going round the world, and that's that. We've waited our whole lives for this adventure. You talk as if I'm going to die on you, girl.'

He regretted that later, as he set down Shelley's bowl.

'Shouldn't have used the D word,' he said to the dog, who wasn't listening, too intent on wolfing down her meaty chunks. 'We don't mention death anymore. Doesn't mean I don't think about it, though.'

He ran a hand along the dog's smooth back.

'Make sure you get Marie out of the house, won't you, after ...' Mac turned and switched off the tinny radio, with

342

a roughness that was out of character. He liked to hear Adele sing, but 'Hello' was too mournful a song to countenance right then.

Later, when Marie invoked the name of Princess Diana in some context, Mac heard his voice raise, heard himself say, 'For God's sake, woman, she was born with a silver spoon in her mouth, nothing like you and me. She would *not* understand what we're going through; she wouldn't bloody care! Can you stop with that?'

He was sorry, and he said so, and Marie understood. 'I made you cry,' he said, ashamed, hating the anxiety that strung him up so tightly and made him shout at the one person with as much to lose as himself.

He lay awake, long after Marie's little symphony of snores set up.

He would prefer to talk about death, now that it never left his peripheral vision. An expert on reading faces, he translated the doctor's expression. His death was a fact of life, and must be faced. They faced everything together, the Mactavishes.

Except this.

It was too much for Marie, and he respected that. His fear of dying was nothing to do with the event itself. He didn't know what lay ahead on the other side; he didn't give that much thought.

It was the leaving that hurt. The idea of not being there, of a Mac-shaped hole. He didn't flatter himself that he mattered all that much; he was just one of eight billion other humans. *But I do have stuff to do.*

Who would pick up the phone when it rang at night and scared Marie? Who would nip out for chips when she was down? He had to be available to pick up visitors from the Tube station, and he needed to know how young Abbo got on. Mac wanted to help Emma and Ollie stay in tune, to see Dan find a good woman, to reconnect with his beloved Lottie, to paint a rock each April and lay it with the others around the magnolia.

He got out of bed, and went to the window. The moon washed the street in atmosphere; even Next Door's dismal front garden looked magical. The magnolia seemed to glitter.

Down he went, one step at a time. The same stairs he used to jog down. Mac caught his breath by the front door, then went outside to fuss over the magnolia. He picked a dead leaf. 'Look after your mum for me, won't you?' he said.

I'm talking to dogs and bushes, he thought. *Perhaps I'm already confused!*

'The household admin's all left in order,' he went on. 'She knows where the folder is but you know what she's like when she's upset. Goes all scatty.'

A window flew up, high above them.

'Uh-oh,' said Mac.

'Marie,' said Mac, taking the phone gently out of his wife's grasp, 'stop, please'. He spoke into the receiver. 'Don't let your mum put you off, Em, we'd love to see you all, and it won't tire me out. Sunday lunch is *on*.'

He put the phone down. 'Darling, I love you,' he said, 'but you worry too much.'

Abbo was non-committal about sixth form. It was, he said, 'All right'.

'You making chums?' asked Marie, as they set the table together. It would be a squash with Tatty as well, but their scratched old table was used to accommodating crowds.

'Yeah.'

'Any romance?' Marie pursed her lips; she longed to marry everyone off, even the youngsters.

'Grammy! No!' Abbo put a table mat over his face. 'Well, maybe . . .'

'Tell. Me. Everything.' His grandmother got him up against the wall.

Tatty didn't ask Mac how he was, and Mac was grateful. He would have had to lie; he had been almost too spent to dress himself that morning.

There was no heart-to-heart, no shocked tears; Tatty took his diagnosis on the chin. Now she accepted a bowl of stew with demure greed; Tatty *loved* Marie's stew.

'So,' said Marie, sitting down last, with her apron still tied, 'we cancelled the cruise.'

'Aw, shame,' said Ollie. 'Probably the right decision, though.'

'Hmm,' said Mac. He agreed, but wouldn't give Death – it

had a capital letter by now – the satisfaction of knowing that. He would go kicking and fighting all the way.

'We'll book again, next year.' Marie's tone made it clear she neither wanted nor needed any comment on her optimism.

There were seconds, and thirds, for those who wanted them, and everyone wanted them, even clean-eating blogger Emma. Except, that is, for Mac, who couldn't finish his serving.

After she shooed them out of the kitchen, Marie's tears dripped into the beef and carrots as she scraped his dish into the bin.

'Oh, Mum, don't cry.' Emma came in and found her. 'It'll be all right.'

'It *won't*.' Marie had no philosophical acceptance of Death; she wanted to duff him up, pull his hair, boot him up the backside. 'The doctor asked us if we had any questions and it was on the tip of me tongue to ask him how was I supposed to live without my Mac?'

They sat. They could hear a raucous game of Scrabble kicking off in the next room.

'You'll get through this, Mum. What does Dad always say? That the *Titanic* wouldn't have gone down if you'd been there to clip the captain round the ear?'

Marie summoned a smile, knowing she was only formidable when she had the quiet, biddable Mac by her side. 'All these years, I've made the most noise, I've called the shots, but it's your dad who's the strong one, the *engine*.'

'I've given it some thought.' Emma didn't pussyfoot; didn't

insist that there would be some magical reversal and Mac would be fixed. 'You can come and live with us. It was Ollie's idea. He'll turn the gym into an annexe.'

'Live with you?' The idea startled Marie.

'You can hardly live with Dan, in his kingdom of cheese. Has he come up to see Dad?'

'He calls,' said Marie.

'That's a "no",' tutted Emma. 'Just give it some thought. I'd love to have you across the yard.'

'How will I live at all? How will my heart beat? Why would it bother?' Marie told Emma about the latest dispiriting hospital appointment. 'I asked about a heart transplant. He was so dismissive.' Marie didn't like the consultant, and was glad he would soon retire and hand them over to a colleague. 'Said Dad's too old, that hearts have to be carefully allocated, and they'd rather see a donated heart go to someone with a higher life expectancy.'

'That's like saying Dad's not important.'

'I was all *Hey you! My husband deserves a heart!* But yer man was very hoity-toity. If only this had happened ten or twenty years ago, when your dad was younger.'

'You know Dad wants to throw a party for your seventieth, don't you?'

'Of course I know. He never stops banging on about it. Has he roped you in to try and persuade me?'

'I told him there's no point.'

'Too right. How could I celebrate with him sitting in the chair, not able to get up and dance with me?'

'How's, you know ...' Even forthright Emma stumbled on this topic. 'His mind?'

'He got up last night, at nothing o'clock, was out fussing with the front garden. I worried maybe he thought it was daytime.'

'He seems *compos mentis* today. Talking of the garden, what're all those white rocks about? Why does Dad keep adding one?'

'I'll tell you another time,' said Marie, reminded of yet another shared truth that only she and Mac knew of.

There were good days. There were bad days.

This was a mixture of both. On the good side, Marie gave up her cherished *EastEnders* so Mac could watch a documentary on puffins.

On the bad side, he knew why she was doing this. *Because I'm dying.*

He couldn't settle and enjoy it, and later, when he went to his man-cave he yelled that there were so many vases of flowers in there it looked like a funeral home.

The next morning the vases were cleared away. A single cactus sat by his computer.

'Look it up.' Marie slapped down *The Language of Flowers*.

He found the page and smiled to himself.

Endurance.

He arrived bearing cheese.

Dan seemed to fill the kitchen. He picked up Marie

and swung her round. Shelley barked and danced on her back legs.

'Where's Dad?' were the first words out of his mouth.

'He's behind you,' said Marie, like a pantomime audience.

Dan wheeled around. 'Whoa, fatso!' he said.

'How long will you stay?' Marie was lit up, apron on, whisking about on oiled slippers.

'Couple of weeks, maybe more.'

She was taken aback. Dan's visits were generally little more than pit stops.

'How's business?' asked Mac. He was in the new armchair they had bought. It was high, with sturdy arms, rather too like the archetypal retirement home model for Mac's liking, but at least it meant he could get in and out of it without help.

'I've had to take on more staff. Cheese is the new rock'n'roll, Dad.'

'And you're being sensible?'

'If you mean did I learn anything from my fall from grace in Lalaland, yes I did. I keep an eye on every aspect of the biz, Dad. It's a success. Modest for now, but we have huge plans for growth. You can come and stay and have a poke around.'

'That'd be fun.'

They both knew it would never happen. Mac went to bed earlier and earlier. Life was effortful; he was the static centre of Sunnyside. His failing heart was picking up speed; Marie gave nightly updates to Bernie. 'I don't like his colour,' she would say, or 'To see him stopping halfway up the garden to summon his strength just breaks my heart.'

'I'm wearing out your poor mum,' said Mac, as he directed Dan in the cutting back of the single-minded ivy. 'She barely sleeps. Sometimes I wake up, you see, and need a tablet.'

'She's fine,' lied Dan. 'So long as she can nag you, Mum's a happy bunny.'

A rap on the kitchen window. They looked over and Marie mouthed through the grass, 'Wipe them feet before you come in!'

'See?' said Dan.

After a run of good nights, Mac woke at 3am, clawing at the air.

'Marie!' The word was a wheeze. '*Marie!*' He patted the bed beside him, but didn't find the hump of his wife's soft body.

Something dark rose from the carpet. It staggered. There was a noise. A deep voice said, 'Shit, my toe!'

The lamp was switched on, and Mac saw Dan hopping in his Calvin Kleins. 'Two ticks,' he yawned, and popped a tablet out of foil. He sat on the bed and handed Mac a glass of water. 'Get that down you.'

'Were you sleeping on the floor?' Mac took the tablet, obedient as a child.

'To give Mum a break.'

'How long you been doing this for?' Mac knew the answer. *Since I told you Mum was struggling.*

'Never mind. Let's get back to sleep. You disturbed a *very* vivid dream about a certain Ms Jennifer Lopez.'

'Who?'

'Goodnight, Dad.'

Mac lay for a while, feeling the tablet work its voodoo, his senses gradually dimming. 'You're a good lad, Dan,' he said, his voice woozy.

Dan scoffed in the dark.

Mac said, 'I don't say it enough.' *Do I ever say it?* 'But I love you, son.'

'You don't have to say it. You've been showing me how to love since I was born.' Dan sighed. 'I haven't always been what you wanted, I know that.'

'Shush now! What a thing to say.'

'But I'm trying, Dad.'

'And I'm proud of you. Now, get back to this Jennifer Lopez.'

When she called the ambulance, Marie couldn't remember her own address.

She raced back to the hated highchair. Mac lay at an awkward angle, head lolling back, eyes closed. 'Loosen his collar, Dan.'

'Dad, stay with us,' said Dan. He was cool, his hair falling over his eyes as he bent over his father.

'Here. Let me just ...' Marie wiped Mac's mouth of the pink, foamy spittle. 'He started coughing, couldn't stop.' She went from foot to foot. 'He said he could feel his heart galloping. Oh, Dan, he can't die on us. He can't.'

'He won't, Mum. We won't let him.' Dan held up Mac's head. 'He's so floppy. Come *on,*' he shouted, willing the ambulance to appear.

The paramedics were swift and wise, and they were kind too; their humanity took in not just the patient but the distraught family.

The doors slammed and the flashing light turned Sunnyside a hectic blue.

The family convened. Shocked, pale, like woodland creatures dumped far from the forest in the sterile bright lights of the hospital.

Bernie got there first, her face free of make-up, phone in hand in case Angus sent out a distress call. 'Tell me he's still with us!'

'Yeah.' Dan fetched her a Styrofoam cup of terrible tea. 'He's stable. But, you know ...'

Bernie did know.

Emma and Ollie came rushing up a corridor that smelt of bleach. Abbo was in a dressing gown.

'Is Gramps going to be all right?'

'We hope so,' said Marie. She was robotic, but kind. The crying was deferred for another day. 'He'll be all the better for seeing *you*, that's for sure. He's having some tests done right now, but the nice nurse'll come out and tell us when we can see him.'

They were surprised to see Tatty, and she was castigated for making her own way.

'Dan would've fetched you, love,' said Marie, wiping a plastic seat for the older lady.

'We're all here now,' said Bernie, and they fell silent.

The clip clop of more feet made them turn. The woman was tall, and in a sparkling gold dress far too chic for the antiseptic surroundings.

Abbo recognized her first. 'Lottie!'

The woman lifted her arms and began to run on her stilt heels.

'Am I in time?' she asked.

The room was dim, and noisy in a low-key way, with the squeak and whirr of life-saving machines that chugged through the night.

The hand that Lottie held in hers was limp, with a canula jabbed into a swollen vein.

'You know what?' she said.

'What, love?' replied Mac, his voice barely escaping.

'I look like you.'

Her famously perfect visage, powdered and contoured, was close to his battered old face. 'Get off,' he said, and stopped himself laughing, because that would hurt.

'I do. I always think that, when I'm getting made up, staring at my stupid self in the mirror. *There's Gramps,* I think.'

No blood related them. They both knew that. They also knew that what tied Lottie to Mac was something much more important.

I'm related to Ed by blood, thought Mac, through the haze of medication. *And look where that's got me.*

'I don't want to go,' he said suddenly, and he felt his hand being squeezed hard.

'Well, stay, then,' said Lottie.

'Life is sweet, love, don't let anybody tell you different.' Mac dearly wanted to stay, for one more dance with his fiery Marie. He wanted to be told off some more, to argue some more, and make up. He wanted to keep an eye on his people. But life had long ago taught Ian Mactavish that he was not in charge.

'Let me fetch the others, Gramps.'

'Don't let go,' said Mac. 'I'm scared.'

She cried. Her mascara ran. She sang, in a tiny voice, the one she used when she turned up at Sunnyside.

'*Be still,*
and hush.
Be warm,
And slumber.
Who's my baby?'

CHAPTER NINETEEN

Her hand floats above the album.

'The last picture,' she says. 'This one'll bring us right up to date.' She trembles. 'What if it's one of them on their own? I have a bad feeling.'

He has waited long enough. There is literally no time left to have the conversation she has been evading. 'Before we look at the last photograph . . . there are changes coming up, and I need to prepare you, to make it simple for you.'

She is vigorous. No more trembling. 'After the photograph.' She holds his gaze; he sees her core self in there, her determination, her refusal to be managed.

The dogeared album is a talisman, he knows that. It shores her up, means something. 'You win,' he smiles.

She turns the page.

It is bare.

29 July 2019

Sunnyside was deathly quiet.

Motes of dust jigged in the sunlight slanting through the hall, the kettle cooled in the kitchen, Shelley pit-pattered about on her delicate paws.

'Tea's brewed!' The shout went up the stairs, for the second time. 'Come and get it, love.' Mac was cheerfully irritated with his wife, muttering to himself, 'Not so long ago I was the slowcoach in the family.'

One foot after the other he set off from the bottom step. He loved to do it now that it didn't bring on a fit of wheezing. No half-way stops for Mac, he fairly bounded onto the landing. Mac was re-learning how to hope; the Mactavish family future would include him after all. *I can worry about them to my heart's content.* To be precise, his *new* heart's content.

He found her. Marie was on her back. She hadn't heard him. She didn't need or want the tea he'd made.

'A pulmonary thrombosis.' The words were clunky in Mac's mouth and he knew he'd have to repeat them later, because Emma was screaming too hard to hear.

'You're sure it's Mum?' she kept asking, nonsensically.

'Yes, love, I'm sorry, I'm sure,' he said, over and over.

*

It had been immediate. A blood clot had lurked since God knows when, biding its time. That morning, on a whim, the vile missile set off for Marie's heart.

'And here's me,' Mac told Shelley with a brave stab at irony, 'with a brand new one.' They were on the high street. It had changed beyond recognition since the day Mac got the keys to Sunnyside. Those times were on his mind since Marie's passing; the past went hand in hand with the present. How Mac longed to push through into their history and wallow in its simple happiness. Instead, he must trudge through the present, with Shelley for company.

'There's been many a boom and bust on this street,' he told the dog, who had stopped to sniff a patch of wall. 'Marie actually cried when Woolworths closed. We never used to have all these chain coffee houses. Suddenly, every other window is a charity shop.' He encouraged Shelley to move away from the filthy but irresistible bricks. 'Marie loved her charity shops. Always came home with a bargain.'

Shelley pulled to take him down the cobbled alley. 'Not today,' said Mac. 'Not yet.' He could not even glance towards the storage lock-up that had once been 'Hair by Marie'.

On the home strait, Shelley sped up. A treat awaited; she knew that. She barely listened to Mac explain how Marie's heart attack was 'just like any other, except, oh how did they put it? *In a far more critical area.*'

The gate made its usual noise and Mac made his usual mental note to oil it. 'It was my illness brought it on. Nobody will ever dissuade me of that, Shelley old girl.' He found his key. 'I'd been at death's door for months, and after one really horrible close shave Marie was practically planning my funeral, when my consultant retired, and the new chap – hang on, let me get your lead off – well, he had very different ideas.'

Mac hung up the lead on its hook. He did everything very properly these days. It helped fill the expanse of time he had to himself.

The younger specialist had brought about a revolution in the Mactavishes' life. 'Too old for a heart transplant? Who told you that?' He cited a study that found that patients in their seventies, if they were fit and healthy with no great underlying concerns, were excellent candidates, with a life expectancy similar to transplant recipients ten or even twenty years younger.

Dizzy with the speed of it, Mac had taken a call to say a suitable heart was ready. All went to plan. Marie held his hand throughout, and made friends with the nurses and baked soda bread for the doctor.

It was miraculous. Slowly, surely, he became himself again. Somebody else's heart ticked and tocked stolidly inside Mac's chest, and he took up driving again and a world cruise was booked and he jogged up and down the stairs like a teenager.

Marie prayed for the family of the donor; they knew their happiness had its root in tragedy. The gratitude used to stop him in his tracks.

Something had changed, though. Now, Mac resented his heart. *It's keeping me alive*, he thought through the sleepless nights. *I want to join my Marie.*

He told nobody. It was such an ungracious, ugly reaction. Until one evening, having dragged himself to Henley-on-Thames for supper at Bernie's, he found himself telling Angus.

It had been a good night for Angus, the pea-souper in his head temporarily cleared. He knew who Mac was, and he understood what Mac had to say. There were tears in Angus's eyes when they spoke of Marie. When he brought up the medical phenomenon of Mac's heart, Mac cut in to say, 'But I don't want this heart, Angus! It's someone else's. Marie's not in there.'

It sounded childish, but Angus didn't laugh. 'Marie isn't just in your heart, you silly fellow. She's in your soul. She's in every part of you.'

So now Mac honoured his new heart, as Marie had done. And appreciated the greatest gift he had ever been given.

The flight to Ibiza took two and a half hours.

Emma had talked him into saying 'yes'. She reckoned it would do him good, take him out of himself. 'You've had two big losses this year. Mum, and poor Tatty . . .' They had all watched Tatty slip away; both major female players in Mac's life taken from him in the space of a few short months. 'We'd go with you if it didn't clash with Abbo's A-levels. I love a good wedding. And so did Mum. So go, Dad, please.'

He could have resisted Emma, but there was no resisting Lottie. He walked her down the aisle, that new heart ballooning with pride.

It was an aisle of lanterns in a ruined *castillo*. Lottie's wedding was bohemian and artsy; Mac saw many outrageous hats among the guests, and not one of them had a job he understood. He met a Tik-Tok influencer at the alcohol-free reception, and a shoe brand advocate by the all-raw buffet. Wondering if there was a burger joint in the old town, Mac sought out SJ, who was smoking on a parapet.

She waggled a hip flask at him.

'Yes *please*.' Mac took a hefty swig. He did a swift inventory of the mother of the bride. 'You look well.'

'I'm great,' said SJ, who would never admit to being anything else. 'You've made Lottie's day, you know.'

'And mine.' He sensed SJ was about to bring up Marie and he couldn't bear it, not at that moment, so he said, 'Her new husband seems . . .'

'Mad? Cuckoo? Loony Tunes?' SJ shrugged. 'He's a tech visionary. Complete genius, and everything he touches turns to gold. But they won't last, Mac.' She shook her head. 'I didn't show her how to have a healthy partnership.'

'You did your best,' said Mac. He almost believed that, and he was fond enough of SJ to want to do so, despite her behaviour over the years.

'She saw it at Sunnyside. Her life there became a touchstone for her. That little room. Your goodnight lullaby. She still has Jeff, you know.'

'I do know.' Mac had been reintroduced the night before. Lottie's tears for Marie, her guilt about staying away, had soaked the poor little chap's velveteen wings. 'I wish Dan had been able to come.'

'Yeah, well, he was never great at showing up.'

Mac could have defended Dan, said the broken leg was real, as was the regret. But there was too much history between the ex-lovers and Mac wasn't up to refereeing.

It's too soon, he thought, hollowly. *I'm not ready for the world just yet.*

There were letters and cards, so many to wade through. The sentiments were genuine, and Mac replied to each one, just as Marie would have done. Visits were rationed; he was thin-skinned, could only bear certain company.

Bridget came, veiled in black, supported by the Adrians. She talked of meeting Marie once again at the right hand of the lord, and the Adrians got Mac pissed.

Glen came. They sat together like two old mongrels, saying little, feeling much. The bearhug when he left said it all.

Dan came. He brought along his new wife. 'Before you ask,' he had said, when he told his parents of his engagement, 'she's actually *older* than me.' Helen was a GP, funny and clever, and she thought Dan was the bee's knees. She had Marie's seal of approval; Mac felt able to stop worrying about Dan at last.

One day Mac woke up and knew something had changed. A miniscule shift within. He had decisions to make.

*

Sunnyside was like a new house.

Repainted from top to bottom, inside and out. Marie's browns and oranges were whited over. Woodchip came down. Shag pile came up. Innumerable china figurines were wrapped in tissue.

The empty rooms echoed. The ghosts of family life were surely there, going about their business, reliving noisy breakfasts and whirlwind arguments and impromptu *craic*, but Mac couldn't see them.

One last walk-through, he thought. Check everything was shipshape.

The ivy on the back of the house was creeping towards the roof again. That was the new family's problem now. The tenacious plant had outlasted Mac and Marie's marriage.

Although, thought Mac, *we're still married. It's just that she's no longer here.* He almost whistled for Shelley, but the dog was at Emma's, settling into her new home.

He would join Shelley after the cruise. The plan for Marie to move into the annexe had been easily cut and pasted for Mac. There were so many plusses. Proximity to Emma and Ollie, and especially to Abbo. His grandson's ambition to 'get into digital art' puzzled him, as did so much else.

I am old-fashioned, he thought, with a jab of panic. It wasn't fun, being left behind. It had been comfortable growing older, becoming obsolete, when he had company on the journey. Now his little redhead had gone ahead, he felt vulnerable.

He heard her then. Loud. Clear. Like an insistent bell ringing in his mind. 'You're not obsolete, boyo,' she told him. 'Nothing old-fashioned about someone who knows how to love, and me and the kids taught you that long ago. Love never goes out of vogue.'

It was glorious to conjure her up, but it was also devastating. Mac hurried through the house, locking, checking, leaving.

The door closed behind him with the familiar chunk/clap sound Mac didn't even know he'd noticed until that moment. Without pause, he took up the spade that lay on the crazy paving that had knocked five grand off the sale of Sunnyside. He dug up the magnolia and wrapped its root ball carefully in polythene. He set the white rocks, all thirty-eight of them, carefully into a plastic basket.

He was all impetus. One last job to be done, and then he could get in the car. Why he needed so badly to be away from the warm little house he'd always hurried home to was not something Mac trusted himself to analyse. It was not his house anymore. There was nobody in there that he loved.

The last photograph must be taken; by cruel coincidence the date for handing over the keys was 29 July, the Mactavishes' forty-ninth wedding anniversary. He struggled, holding the tree with one hand and the phone with the other. 'Dammit,' he said to himself.

'Can I help?'

'What?' Mac had never before heard that phrase from the lips of Next Door.

'The picture. Maybe I can . . .' Leaning against his walking frame, Next Door extended a filthy hand over the fence.

Imagining the farce of explaining the phone to Next

Door, Mac gave an effortful smile. 'Thanks, but I'm fine.' He had hoped to get clean away, without one last disappointing encounter with his neighbour.

'She was a lovely lady.' Next Door's voice creaked from lack of use.

'She was,' agreed Mac, flabbergasted.

'You off now?'

'Well, yes.'

'Ta ra, then.' Next Door shuffled his walker around and turned his back. 'You take care of yourself.'

'And you,' said Mac. 'And you.'

Then he got into his car and drove away from Sunnyside for the last time.

He was early. *Nothing for her to moan about today!* thought Mac. Her hand floated above the album.

'The last picture,' said Tatty. 'This one'll bring us right up to date.' She trembled. 'What if it's only one of them? I have a bad feeling.'

Mac had waited long enough. There was literally no time left to have the conversation Tatty has evaded. 'Before we look at the last photograph . . . there are changes coming up, and I need to prepare you, to make it simple for you.'

She was vigorous. No more trembling. 'After the photograph.' Tatty held his gaze; Mac saw her core self in there, her determination, her refusal to be managed.

The dogeared album was a talisman, he knew that. It shored her up, meant something. 'You win,' he smiled.

She turned the page.

It was bare.

Mac drew a photograph from his jacket pocket. He was all fingers and thumbs with the old-fashioned sticky corners, but he managed to fix it down.

'He's alone,' said Tatty. She had the air of a cat when it's working out whether to jump or not. She looked from Mac to the snap, and back again. 'The same jumper . . . that's you.' She pointed.

'Yup. That's me. Taken a couple of hours ago and printed out at Snappy Snaps.' Mac saw her humiliation at having missed the glaring clues. Every week he had sat beside her, and they had looked at photographs of him. The younger Mac looked very different, but recent photographs were clearly of the elderly, patched-together chap in front of her. *She still doesn't know who I am.* Mac knew she wouldn't use his name.

Tatty frowned at the photograph. 'You're alone,' she said, and her voice was furry with compassion.

'No, I'm not. I have you.' Mac didn't tell her about Marie's death; he never would. Now that he had her full attention, it was time to talk. 'Tatty, I have some news, but I don't want you to fret about it.'

As if I can stop her fretting.

Nobody could do that, not even the kind staff. He had never heard of Rapid Progress Dementia until Tatty's diagnosis; from that first flicker of unease at a family Sunday lunch – she had been unable to remember Marie's name – to her retreat into a personal fog had taken seven weeks.

'When do I ever fret?' Tatty was imperious, but mildly so. She seemed genuinely eager to put his mind at rest. 'I have plenty to do.' She leaned closer. 'Keep an eye on *her* for a start.'

A few feet away, her nemesis was deep in a wordsearch.

He had to keep talking, keep her focused. 'Tatty, we're on the move. To somewhere greener.'

'I like it here.'

You complain about it every week! Mac never missed his weekly hour with Tatty; just once, Dan had taken his place and flirted with everyone from the receptionist to the cleaner, telling his great aunt she was "bloody gorgeous". 'I promise you'll like your new place, too. Emma, your great-niece, has found a homely, professional, caring home for you. She's very picky; her standards are as high as yours. The best part is, I'll be five minutes down the road and I can drop in much more often. You'll be sick of me!'

Tatty didn't laugh. She stared, instead.

Big Legs hovered, ready to lend a hand if necessary; Tatty's meltdowns were rare but they were spectacular.

'You have a great-*great* nephew, and he's dying to pop in.' That was an exaggeration, but Abbo would show his face now and then. 'A move is never easy, but we'll be with you all the way. If we embrace this, it might be marvellous.'

She shrugged, suddenly blasé. 'We'll be fine.' His obvious relief seemed to amuse her, and she patted his hand. 'You're a good boy, Ian,' she said.

*

Mac stood by the car for an age. To hear his name on her lips, after all those sterile hours spent sitting with her, pleading for recognition. This was a crumb he could feast on, even if she continued to bite off his head every time he visited.

He got in, still high, and looked forward to telling Marie. Again, it hit. The reality of his wife's absence. It broke over him like a wave as he gripped the steering wheel. And it passed.

I'm getting better at handling it.

He had a long drive ahead. Dolly Parton kept him company. Dolly understood about loss; he could hear it in her voice.

The precious anniversary album had been hard to part with, but he had tucked it into Tatty's bag during that long, *horrible* day when he'd moved her into the care home. He had hoped it might nudge her memories into the open.

At first, the book had oppressed Tatty, the photographs only serving to underline how much she had forgotten. So Mac stopped asking did she recognize this one or that one; he slipped into a pretence that he didn't know the messy, happy little family either.

He and Tatty got to know them together.

There was no captain's table. No swimming pool, no cabaret nights. Marie would have turned her nose up at the MS *Oldenburg* but Mac stood on deck the whole way, his yellow sou'wester a jolly smudge in the grey snarl of the storm.

The boat lurched against the stone quay of Lundy Island.

Mac gallantly helped his fellow passengers off, and let them swarm ahead. It was bleak and cold and wonderful; days of bird watching lay ahead.

Mac stared into the lashing rain. He saw the bird waddle, as if heading over to say hello, but of course it had no such intention, and took off and flew over his head.

My very first real-life Atlantic puffin. It would, no doubt, be one of a pair. Absurdly, he wondered if it could be the puffin he had sponsored in Marie's honour, just after she died. For thirty pounds a year he received updates on the colony and was allowed to name 'his' bird.

He decided that it was indeed his bird as it swooped above him, its paddle feet dangling.

'Good morning, Princess Di!' he shouted, but his voice was stolen by the wind.

She sits in her easy chair, at a loose end.

Something catches her eye on the low table.

A book. No, a photograph album. She takes it up, turns it over. She holds it up over her head. 'Does this belong to anyone?'

'Not me,' says her nemesis.

Tatty doesn't deign to answer.

'Why don't you keep it?' suggests a care assistant, pulling on her coat at the end of a long shift. 'You can show it to your visitor next week.'

'I might just do that,' she says.

Acknowledgements

This is as much Clare Hey's book as it is mine. Thank you, Clare, for letting me loose on your cracking idea.

Thank you, Simon & Schuster, for lending me the wonderful Louise Davies and, once again, the incomparable Sara-Jade Virtue.

I know I'm biased, but my agent really is the best. Thank you, Charlotte Robertson of Robertson Murray, for your wisdom and your kindness and your endless store of solid gold advice.

And lastly thank you, Neevo. You've made a tough year bearable, and I hope I've done the same for you.

booksandthecity.co.uk
the home of female fiction

WS & EVENTS | BOOKS | FEATURES | COMPETITIONS

Follow us online to be the first to hear from
your favourite authors

booksandthecity.co.uk   **@TeamBATC**

Join our mailing list for the latest news, events and
exclusive competitions

Sign up at
booksandthecity.co.uk